"COMPELLING"
—Richmond Times-Dispatch

"INSPIRED"
—Richmond News-Leader

"STUPENDOUS"
—Buffalo Evening News

"In the novel, the name is 'Lenora Malcolm'—but the pattern of the plot follows the career of Isadora Duncan . . . and covers her unconventional story, her search for lovers, her illegitimate children, her heavy drinking, her rapid decay, and the famous sick-minded episode with the mad Russian poet"

—VIRGINIA KIRKUS BULLETIN

"Mr. Weiss with remarkably sensitive perceptivity has caught in all its splendor and in all its misery the spirit of a great artist"

—BUFFALO EVENING NEWS

Diana J C Sweeney

1964/5

About The Author

Born in Philadelphia, *David Weiss* did editorial work for motion pictures for twenty years.

He is the author of *The Guilt Makers* and the best-selling *Naked Came I.* His latest book is *Justin Moyan.*

Mr. Weiss lives in New York City with his poet-painter-playwright wife, Stymean Karlen.

THE
SPIRIT
AND
THE
FLESH

DAVID WEISS

POPULAR LIBRARY • NEW YORK

To the memory of
IDA GOLDBERG
who lived for art and beauty
and thus still lives in us.

AUTHOR'S NOTE

This book is a novel, not a biography. The story follows the known facts of Isadora Duncan's life when it fits the purposes of fiction; when it doesn't, it follows the dictates of the character created in the novel. It is essentially a work of the imagination. The characters are my creations, no one else's. No living people are portrayed; this is a novel of a time that was, of a world that has vanished.

The names of real people no longer alive have been used only for those characters whose identity is an outgrowth of their public personality, such as Rodin, Duse, Pavlova.

Thus, while this novel is inspired by an actual life, the resources of fiction have been used to permit the fullest freedom in the interpretation of this life. And since Isadora Duncan was poetic and romantic, this novel has sought to capture such qualities in the character of Lenora Malcolm. I believe there is little here that Isadora Duncan did not feel or do, and very little that she might not have felt or done.

A DANCER SPEAKS

*I speak for every one of you, for the first to the very last
    of you,*
I say for you since no one will say it for you, nor will you,
I say for you the Unknown as well as the Most Famed
That the moment has come to you and will come again
*When you have felt and will feel again unsung, unnamed
    and unknown;*
*As well I speak for myself who has danced five hundred
    dances*
*And I feel for you as I feel for myself in your dressed un-
    dress*
In a way that none of my dances has yet expressed.

*As well I speak for the jungle and I say the same for the
    wild*
And why they are wild, she and he and their young,
The moment has come to them and will come again;
As well I speak for the flower in her puzzled fields,
*True to her nature she sprouts buds but the moment has
    come to her*
And will come again when she will feel uncalled;
And I speak for the winds on their perpetual search,
*And why they howl, feeling unessential in their unknowing
    void.*

*And I speak for the unfettered bird free in his nameless
    lane,*
The moment is with him in every flap of his crying wing;
And I speak for the earth. We walk across her heart but
What have we heard her say? Who calls her and why?
*I speak for the undying and the dead. Who of us knows
    which he is?*
I speak for the ocean waves with their vain crests
*Rushing to their Place but falling to the level of the sand
    grain*
Long ago fallen to unrest.

I speak for Creation itself that started in each one of us
And must go on laboring and starting in every seed that forms,
Impelled into Becoming by the nature of nature's ways
And the moment has come to Creation and will come again
When Creation will feel itself admonished by an angry abyss;
And I speak to this bottomless depth which holds your heart
And your face and I say you are its unfathomable self
And I will say it again with my first and my last dance.

STYMEAN KARLEN

BOOK ONE

1

A woman comes to womanhood by many ways. Some come quietly, with care and deliberation; some come so calmly they seem disembodied. Thousands of women follow the routine paths, and most of these ways are lost in the past. And there are those whose very entrance is an upheaval, is both an anguish and a joy.

They are the free ones, they say. They come with exultation, and a compulsion to defy, to proclaim, to ride the whirlwind, to shatter the commonplace and bend space. They seize fortune even at birth, for they know that fortune is male. Yet they are always female, for they are most aware of the male, and in nakedness or velvet they are adorned for the admiration and consciousness of the male.

And occasionally a woman comes to womanhood with a cosmic passion, seeking a new language of communication and new worlds of experience.

Such a one is being born now, and this is her beginning.

All the long, windy May day, imprisoned in her bed, Lena Malcolm lay silently and brooded. She thought of her other children, Archer and Amy, and wondered what would become of them now that they were without a father; she thought apprehensively of the life about to emerge from within her; she thought of San Francisco this windy May day of 1878 as a grubby patch in the wilderness, although it was a city of over two hundred thousand souls.

Youngest and wildest city on earth this year of 1878, legend had it that the city had been founded by gold seekers believing it would be an Eldorado. San Francisco was a cluster of many hills, she recalled in a sudden rush of memory, wanting to find virtue even where virtue did not exist. For in the next moment she saw it as a loud-mouthed slut of a city, with all its vitality. Most of the dwellings were of wood, and when it rained, most of the streets became mud. One heavy rain, and there were many from the great rim of the Pacific, and nothing moved, neither horse, nor carriage, nor cable car. Fog was frequent, and fire, and sudden earthquakes.

Lena could not fall asleep. She heard the midwife telling her children, the oldest not quite six, that the baby would be along soon, and their shrill voices asking, "What will it be?"

For a dreadful moment she wanted to cry out, "An idiot." She had hung lace curtains on her windows, and this shingled house was in a clean neighborhood although the street was greatly in need of paving. Like all respectable women, although she had borne two children no doctor had ever beheld her body. And would not now, she thought, with a midwife in attendance. But in the processional of years she knew this year would always remain a heavy burden. Neighbors no longer dropped in on her or received her on their "days at home." She was about to obtain a divorce, and nice women did not divorce.

"It it a boy, Mama?" asked Archer, standing in the doorway. He was feeling like the man of the house, being the only male in the house. "We'll have fun if it is a boy."

Before Mama was able to answer, the midwife was hushing him. Too roughly, thought Mama, hoping that the white-haired midwife, who had no children of her own, was not a scraper.

Archer was arguing with Amy that it should be a boy, one girl in the family was enough, and Mama turned inward.

My husband will not come back, I can be sure of that, rang through her mind. He had dismissed her, although she was obtaining the divorce. James Donald Malcolm, art collector and dilettante poet, had violated the seventh commandment and sought other shores. But his refrain had been the same as all the others: nice women did not divorce. His wife's duty was to forgive. Her decision threatened the very structure of marriage, agreed James Donald and his friends. Whatever you did—hate your husband, ignore him, sleep frigidly by his side, bicker with him until he had splitting headaches and so did you, one thing you avoided; you did not divorce. This very day he was able to promenade wherever he wished, she thought with a surge of resentment, while she lay imprisoned and isolated. In this moment she resolved that she would have no man again. She began to design her life for the days without sexual love. This pregnancy would be a last encounter. Yet, her emotions reversing themselves, she was glad that this child had been conceived in the last brief instant of love.

The more she reflected on her husband's lack of character, the more she was determined to create a child with a sensitive and significant nature. She recalled her own childhood and how she felt cheated, lacking the privileges of the boys. This child, if a girl, would lead her far beyond the limitations of her own personality and society.

Lena Malcolm lay back in her bed and imagined it a patch of grass in a lovely garden. The bed was large enough for her tall figure, but the mattress was worn and hard; yet she told herself she would not have it otherwise. This hard soil pressed firmly against her flesh and made her aware of her body. Suddenly she was proud of the great flare of emotion within her.

Something was rustling within her, and she was aware of the presence groping toward the light. By now she had a feverish wish that this child must be perfectly formed, must be a girl—an expression of herself.

It had grown dark suddenly, and still. She became conscious of a spreading on all sides, of being unable to see or reach her extremities. For an instant she felt helpless, and then she was irresistibly impelled to the achieving of this moment. The midwife and her sister Jessie hurried to her side. Then there was only pain and an inner voice shouting: *The kettle is boiling, the cloth is spread, the door is open. Hurry, hurry, here dwells the familiar mystery. Come, come quickly, before the soil is impoverished and the seed is dust. Here grows a life, new, tough, energetic, yearning to be active.*

But the child was a long time getting born. The inner voice died away. It was almost midnight when Lena Malcolm heard the cry of the newborn child. Not a whimper like most infants, but proud, almost defiant.

Lungs are good, she thought dimly.

She heard the midwife say, "A perfect specimen."

"What is it?" she murmured through bleeding lips that she had bitten in pain and which her sister Jessie was swabbing.

"Relax, dear, it is a girl," said Jessie. "A pink and white girl child. What are you going to call her?"

A far-reaching name, a name which would extend out of this world of bustles and whalebone corsets such as Jessie was wearing, and she was possessed with a brazen thought. She would place herself on the same level as a man: if a son could be named after his father, a mother deserved the same privilege. "Lenora," she said, "after myself." It was not precisely after herself, but it was close enough, she thought.

The midwife and Jessie placed the infant in the wooden bathtub, a recent present from Jessie, and Lena stared at them. Jessie was a dear, thought her sister, if too formal sometimes. Lena's gaze turned to the rubber plant, but it was really quite ugly, too ugly for her children, she decided in this continuing flare of independence, and she knew she must dispose of it as soon as she got out of bed. The other children were asleep, for they had been unable to outlast the night, and Jessie was advising her to close her eyes and take advantage of the few remaining hours.

"After I see my baby," said Lena.

Jessie held up the new Lenora, and there was a sudden waving of legs and arms as if the infant was dancing in acknowledgment of its birth.

Jessie cried, "Did you ever see such an active child!"

"I was the one who was active," said the mother. She noticed that the midwife was homely, when she knew that her children from now on must be surrounded with beauty. "Put her down, next to me."

The infant tumbled over, her mother's hands still weak, but the mother merely smiled as even the midwife looked concerned. Lena Malcolm did not hold with the superstition that if a child fell at birth it would be a fool at maturity. Even as the newly named Lenora lay in her mother's arms, her little arms and legs continued to wave.

2

Mothers search for signs. Mothers search for lovely portents of the future in their infants, and signs of genius and a purity seldom found. And some expect their children to be born without sin, searching for signs of a child so washed in a happy energy that their own flesh seems born again. But motherhood comes in strange and private and unexpected ways. A mother may suffer womanhood for many years and never cry out, but let a single blow be aimed at her infant and she will raise all the demons of hell. Let births be as plentiful as the locusts, the birth of her child has a special significance, and the man who would deny that, beware. Where a mother lies beside her infant, the signs are rich with light and loveliness, and this, then, is the pendulum of birth.

Passing through such a world, Lena Malcolm awoke the following morning with new courage. It was very early, the sun was almost white in its rising, and she felt as if she and the world had altered overnight. Yesterday's fog was gone. The bedroom was as quiet as the street outside. The other children seemed safely asleep.

Not out of chance had this child been born, she assured herself, not crudely or blindly, but out of grandness and an overwhelming desire for beauty. Not out of a brief, hurried moment of longing, but out of the flowering of the blood and the holy life-giving of love.

The infant stirred in the cradle, and the mother felt she had defeated the foe; quickly now she would recover her strength. The infant's arms and legs circled curiously, as if discovering the facts of motion for the first time, as if taking her first genuine plunge into this thing called existence.

It was not that easy, thought the mother. Not all the signs were favorable. She gazed past the baby and saw the wooden sidewalks outside the house, the muddy streets with ruts torn deep like wounded flesh. She remembered the constant smallpox epidemics, the sensuous abuses of the brothels along the Barbary Coast and a city that was acquiescent. She was revolted suddenly, hating all this and the dreary poverty which had settled upon them like a plague.

But the infant was still moving, and the mother stared only a moment more at the impoverished house and then sought to concentrate on Lenora. Once again the mother was certain that this infant born in such a time of anguish would be the one most capable of wonder and ecstasy.

Then she focused on the other children, who had begun to stir. Archer, the eldest, wanted to recite Longfellow to her, while Amy had just suffered a tragedy. Amy's padded diaper, heavy enough to be a bath mat, was hanging around her knees, and Amy was unable to walk. Lena adjusted the diaper, wondering why even a baby's things had to be so ugly and concealing. She knew she would have a sense of even greater achievement if they all became advanced children. A little later Archer ran off, and when his mother asked him where he was going, he blushed and said, "To play."

She had a feeling he was not telling the truth, that he was hoping to earn a few pennies somehow, but she had not the heart to expose him.

When Archer returned he was mighty proud, having earned

several pennies by running some errands for the butcher down the street. The boy held the money as if it were a great chunk of wealth, and she said, "Marvelous," although she would have preferred to hear him recite the "Curse of Cromwell," like a fine Irish-American lad—although her husband's side of the family was Scotch—or to narrate the story of Prometheus as told by the poet Aeschylus, or better yet the lines from Milton, "First there was chaos, the vast immeasurable abyss, outrageous as asea, dark, wasteful, wild . . ." which he gave such a soaring sound although he understood scarcely a word of it.

Lena was reflecting on that when Jessie interrupted her.

Jessie said, "You look distracted. Have you eaten?"

Lena had become so engrossed in the infant she had not.

Jessie said, "You cannot be so impractical. It is impossible to think that you can ignore the world or forget to eat. You have even avoided our parents since you decided to divorce James Donald. Your children will suffer for it."

"They will get the best kind of a bringing-up."

"Without a father? Rubbish! You are in no position to support such an extravagance as divorce. You ought to realize that what I am advising is for your own good." But Lena did not seem conscious of anything but her own thoughts.

Compared to Jessie, she was regarded as the plain one. She was tall, with good eyes, but everyone agreed that Jessie possessed the beauty in the family. Her own profile was gaunt, as if carved out of rock, but Jessie's was perfect and striking. Her skin was pale, where Jessie's was blooming. Jessie could have been a fine actress, Jessie was so attractive, but she would have preferred to be dead than be seen on the stage. So now she was married, and respectably well-off if not happy. Jessie stood in queenly dignity, her high voluptuous bust accentuated by her narrow corseted waist. If this was the best man could do, reflected Lena, it was indeed a world of dubious virtue.

But Jessie was insisting, "You must realize that what you are planning is immodest, that all you will succeed in doing is attracting attention."

"Despite my quarrel with James Donald?"

"It is not that serious. I have quarrels with my husband."

"Oh, I agree, it is not at all serious, only irreparable."

Jessie was not as imaginative as her sister, but she recognized a touch of hysteria when she saw it. Whatever betrayals Lena's husband had committed, the years would be more wretched without him; San Francisco would be tolerant of him but not of his wife. They would have no mercy for a divorced woman, even if she were the victim. To be so reckless as to dare divorce was a monstrous foolishness, and no hurt pride was worth it.

Jessie said, "The children need a father. Especially the girls."

This was a violent challenge to Lena, and she retorted, "They need a mother more. All of us are, basically, the products of mother love. Fathers are the surface which society places upon us in the form of marriage. If we had to depend on men, the human race would have come to an end long ago."

"No man will accept that."

"Perhaps." Lena stared lovingly at her children. Love for them at this moment pressed heavily upon her head like a crown of iron, but distraught as she was, there was a vital and growing conviction in her that her children must move from sunshine to sunshine.

"Lena, your doctrine is not nice."

"Not nice?" Her husband could spend night after night with disreputable tavern crawlers, and Jessie ranted on about being forgiving and sensible. Yet Lena knew she must not regard her sister as silly, for her sister meant well. "Pick up Lenora," she said, in a gesture of conciliation. "The child is as light as a feather."

Jessie lifted up the infant, slowly at first, then gladly. The infant was very light, and yet she could feel a sense of energy and growth, and she said, with a hard-wrung smile, "She is a finely formed child."

"Perfectly formed," Lena said proudly, and declared in a flare of independence which surprised even herself. "My baby is not going to wear padded diapers, bibs, and dresses. My baby is going to dress more sensibly. She'll be proud of her body and won't hide that."

Jessie, for the moment, surrendered to her sister's determination. Holding the infant in her arms, she wondered: did the infant actually comprehend? The infant seemed to be reaching for her milk, even though she was covered with whalebone, and she blushed. Jessie shook her head and looked away. No children of her own, there would never be any children of her own, she knew, but she could not tell anyone, not even her sister. Here she stood with two tiny hands reaching for her, and it was acutely painful. In this moment the world outside ceased to have any existence. Jessie stared bewildered at Lenora, wondering why she, so much more practical, so often wiser, should want this infant to be radiant with self-expression. She held the infant tighter then, yielding herself up to an unfulfilled desire, and thought, which indeed of all of us are sane?

Lena whispered, "Lenora has energy for a hundred. She has been full of emotion ever since she was born."

3

The days of infanthood are least remembered, yet they are most deeply felt by the young Lenora. Every sensation is new and infinite, untouched by experience, and thus startling, tumultuous, and often shocking. Every sensation is profuse with impression, a deluge of feeling, and almost too intense to be endured. It is a labyrinth, and sometimes the infant feels lost. The days of infanthood are also a long climb out of the darkness and into the light.

Here, in these first years of her life, there is hardly any remembered consciousness; the memories which recur and draw her back are the forces spreading increasingly to her fingers and toes, forces she cannot control or define, and yet they threaten to overwhelm her.

For Lenora can move. At first she is scarcely aware of that. Yet to move is her initial essay in living. She has been equipped with an elaborate apparatus for these ventures, but sometimes she lacks the coordination but never the desire. Lying pink and pretty in her cradle, she yearns to go far. Her brother shouts teasingly in her ear, and she is startled, although she is not aware why. Communication evades her. Not all the flattery in the world interests her. She has not yet been vexed with language. It is in movement that she expresses herself, it is what she is. Often it is all she knows.

And three years pass before Lenora experiences an event she is able to recall.

Lenora was sitting on the floor, playing with her toes and wondering why they bent so easily, contemplating them as a source of entertainment, wondering too why she could not walk on her hands as easily as on her feet, and she was bored. She had been told to rest by her mother, and she did not want to rest.

Seeing no sign of her mother about, Lenora sought to find relief from boredom by balancing on one leg. Succeeding, she rocked back and forth, pleased with the motion, twisted

around, retaining her balance. Next she tried to stand on her
toes, but she discarded that, for it hurt. She felt more comfortable on the balls of her feet, and as she skipped about the
room a new consciousness seemed to clamor in her.

The child did not comprehend the meaning of this, but a
thrill went up her spine; this was fun. No longer was she
bored with the old room. When she jumped off the ground
she felt a new, wonderful satisfaction; she knew that she was
the bravest little girl her mother had ever seen.

Lenora was becoming conscious of other memories, too.
Past four now, seeking to recapture the triumphant excitement of balancing on one leg, of skimming over the ground, a
new joy washed over her. She could not remember a day now
when she did not feel in terms of motion.

Lenora's most vivid early memory was of the bay, however,
and how it attracted her with its enormous energy. The water
surrounded them on three sides, and it contained a prodigal
odor; it gave her a delight which she could not name but
which drenched her in a joyous world of sensation. The bay
was never the same two days running. More and more, as she
was left to her own devices while her mother was away teaching piano, her footsteps turned to the waterfront. The water
was colder in summer than in winter, which puzzled her, for
she had been taught that summer was the hottest time of the
year. It was often foggy, but never quite the same way.

Once she almost slipped into the water. She got wet to her
knees. And even as she was frightened, her inner excitement
was intense. Everything else was blotted out; she felt as if she
had lost all fear, and her vitality was tremendous. She told no
one of these adventures. When Amy, who was supposed to
watch her, asked, "Where were you?" Lenora replied, "I
was . . . anywhere. . . ."

Amy gazed at her as if she were a silly, knowing there was
no such place as anywhere, but for Lenora it was a place. It
was where she could float through the air like the clouds,
where no one bothered her and she had no need of anyone. It
was the cliff she could climb by herself; it was where she felt
she had the legs of a centipede. It was where the wind seemed
to lift her as she whirled through the air. Anywhere, she knew,
was here and there and everywhere, although she could not
make head or tail of it.

Lenora was now not quite five years old.

4

Then there came a time when Mama was home often, when her piano lessons slackened, and she read the masterpieces to them. All roads now led to her readings, which became the heart of their lives. Lena Malcolm had become Mama to her children. This metamorphosis was of her own choosing. She resolved that she would not compete with her children. She would keep their birthright uniquely their own: she would divide her capital equally among her children, they would all be artists. She was certain this was a safe investment, would bring them happiness and the creation of a beautiful, sturdy life. Intensely now, Mama concentrated on the poets of beauty. "Read this, Archer," she requested, and handed her eleven-year-old son Wordsworth.

Archer recited with pride and devotion: *"The world is too much with us; late and soon . . ."*

No one cared that his pants resembled burlap or that his cotton stockings were torn. The other children loved the ringing quality of his voice. But Mama was not satisfied. She said, "It sounds nice, but it needs more feeling. You try it, Amy."

Amy was too grave to suit Mama. She handed the volume to Lenora who recited it with eloquence, although the child understood only a little of it.

Mama, pleased with Lenora's emotion, had her repeat the recitation. The child was blessed with a gift for feeling, she reflected joyfully.

San Francisco might be a new Sodom and Gomorrah these boisterous days of 1883, she thought, but her children were made of braver stuff. Their heroes, she told them, must be the courageous artists such as Byron, Wordsworth, and the Brontës. She added that the only sin was to oppose oneself, and that love should encompass the universe. Mama paused, reluctantly. Lenora was nodding, almost asleep.

The child was thinking that everybody was so eloquent, but occasionally dull. Then Lenora was wide awake, for Mama was asking her to act out Archer's reading of:

"O wild West Wind, thou breath of Autumn's being . . ."

Lenora, intoxicated with excitement, knew she was the leader and that her brother should follow her. The others forgot the reading, although Archer's voice swelled. Lenora moved like an ocean wave curling before the wind; she was dancing, although no one had suggested it.

Mama was delighted with Lenora's grace, with Archer's elocution. Absorbed, she did not hear Jessie enter. Jessie thought Lenora possessed a raw, unstable look. And the child's white pinafore, which she had given her, was dirty. Jessie asked, "What is this all about?"

Jessie's interruption botched the scene, and both children halted in disgust, united in anger against this interloper. Mama, feeling protective, refused to explain. If what her children did was not understood by others, it was the fault of others. After all, she did not expect Jessie to comprehend the ways of children, never having had any. Mama smothered her children with a shower of kisses, which they accepted as their due. Baffled, Jessie sought to win them to her side, kissing them also. Archer was annoyed, thinking it sissylike, but he was dutiful; Amy acted as if it were appropriate and was pleased, calculating that Aunt Jessie did have the power to give her elegant pinafores; but Lenora, without hesitation, fled from Aunt Jessie and embraced Mama so passionately, Mama was in danger of being strangled.

Jessie was even more hurt. Jessie knew that her mission was one of high-mindedness; she felt grievously wounded. She cried out, "You don't teach children to enjoy themselves, you teach them to improve themselves."

"I teach them to be themselves. I believe," said Mama, with an eloquence which surpassed her children, "as Jean Jacques Rousseau did, that it is unnecessary to worry a child's brains with rules during the early years of their life. One must offer poetry, music, dancing. These are the spiritual experiences which will last a lifetime."

"Under what moral law? You have to teach the children some rules, some properness. Otherwise, they will become outcasts."

"The laws of Nob Hill, or should I say Snob Hill? They create a world so respectable it could only be endured by a society that has nothing else to think about."

"Lena Malcolm, it is useless to reason with you."

"You forget that artists are the first citizens of the world."

"Bosh."

"My children trust me."

"Why not! You allow the children to do whatever they please, you even allow them to participate in discussions such as these, which we were never allowed in our day. No wonder they agree with you. I do not blame them. I would too, if I were their age."

Mama replied, "I give them the same freedom that I want, with a few limitations and some guidance."

"You are as much of a child as they are!" Not waiting for an answer, Jessie went swiftly out of the room, not defeated, however, in her own mind. Her sister might reside in an unreal world, but she would yet find the way to teach the children, such dears really, that custom was man's effort to establish an orderly set of values, which, if you obeyed them properly, made living easier.

Mama, meanwhile, incapable of holding a grudge against her own flesh and blood, put aside the quarrelsome feeling and returned to the children. As the final bit of magic for the evening, Mama told the children about the Brontës. She took them through the old vicarage on the dark Yorkshire moors. Mama quoted how clergyman Patrick Brontë had not condescended to read his daughters' works, that he had been heartless, and yet the talent of Charlotte, Emily, and Anne had grown in glory. She made it sound as if the Brontës had dedicated their lives to art and said this with such emotion the children were brought to tears. But their blood also leapt at the drama of these lives, and they knew they were more fortunate than the Brontës. Mama would aid them where the Brontës had had no such aid: Mama would lead their advance on the capitals of art.

Reclining about Mama, the children were also thinking that to be born in a time of anguish was exciting, especially if they lived forever after in immortality. They were wondering, in their own fantasy-soaked manner, what glorious events might happen to them. They were full of pride and tenderness. How interesting to suffer when one was an artist!

And Lenora could not fall asleep that night. All was silent except for the occasional clatter of hoofs on the cobbles of the street, and yet it was as if there were sound all about her. Fragile voices whispering and whirling past her, and she tried to lie quietly, but it was impossible. She longed to move with these sweet, musical voices. She would be the West Wind and the South Wind. She would be Emily Brontë, while Amy could be Charlotte, and if Mama had another daughter she could be Anne. She glanced across the room at Amy, but her sister seemed sound asleep. But she could hardly contain herself. Driven by depths she did not comprehend, Lenora slipped out of bed and balanced on her bare feet. It hurt a little, but her feet were flexible and she did feel free. She arched her back, her legs—why hadn't she thought of this before?—and rose, seemingly higher than she had ever risen before. Then she was able to fall asleep.

5

Mama, as a wanting-to-be emancipated woman, found it essential that she continue the education of her children at an accelerated rate. Every night when Mama was home she read aloud from Homer and Sophocles and Blake and Byron and Milton. The deep wound in her began to heal as she saw more signs of creativity in her children. Archer's acting had force now; Amy played the piano efficiently, if not brilliantly; as for Lenora, it was impossible to tell yet whether she had talent, but she moved with such energy, always on the go, and was so pretty, Mama was sure she would amount to something, although Mama was not quite certain what.

Mama, when she was not exhausted from her piano lessons, also played for them. Scarlatti and Liszt were their special favorites, but Mama also gave them the music of Bach and Haydn. If not as ably as she preferred, she was consoled with the thought that she was giving them a sense of the beauty of life. Although they were not enchanted with Bach and Haydn, Mama was rigid now. Mama believed there would be a time when the children would be grateful for this early grounding in these composers. But she never played the scales for them, or exercises.

How could you be a romantic, Mama asked herself, and play scales?

Lenora enjoyed moving in pantomime to Scarlatti. It was not dancing, as such. There were no formal movements. No one, not even Mama or Amy, who displayed a penchant for teaching, attempted to teach Lenora. But this activity became the child's reason for existence. In this lotus land the poets and the Greek gods were far more real to Lenora than their neighbors. She seldom saw them, the Malcolms moved so often these days, and when she did, it was usually unpleasant. The family's growing reputation for eccentricity weighed heavily on their neighbors. Most of the neighbors not only possessed fathers, they possessed fathers who earned a living.

Mama blamed this on what she called "the cultural apathy of San Francisco." For her, and gradually for the children, culture came to be an ideal which existed far away, in London, Paris, Berlin, and most of all, in Athens. In what Lenora came to call, "the land of far away."

Mama also believed that most parents limited their children's talents but that she was developing those of her children. The world she was putting before them, as she expressed it, ". . . is best explained by Goethe." Mama shifted on the uncomfortable horsehair-covered chair this autumn day, a Sunday on which she had no lessons to teach, and said to her children, "The great Goethe believed we must find the right model, to best coin the metal that is within us."

"But what is a good model?" asked an intent Archer.

"What do you think?" Now that her children were on the correct path, she was resolved not to influence them unnecessarily.

Amy said, "I would like to be Athena, the goddess of wisdom."

"I am going to be Hamlet," said Archer.

"And you, Lenora?" asked Mama, for her youngest had not answered.

How boring all this was, thought Lenora. They thought they were going to be something magnificent, but she knew she was already.

Mama asked, "What model fortifies you, dear?"

Lenora stood up boldly, pirouetted before the one mirror in the house, and stated, "Venus." The other children laughed at what they regarded ridiculous, for how could their baby sister know about the goddess of beauty? But scorn was not the way to halt Lenora's tongue. Lenora burst out, "Mama, you did say you had me because of Venus." She knew this dramatic tale by heart. "You told me that I was a true child of beauty." The drama of her birth was a treasure, and no one was going to take this glory away from her. She trembled with emotion. She was full of an unexplainable joy, and she felt a little wicked too, for Mama had confided this to her privately, but she could not allow the others to get the better of her.

For a moment, however, Mama felt betrayed. Lenora never should have exposed this; she favored none of her children. Yet she could not scold Lenora, the child looked so lovely, her hazel-green eyes glowing, her skin fresh and bright, and her little nose—Mama's particular delight—straight and perfect, except for a slight Irish tilt.

The other children were not so enchanted. "You are a little girl," said Archer, "and little girls should be seen and not heard."

The next instant there was a hubbub of voices, an angry blur of faces, and then Lenora announced, "Archer can't catch me." They raced around the shabby room, and Archer, much to his exasperation, could not catch her.

Archer, usually the mildest of the children, then tried to hit

Lenora. Mama, horrified, stopped him immediately. She said that boys and girls were equal and that neither should seek to surpass the other. Mama spoke decisively, but things were still not tranquil among her children.

The instant Mama halted, Lenora was refusing to admit she had been wrong; Archer was on the verge of striking Lenora; Amy was trying to outshout everyone. Mama sighed wearily. She was trying, with all the intensity of her passionate soul, to be a good mother, but she was thinking it was too difficult. Yet she did not wish to deny her children the pleasure of mother love, and so she made one more effort at reconciliation. Mama kissed all of them and then, to prove she had no favorites, requested Archer to read from the *Iliad* where the male gods seemed to have their way, at least part of the time.

But putting the children to bed a little later, Mama could not contain herself. Mama kissed Lenora good night with extraordinary intensity. Mama was thinking that Lenora, although she was giggling because Mama's embrace tickled, seemed most of all to be possessed with the undeviating faith in herself that was beyond logic, that Mama knew all artistic souls, even at a childish five, should have.

This faith however, did not make life easier. As Mama had expected and as Jessie warned, Mama was condemned for divorcing James Donald. In self-defense Mama told her children that most husbands, after the first few years of marriage, regarded their wives with distaste, indifference, or took them for granted, and that most marriages became emotionally bleak and sterile. She taught her children to resent the clothes of the time, finding in her hatred of corsets and stuffed bosoms a hatred of convention and commonness, although she did not have the courage to dispense with them. Which was wonderful and terrible.

This became a family which week by week did not know where the rent was coming from. The frequency with which they moved was not wonderful. And Mama was not skillful at hiding her distress. However, she pretended indifference to this gypsy life, to the constant evictions; when she had to find a new lodging, usually worse than the last, she grew frantic and nervous. Lenora noticed that Mama dropped things when they had to move, or sat in the family rocking chair and rocked incessantly, as if that would drive away the eviction. Mama had no suspicion this caused her children to suffer more. They never complained. What was the use of complaining when nothing could be done? And then it was against their faith, and yet often the movings were very painful.

Lenora was counting the weeks to her sixth birthday, certain Mama would give her something wonderful, when a moving became a humiliation she was never to forget. They were still rooming on the second floor of a dreary house close to the Barbary Coast. Mama was away teaching, in far-off East Oakland, and Lenora was in her favorite dreaming spot, her bed, while the others were playing outside. Left much to themselves, the children had discovered many ways to entertain themselves, and one way was to act out scenes from plays they knew, but this afternoon Lenora was not included. Lenora had become angry when Archer had refused to read from Shelley so that she could dance to the poet's words. Archer and Amy had wanted to do a scene from *Twelfth Night*, where all of them could perform; when Lenora had refused to abide by their decision they had gone outside without her.

Lenora now, dreaming on her bed, was imagining herself a gypsy queen. She was wondering whether she should forgive Archer and Amy for not playing her way, and if school, which was to start soon, would be as much fun as Mama, and she did not hear the sound of the footsteps on the stairs. She was startled by the loud knock on the door, the sullen, unshaven stranger who stumbled in.

He grunted, "I'm the mover."

"The mover?" Were they having to move again?

"Yep. Get going." He motioned for her to lift herself out of bed. He was half drunk; he sniggered as he saw the child's bare legs, mumbled an obscenity, and suddenly, while she was too stricken with fear to budge, he leaned close as if to touch her. He had the stench of whisky, sweat. He put his fat limp hand on her; it was hairy, repulsive. As he leaned closer she stuck out her foot and he tripped. He cursed, and Lenora, terrified by his stench, his hands, his swollen nose, his little sunken eyes, his vulgar face, wanted to flee, but he stood over her.

She prayed to God, but Mama said there was no God; she prayed to the Greeks, but they were far away; she prayed for her family to appear, but they were angry at her. She wished she had not fought with Archer and Amy. She jumped out of bed, but this only inflamed the mover. He growled, "Come here!" Crouching against the wall, her retreat blocked, Lenora was just about to scream her lungs out when she heard Archer's cheery whistle as he came up the stairs to see that their books would be moved. Quite beyond reason, she embraced Archer. The mover was gone before she could remember how he had left, and then she did not know what to say.

Her brother was puzzled: what possessed Lenora! He knew his sister really liked him, the Malcolms had to stick together, but she was such a vagabond already and so determined to be first in everything.

Lenora was able to keep her secret while they moved, but that night it was more than she could bear. The new rooms were gloomy, pitch black, the bed creaked with every restless movement of her body, and they were just a short distance away from the ugly encounter and she was sure the mover was returning, and suddenly she was sobbing as if her heart would break. When Mama calmed the hysterical child, she heard the whole sorry story.

Mama, investigating the next day, learned that the moving crew had been recruited from the nearby Barbary Coast, on the promise of earning money for drinks. She decided, that whatever the sacrifice, they must move to a better neighborhood.

Castro Street was highly recommended. It was a more attractive neighborhood, with a wide lawn in front of the house and a spacious back yard. But the Malcolms were not allowed to play in either. The rooms Mama could rent were tiny; the precious piano had to be stored in the hallway. The rooms were poorly heated, and the yellow wallpaper was nauseous. Nonetheless, to afford this neighborhood Mama had to sell most of their furniture and even their Nottingham lace curtains. And this moving did not deliver them from the tyranny of poverty. In debt already, Mama was forced to hire an old moving van which everyone knew was the cheapest in the neighborhood and which, most of the time, was used to collect rags. It had no top, and their neighbors gaped critically at the skimpy possessions tossed carelessly upon the van. When the Malcolms arrived at Castro Street, their new neighbors indulged in an inventory of the Malcolms' worldly goods and, finding them insufficient, promptly rejected them.

Lenora could hardly contain herself. Faces peeked out of nearby windows, but no one greeted her. She sensed their curiosity and that they were unfriendly. She felt like a fool, wanting to be friends with everybody. She was so much alone these days it became very difficult for her. Mama was away teaching almost all the time now, Archer and Amy were in school, which she was still too young to attend.

One afternoon, caught in a torrential downpour, Lenora sought refuge on a spacious porch a hundred feet away from Castro Street and was ordered off. The child was too confused to argue. She knew it was ignominious, but she fled. She was drenched to the skin when she reached home. She was frightened, she felt naughty, something that seldom happened to her, and she was very cold. Mama, arriving home, filled her with hot tea, but Lenora could not stop shivering.

And Mama came to a most unladylike boil. She was in a foul mood suddenly, unable to be resigned. Mama had been seeking to reawaken the child's desire to imagine, feverishly she had been reminding Lenora that together they would gather strength if they lived by Shelley's noble creed—". . . *a man to be greatly good must imagine intensely and comprehensively; he must put himself in the place of another and of many others . . .*"—and all at once her words mocked her. Lenora's shivering had increased. Mama abruptly halted her reading. For once even her beloved Shelley was no relief. "Don't cry, dear," she said. "Please, don't cry." She could not endure tears.

"Mama, I did nothing wrong."

"I know."

"But I feel so ashamed, as if I had."

"We will move, dear, we will find a better place to live." She wrapped the child in warm blankets, in all the blankets they owned. She kissed Lenora until they were both tearful. But her daughter did not ask that the reading be resumed; Lenora, even as she held her close, seemed far away.

6

So this year of awakening memory seemed an age to Lenora, and not always a golden one. The child began to realize that between the spirit and the striving there were many gaps.

When Mama became aware that such flaws were inevitable in their present way of living, she agreed to let Aunt Jessie keep Lenora while she was away teaching. It was enough to shatter her heart, but the stringency of the situation left her no choice. Mama had acquired more pupils in distant East Oakland, and she was home less and less. The other children were in school, where they were occupied safely and busily at least, but Lenora was alone most of the time and Castro Street remained hostile. Mama decided, reluctantly, that Jessie's properness could not cause Lenora any permanent harm. But Lenora refused to go until Mama assured her it would be for only a few weeks.

"No longer, Mama!" insisted Lenora, while Mama sadly prepared for the child's departure. "Promise!"

"I promise!" But Mama felt anxious, as if somehow, after this separation, things would never quite be the same between them.

Aunt Jessie's home was a three-story monument to Victorian splendor. The wooden turrets and the Gothic arches were far fancier than any house Lenora had lived in, but the rooms were dreary, crowded with overstuffed furniture. Lenora did have a bed all to herself, but she was not allowed to remain in it past rising time, or dream or play in it, and she came to hate the four-poster. She never wanted to go to sleep, and Aunt Jessie put her to sleep many hours before Mama had. Aunt Jessie had many rules, informing Lenora, "You must not skip, you must not play with your hair, and, goodness gracious, you must not squirm so!"

When Lenora sprawled on the floor as she had for Mama's readings, she was hoisted abruptly to her feet. When she happened to do it again a few days later, absorbed in reading about Apollo and Diana, she was spanked. Lenora had never been spanked. Lenora was so furious she refused to cry when Uncle Rufus vigorously performed what he called his "solemn duty," although he enjoyed doing it.

One lovely day, one of the few days without fog, Lenora was hopping up and down just for the sheer joy of it when Aunt Jessie caught her. Shocked, Aunt Jessie declared, "It is most unladylike." Just as Lenora was wondering whether it would be better to run away in the afternoon instead of the morning, after she had an extra good meal, Aunt Jessie decided to give her a party for her sixth birthday. It sounded wonderful to Lenora, and she put off running away; parties meant presents, games, other excitements.

Aunt Jessie also thought the birthday party a stroke of genius. It would endear her to the child; it would introduce her niece to the neighbors with the proper flourish. It would be a most vital step in the discriminating education of a young lady.

Lenora was happy for almost a week. Aunt Jessie was busy preparing a special dress for her, and there were other garments to be fussed over. Lenora began to feel affectionate toward her aunt. The morning of the party, however, the fitting did not go well. In Aunt Jessie's opinion foundation clothes were character-forming, unmentionable, and essential. By the time she draped all the essentials upon Lenora, the white cambric petticoats, the white cambric drawers, the wool challis slip, Lenora felt the weight of the world had fallen upon her shoulders.

Aunt Jessie cried, "You look downright delicious!"

"Do I have to wear three petticoats?" asked Lenora, her misery growing.

"Petticoats are of paramount importance, child. A lady's character is judged from the way she exposes her petticoats."

"But they are so uncomfortable."

"Dear, I have a real surprise for you." Aunt Jessie brought forth an embossed velvet dress, and Lenora admitted it was lovely to touch. Aunt Jessie pointed out, "You will be the quintessence of refinement."

It took a long time to be fastened into the dress, and then Lenora could hardly move. She was not finished, however, for the shoes Aunt Jessie had obtained for this occasion reached above her ankles, and they were so tightly laced the child thought her feet would die. But at last it was all done, at last Lenora was a model of a proper young lady, and she had never been so miserable. Her feet ached, she could hardly breathe. She took a few tottering steps before she was even certain she was able to walk.

Aunt Jessie said, "You do have feet that are a little too large, due to the way Mama has been dressing you, but then American feet are seldom as small as they should be. Still, you do look smart."

Lenora tried to feel happy, as she was supposed to feel. Perhaps her aunt was correct, fine clothes such as these were a comfort and a blessing. Now if Mama and Amy and Archer approved, the discomfort could become unimportant. She hopefully imagined their surprise; they had never seen her so adorned.

Then Uncle Rufus inspected her. Wanting his admiration even as she was indifferent to winning his love, Lenora tried to stand straight, but it was impossible.

Uncle Rufus was a stocky man with General Grant whiskers which compensated for the lack of hair on his head. He looked what he wanted to be: a bearded dignitary who impressed and ruled. But what puzzled Lenora was that Uncle Rufus, though a head shorter than Aunt Jessie and homely by comparison, was the unquestioned master of the household. He made it quite clear it was *His House, His Food, His Servants*. The child knew she was in the house only on his sufferance and that it was vital, in Aunt Jessie's opinion, that she win his approval. So while she had no intention of remaining any longer than it suited her, she had no desire to bring criticism down upon her aunt, who was her blood relative. Lenora also sensed that Uncle Rufus regarded her entry into his household as an invasion of his property rights, but he was allowing the party to be the test. If she behaved like a proper child, he might consider an extension of her stay. He agreed with Aunt Jessie that she was a pretty child and could be useful as a companion for his wife.

Aunt Jessie said, "Pirouette, so Uncle can see all of your lovely outfit."

Lenora, normally very graceful, almost fell, but she managed to make a complete turn.

He asked, "Where is the hair bow? All small persons should wear bows."

She longed to shout, why don't you wear one if you like it so much, but that was no use she knew. Grownups like Uncle Rufus never listened to her.

Aunt Jessie said, "She will, dear. Lenora, kiss your uncle like a good little girl."

Lenora dutifully absorbed the prickle of his beard, although she loathed it. Aunt Jessie was proud of her, and surely after a few minutes of wearing this harness she should be able to walk without each step being such an ache.

Lenora was preening herself before a mirror when Archer and Amy entered. They stared at her with such shock she knew it was not flattering. A little later, catching Amy glaring at her, she felt like a traitor. Amy, alongside of her, looked drab and dull. But before Lenora could explain to Amy that it was not her fault, Aunt Jessie was continuing their education.

Lenora was flanked by the homemade clothes of Amy and Archer, which gave Aunt Jessie joy that she had delivered one child at least from bondage. And as she had bettered Lenora, she would better all of them. She established herself in the center of the parlor, an authority on manners, and read to the children from her cultural bible, *Harper's Bazaar*.

Lenora interrupted suddenly, "Aunt Jessie?"

"Child, it is not polite to stop an elder in the midst of a lesson."

"But the stockings itch."

Amy giggled, then Archer, and Aunt Jessie said, "Alas, I had the illusion that my sister's children might yet become little ladies and gentlemen."

"But they do itch," repeated Lenora.

"You are not accustomed to them," said Aunt Jessie.

"I am so!" cried Lenora, sure this was criticism of Mama.

Aunt Jessie was angry too. They were behaving like little barbarians. Sternly she ordered Lenora to demonstrate the proper curtsy with which to greet guests. Lenora bowed an inch or two, but that was all, she felt so confined by the clothes. Aunt Jessie said, "It is difficult for me to believe that a child who cannot curtsy properly deserves a birthday party."

Lenora said, "Everything is too tight."

Aunt Jessie said, "Or you cannot do it."

There was no such word as cannot to Lenora. She bent to curtsy. She knew she was limber enough, and she hoped the velvet would stretch. But as she settled into the proper curtsy position, the dress ripped. Lenora straightened up to avert further damage, but the rip widened along a seam and the petticoats underneath became visible. As Lenora stumbled into a corner to hide, Archer and Amy roared with laughter. It made her feel more wretched. She throbbed all over; she felt she would come apart at all her seams. And suddenly she hated the clothes, the party, all the instruments of her humiliation. She fled.

There was no consolation until she reached the bay. No one had followed her; she had run so swiftly it had been impossible. Lenora stood upon the rocks that bulged over the water and now, more than anything else in the world, she desired to move as gracefully as the sea. The waves washed through her, and she felt far away from strife. There was no joy but motion. There was the foam and the surge of the water, and it was all motion. It quickened her blood, and all the muscles of her body. It brought her joy that here, by the bay, she felt triumphant over humiliation and pain. The sea was never overdressed; the sea knew the simplest appearance was the best.

Quickly, then, Lenora ripped off what was left of the velvet dress, the petticoats, the drawers, the slip. She was especially happy to be rid of the stockings and the horrible shoes. Then, naked, she felt the salt spray of the water, the sensual heat of the sun, the gentleness of the wind. She felt suspended in the air like a gull, and a flood of feeling and motion rushed through her. The air and water seemed to lift her above the ground. The sun and the wind and the spray seemed to create a harmony which carried her wherever she wanted to go. She looked like a tiny pebble beside the immense bay, but she felt delivered from stupidity. She felt born again, felt joy and love swirling through her, felt she could love everybody, even Uncle Rufus.

After an unmeasured time Lenora stopped dancing. Her spirits still longed to soar, but her body had become weary.

The wind had shifted, and she heard the church bells announcing the time. It was much later than she had realized, and Mama would be worried. Lenora gathered up the clothes. Mama must return them to Aunt Jessie; they belonged to Aunt Jessie. The child donned the velvet dress and one petticoat. She was not troubled by the rips now.

Motion was language also, she was realizing, although she was too young to put it in such words. Motion was a language which could speak of heaven and earth, which expressed so many things she could not express any other way. It made her feel so glorious, so intoxicated. What could be more wonderful!

Mama was deeply unhappy about the flight. It had been very rude, she told Lenora, "And you behaved badly." But she did not send Lenora back to her sister. Jessie was not having a thing to do with Lenora, unless she apologized, and Mama had no intention of submitting the child to such an indignity. Mama thought Jessie had been wrong too, forcing Lenora into those unnatural clothes. When she had to be away teaching again, with school still a few weeks off for Lenora, she left the child with her parents.

Lenora liked her grandparents. They lived simply, in a small house with a pitched roof, and none of the rooms were forbidden to run or jump in.

Grandma flew the twin banners of Puritanism and Pioneerism, and Lenora admired her spryness. There was hardly a thing Lenora could do that Grandma could not do. Grandma was past fifty-five, but she had grown up in a hardy tradition. And though she did not always approve of Mama's attitudes, she believed in minding her own business. Her own parents had made her very unhappy with their strenuous objections to her coming to California with Patrick O'Dea during the gold rush; she had no desire to repeat this mistake. Instead of halting her, it had made her even more anxious to go, although she had been pregnant at the time.

It was Grandpop, however, who was Lenora's favorite. Patrick O'Dea regarded his grandchildren as cherubs; he was never happier than when he had them on his lap and told his stories. Such as now, relating how he and Grandma had come over the prairie. Lenora felt she was riding right beside him on the prairie as he said, "Grandma was carrying your Mama then."

"In the wagon?" asked the excited Lenora.

"Inside of her." He did not hold with lying to children, whatever their age. "We were ambushed by redskins, and I was busy, with the rest of the wagon train, shooting redskins, when——"

"Did you kill many, Grandpop?"

"Six or seven." Each time he told this story the slain grew, but Lenora did not mind, for it made him more interesting. "But your Grandma, she was the one you couldn't tame. I get through shooting redskins, I tell her everything is fine, and she tells me not to worry, the child is all right. She is acting like a filly who has just won a horse race."

"Why not?" said Grandma. "I come from good Irish stock. I knew the baby would be all right."

Lenora asked, "Were you scared much, Grandma?"

"No," said Grandma. She kissed the child and then, to give her an ancestry which would make all the fools who snubbed her envious, added, "We come from fighting blood. O'Deas fought in the Continental Army, Grandpop was an officer in the Civil War. You should be proud of your family."

"I am, Grandma." She was, almost as proud as when she had danced by the sea. "Did you really jig, Grandpop, when you came home from the Civil War?"

"Sure," said Grandma, "because I taught him."

He played a jig on his mouth organ while Lenora tried to follow Grandma's brisk step. Lenora liked the tune, but the step was mighty fast and Grandpop was not much in rhythm. But when he played a more romantic tune, "The Song of the Irish Emigrant," she was able to follow him. Then he went on to "Three Little Drummers," and Lenora caught some of Grandma's flourish. Aware they were applauding her, the child felt on wings.

The following afternoon Lenora wanted another performance, but it was impossible. Grandma had all the wash before her, and it was vast and had to be done. This struck Lenora as silly. How could you waste an afternoon on such dullness, when you could jig? But when she helped Grandma hang the wash, she was given a new jig to learn. It was called "Wink and She Will Follow You," and Lenora, who had been practicing secretly, learned more quickly now. Though it was in triple time instead of the six-eight of the ordinary jig, Lenora caught the correct beat. Lenora learned something else. When she felt joy, the jig was easy.

7

School is a serum which sometimes takes and sometimes does not. When it does not, Lenora believes that the flock is wrong and that she has been driven toward new impulses, powerful and swift and better focused. She is willing to turn somersaults to prove this serum is a poison, that in her contempt for school she has destroyed sham and subterfuge.

She is a little girl with hair that tangles in the wind, who loses buttons and hair ribbons and hates heavy woolen stockings, who slides down banisters and giggles too loudly to please Victorian politeness, but she has learned with a wisdom far beyond the resources of school that she is beautiful, even at seven. She senses that when she runs and skips and dances on her long slender legs, she speaks with an eloquence far beyond a school child's power.

Much of this was felt by Mama too. Lenora is beautiful, she told herself, as Shelley must have been before he died upon the wild waters. All my children must be beautiful, even though not all of them possess Lenora's grace. Nothing must ever make them indifferent or blasé. Amy will probably never be as pretty as Lenora, with her thin, bony features, and Archer's face is too round to be handsome, but all of them have the same vital spark. A roof over their heads is important, but I must give them greater resolves. I must not harp on it, but I must be persistent.

No one regarded my education as vital. I was withdrawn from school without even finishing the fourth grade. Girls do not need learning, my parents said, if anything they suffer from it, acquire false ideas, are inclined to become melancholy. Learning is like a fever, they told me, and you will get over it the day you marry. But I have not got over it, Mama thought, and I never will. Why had they not known that without education I have no thinking power? Why had they not known that I could not mature without education, without thinking power?

She thought of her children again and how they would bless and appreciate her. With the resources of education they would not have to depend on piano lessons, sewing, or marriage. They will be artists, they will be neighbors in happiness. Not like myself, untrained, self-taught, a lone bird struggling through a dense mist.

Oh, Mama will never forgive her parents for this lack. She could weep like a child because of their short sightedness.

The public school was a surprise to Lenora. After the magnificence of Mama's teachings she expected the schoolhouse to be beautiful and majestic, but it was a broken-down building in a decaying section of San Francisco. It had been a beer hall a few years before and only recently had been converted into a school. The windows were dirty, plaster dangled overhead, and potbellied stoves furnished insufficient heat for the chilly rooms.

By the end of the opening day Lenora had a miserable headache. She longed to quit. Other children were running home, crying that they did not wish to stay in school, but she was too proud to admit defeat, and Mama had promised it would be a fine adventure and Mama almost always was right. So Lenora hoped her teacher would make the disagreeable surroundings more pleasant, but these hopes were dashed quickly. Miss Stahlback was scrawny, with pinched features and severe black hair parted tightly across her small skull. She was even uglier than the school.

Miss Stahlback had been teaching for many years and had long since settled into a labor-saving routine. She was paid according to the number of pupils she taught; she crowded as many into her classes as the room would hold. She believed her pupils should be constructed for endurance; if at the end of the day they were exhausted, wonderful! Then they had no energy to dispute her and kept out of mischief. Discipline and manners were also of prime importance to her, as were attendance and memorizing.

Miss Stahlback, roving through the class, was having the children recite nursery rhymes and was distressed by their errors. She decided that teaching was a waste. How nice it would have been to have married and not have to make children think.

The class stirred restlessly as Miss Stahlback paused to meditate, and she snapped to attention and ordered little Bobby Rock to recite "Jack and Jill."

Bobby's voice came falling down, and suddenly it was more than Lenora could endure. She had not been called on for weeks; she knew she could recite so much better, and it was wonderful to win the class's attention. On her feet in the next instant, Lenora was quite dramatic, declaiming:

Thou still unravish'd bride of quietness,
Thou foster-child of Silence and slow time . . .

The expected applause did not come. Miss Stahlback cried. "How vulgar!"

Lenora replied defiantly, "It is Keats, and I know more."

"Have you no conscience, Lizzie Malcolm?" The class was attentive now.

"My Mama taught it to me."

"You do not expect me to swallow that!"

"But she did, she taught us Emerson and Byron and Whitman and——"

"Horrid writers! I dare say they have a kind of cleverness, but there is no godliness in any of them."

The class tittered at this rebuke, and Lenora thought bitterly, they think I am stupid when they are stupid because they have no courage.

Miss Stahlback declared, "The next child who recites without my permission will be severely punished."

"But I know more," said Lenora. "I really do."

"You are a vulgar, vulgar child," said Miss Stahlback.

"I am not!" Lenora shouted back, jumping up and down in anger.

Miss Stahlback cracked the child across the ankles with her yardstick until the child felt numb with pain, but she did not cry out, she would not give any of them the satisfaction, and so Miss Stahlback placed her in the rear.

Lenora's ankles ached for days, but she did not mention the beating to anyone. She tried to be patient; the term was ending soon, and then she would have another teacher. The next term, however, the second-grade teacher was Miss Stahlback, and Lenora came to believe she would have her forever.

So Lenora embarked on passionate explorations elsewhere. She seemed to be listening to the teacher even as she felt imprisoned at her desk in the rear of the room, but her imagination took her on daring far-off adventures. She saw herself as Diana and Helen of Troy and George Sand; she composed a tableau in which she met Byron. Pulsing with dreams, the teacher's face dissolved, and Lenora imagined the boards of the Grand Opera House beneath her feet and three thousand people applauding her as they applauded Edwin Booth. And as her dreams expanded they became more familiar than the drab schoolroom. She felt within her the surging power of her imagination, a strange blazing power which had no form and yet took her everywhere. Tomorrow, a year from now, five, ten, what voyages she would take. Mama would come too, and perhaps Archer and Amy, but no others; she would punish those who humiliated her now. Oh, what immense voyages she would take! How wonderful!

But it was not wonderful to sit through a succession of aimless days, waiting for the dismissal bell to ring. Lenora had decided she would prefer to die in battle, but as the months dragged by without change she was afraid she would expire right in the classroom. Then the passionate explorations became futile. Then she could only sit silently and stare out the window. She had learned that even one who danced with the gods had to suffer and that to be a good teacher you had to love teaching and Miss Stahlback loved nothing, not even herself.

Lenora was eight now. Constant dreaming and suffering had given her a groping, fragile air, and the success Mama had expected for the child in school seemed further away than ever.

The child is taller, thought Mama, but her mind is afraid to reach very high. Her slender body is physically erect, but she walks stiffly, and her head sags too much of the time. Her imaginative ideas are frozen by the rules of conduct. Loneliness shuts in her heartbeat, and her face is tense with a little girl's frown, and her thoughts have become hit or miss. She does not talk enough any more, and the character of her silences is becoming fretful. Getting used to it, that is all they are really teaching her, Mama's mind ran on, a little distraught. What a stupidity that is! They are not even teaching her to be conversant with the laws of nature—or to wonder!

So Mama, believing that much of growth had ceased since school had begun, that perhaps she had placed too much dependence on what she herself had lacked, resumed the after-school teaching of her children.

Most wonderful of all to Lenora was to see Mama smiling again, to be able to ask questions again: "Mama, why is fog?"

"Because, well, Lenora, because . . ."

Lenora needed no answers, just so she could ask. "And why do women have to do washing and not men? I don't like to do the dishes any more than Archer does."

"Because, well, because . . ."

Lenora was off on a new torrent of emotion, asking, "Is it wrong to dance?"

"Who said that?"

"Oh, people."

"Dear, was it Miss Stahlback?"

"Mama, why is she so afraid of everything?"

"There is no other place in the world for her but teaching. If she loses that, there is nothing else she can do to earn a living. As a spinster all she has to look forward to is being an old maid."

"Mama, are you afraid?"

Before she could reply—not when I am with my children, they are the best luck I can wish for myself—Lenora had lifted the shawl off the piano and thrown it over her shoulder like a Greek drapery and was dancing. And when Mama suggested, "Would you like me to play?" Lenora nodded, and as Mama played one of Schubert's art songs the music seemed to flow into the child. The tall, gaunt woman played on and on, but most wonderful of all to Lenora, again, was Mama's smile. That evening Lenora composed a poem which she hung over Mama's bed:

> When my Mama smiles
>   She is an angel;
>
> When my Mama smiles
>   I feel good;
>
> When my Mama smiles
>   The clouds run for miles;
>
> When my Mama smiles
>   We should!

Mama was so moved she was unable to sleep. Teaching was becoming its own reward, it would deliver a glowing future for her children. She would get her artists after all; it was not a mocking jest. People might slam doors in her face, but her children would break them down, they must break them down, they must not be trapped by conventions that turned artists to stone.

At the same time Lenora began to read omnivorously. Because she had no father, she was still regarded as an outsider by most of the neighbors. Some of the girls sneered that she was "common," and her answer was to slap the girls. She knew that Mama had been married. But Lenora assumed that her father had deserted them and considered this a personal affront. It became easy for her to have a prejudice against fathers, and not having a father became the natural way to grow up. Lenora was sure that marriage was a state of bleakness; she did not understand the hows or whys; it was exciting to shock adults with her frank statements against marriage;

the actual facts of life were a mystery to her. When Amy whispered to her the way children came it seemed ugly, and she was not sure her sister was right. When boys tried to kiss her, they were clumsy—grabbing her too hard—and she repulsed them. She was positive this could not be love.

There were few of the cruelties of most families. Where other brothers and sisters teased constantly, deliberately hurt one another, the Malcolms were drawn closer together. Sometimes Amy sought to impose her will on the others, but Archer was gentle almost always, now that he was becoming a young man. There were moments when they were quick to quarrel, for each of them had an independent mind, but one thing brought complete agreement: when the neighbors treated a Malcolm as an eccentric, which was frequent, they became united as one. Some instinct stronger than mere reasoning mounted within them at such times. And whenever the world in its realism grew too harsh all of them were able to create a world of fantasy, as if that existence had been here all the time and only had to be discovered. Often, performing with each other, they would battle fiercely to outdo each other, but God help the outsider who strove to outdo a Malcolm—it was all their life was worth! This was as natural to them as it was to be a Malcolm and an artist. So Archer and Amy agreed with Lenora's dislike of school.

It became natural for the twelve-year-old Lenora to tell Mama that she had enough of school, that it was absurd, ugly, and stupid.

Despite Mama's efforts at self-control, she cried out, "No school? That's impossible!" What possessed Lenora now?

Lenora said, "I love school, but as you teach it."

"Only I do not teach it, and Miss Stahlback . . ."

"Does, Mama?"

By instinct she avoided lying to her children. And she preferred not to argue with them, although now she sensed a little intrigue, rather deviously managed by Lenora. She said, "You cannot just do nothing."

"I can dance."

"Dear, you have talent, but . . ."

"Mama, you could teach me," said Lenora, using all of her charm.

"I have no real knowledge of dancing."

"You have the greatest knowledge of music and art of anyone we know. Amy can accompany me on the piano, and Archer can fill in with his acting. We will be the touring Malcolms, we will always be together."

Mama had to admit it was tempting. She knew that if any of them would have suggested going into a shop she would have heard it with consternation.

Sensing that Mama was weakening, Lenora said, "You have taught us all we know. You have taught us such fine things, and can teach us more."

It was a great challenge, thought Mama. Her teaching could be the outlet for her love; she could keep the children gainfully occupied; she could focus them even more on art. She changed her mind four times, however, before she could agree to the departure of the children from school.

When Mama announced her decision, Lenora was triumphant. Archer and Amy agreed that Lenora was smart—school was unnecessary—and Lenora hugged Mama and cried out, "I will dance as much as I like, and no one will say I am jumping too high, or running too fast, or that I must not hurl myself into the sky. I will hurl myself wherever I please."

Mama reminded, "Within reason, dear."

"When I go on the stage and have children, you can take care of them."

Mama said, rather annoyed, "I took care of you. I think you should take care of your own children."

"Then I won't have any."

"Children can be a source of great happiness."

Dancing about, Lenora shouted, "I will dance in the houses of the most important people in San Francisco, you see." Anything seemed possible when she was in motion. In school she was a nothing, but Mama was smarter.

Mama said, "You will have to take dancing lessons."

"But that isn't any fun." Lenora halted, feeling about to be squeezed in.

"Shouldn't you dance according to the rules? Everybody else does."

Lenora leapt away again, saying, "You cook from a recipe. Don't expect me to dance from one." Yes, yes, anything was possible when she was in motion.

BOOK TWO

8

Lenora cannot rest. There are no impossible horizons now; all of earth seems within reach and it is essential to soar. She has discovered there are many ways to heaven, and that dancing is the one she prefers.

There is a delirium of joy within her when she dances. Dancing, she feels she is a creature of air, of fire, of water, that she is returning to the elements from which she has come. These are dreams come to life. All the days now, even when she was home alone, she danced.

Nimble, quick, some steps came easily, but today Lenora felt awkward. This stormy November afternoon she sought to move with the speed of the wind which howled outside, but it was too fast. She took off her shoes, but even in her stockinged feet she was behind the wild speed demanded by the driving wind. Lenora paused, but the wind did not pause. She sought to capture its speed once more, but though she flung herself about the room, it was not enchanting as when she had danced by the water.

Today Lenora was searching for a new step she could not name, a spontaneous step which grew out of her own emotion and the wind. Today she was seeking to capture in motion the rapture Shelley gave her. How her art must be fashioned to his fine words, for they gave her an exalted feeling. Today, posing in front of the fireplace, repeating the opening lines of Shelley's "Ode to the West Wind," she tried to be the essence of abandon. But as she listened to the wind, to all the voices within her, dancing as she imagined it now seemed so much vaster than her reach, her resources.

It had grown quiet outside. The wind had died down. Something seemed to be rustling within her. By now she had a fanatic wish that this dance step be perfectly formed; she felt irresistibly drawn to the achieving of that moment. But she stood in poised fragility as Mama entered, with Aunt Jessie close behind, and Mama asked, "What are you doing?"

"Dancing."

"You are not moving," said Mama, while Aunt Jessie waited to be greeted.

Lenora drew a little away from Mama, as if communication had been severed. She could not explain that inside she was dancing.

Mama said, "Doesn't Aunt Jessie look lovely, dear?"

"Yes," said Lenora, and nodded hello to her aunt in a measured way.

Aunt Jessie had grown stout, but her skin retained its color, and she was elegantly dressed and still the beauty of the family. A truce had been established between Aunt Jessie and the Malcolms, which made Mama happy. Mama believed in keeping the family close together, and she liked her sister even when she thought Jessie was obstinate and narrow-minded. And Jessie had forgiven Lenora, in the name of home and children.

Mama said, "Lenora, I have good news. Aunt Jessie may be able to get you a sponsor. A friend of hers, Mrs. Fanning, has great influence in art circles."

Aunt Jessie said, "I have a natural reticence against dancing, but since Lena thinks it may be useful, perhaps something can be arranged."

"The child has talent," promised Mama, having to promise something, for there was no promise in Lenora's icebound posture.

"Might not Lenora be more gainfully employed in embroidering book covers, or knitting?"

"I know you speak in good faith, but you are in error."

"I speak because I am practical. There is too strong a tendency among young women to rise above their station in life, spoiling good dressmakers and cooks and wives in order to be incompetent musicians and teachers of music."

Always criticism, thought Mama, and suddenly humility was just as impossible as being a cook or a dressmaker. Risking the aid half promised by her sister, Mama stated vigorously, "I am certainly not going to waste talent and send a hummingbird into the hen yard to scratch the earth and hatch eggs."

Aunt Jessie replied coldly, "I am trying to think of everything. It is easy to be clever but not so easy to support oneself."

After a long pause, Mama said, very softly, "I know."

"Moreover," said Aunt Jessie, "the child is not unique."

Lenora saw her dreams being stepped on. She said, "I do not need a patron." She took a deep breath and danced about the room, on her toes and yet not on them, bouncing up and down in a graceful lifting motion. As she came close, gathering intensity, Aunt Jessie cried, "You must not jiggle your body!"

Lenora halted abruptly, all the desire to dance out of her.

Aunt Jessie said, "You cannot romp like a boy. You are not a boy."

Aunt Jessie was frowning, and even Mama looked disturbed, and Lenora wondered what was wrong now. She felt betrayed, even by Mama. Lenora was not aware that she had embarrassed the adults, for her breasts growing into form had bounced up and down, and the illusion of childhood had vanished. She was no longer neuter, but possessed something which had to be regarded furtively. She had become adolescent, and something to be worried about.

Aunt Jessie said, greatly aroused, "I have been dealing with Freud's Corset House, and their Marguerite corsets are fine for young ladies. I hesitate to speak on such an immodest subject, but one would be quite suitable for Lenora."

Mama, who in theory wanted her children to grow up, was unwilling to recognize these first signs of maturity. It was too upsetting; it did something to her that she could not analyze, but she found herself wanting to conceal the child's first sign of physical maturity. Mama said, "A corset is not necessary . . . not yet."

Lenora longed to flee, for she was discovering feelings she could not share with anyone. But she knew that if she deserted Mama while Aunt Jessie was here, it would give her aunt an advantage that would serve neither her nor Mama well. Lenora stood completely still, but before Mama, presenting an image of romantic, yet modest, decoration.

Aunt Jessie said, "That is better. A lady must make no display of her feelings. She must stand quietly and have perfect balance."

Mama tried to reassure Lenora, saying, "Child, you were graceful."

Still mute, Lenora had very little identification with Mama now, feeling she was not really her recognizable self but that she had a double life and no one would possess the second existence but herself.

Mama sensed that. She kissed the child with all of her

emotion, but the child's lips were dry, unresponsive. She asked, "Don't you feel well, dear?"

"I feel fine," answered Lenora. Lenora was sick of how she felt. She yearned to be so distinguished, and they were talking of such stupid things.

9

While Mama waited for Jessie's patron to materialize, she planned to send the child to dancing school and invited her parents to watch Lenora perform.

Mama dressed the child in a lovely, simple frock which stopped halfway between the knees and the top of her shoes. She knew it was the fashion for girls from twelve to fifteen to wear their dresses to their shoe tops, but she told herself Lenora must have the freedom to move. At the last moment Mama placed a flower instead of a bow in Lenora's hair, deciding it was more appropriate for spring. Archer and Amy gathered around Lenora and agreed she was Spring, although Archer preferred her as a daisy and Amy wished someone would give her such a nice dress.

Lenora was not certain whether to be proud or ashamed of her costume. They wanted to keep her a child, she decided. She felt these clothes were not really necessary, yet this new development could be the start of an exciting life. But all at once she was irked. She was realizing that the money to pay for her dancing lessons would have to come from her grand-parents, if they thought them worth while. She had no doubts about her chances with the future.

Grandpop wore a formal frock coat, for he knew this was an occasion. The coat was so old the black had a green tint, but he acted as if this was a recital worthy of a grand duke, and Lenora dared him for such make-believe. Grandma was not as rhapsodic as Grandpop, for she saw problems. Dancing might be only a whim with the child, she thought, or a need to get rid of discontent. Moreover, she and Grandpop were living on a small pension, and any new expenditure had to be justified.

Confronted with Grandma's disquieting severity, Lenora wanted to beat on their feelings with her bare feet. Listen with faith, her heart cried, listen as you listen to the wind and the sea, listen, listen, for I will not be a traitor to what they have taught me. Instead, Lenora shuffled uneasily, feeling that her slippers were an encumbrance, and yet no one da~ ~ed in her bare feet. She said, "I can jump high."

"Why?" asked Grandma, staring at her sternly.

"Why!" Lenora paused in mid-air. What had the sea to do with being wet? But it was.

Mama came to the rescue, saying, "Some people cry when you play 'The Last Rose of Summer,' others are moved only by a Bach chorale."

Lenora said, "I want to be as famous as Sarah Bernhardt. I want to dance on the stage and die like she does."

Grandma asked, "You won't be afraid with so many people looking at you?"

"It is ever so nice to have people watch you. I like audiences. I just look past them and dance so pretty they have to watch me."

"Wouldn't you like to have other little boys and girls to play with?"

"I am not a little girl. And I haven't time. I am busy dancing."

"But when you grow up, you will want to like those boys, won't you? Almost all great dancers and actresses get married. Even a Bernhardt."

"I don't care. I am not getting married. When I come on the stage I don't want to be anybody but Lenora Malcolm."

Grandma believed in free thought, but this talk of nonmarriage was too free. She said, "You are putting too severe a strain upon people's faith."

Mama said, "People will be tolerant if she is an artist."

"Let us not be enchanted with unreality. People will say—"

Mama cut in, "People gossip about us even when we do nothing. She is only twelve. How can you take her so seriously?"

Lenora, very determined now, skipped around the room in time to the waltz Mama played on the piano.

Grandpop said, "Real pretty."

Grandma said, "What else can you do, child?"

"Jig, waltz, pirouette."

"Can you dance on your toes?"

"Of course she can," said Grandpop.

Lenora rose on her toes, but within a few moments she thought her foot was going to break. A dreadful ache spread through her foot, but she managed to hold a semblance of a toe position until Grandma nodded approval, although the pain increased and she thought she would faint.

Grandma said, "That is more like dancing."

Grandpop said, "It's in her blood. The child has inherited talent."

Lenora's gestures grew vigorous and assured as she danced a waltz which appealed to her since Strauss had written it, but her ache returned when Grandma said, "I am not certain about the talent, but dancing should not do her any harm, and it may even help her posture, although I was learning to sew at her age."

Grandpop said, "You won't discourage her. She has the strength of a mule. You might as well let her have her head."

Grandma said, "Maybe. Lenora, what dance do you prefer?"

"Whatever I am doing."

"Why do you want to dance? The real reason?"

"Because it is natural. And beautiful." And for many other reasons not so easily answered. But as she felt, she danced. "I want to dance to the end of the world," she said as she danced about the room but not on her toes.

Grandma said, "With all this energy, you could pull a mighty fine buggy."

Mama, correcting her as politely as she could, explained, "She will become more finished. She will grow."

Grandma said, "Little warts grow too." Then, seeing Lenora looking mournful and desiring to clarify her own mixed feelings, she added, "But the child does have unusual energy." She told Grandpop to turn over his gold fob to the pawnbroker, their routine method of raising money.

When their grandparents were gone, Amy said, "You were not good, Lenora."

"I know."

"You were too nervous."

"Yes," said Archer, who was developing into somewhat of a philosopher, having just read Aristotle and Goethe and Hazlitt on the theater. "You were nervous because you had no philosophy of style, no point of view. But you are never nervous when I accompany you with my readings."

No, thought Lenora, they were all wrong. Archer was a fine reader, but it was not nerves, it was far worse. For the first time her courage had failed her. When she danced by the bay it had been natural, but on her toes it was cruel—so cruel she was not sure she could endure it again.

Mama was elated. She said, "Grandma is going to help me send you to one of the best ballet masters in San Francisco. She is not certain you will be a dancer, but she will pay for your lessons."

The ballet master had none of the abandon Lenora craved. She had imagined a graceful, charming man, with a sense of urgency. In her naïveté and as a result of Mama's teachings she expected a professor of ballet to feel for everybody, to be inspiring, but Henri Roubert was a prim little man with an aloof air. She heard that he had trained with the Paris Opéra, but what no one knew was that he had been only in the chorus. In San Francisco, however, he was an authoritiy on the ballet, although he preferred the minuet. He had been born of bourgeois stock in Paris, which he regarded as vulgar. He was happiest when he minced across the floor in a minuet, when he felt he was a portrait of the eighteenth century, his favorite time to him, an aristocratic time.

The studio was another disappointment to Lenora. She had assumed it would have grandeur, but it was dusty, drab, and circled with mirrors that made her self-conscious. Then, from the start, Roubert greeted her with the five ballet positions and spoke of them as if they were divine. This was not a magical formula, Lenora thought with a shudder; this was waddling like a duck at the oddest angles. She wished for a sensuous perception commanded by her own beat, and he ordered her flesh to be as hard as bone. No emotion allowed, no exaltation or joy in any of these steps, nothing but the five positions, and her toes began to ache once more. Seeking to stand on one leg, she was taut; she was sure she looked like a crane. She stumbled and felt dishonored.

He examined her to see if she possessed the proper kind of feet, torso; but what about her intensity, her understanding, her imagination, her soul, wondered Lenora. Mama said the soul was the seat of everything.

He said, "You are too tall for your age." She noticed she was as tall as he was. "And your hips, alas, are too broad, and your feet, alas, are not strong enough, and you are much too old! Twelve, much too old to start ballet. Nine, ten would be far better. The exercises are most difficult, your body is already formed, but with perfect discipline and my teaching —— No, no, you must not flap your arms and legs like a stork."

Lenora felt as stiff as a ramrod. She realized she was supposed to rely on what the professor knew, but that was contrary to Mama's teachings. And so much emphasis on balance was against her own feelings. Within a few minutes she came to feel that the only balance was the avoidance of it.

During the lesson the following week the class was ordered to stand on their toes, and the shuffling was frantic. Roubert watched coldly, for there were no Mamas present now. As the class spun around, Lenora stared into the mirrors, and what came whirling back was awkward enough to make her weep. What was even more painful, she felt so ugly. Lenora knew she could never get herself beautiful in these fixed five positions. And he was telling her, "You have absurdly weak feet. This climate does not suit grace."

"Did you see me waltz?" she said abruptly. "Everybody thinks I waltz very well." She moved now with all of her charm.

He thought her ridiculous. He ordered her to exercise. He accelerated his count. It was his drastic cure, and he leaned against the rail while she attempted to move with the class. But Lenora felt, after what seemed innumerable efforts to stand on her toes, that they would snap off. Lenora tried again, in a kind of frenzy now, and Roubert smiled cynically and said, "You cannot dance solo. You are far away from that."

"How far away?"

"In seven or eight years . . . perhaps."

Lenora was stricken. He ignored her as he talked about the necessity of the rigid stretch of knee, ankle, and instep to form a single straight line, and that was another slight. She told herself it was not natural to turn out the feet, but awkward to the breaking point. Suddenly Roubert struck her as stupid. He was ordering her to renounce the easy natural movements of running and skipping, and she knew that was wrong. Mama had stated that she should form her own conclusions about dancing, and Lenora did, with determined finality. Ballet dancing made her hate her own muscles. There was no challenge to imagine. She wondered if the sea ever felt so useless.

So Lenora turned reckless. Roubert ordered everyone to rehearse the first position as punishment for his own dissatisfaction with his present situation, and she did not want to keep her heels together while her toes pointed out. Rebelling, she danced into the center of the room. There was a tempest within her, and she gave herself up to it, not caring what anyone else thought. The amazed Roubert allowed her to take a few steps, and then he halted her. She seemed to be hanging in mid-air as he asked, "What is this supposed to be?"

"I am dancing the moon."

"You want to be the moon? You want to dance the moon? Who can dance that!" He glared at her, for once admitting bewilderment. He wiped his forehead, then reasserted himself. "You dance Giselle, but the moon? Fantastic!"

"I do not like ballet."

"Miss Malcolm does not like ballet. How thoughtful. You are always behind everybody, and you do not like ballet. You ought to go into a shop, sell moons. Now turn out your legs."

She did not obey. She remembered Grandma and asked, "Why?"

"Why!" Now he was really shocked. He exploded, "My God, it is essential!"

"It is not," she said, and shivered at her own audacity although this also pleased her. "Ballet is stupid, corrupt, and cruel."

And that was why she quit, she told Mama. "I could not do anything else." She told Mama about the many difficulties, and this time there was no questioning. By now Mama was aware she had borne a child with such a strict intensity of purpose that no arguing would alter her. But Mama began to treasure Lenora's childhood things: a lock of infant hair, a stocking half knitted, trivial things, yet in some ways more familiar to Mama than the child becoming a stranger in unexpected ways.

And considering all this carefully, Mama spoke to Jessie about the audition with the hoped-for patron. She implied that her sister could be a fairy godmother to Lenora, which prompted Jessie to make an appointment for Mrs. Fanning to view the talents of the Malcolms, especially Lenora.

Aunt Jessie enjoyed having the family dependent upon her. She put the major portion of her energy to this high purpose. She insisted on the girls wearing white, the color of innocence. She bought a calisthenic dress for Lenora. Since Mrs. Fanning represented opportunity, Lenora sought to be a good niece, but she resented the calisthenic dress with its wrist-length sleeves —no one would see her lovely arms. And she did not care for the slippers, although the slippers were more comfortable than toe shoes.

Mrs. Fanning lived at the top of Nob Hill, and Lenora could not be casual about such a significant audition. Once, in her resentment of this section which dominated San Francisco with its wealth, power, and exclusiveness, she had vowed to dance up all the way. This afternoon, however, Lenora was content to sit quietly in the hansom cab Aunt Jessie had hired for the occasion. Despite Lenora's resolve not to be impressed, she was fascinated by the magnificence of Mrs. Fanning's mansion. More of her resistance to the rich vanished. She decided that perhaps not all wealth was sinful.

Mrs. Fanning kept them waiting, which was the custom, but she looked so delicate with her alabaster skin and dark hair and fragile features that Lenora was certain she must be a cultivated lady. Mrs. Fanning asked Lenora, who seemed to be the leader, "Why do you want to dance, child?"

"Because nature dances, and I want to be beautiful."

Mrs. Fanning turned to Archer and asked, "How goes it, boy? 'If you have a voice,' said Ovid, 'sing, but if you have good legs, dance.' ' "

Archer said, "You honor us, Ma'am." At a signal from his aunt he planted himself firmly as he had seen Richard Mansfield do and recited:

> We are the music-makers
>   And we are the dreamers of dreams,
> Wandering by lone sea-breakers,
>   And sitting by desolate streams;
> World-losers and world-forsakers,
>   On whom the pale moon gleams:
> Yet we are the movers and shakers
>   Of the world for ever, it seems.
>
> With wonderful deathless ditties
>   We build up the world's great cities,
> And out of a fabulous story
>   We fashion an empire's glory:
> One man with a dream, at pleasure,
>   Shall go forth and conquer a crown;
> And three with a new song's measure
>   Can trample an empire down.

Archer paused for the climactic explosion of emotion on the third and last verse, and Mrs. Fanning applauded and said, "How lovely. What is it from?"

Archer said, "It is by Arthur O'Shaughnessy."

Mrs. Fanning sighed, "Alas, too many of us are afraid to dream."

Lenora asked, "Why?"

Mrs. Fanning looked disconcerted for an instant, then gave Lenora a gracious, blank glance. "I think, child, you should realize that the understanding of a thought does not necessarily provoke the expression of it."

Animated discussion followed between the Malcolms, led by Aunt Jessie, in which they agreed with the wisdom of Mrs. Fanning's words. Prodded by their aunt, they decided it would be best to begin their audition with a melodrama. They performed a scene from *The Corsican Brothers*, which they had seen at the Grand Opera House from the gallery. Lenora played outrage with burning vigor, and Mrs. Fanning said,

"The child has a knack." Lenora felt strangled; she expected to be called talented at least, she had acted with such exertion. Then the patron said, "May I see some more, children?"

The Malcolms embarked on the comedy scenes from *Twelfth Night*, and Mrs. Fanning said, "Splendid," but sat unsmiling as if anticipating a calamity. It paralyzed their initiative, and they did not know what to act next, whether to attack with drama from *Hamlet* or from *Romeo and Juliet*.

While they debated, Lenora noticed that Mrs. Fanning had very pretty hands and was toying constantly with them. Small, white soft hands, thought Lenora, so unlike Mama's callused ones. What Lenora did not know was that Mrs. Fanning had a tiny watch inserted in a corner of her card case, which she was consulting without being observed.

Mrs. Fanning asked, "Do you have any other gifts?"

Lenora said, "I dance."

"Oh, yes. Perhaps some other time we can have a dance program."

"Thank you," said Aunt Jessie, "You have been most kind."

Mrs. Fanning stood up in a gesture of dismissal, and Lenora, angry that the best part of their program—her dancing —had been ignored, paused just an instant to get her breath and then whirled about the room as if blown by a great wind. Her grace, after the postured and declamatory reading, was all in her favor. And her audacity was appealing. Mrs. Fanning sat down. What was most appealing of all was the surprise. When Lenora finished, Mrs. Fanning said, "This is not quite what I had in mind, but it is sweet."

Lenora said, "I have an encore that is even nicer."

Mrs. Fanning said, "I am sure it is. You have a nice natural tempo." She felt an urgency in the child invading her and she looked away.

"I could perform this way whenever you wish, ma'am."

"You could appear at our tea parties."

Aunt Jessie said, "Thank Mrs. Fanning, dear."

Happy, Lenora had to feel this like a dancer. She composed a graceful bow to express her thanks and asked, "When do you want me to dance, ma'am?"

"Later," said Mrs. Fanning. "When I come back from Europe."

They were at the door when Mrs. Fanning asked, "Child, why don't you dance on your toes?"

"Tipsy-toe dancing!" Lenora's voice grew scornful. "I don't like it!"

Aunt Jessie and Mama stared at each other and for once,

agreeing on Lenora's perilous ways, understood each other very well. But Mrs. Fanning smiled pleasantly and said, "Perhaps. Only you should tolerate it, since you expect to become a dancer. And you may become one. You are highly charged. You have an interesting emotional quality, if you survive it."

"Ma'am, I dance only what I feel."

"And you feel extremely. If you are serious about being a dancer all that may help, and your aunt did not exaggerate, you are very pretty."

"I am going to be an artist . . . all of us are going to be artists."

"I can believe that," said Mrs. Fanning. "You, all of you in fact, have a great deal of confidence in yourselves. I will speak to some of my friends about you before I go to Europe."

The children, led by Lenora, marched out as if this performance had made them professionals. Or at least changed them to something higher, better. They were returning to a shabby, ugly boardinghouse, they had even less capital then before, for the preparations had cost money, but they owned something far more precious. They were artists. They had faced their first audition and done it with a flourish. Lenora, having taken the initiative, felt this particularly. Never again, she informed Mama, could she refuse a challenge. They even thanked Aunt Jessie. As for Mama, she was certain now that there was noble music in them and felt greatly rewarded.

10

Mrs. Fanning did recommend the Malcolms to other patrons, and this gave them a fresh boldness and the impetus for further explorations.

It was one of Mama's great times. It was as if she had communion with the future, a future which would be unique and eminent. Mama was not certain she had got her genius, but she was certain her children were artists.

It was a great time for Lenora also, despite the pseudo-genteel boardinghouses, the day by day uncertainties, the chronic poverty.

The first public performance occurred shortly after the visit to Mrs. Fanning. She recommended them to the rich, influential Mrs. Vogel, and at the latter's tea party the Malcolms repeated the scenes from *Twelfth Night* while Lenora improvised a solo dance as well as acted.

In San Francisco itself Lenora began to get solo engagements. By the time she was fourteen she danced at the Pandora Dramatic Club, at a Golden Gate Fashionable, and was thought so talented she was offered a chance to play Eva in *Uncle Tom's Cabin*, but that bored her and she turned it down.

There were many able, experienced soubrettes at liberty that season, and Archer wondered if she was not being hasty, but Lenora was determined to succeed as a dancer. She believed hers was a new way of dancing, although she could not name it and actually much of it was not new. It was sentimental, graceful; she wore comfortable dancing shoes and a lovely lace dress. Her dancing was sometimes free and sometimes waltz, and sometimes it had the sea and wind in it, but always it had part of herself. That much she had learned. This was her only rule. She never danced on her toes, however, and continued to insist that she never would. She told Mama, "It is silly to depend on one inch of your body for everything you do."

Mama said, "Some of the discipline might be valuable."

Lenora stated, "No. Ballet is all outside dancing."

Mama was not so sure, but she said nothing, afraid that criticism might blow out the child's flame.

More and more Lenora did not wish to be bothered with Mama's ideas. More and more the child was not a child, getting adolescent headaches, saying she looked a fright, worrying about her hair, her skin, caring intensely about her appearance, worried that she was getting homely although she was becoming even prettier. By the time Lenora was fifteen she was tall and slim, with lovely reddish-brown hair and a tip-tilted nose. She was pleased with the curve of her neck and shoulders, but she was afraid that her firm but small breasts would grow no larger. When Lenora imagined herself a nymph, artless and chaste, she was almost content with the way she was maturing, but later—it could be the same evening, when she yearned for Albert, a young actor she admired and was certain he regarded her as a child—she felt she was a failure. She was humble then, fearful that she would never mature, and yet she could not face any questioning. After she recovered from Albert she thought herself in love with a tenor whom she worshiped from the gallery of the Grand Opera House. And even as she felt frustrated there was a kind of fulfillment, as if the very wanting was enough, was a kind of maturing, for now. But to talk about it disfigured her illusion, and so she kept silent. Yet there were times when dreams, dancing, and reading were not enough, when a deep and secret longing threatened to undermine all her vows to keep herself chaste for her art. So her desires went up and down, but never to a logical end; she felt vivacious and vulnerable at the same instant, tense yet poised, an amorphous unrest intruding, making her ache with life.

There were also times now when Lenora wanted to say, Mama, tell me about my father, but she did not, sensing that the reply would be confusing or irritable. James Donald had remained an unspoken subject, and Lenora considered herself immunized against fatherhood, but now she began to dream about him, only in her dreams her Papa was young, fearless, gallant, attentive, and he took her into his arms, and her joy was almost unbearable.

And he was asking her:

"Do you love your Papa?"

"No, sir."

"Why not?"

"Because you treated my Mama badly."

"How do you know I treated your Mama badly?"

"Because she told me."

"What else did she tell you?"

"That you left her."

"Do you want to love your Papa?"

"No, sir."

"Why not?"

"Because I must hate him."

"Why did your Mama tell you that I was cruel?"

Because I asked her. I have no father. But she kept hearing the words behind these words: does he care, he must care for me, his daughter, if I succeed, if I am not commonplace.

Disturbed, for when Lenora was awake she was always assuring herself that her father was faceless, she sought even more to focus on her dancing. As time went on this was not enough. She longed to dance heroically, to take in the whole world, and San Francisco seemed so small and unheroic. A new and increasing restlessness spread within her.

Driven yet drifting, she often ran away alone to the bay. Then she danced, then she felt, as she had years before, that her clothes hindered her. Impatient, for there was so much of new life stirring within her, she took off everything. She knew she was old enough to look after herself, yet she had moments of doubt at this daring. But when she was sure that no one was watching, she danced naked by the water and felt free as a nymph and unconquerable. How right, how beautiful to worship only nature, she thought, and be in communion with all of creation, to draw exhilaration from the world of the senses. All things seemed possible, all the bonds seemed to fall off. She was exalted by the winds, the rush of the waves. Her blood ran fast. But it too, finally, was not enough.

Lenora had assumed that when she danced in the resplendent homes of the nabobs, the Comstock millionaires who lived in the castles on Nob Hill, she would meet San Francisco civilization at its best, or at least at its most interesting. But when she was sixteen, when she met Mrs. Fanning again, the encounter was different than she expected.

Mrs. Archamp was Mrs. Fanning's aunt, and she ruled over much of the city's society with an iron hand. Mrs. Fanning, who had been abroad the past three years, had just returned, and the party was in her honor.

Mrs. Fanning remembered Lenora's energy and, having heard that the girl's skill had improved, recommended her— but none of the others—to Mrs. Archamp, saying the child was rather interesting and attractive.

It was a midweek afternoon when Lenora and Amy, her accompanist, arrived at the Archamp mansion. Lenora felt overwhelmed by its size. The appointments were dark and formal and made her sad. She was not certain she could summon the energy to dance romantically here. Just as she had an intense urge to flee, she saw a friendly face, Mrs. Fanning, sitting behind several fat dowagers, looking lustrous by comparison with the unattractive older women.

Mrs. Archamp said, "Proceed."

In a sudden, reckless mood Lenora went around the room with a rush of vitality. She realized she was splashing out emotion as she danced, but at least it was natural, felt. There was no applause. Mrs. Fanning suggested, "Do something . . . softer, dear." Lenora's recklessness did not alter, however, for though she did not rush around the room this time, her dancing remained free. Only the mood mattered, only the movement and grace, emerging from her memory, from beginnings known and unknown. She was treating her feelings as if they had to be aired and nourished. But as she slackened a moment, to regain her breath, she wished the audience would co-operate—just a little. No one's expression had changed. She wondered what Venus would have thought of her dancing. She thrust herself forward in a new gush of emotion, and Mrs. Archamp coughed, and suddenly everyone else did also.

Mrs. Archamp said, "My dear, this is not what I had in mind."

Lenora found herself blushing, to her dismay.

Mrs. Archamp said, "I wanted a few felicitous gestures."

Mrs. Fanning said, "Something cool, restful."

"But this?" Mrs. Archamp spoke with scorn and malice and the knowledge she had the power to say whatever she pleased. "Your dancing is so rude."

Recoiling, Lenora longed to cry. You were not allowed to expect anything, and why did anyone have to make the best of it when it only depressed you? They did not like her dancing. Indeed, they seemed to despise it. There was no inspiration here. There was no use prolonging this appearance.

Lenora turned to depart, but Mrs. Archamp was not finished. She spoke with arrogance, and, wretched as Lenora felt, she found herself forced to listen. "Child, your intensity is excessively tiresome. It is a kind of emotional Saint Vitus' dance."

"Is that all?"

"How very odd to want to dance this way? How old are you, child?"

"Sixteen."

"And you want to dance without your mother present?"

"I am grown-up."

"You are a child. Miss Lake's School for Young Ladies is opening next week. You would be wise to enroll there."

"I am a dancer."

The *grande dame* was withering. "The truth is, you are inexcusably rude."

Lenora had such an overwhelming impulse to be gone she did not reply.

Mrs. Archamp declared, "The goddess Terpsichore floats through the air, is pleasing. The pleasing are truly happy. But I shan't be angry with you, despite your impertinence. My housekeeper will see you in the kitchen."

Lenora had no desire to be paid in food, although Amy said she was silly. Amy did not like the fat dowagers either, but Amy was hungry. As they reached the entry Lenora was mimicking Mrs. Archamp's bulldog expression with such accuracy Amy was giggling, when suddenly Mrs. Fanning appeared.

Mrs. Fanning gave the sisters a searching look. Lenora expected a new inquisition, but Mrs. Fanning merely said, "You have a restless foot."

Lenora nonetheless felt irritable, recalling Mrs. Archamp's

words and said, "If this is part of the engagement, that is finished."

"Child, I——"

"And I am not a child. Not any longer."

"Whatever you are, you do not belong here." Lenora was astonished. This was what she had been thinking. "I have just come back from Paris and New York. What do you know of these cities?"

"I know they are far away."

There was a queer note in Lenora's voice, and it was Mrs. Fanning's turn to be surprised. She said, "I think you are jealous of my being able to visit Paris and New York and London."

"I am not." But Lenora was, dreadfully jealous.

"You sound as if travel is an enormous thing. It isn't at all."

"Perhaps," replied Lenora, with one of her changes of mood which were frequent now, "San Francisco is still too young to endure criticism."

"In any event, here you are likely to become just a vaudeville performer."

"Never."

"Never is a long time. You cannot be sure."

Lenora was sure. What did they understand! Dancing was a language in itself, and she was tired of rules, made for those who had the sense of stone, or maybe stone had more sense. Soon they would confine the very air and allot just so much to breathe, and if she dared drink more than a pint a day she would be a criminal. She was not prepared for any simple solutions.

Amy asked, "Mrs. Fanning, why do you think Lenora ought to travel?"

"Some people are different, dear, and need different worlds."

Lenora said, "It was because I stood up to your aunt."

Because you did what I have always wanted to do but never dared, thought Mrs. Fanning, but she said, "It takes two to see the truth, one to dance it and one to appreciate it. In New York, even Chicago, more will see your dancing." When Lenora agreed with that, Mrs. Fanning added, "If you are really serious about going to Chicago or New York, let me know. I have a brother who is a newspaperman, who knows many people in Chicago."

Lenora ran home, thinking, Mama will say we lack money even to pay the fare, but Mrs. Fanning's offer is too providential to ignore.

Mama pointed out that Mrs. Fanning's help did not include money.

"We will manage," said Lenora, although she had not the slightest idea how. Lenora felt grown-up now. And when Mama said their roots were here, that it would hurt to pull them out, to give up the piano teaching she had labored so many years to develop, Lenora retorted, "We'll return. When I get an engagement with a great manager, a manager who will understand my art, like David Belasco or Augustin Daly."

Lenora quickly excused herself and went to her room. She stripped and stared at herself in the mirror for a long time. It was unladylike, daring, but she was maturing; she was positive now. Her breasts were larger, they had been tight under her frilly frock, and now they were firm and full. Yielding then to her emotion, she danced around the room and found delight in the lightest movement and she knew she was not mistaken. She must exist with the energy of the explorer.

Hurriedly, then, Lenora sought out Mrs. Fanning. It took weeks before Mrs. Fanning could see her again, but the patron remained sympathetic, and finally she arranged for her brother, DeWitt Hale, to meet Lenora. It was early afternoon of a spring day in 1895 that Lenora went to keep this appointment with Mrs. Fanning's brother. He was a wiry, tense, harried, middle-aged newspaper editor, who eyed her apprehensively and said, "But you are too young. You have no manager. No one will even give you an audition in Chicago."

Lenora said, "I have a manager," and hastened to collect Mama, who was waiting outside, introducing her as "my manager, Mrs. O'Dea." Lenora was not sure he believed her, for he stared at Mama as if she were a chaperone, but evidently his moral qualms were assuaged, for he told her he would give her an audition.

Lenora rented a small studio, Mama accompanied her with great sympathy, and Lenora appeared in a short revealing dress which brought upraised eyebrows from DeWitt Hale and even startled Mama. Mama could not halt, for that would be disloyal, and Lenora would not heed her. Lenora knew that some people might consider this garb improper, but the surprise would be useful and it set off her lovely figure. The dress seemed transparent, but it was not, and she looked eager and eloquent.

When she finished dancing to Schubert, DeWitt Hale sighed and said, "I've never seen anything quite like it, but . . . where did you say you want to go?"

"Chicago, New York, London, Paris!"

"At once?"

"At once! At least to Chicago!"

DeWitt Hale stared at her a moment more, thinking, she is very pretty and appealing, and that has its advantages. And now she was especially appealing, looking wistful rather than audacious. He wrote a flattering letter of introduction to a good friend of his in Chicago, Ralph Went, an important member of the Chicago Press Club.

Lenora held this letter of introduction as if it were worth a fortune and announced to her family that she had to take advantage of this great opportunity. But Grandma was not as easily convinced as the others. Still spry at sixty-seven, although Grandpop was bedridden now, she expressed herself directly. "Your dancing has improved, Lenora, but can you work like a horse?"

Grandma was not always a comfort, thought Lenora, but she replied, "If I have to work hard, I can. And Chicago does have many more opportunities."

Archer said, "We can work just as hard as Lenora. We want to perform too," looking at Mama for support.

"You will act," said Lenora, "as soon as I get a decent engagement." She meant as soon as she was successful. "Then you will come. With this letter of introduction I'll get an engagement quickly."

Mama said, "In a few weeks, undoubtedly. We won't be separated long."

Lenora grew irritable. "Maybe you have as much endurance as I do, but I have had more engagements. Don't you see that the vital companies are in Chicago and New York, and right now we can't all leave San Francisco. There isn't enough money"—there wasn't any at this point—"but as soon as we accumulate any savings we will send for you."

Grandma said, "You can be so ambitious you will get nothing."

Mama said, "If you wish to be happy, it is best to start at the top. The bottom will be envious, and the middle will be indifferent, but at the top, if you have genius, you will be welcome."

"Exactly," said Lenora.

"I apologize," said Grandma. "I did not realize how important this is."

"That is all right," said Lenora, missing the sarcasm in Grandma's voice. "Only the truly creative artist knows what is in herself."

Grandma reminded, "Failure can be very disagreeable."

Lenora said, "If I stay here it will be the end of us." Her mind was made up. There was such an intensity in her, such an immediate desire for migration, for exploration, she was so certain that distance was merely an inconvenience to be conquered, that even Grandma finally agreed—against Grandma's better judgment—that Mama and Lenora could risk the theatrical world of Chicago.

To reach the promised land Mama and Lenora accepted a loan from Grandma, enough to pay for fare and a few weeks' room and board. And Mama, who often believed that a widow of forty-seven was of little value, felt as if she were embarking on a spiritual mission—Lenora seemed so dedicated to dancing.

Mama was overwhelmed by the impact of Lenora's will and stricken by her emotion for the children she was leaving behind, but she prepared to accompany Lenora anywhere, since Lenora was Mama. Mama could not resist the distress in her other children, however, and suddenly she kissed them and said, "We will pretend that we are together wherever we are."

"Yes," said Amy and Archer.

Good-bys came hard, however. Amy was kissing them with unusually moist eyes; Archer and Aunt Jessie were tearful; Grandma was blowing her nose as if stricken with an attack of sniffles. And Lenora was bewildered. Instead of feeling inspired by the joy of departure, there was a painful gulf, and furtively she wanted to cry also. But she must not, she told herself; she was a young woman now. She took Mama by the hand and boarded the train with the nobility and grace of a queen going to be crowned. Such gravity was the only way she could avoid bursting into tears.

Amy and Archer were marshaled around Grandma, who promised to keep an eye on them. But though they were grown-up it was as if this parade of torchbearers had become confused and lost their way. It was more than Mama could bear. Mama stuck her head out the train window and said to Grandma, loudly so all could hear, "If I temporarily forsake Amy and Archer it is only to bring them a world in which they will be crowned too."

The train was moving then, in short, erratic jerks, and suddenly Lenora was holding onto Mama. It seemed so long ago that she had clung to the sand with her bare toes, dancing to the song the wind had taught her. Answering her own feeling, she whispered, "Mama, it was a very proud thing you said."

11

Chicago was far different than Lenora had expected. She had visualized a city of bright, vital beauty; instead she saw a city that seemed preoccupied with ugliness, with the same brawling energy that was typical of San Francisco. Even when she explored the streets with the historic names she was disappointed. Washington and LaSalle and Madison were so prosaic. Cross streets such as Schiller and Goethe with their weighty mansions of stone had none of the romance she associated with those great men. Everybody was too much on the go, even for her. It was her first encounter with steel works and stockyards, and she disliked their harshness. She thought what a fool our imagination and anticipation can make of our hopes.

Where was the city's soul, Lenora wondered. Where were its dancers? Where was its freedom? The kind of freedom she always desired but rarely realized except when she danced. She half expected dancers to greet her at the railroad station, although she would not have admitted that to anyone, not even to Mama. She did admit to Mama, who was more tolerant of Chicago, that the business center was energetic. "But it isn't pretty or inspiring," she argued in defense of her quick distaste for Chicago.

"Let's not be so quick to look down our noses. This is not Paris or London, but Chicago has more theaters than San Francisco, more genuine opportunities." Mama paused, feeling awkward and exasperated. Lenora was not listening. Her daughter's inattentiveness came at Mama with such force it was unpleasant and disconcerting. Lenora stood on Michigan Avenue, staring at the houses of the wealthy with such a conviction of her own righteousness that Mama wanted to shake her. The next instant she decided that her daughter had not altered too much, or too painfully. No, no, that was unthinkable; Lenora was still fleixble and imaginative, thought Mama, perhaps too imaginative at times—with a rarefied notion of beauty, sometimes too self-absorbed and with a restlessness that could be exhausting, yet with an ever increasing sense of wonder and discovery. And even as Mama was uncertain whether she was ahead or behind Lenora, she told herself: if you cannot help her, do not criticize, say nothing. Our world is hardly crumbling as long as we do not lose our sense of direction. Mama could not resist saying however, "You are too bright a girl to be intolerant."

"I am not intolerant," said Lenora. "I just do not like Chicago." But she was determined not to go back to San Francisco.

Lenora refused to go back even when they discovered, to their dismay, that Ralph Went was out of town and the treasured letter of introduction was useless for the time being. No one in his office knew when he would return from New York. Although Lenora stopped in his office several times the following week, each time leaving her name and DeWitt Hale's, there was no consolation in the repeated, "Mr. Went is away indefinitely."

Lenora refused to be discouraged. She had set out to conquer the world, and she continued to confront Chicago with the imperious demand that it conform to her desires. She was positive that nothing on earth could stop her. Only no one seemed to desire her to push back horizons.

The first producer she approached for a job said, "Can you do hootchy-kootchy dances?"

"You are too thin," stated the second producer.

"You are too dull," said the third.

Then there were those who said:

"I want something more lively."

"Too lively."

"Not lively enough."

Finally, there was the kindly, fatherly producer who asked her to sit down, who was willing to listen to her aspirations, who even tried to advise her, touched by the paleness and beauty of her face. He said, "Your ideas are nice, but you are just a child. You ought to go home to your mother."

"I am over twenty-one," she said defiantly, but she felt herself blushing to the roots of her hair.

"No, child, you are not a day over sixteen."

That made her furious. She was over seventeen.

"Then you are not even a professional, I can see that," he added, the stout, gray-haired producer growing friendlier with each bit of advice.

"What do you mean?" This was even more upsetting.

"All this talk about the Greeks." His honest face lit up with laughter. "The only Greeks I know in Chicago run restaurants. Look, child, why don't you go home to your mother? You are rather pretty, you look like a nice girl. Why don't you find yourself a decent young man, marry him, and raise a family?"

Lenora stared at him, thinking how dare he, but his manner

was bland, and he wore an air of moral superiority that was beyond offending.

He said, "I do feel sorry for you. You know nothing about professional dancing. You will starve, as sure as I am sitting here. I am telling you this for your own good."

Furious, she rushed out, determined to obtain a dancing engagement at once, but the answers continued to be "No." There were many want ads for chambermaids, cooks, and dressmakers, and after several weeks when there were no dancing engagements she applied for these jobs, and so did Mama. But they said Lenora was too young and inexperienced and Mama too well-bred to be properly humble and respectful. And moreover, Chicago had many unemployed, grateful to work for four to six dollars a week.

Unable to endure the continuing rejections, Lenora approached a vaudeville house on State Street where the cheap theaters were located. It was in answer to an ad for a theatrical company, and the owner regarded her with incredulity, saying, "I want a company, an act, to complete my vaudeville bill."

"I am the act," she stated, with far more conviction than she felt.

"But I don't want a single."

"I am not a single. I can create enough movement for a troupe of ten."

He laughed skeptically, but before he could halt her, she whirled in front of him, jigging and spinning so energetically it took his breath away. She was very lively, although she hated what she was doing, and the florid, heavy-set owner was taken with her energy, audacity, and appeal. He agreed to give her a chance, for one performance.

When Lenora showed Mama the bill, Mama said critically, "It sounds like vaudeville." It consisted of Haber and Peden in a collection of witticisms; Rosa Elmore, a petite comedienne; Brack and Burke, with their performing cockatoos; a fat-woman sewing contest; Frank Ash, contortionist and banjoist; and Lenora listed as "Lenora, The Marvelous Malcolm." Mama added, "I suppose that is the way they must list you, but it isn't very poetic."

Lenora was more concerned with her performance. This introduction to the theater was not wonderful as she had expected back in San Francisco, or beautiful, or heroic. Heroes chose their battles, she thought, and were not compelled against their faith. Part woman and part child, Lenora stood in the wings as the fat-woman sewing contest ended, not sure she could go on. Mama was frowning already.

Mama was unhappy about the dime museum next door with the fire eaters and the snake charmers and the bearded ladies. But as Lenora wavered she saw Rosa Elmore regarding her with a cynical smile, and Lenora, as if pushed by an arbitrary force, stepped forward. She was certain she was better than this soubrette. And every challenge had to be fought to the bitter end.

The band struck up a waltz which the owner had suggested because it was simple. Lenora could see Mama, sitting out front, wincing at the obvious music. Yet Lenora sought to be lively. She was energetic; she kept her balance, which in itself, considering the music, was a feat.

When the waltz finished there was a hush, and then Lenora heard laughter. Suddenly she was furious. She ignored the motion of the owner to get off so that Brack and Burke, with their performing cockatoos, could get on and save the bill. She ran down front, creating as she ran. She bent gracefully, then swung around as if caught by the wind, glowing and ecstatic. She lifted her skirt until an audacious amount of body showed. In this convulsion of emotion, of risk—calculated and otherwise—Lenora was very pretty and personal. She pulled the audience toward her with an appealing gesture of her arms, and all at once the crowd applauded loudly.

The owner forgave her earlier failure. He hired her for the entire week, at twenty dollars a week. Mama, with a patience and fortitude that surprised Lenora, made no comment although it was obvious she considered this engagement a venture of dubious merit. For reasons Mama could not fathom, there were things about Lenora's routine which were disturbing.

Lenora agreed, yet she was proud she was a success. She went to see Ralph Went again, but he was still away, although this time his office thought he would be back soon, and she left her professional address with them—to make sure he knew she was a professional.

The next few evenings her spirit and emotion were infectious. But she was unhappy. She had imagined that her metal would be forged in a fiery crucible, but doing twists, spins, showing some of her body, it was plod, plod, plod.

The owner asked her to stay an extra week and she said, "No."

He stared at her as if she were crazy. He knew she was just a beginner, although quite ornamental. He said, "You are energetic, attractive. Fatten up a little, show more leg, who knows how far you can go?"

"No," said Lenora, "I don't like this. I don't like it at all."

"You won't get another chance. Not as good as this one."

Lenora did not change her mind, even though twenty dollars a week was the most she had ever earned. Mama agreed with her, saying, "This is just a brief stop on our way." The salary was useful however, Mama admitted, but Lenora, once she gave her notice, was concerned with loftier ambitions.

Lenora was packing when Brack of Brack and Burke, with their performing cockatoos, approached her. The bald, wizened man asked her to join their act.

She said, "But I don't fit."

He said seriously, "You'd go good with the birds. You'd like them in no time. We could break you in in about a week."

"Would that be a good idea?"

"Sure. You're just impudent enough to be effective on stage."

"I see." She did not see at all. For once she was almost without words.

"And we'll be hitting New York one of these days."

"Thanks, but . . . I have another engagement." He congratulated her, as if he believed her, as if it were his loss, and then he waddled away, a small man, not a bright man probably, she thought, or a reading or thinking man, but in a curious way he had given her a sense of accomplishment.

After this last performance Ralph Went also came backstage to tell her how much he had enjoyed her dancing. Pleased by Lenora's attractive youthfulness, he was attentive at once. Her performance puzzled him, but she had moved him with a suggestion of amorous excitement.

He was flattering beyond Lenora's dreams, and his praise made her feel grown-up. He listened thoughtfully when she told him about her ambitions in a spurt of impulsive affection. She was certain he had intelligence and integrity, for he did not make her feel clumsy or impractical or silly. Ralph, as he asked her to call him a few minutes after they met, agreed that she was too fine for vaudeville, that she was correct in seeking out the great manager who would appreciate her. He was outraged that discerning managers had not been available; he deplored a world that did not understand her art; he promised to introduce her to the famous producer-manager, Augustin Daly, who was bringing his company to Chicago soon. Ralph had interviewed him in New York a few days before for his newspaper.

Lenora told Mama later, "Ralph is creative like we are. He understands my aspirations. And he is a fine-looking man, with deep gray eyes, a splendid head, and the high forehead of a scholar." It was her first romantic situation, and she was eager to make the most of it.

Ralph Went was too old for Lenora, Mama thought the following evening when he called upon them—a man in his late thirties. She also thought that his gray eyes were too cold to suit her. She did not think he was handsome, although Lenora did. She also wondered whether he was really as erudite as he sounded, with all his admiration for Swinburne and Wilde. She could not share Lenora's enthusiasm, but all her life she had avoided saying "don't," and she could not begin now.

Lenora did not understand everything Ralph was discussing, but she enjoyed having her emotions so strenuously involved. Mama looked at her questioningly when she said, "I am spending Sunday with Ralph," but Mama did not object openly.

It was the first Sunday since they had come to Chicago that Mama and Lenora were spending the day apart, and this was a new pang for Mama. Lenora felt uncomfortable too, but only for a moment. The idea of falling in love was something to contemplate with enthusiasm. Sunday, she told herself, she would put away childish dreams and live and Ralph would introduce her to Daly and she would be on the road to stardom. She glowed with anticipation.

Sunday was a lovely day, and Ralph and Lenora went along the shores of Lake Michigan and into Lincoln Park. They walked hand in hand, laughed, talked, picnicked. In a few hours they were close friends, and he became the creation of her illusion. When Ralph leaned so their bodies touched and his hand tightened on hers, she desired to cast a spell over him. He continued to agree that she was wonderfully talented, and she felt a fine personal current between them. There was a moment of distress when Lenora recalled that she had expected her first love to be an Adonis with wide shoulders and narrow hips, and Ralph's short legs and wide hips were quite unfit for dancing. And when he squinted at the sun the lines around his gray eyes made him look more than his acknowledged thirty; then she knew he was closer to forty, as Mama hinted. But his persuasive voice remained caressing, especially when he stated, "You are an artist, and an artist is an exceptional person." By the time he brought her home it seemed inevitable to be in love with him. Because he did not kiss her good night she desired him to, and more, but more of what she was not certain.

Daly did not arrive in Chicago the next week as Ralph had promised, but the following Sunday was a day Lenora knew must be without blemish. He invited her to his studio where he painted and wrote, and she accepted as a tribute to her charm, although she told Mama she was going on a picnic.

Ralph showed her pictures of Greek art and said, "They lived the freest, loveliest life on earth." He quoted Homer as proof, and embraced her, but what followed seemed mostly a violent muscular spasm.

She wondered if Venus would have done it better. There were kisses, only she did not feel incomparable as she had expected, but awkward and silly. Ralph made it plain that he was bewitched by her beauty, and Lenora, who desired to be chastely unattainable even as she wished to be wildly possessed, was confused. When his arms strayed to untouched parts of her body she pulled away. He expressed fervent interest in painting her in the nude, so he could capture her lovely body for eternity, and she replied that she was too thin. He frowned, and she did want to remain in love and meet Daly, and she added, "I'll pose later, in a few weeks, when I am more worthy of your art." She kissed him good night with what she thought was ardent womanliness.

He assured her that Daly would arrive in Chicago the coming week and that his introduction would get her a part with the great producer. The next few days Lenora read everything she could find on Daly. She became positive this producer was remarkable. He had established many stars: John Drew, Hobart Bosworth, Cecilia Loftus, Maxine Elliott, and his present star, Ada Rehan. He was a producer of taste and invention; Duse and Bernhardt admired his art. Lenora, reviewing his thirty years of successful producing, was certain that he was just the producer for her.

When Daly arrived in Chicago, Ralph gave her a flattering letter of introduction, and she decided to approach Daly as an experienced performer. Lenora arrived at the rear of the theater where Daly was rehearsing, demanded an immediate interview, waved the letter of introduction as if it were a battle flag, and was halted by the doorman. He took Ralph's letter inside, and five minutes passed, ten—an hour, another hour, and there was no request for her to come inside. Finally, when she tried to push her way in, the doorman said Daly was not seeing actors, if she wanted a part she must talk to his general manager, Oscar Drury, which made her angrier.

A few days later, not telling Ralph that his letter had been ignored, not wanting to hurt his feelings and their love, she took matters into her own hands. After a matinee she slipped past the doorman in the guise of a waitress bringing in the great man's supper. The doorman looked suspicious, as if he had seen her before, but she was out of sight in an instant. In

Daly's office she discarded the apron, put down the tray without any damage to the crockery, which had been a worry, and stood in front of Daly in a tight red velvet dress. She hoped the producer was impressed. She expected the words to roll off his tongue, but he was startled.

Finally, he did ask, "Is there something I can do for you?" and stood up politely, automatically, as one should in front of a lady.

Daly was tall, slender, attractive, reflected Lenora, but it struck her as extraordinary that with all his success he seemed melancholy. His gray-green eyes were sad, and he was preoccupied. He said, "You have a message for me, miss?"

She said, "I am a dancer."

He looked bewildered, as if to say what did he need a dancer for?

"I also act," she blurted out, in this instant deciding it would be just as wonderful to be a great actress as well as a great dancer.

Lenora was seeking to be a captivating ingénue, and Daly composed himself; he knew how to deal with this situation. She was lovely-looking, he thought—and could you think of anyone more virginal! But to have her dance for him was out of the question; she was just an adolescent, although a very attractive one. He said, "You are young, girlish."

"I am not a girl. I am a woman."

"How old are you?"

She hesitated, thought she detected a smile in his gray-green eyes, and decided not to exaggerate too much. "Twenty-one, sir."

"My, that is rather old to begin."

"I am not a beginner. I have played stock here at the Schiller Theater, at the Grand Opera House in San Francisco, and elsewhere."

"Elsewhere?" Daly looked thoughtful. He took in her upturned nose, her provocative smile and asked, "Are you Irish?"

"Yes," she said proudly, "I am Lenora O'Dea Malcolm." For the first time he really seemed interested. "I am very graceful on stage, Mr. Daly."

Personal appearance was something Daly never seemed to study in himself, but he believed it vital to his performers.

He examined her more closely and itemized: she was Irish and audacious, which was all to the good; she had lovely arms; she was over medium height, which was fine; the line of her neck and shoulders, although narrow, was excellent. There were moments when she moved effectively, particularly when she was aroused, as now. He said, "Casting for my permanent company is starting in New York next week. Report to my general manager there, Oscar Drury, and perhaps he can use you."

A jubilant Lenora told Mama that success was inevitable. There was just one difficulty: they had run out of money again, they did not even have enough for train fare. But nothing was halting Lenora. When she saw Ralph that evening she told him, "It was your letter of introduction that got me the engagement, Ralph. Daly remembered you very well. He sent his regards, he was almost as sweet as you." She threw her arms around him and embraced him as if he were a Lord Byron and whispered, "You wouldn't want me to lose this opportunity that I only got because of you?"

"No." What favor did she want now?

"All I need is the fare." She kissed him as if he were the finest man in the world. "You wouldn't allow that to halt my career, would you?"

"No, but . . ."

"It won't end our love. We will be much happier in New York."

"Yes."

She kissed him again, but somehow it had the touch of a child—natural and simple, without passion. Yet even as he felt deprived, he found himself giving her money for fare, for her mother too, and a little over, although he did not care for her mother and he wondered if Lenora was really in love with him.

"Ralph, it is sweet of you to do this," giving him a quick, light embrace, "but we will be together soon again . . . within a few months."

Ralph found himself pledging his life to her as he added a few dollars to what he had given her already, although he meant it as a loan, and in his mind he was determined to get it back one way or another.

They agreed that they were engaged, and several days later, when it was time to say good-by, he wanted to say it by way of a farewell dinner at his studio, but she insisted they must be Spartan. What Ralph had expected to be a racy good-by became a simple kiss and hug at the railroad station. But once again Lenora assured Ralph that she was his—heart and soul —and that when he came to New York their engagement would be official.

Mama heard this, but Lenora did not elaborate, and Mama was too hurt by Lenora's secrecy to inquire further. Mama did not like feeling suspicious of Lenora, and distance might

stave off this absurd situation, she told herself, for she was
afraid Lenora was really infatuated with this older man, this
journalist.

Lenora's mood changed the instant the train was out of
Chicago. Now she was certain she would be discovered. She
was a few months past seventeen.

12

This is the would-be conqueror, the would-be world shaker.
This is the girl who is determined to blaze a new trail. She is
untrained in any of the formal ways. She has no father to
support her or relatives who are impresarios or patrons
wealthy and well placed, and the world has many like her,
searching to discover and to be discovered. Indeed, she seems
to possess little but an earnest conviction of her own talent.
But discovery, as long as she can remember, has been the
omnipotent moment. She believes that once migration leads
her to a favorable climate there will be no barriers to self-expression and discovery and that all of experience will be
within reach. Dancing is discovery, beauty is discovery, and
Lenora is determined that Daly will be discovery too.

Everyone told her that she should be frightened out of her
wits in New York, but she was not the least bit frightened.
She felt very brave. Indeed, she was the only Lenora Malcolm
in New York, and never had she felt in better health or in
higher spirits.

Lenora even found the streets of the city inspiring. The
great names she saw everywhere took possession of her heart.
They were a dream coming true. Henry Irving and Ellen
Terry were opening in *The Merchant of Venice*; John Drew
was appearing in *Christopher, Jr.*; David Belasco had a new
hit, *The Heart of Maryland*; but lifting Lenora's heart above
all else were the announcements that Bernardt and Duse were
appearing in New York soon.

She arrived at the Daly's Theater, trying to look at home,
and announced that Augustin Daly had engaged her for his
permanent company. She spoke with such assurance she was
ushered into his office at once. There were two persons in his
magnificent office, Daly and his general manager, Drury, but
they did not notice her entrance. Drury kept saying, "Yes,
Governor," and "No, Governor," and her eyes wandered to

the walls lined with pictures of Kean, Booth, Wallack, and Macready. This was theater, she thought enthusiastically, this was discovery, and nothing seemed out of reach at the moment. Then for an instant she felt she was betraying the dance, and she told herself she must make the theater and dance one.

Drury was gone, and Daly stared at her as if he had never seen her before. She said, after a difficult pause, "I am Miss Malcolm."

"Did I ask you to come in?"

This was no way to start, she thought, but she mumbled, "Yes, in Chicago."

"Oh, that is a dreary place, isn't it?"

"Well, it is not like New York." She had been here two days.

"I have never had much fondness for Chicago. I only tolerate it because of the hearty welcome my company always receives there."

"I am from San Francisco myself."

"Yes. Now what did you say your name was, miss?"

"Malcolm. I am Lenora O'Dea Malcolm." He did not remember her. He did not behave like a discoverer; his behavior was outside her experience, a new disillusionment. He had a reputation for being severe, but she had not expected this. "You interviewed me in Chicago, for your permanent company."

"Oh, yes," he said, with his first show of interest. "What have you done?"

"*Twelfth Night*, and many plays, but I'm mainly a dancer."

"Can you do pantomime?"

She nodded, although she never had professionally.

They went to the stage. Daly stood in a remote part of the dim theater, deserted except for the cleaning women, and waited for her to audition. He leaned against a pillar, looking bored.

Not at all self-possessed now, Lenora moved forward, kicking front and back and doing the other fancy steps which were the fashion of the musical theater. She swayed, looking eager, although she did not feel eager. The light fell on her badly. There were no waves or wind to inspire her. She felt she was moving in many directions without arriving anywhere; she felt ugly.

Daly said, "You should move quicker. Let me see you gesture."

"But I am a dancer."

Daly seemed unable to classify her for a moment, as if in

his theater there were no dancers. He said, "Go upstage. Lift up your arms."

She lifted, but her arms felt like lead. She felt overwhelmingly futile.

"Move your arms more. They must be emphatic, yet light."

She reached until her outstretched arms throbbed with pain. Daly looked dejected, and she repeated the motion, certain he was not interested. As she stepped off the stage, her nerve gone for the moment, he said, "Report for rehearsal tomorrow. What did you say your name was?"

Lenora knew she should be grateful, but she was angry at his forgetfulness, and so she said, "Sarah Malcolm," after Sarah Bernhardt, her idol.

"A pleasant name," he said, "Give it to Mr. Drury."

Lenora appeared the next morning, expecting to be cast for his permanent company, sure she would be playing with Ada Rehan or Cecilia Loftus or one of his other famous stars, and discovered to her disgust that she had been hired for just one play, an experimental production of an English farce, starring an English actress, Irene Vollen, and that she had no lines to speak. But when Daly appeared, after the casting was finished, she decided to remain with the farce and show him that she was worthy of his permanent company. She plunged into the rehearsals, and her confusion grew. No one included her in any intimacy but focused on Irene Vollen, who was playing the title role, *Mistress Candor*; nothing in her role had anything to do with dancing. Yet when the director gave her gestures that were artificial and mechanical, she turned them into the tempo of the dance. She strove to prove to Daly that she could be both dancer and actress.

Daly found himself watching her, thinking she was a pretty, virginal thing; men would like her eyes and arms, but would she end as merely another would-be actress? She was not impressive in her acting in spite of her natural attractiveness, and he felt sorry for her, and he knew he must not . . . no place for being sorry in the theater. The only way he could have a profitable company was with strict discipline and stars such as Irene Vollen and Ada Rehan. Something hard, something far beyond the moment came to Daly then, and he thought, she has to prove herself as I did, find a method to make her individuality and skill come together in a kind of magic, if she has any genuine talent in her. And even that might not be sufficient, for there was plenty of talent available. Daly did not abandon his reserve and express any of this. Already he felt he had gone too far. From this rehearsal on, he was even more distant.

By the time the farce opened, Lenora was miserable. Irene Vollen dominated the stage, everything remained mechanical despite Lenora's effort to feel her role. Opening night she was too unhappy to care much about her performance, and this frightened her. Until now she had cared very much how she performed. Lenora was even more miserable when she saw the reviews. There was not a single mention of her, and most depressing, her name in the cast of characters, even the assumed one, was spelled wrong: Sara Malcolm.

As Lenora's temper exploded Mama said quietly, "It is a start, dear, and from this you will go on to better roles." Mama did not believe this, and she had an almost uncontrollable desire to return to San Francisco, but she was also aware of Lenora's need for discovery, however many painful ways it cut. And no one, not even myself, Mama said passionately to herself, must extinguish the fire in Lenora. So Mama, who had thought Lenora's performance only adequate, put her arms around Lenora and spoke about the virtues of self-control and patience and said that the Greeks had worked a lifetime to capture one perfect movement.

Lenora looked happier, the way Mama wanted her to look, and said, "You are right." She kissed Mama tenderly, as if nothing else mattered. Now she did not mind the bad reviews, since they were what Irene Vollen deserved.

A few weeks later Lenora was hopeful again, for Daly cast her as a gypsy in *Much Ado about Nothing*. One performance, when she became aware that she had the stage to herself for a moment, she lost her uncertainty in a state of nervous exhilaration. The music was Schubert, and she was supposed to make a few simple gestures with her hands. But as she ran forward with arms outspread she seemed to embrace all of the audience in an ecstatic hug. The audience reponded warmly, and she ran off, certain she had established her right to dance in the production. Instead, the next time Lenora came on at this part of the play, three other girls came with her. She protested to Drury, for Daly refused to see her, and was told either she danced with the other girls or not at all.

When she said, "The audience liked my dancing," Drury retorted, "They liked your brazenness. You also destroyed the mood for Miss Rehan's entrance. She almost did not go on because of your dancing. No one must focus on you; that will ruin Miss Rehan's entrance. If I catch you dancing by yourself any more, you are finished here."

She was allowed to continue in *Much Ado about Nothing* as long as she remained pictorial and took no attention away from anyone else. She learned to dance without expression, although she hated that. She did not feel Schubert at all now, although he was a favorite composer.

But Lenora, with all her discontent, made several vital discoveries. She knew now that she had been the reality—not the stage. And when the production remained in New York, she was able to see the actresses she regarded as the greatest women of the time: Bernhardt, Duse, and Ellen Terry.

Lenora found Bernhardt a creature of fire, with amazing energy, who moved with the grace of a life-loving cat. Duse was an even more profound influence on Lenora. The young dancer came away from Duse's acting in a kind of trance, as if, in Duse, she had been living on the stage. It was Ellen Terry, however, who most fitted Lenora's aspirations. Here was the romantic figure which she fancied herself becoming. Ellen Terry, playing Portia in *The Merchant of Venice*, was a queenly portrait, her voice like a deep bell. She was enthralling to Lenora, although she was actually a middle-aged, gray-haired woman of matronly build, still handsome but no longer beautiful. Yet when the play ended it was an unforgettable moment for Lenora. It was as though a glimpse into a brighter, more magnificent, beauty-laden world had come to an untimely end.

Lenora resolved that this was the kind of a world she must create. But as she identified with these goddesses, they made her ask many questions.

"So then, am I talented? Are there any adequate measurements? Can my body span the universe? How far is it to fame? Paris and London and Rome are many days away, but New York is here, yet fame may be an infinity away, may never come. Fame, this is the creation of histories and romances; it is a sentimentality; it is a promotion, usually too late. Shakespeare dead, is dead, but Shakespeare is also a body of work, is a map of the universe, is setting fire to many hearts, is a significance, a wonderful moment for others. Life is a risk, but fame is a greater risk; will I have anything to say in the verdict?"

Even as Lenora knew she could not accept anyone else's verdict but her own, Ralph arrived in New York with another verdict. Almost a year had passed since they had parted, and she believed that she had matured, although the world had remained unconquered. She was eighteen now and proud that her body was assuming a womanly shape. But Ralph, whom she expected to be the ardent wooer, rescuing her from the tedium of Daly, greeted her critically and complained about the production of *Much Ado about Nothing.* "As for your performance," he said, "where was it?"

"It was atmosphere," she answered, but before she could explain further, he was off on more criticism. "You shouldn't allow yourself to stay with such a stupid producer."

Her yearning heart expected speedy relief now. His encouragement would ignite her into a glow of artistic ecstasy, but all he was doing was growling that he was unappreciated, that he was going through hell—spending the last six months writing a play which Daly had just rejected.

He read it to Lenora, to show her what a terrible mistake Daly had made. Lenora thought it nice in a pseudo-modern imitation of Pinero but hardly inspired, and he found no comfort in her hesitant praise. She sensed she should express some enormously felt emotion, but as he continued to pour out his troubles she could not sparkle. Even as his arms tightened around her, he went on complaining. It made her self-conscious. His rhetoric did not fit this experience. This bore no resemblance to love as she imagined it.

The longed-for visit of Ralph's dwindled away without any consummation, and then on the day he was departing Ralph altered his strategy. He said, after seeing her dance in a fluid manner for some society women—an engagement that gave her a chance to express some of her own ideas—that although she was still too frail for full satisfaction, she was improving, she was capturing an air of insouciance that was stirring.

It brought Lenora back to his vital qualities. The thickness of his chest, the strength of his legs—even if they were not graceful—gave an impression of earnest vigor. She liked again the virility of his jaw. He did care for her honestly, she reflected.

Ralph said, as he narrowed the distance between them, "To be platonic, Lenora, is to be disinterested. You wouldn't want that."

She agreed, but as he drew closer that was not what she wanted either. There was something coarse now about his insistence; there was a strange, disturbing lack of pleasure in this. Even his fingers seemed awkward, possessing a third personality, not his or hers.

He said, "It is only the conventional who consider innocence intelligent." But when he clutched her, even as her heart pounded so loudly she was positive he could hear it, her dismalness increased. This was not what she desired either. His kisses were wet, flabby. He had lost his self-restraint. Instinctively the virgin now, her arms went up between them like a fence. It was too soon, her heart cried, too hurried, too imperfect. Ralph was even angrier when she refused to go to his room and help him pack. She was talking about her dancing and how she needed to rest so that she would be fresh for tomorrow's performance, and he exploded, "What performance! Your dancing in the play is meaningless."

It was true, but it was dreadful for anyone else to say that.

"You ought to settle down. Look, dear, no one is really interested in what you call creative dancing. Be content with marriage. Everyone else is. Why, in a few years we could have a lovely family."

"Is that what you think of my art?"

He shrugged. "It's nice . . . but what else!"

"And you were so understanding in Chicago."

"That's another thing, you promised to return the money I lent you."

"I will."

"When?"

For a moment Lenora stared at him, shocked, and then she said, "Love is cruel. Very cruel. You have no sense of obligation, Ralph, none at all."

It was his turn to be puzzled and shocked. She acted as if the money was coming to her. But what angered him most of all was that he, the worldly one, had been fooled by the innocent. Suddenly he was so angry he could not ask her again for the loan. In a curious way she was making him feel like a devil unless he was completely magnanimous. She was saying now, "Nonetheless, Ralph, it was nice of you to help me when you did," and he found himself saying, "Let's forget about it."

"Oh no," she said softly now. "It was a lovely gesture, and I'll always treasure it."

He felt he was losing his sanity, and he did not know whether to hit her or embrace her. Instead, he found himself shaking hands, saying good-by almost formally, doing it just the way she seemed to want it.

Yet for a moment she looked stricken. As he turned to go her eyes filled with tears. But she could not say it, and a minute later he was gone. He felt even more alone when he got his things from his hotel room, and sad and baffled by her talent for provoking love without satisfying it.

Lenora felt sad and baffled too, but for different reasons. She told Mama, "I failed Ralph. I did not love him enough. If I had I would have been willing to live with him, I would have convinced him that was more sensible than marriage."

Mama said, "That is nonsense."

But Lenora was feeling better with that announcement. She struck what she considered a magnificent tragic pose, imitating Sarah Bernhardt in the role of Marguerite Gautier giving up Armand Duval.

Mama laughed critically. Mama wanted to whack Lenora on the backside. Sensing however, that Lenora was on the verge of rebellion, Mama postponed a showdown on their diverging ideas of marriage and suggested a new interest. "I hear that Daly has great plans for next season. If you get a good role, we can have Archer and Amy come east."

13

So Lenora decided to give Daly one last chance to discover her. She became convinced that his new season, which promised to be a flourishing one, could be her season of achievement and recognition, and she resolved to apply for a principal role.

Mama agreed. "You have experience now, dear, you are very pretty, you move gracefully, you speak properly. You really could become one of his notable discoveries." Mama, moreover, was looking forward to Lenora earning more money so she could bring her other children to New York.

Lenora appeared at Daly's Theater for casting, anticipating a new career, certain she would win a lead in his first production, *Lotus Land*, for this operetta contained dancing for the principals, and she was virtually ignored. Casting for *Lotus Land* began at eleven in the morning, and it was past midnight when she came on to read for one of the principal roles. Then Daly wanted her to be motionless, to get the quality of her voice, and she could not act without moving. Daly's reaction was inevitable: he said she was dreadful.

When *Lotus Land* opened at Daly's Theater, Lenora was one of twenty attendants to the ingénue lead. She resented the long trailing robes which hampered her movements, the rocking back and forth while waving a fan and parasol. She thought this ridiculous. She knew she was no better than a chorus girl, with all her fine ideals. Another disappointment was the new roster of Daly's permanent company: it held the place of honor on his programs; there were forty names on it, some new, but no mention of her. And she thought this musiical play about Tibet an absurd tale. When the reviews were ecstatic and the show settled down for a long run she felt imprisoned.

When Mama became certain *Lotus Land* would run the entire season and perhaps into the next season, that Lenora's steady salary was assured, she wired Amy and Archer to come east. She sent them money she had been saving, unknown to Lenora, knowing that Lenora would never have saved it, and assumed that Lenora's connection with Daly would be valuable to Amy and Archer.

Lenora, however, had no intention of remaining imprisoned. She asked to dance in the forthcoming production of *As You Like It*, and Drury, supervising the casting, was shocked that anyone would think of dancing in this play, where in his opinion language and décor were all.

Yet Lenora felt she had to give Daly one more chance to discover her. Once again she approached Daly with a plea for a speaking role, realizing now that there was no place in Daly's Theater for dancing, and Drury said, "You're too thin, too young-looking. We could only consider you for our next New York season"—now almost a year away—"if you strengthened your body, filled out, especially where you could make it count. I recommend exercises for your upper chest, shoulder blades, lateral trunk, and general equilibrium." He intended it helpfully; he was convinced she needed all this to look womanly and elegant, to develop the large chest and bosom so she could speak properly in the swelling tones of an Ada Rehan and an Ellen Terry.

But when Lenora refused to take his advice and, worse, insisted on creating a dance out of her one solo moment on stage, despite his repeated warnings, he dismissed her. It was a relief to Drury, and to Lenora, who could no longer endure being just a chorus girl, but Mama was stricken by the news, for Lenora had saved no money and Amy and Archer were due in New York soon, and Daly was unmatched in the theater as a producer of taste.

Lenora explained, "There is nothing spontaneous in Daly's work. His artists are the scene designers and the costumers."

"There is nobody better than Daly in America."

"We will go abroad."

"Just a moment! It's not an overnight trip you are talking about. And you were so pleased when you got this opportunity with Daly."

"That was long ago."

"Do you really know where you are going?" Suddenly

Mama wanted to shock Lenora, as Lenora was always shocking her.

"Mama, don't sound so majestic and all-knowing."

"Do you really know?"

"I know I have no intention any more of dancing in a theater with a stupid, confining, boxlike stage."

"Who put this in your head?"

"You. You told us the Greeks regarded the theater and dance as a religious rite."

"And Lenora Malcolm will step down from Mount Olympus and create it?"

"Isn't that what you have been teaching us?"

Yes, but this is no compliment, thought Mama. It was as if Lenora regarded her as a jailer, yet was resolved to go ahead whatever the cost. Freedom to her daughter might mean freedom from her, and that was neither generous nor heartwarming. No, Mama cried to herself, I am wrong, these doubts are reflections of my own fears. So it became essential at this moment to show her trust of Lenora. She said, "I want you to be a fine dancer, but I don't want you to go too fast and then be disappointed."

"I haven't gone fast enough," said Lenora. She went on to justify her decision to give up the commercial theater and to earn her living as a creative dancer as the only possible step toward her true aim.

"What kind of a true aim?" asked Mama.

"You'll see . . . some day."

Lenora was standing before her, but somehow it was as though they had changed places and Mama was back in her own childhood. She was staring at Lenora with the eyes of her own youth, and now she saw that Lenora was possessed with many rare essences. She said, "You are right, dear, you must not be afraid."

"I'm not," Lenora said proudly. "I've learned that to be a dancer is to die many times, but also to be born many times. I have been reading Hawthorne, as you suggested, and he says we should 'do nothing against one's genius.' " And already, thought Lenora, she had not done too badly. Tomorrow, or the day after tomorrow, or soon thereafter, she would achieve her own changing vision of herself. Oh, absolutely, she repeated to herself for confirmation. She had to be sure of this, before the world closed her in.

Mama said, "But what about Archer and Amy? They are coming east and counting on you helping them with Daly."

"They will manage," said Lenora. "I have."

A week after Lenora quit the long-running operetta Archer and Amy arrived in New York. They were stunned to hear she had severed her favorable connection with Daly. They were discouraged for about an hour, and then their natural vitality and optimism gave them fresh energy and hope.

A dance studio was rented in Amy's name. Amy, shorter and slighter than Lenora, was brisk and purposeful. Quite sure of herself, Amy opened a dancing school as if she had many years of experience, while Archer caught on with a stock company, playing walk-ons, although he was determined to become another John Drew.

Mama recaptured the high velocity of her daughters as pupils came to study with them, although the Malcolms had to sleep on the floor. This was no sacrifice to Amy and Lenora; they were so exhausted after a day of teaching and practicing they fell asleep at once. But Mama often lay awake for hours, thinking she was the housekeeper in this temple of art, she was the island which anchored their emotions, and she wondered about the future of her daughters. The goal was not as pure and simple as it was once, her children were no longer children, and yet they seemed so inseparably tied together.

They were not so tied together, however, when Amy chided Lenora for practicing with excessive emotion, saying, "You extend your arms out as if you want to encircle the entire world, and that is impossible."

"You don't like it?" said Lenora.

"I don't like it," said Amy. "You shouldn't be so abstract. Choreography is not to be understood in a few minutes, or even a year. You are quick and graceful, but that is not enough. You should study more."

"With you?"

"Don't take offense. With me, with someone who knows more than you do."

Lenora did not accept this advice. She thought it jealousy. But whenever Lenora was alone now, she studied her anatomy. She spent many hours noticing the way her bones were set. She realized she could assume many shapes, even though the meanings were often confused. While she stumbled when she could not compel what was still an underdeveloped body to reach her grandiose conceptions, she was finding moments of ecstasy. They were brief, but she was perceiving new things about her body and its deeper self. And as time went on Lenora came to believe that since her body was shaped by nature's design, it must reflect nature, that for the real source of the dance she must go to nature. Then no tree stood straighter than Lenora, no tree was more graceful. It was as if she were just starting to live in her body. Nature became her greatest passion.

There were no rules she could put down on paper, but she practiced constantly now, grappling with the intricacies of her body, exploring, experimenting, and always searching for the original emotion. There were the first steps which became intrinsic steps, there were those which were a mistake. Sometimes she felt she was in a mire, or stricken with a fever, but other times she felt fleet and mobile.

She felt with the urgency of youth that she could not make up tomorrow what was lost today, that this must be the year the prima ballerinas became mad with envy. Even as she disliked the dowagers stiffly elegant in their satin gowns, she wanted them to admire her.

Thus for a long time there was nothing in life except practice and the constant searching into the whys of dancing. It remained a time of exploring emotions which would direct her energies to perfecting her flesh and imagination. Sometimes it was a slow and stumbling time. Often, trying to find the origin of her inspiration, she was as stationary as a statue. She noticed that when she was this way, her eyes closed, her concentration intensely upon herself, an energy and emotion that was new and powerful grew inside of her. Then there seemed to be a fountain of inspiration pouring through her that would never end. In this new vigor she found herself walking and running with a simple, natural motion. This went on for hours. And Mama would shout, "You've worked all day without a rest. Come to dinner now." And Lenora would pause, waving away Mama's repeated, "Your food is getting cold," listening attentively only to the meanings stirring within her. During these explorations she felt suspended in time and space, and her flesh and emotion seemed to take on an artistic harmony.

But this privacy became rare when the family need to earn a living encroached on her practicing. Lenora was not disturbed that there was very little money in the household or by her family's startled, almost shocked looks when she rehearsed in her scanty white tunic and exposed more flesh than was considered proper, but she did not like being encircled by their activities. It prevented the best interior conversation, but she had to accept one corner of the studio and the use of the gramophone as accompaniment, for Archer declaimed Lear and Hamlet in the second corner, Amy taught dancing for the rent in another, while Mama cooked in the fourth.

Soon too, spring returned with a profusion of warmth, and

reminders of Ralph were plentiful once more. By day that was not so painful, but at night, seeing lovers walking hand in hand, there was a quick intense hurt in Lenora. It was almost more than she could endure. Then she practiced until she was too tired to feel anything.

Yet in her dreams she could not deny Ralph, where he gathered her in his arms and carried her to a huge bed, strong and compelling. But she kept this a secret from everyone, although it added to her unhappiness.

Love could be such a magnificent contribution to art, thought Lenora, but why man should have to assume the initiative struck her as absurd, as if half of the human race had lost its individuality. She told herself love should be life-giving, not a restriction such as marriage, even if it meant standing alone, and she was even more certain now that her romance with Ralph had perished because of marriage. In her growing pride she decided she would prefer to lose a lover than hold him because of a legality. If Ralph had failed her in any way, she thought in retrospect, it was because he had suggested marriage because he was a small talent, not a genius.

For more months now there was nothing essential but dancing, and even that continued to leave Lenora dissatisfied. Achieving a lovely dance movement, it gave her a moment of pleasure, but it did not last. Whatever she was doing, this waiting was not right. She longed for stimulation with a voracious appetite, but boiled eggs and oatmeal and cleaning the windows of the studio so their patrons would know they were not fly-by-nights was a kind of no. She yearned for excitement and romance, and nothing was happening now that was inspiring.

Then Mama talked her daughters into creating a family entertainment. But even as Amy instructed Lenora, Amy was aware that her own precision and economy of movement was not favored by her moody sister. Yes, thought Amy, Lenora has the grace of a young savage, but it is all emotion. Much of the time, too, it was obvious that Lenora's attention was drifting away, and yet Lenora could pay the most flattering attention if the person interested her. One minute Lenora could be passionately affectionate, the next nothing prevented her from doing and saying anything she wished. But it seemed to Amy that Lenora was never tired of listening to the gramophone.

Lenora continued to regard Amy's instructions as superfluous, but she tried not to object, for Amy had begun to make important contacts. The Malcolms were still no more than a quick step ahead of eviction, and so Lenora agreed to coax money out of rich society patrons, although she called them Philistines and thought them dull and unworthy.

It was many months after Lenora's last performance for Daly that the first family concert took place. She approached the performance itself with her usual confidence, even as Amy was apprehensive; they were appearing in the drawing room of one of New York's Four Hundred. Lenora wore a white dress with a short skirt and pink stockings and pliable slippers which had no heels. She danced while Amy read several poems, and then Amy lectured on the philosophy of the dance. It struck Lenora as all very dull until she saw it written up in the newspaper the following day. They gave her more space and praise than Amy, which was encouraging; it was her first public mention as a solo dancer.

When Lenora heard that the renowned composer, Ethelbert Nevin, had rented a studio nearby, she had a brilliant idea: he would accompany her, not Amy! Nevin fitted her conception of what an artist should be. He had composed in far-off, picturesque Italy; he was romantic-looking, pale; he was well known. She adored his sea pieces; she found them poetic, melodic, and charming. She decided he owed it to himself to become aware of the skill with which she interpreted his art.

When she entered his studio and offered to interpret his music, she expected him to glow with appreciation. Instead, Nevin ordered her to halt as she began to dance.

"But your music is beautiful," she insisted.

"It was not written for dancing," he said angrily.

"But it was."

"Don't tell me why I wrote my music!"

"Dancing will give it a new dimension," she argued. She felt Machiavellian. It was a wonderfully reckless feeling, and moreover, he was as slim and sensitive-looking as his pictures, as a genius should look, and he should have the intensity of a true lover. She was prepared to be deliciously overwhelmed by Nevin.

He stared at her as if she were an odd little girl, pretty no doubt but so young, as she stood in front of him and claimed, "When I dance, it is like a sea piece." She was dancing again before Nevin could halt her. Lenora was certain there was no better body in the whole world than hers, and all it required was a genius, an American Chopin like Nevin, to lift it out of obscurity. When she finished dancing she was certain Nevin would be greatly moved. But he was dry-eyed, although he admitted, "You do have the texture of the music, in some ways."

"It is magnificent. The music, I mean."

" 'Narcissus'—magnificent? I think it is a nasty little piece!"

"Oh, no, it is really quite wonderful!"

Nevin did not tell her how unhappy it made him to be known for the composition of "Narcissus," when he had nobler dreams. He wanted to compose large, serious pieces, to be the American Mendelssohn, and people talked only about his trifles. But when she went on to dance more of his sea pieces he agreed that her feeling was accurate and that she made them pretty.

Lenora knew Nevin really meant adorable. His vague likeness to Chopin made her heart leap again, although she noticed, glancing at him more closely, that he was sallow and anemic-looking. He did seem to trust her interpretations now, however, and agreed to have her on one of his programs.

A month later Lenora danced to three of his sea pieces while he was at the piano. But feature billing was given to the soprano who sang eight of his songs, and Lenora became just a footnote on his program. The critics neglected the concert; there was only one curt review, and it was a small item in the society notes.

She realized she had obtained more space when she had danced with Amy. When she recovered from her disappointment, she told herself this minor billing was a test of character, and she was proud of having danced to Nevin's music with the composer himself at the piano, and Nevin did say, "You were sincere, Miss Malcolm."

Mama added, "There were moments, dear, during the recital when you brought a radiance to the stage."

Lenora said, "It was not enough. I couldn't express many of the things I wanted to." Nonetheless, she believed that she and Nevin were ideal partners. She still felt deliciously overwhelmed by him, but he displayed no personal interest in her. A few weeks after this concert it was announced that Nevin had closed his studio and left New York, on the verge of a nervous breakdown.

Lotus Land was running still, in its second year at Daly's, and Lenora did not feel a part of New York, telling herself that the city was without character, failing to recognize her talent. And in a sense Nevin had failed her also. Suddenly she was full of self-pity, like his music. She was loathing her present existence, and a great idleness seemed to settle over her even as she continued to practice and dance.

14

The following year was the year of Omar Khayyám. *The Rubáiyát* was sung, recited, and pageanted throughout the land. Lenora was fascinated by its bittersweet promise of wonder unending. She shook off the apathy of the last few months, and, breathless with a new, intense energy, she rose poetically to the occasion. She practiced beauty as well as dancing. She was resolved to combine all the arts in one: music, dancing, painting, sculpture, and literature. She felt in every curve of her body an excitement which compelled her emotions as she danced to:

> *Here with a little Bread beneath the Bough,*
> *A Flask of Wine, a Book of Verse—and Thou*
> *Beside me singing in the Wilderness—*
> *Oh, Wilderness were Paradise enow!*

She fancied herself a goddess then, and as she danced to this verse she imagined herself in full sunlight, her arms lifted, her lips laughing, her slim, tall body passionate in the passionate atmosphere.

How deeply she felt, how conscious of her unique mold!

Mama was puttering around the other end of the studio, being practical, saying it would be cozy if they had a real kitchen where she could make a good hot meal, and suddenly she was an alien spirit to Lenora.

Amy was cultivating the wealthy, and soon the Malcolms, led by Amy, were performing their entertainment for many society women in lawn fetes. At the instigation of Archer, he was included, and he read verses from *The Rubáiyát*, while Lenora gave a dance of her own composition and Amy lectured on the arts.

They were so well liked, they were asked to perform at Newport. Amy felt this was a memorable occasion: there were twenty patronesses who paid five dollars each to see the verses of Omar Khayyám done into dance.

Even more exciting to Amy was a request to perform for Mrs. William Astor, one of the richest women in the world and one of America's social celebrities. Mrs. Astor sat under a magnificent canopy while the Malcolms performed on the lawn. Several reporters were permitted on the estate, but they had to observe the fete from a distance, with the servants. The guests were dressed in the height of fashion, but they seemed parasitical to Lenora, expecting her to extend herself without extending anything in return. Even after she made her entrance, with what she thought was a compelling beauty, they gossiped about food, gowns, and cotillions.

Amy believed that she had been wise in specializing in society, that the Malcolms had arrived. Her tiny, pert face glowed as she told Lenora that the most exclusive society of Newport was watching their entertainment.

Lenora sought to give a feeling performance, but she had to dance with her hair heaped up in a huge pompadour, on Amy's orders, and this weighed her down. She wore a lace dress and ballet slippers, which were supposed to be proper but which struck her as vulgar, as if she were mocking nature. She felt nothing spontaneous. A reporter was describing in great detail what Mrs. Astor wore, but nothing about the way she had danced. This was absurd to Lenora.

Determined, however, not to succumb to pessimism, Lenora went to extra effort at another lawn fete to give the luster of Omar Khayyám, dancing in bits of gray gauze over a white tunic, and the dowagers were shocked and declared, "Child, this isn't art, this is embarrassing." Foolishly angry then, in Amy's opinion, she danced next in just her white tunic, and several dowagers said, "She dances in her undershirt." She returned to her lace frock only to be told by another dowager, "You should be raising a family. If you keep on dancing this way, you will never be able to have children."

Lenora decided there was not any promise of a brighter day here.

Lenora had read that in London and Paris artists met people who were doing inspiring things, that she might even sit next to someone who had known Edward FitzGerald, whose translation of The Rubáiyát was world famous. In New York, she decided, the great men were not about or were too difficult to meet. Perhaps they lacked artistic eloquence, she speculated, because the climate was too thick with cant. Or perhaps there were no great men here, at least in the arts. Lenora came to believe that art in America was in the hands of the wealthy, who were occupied chiefly with holding silk parasols to protect their delicate complexions, yet none of these society women had a complexion that compared with hers. They were afraid of her, she told herself, and she translated their indifference into hostility. Her yearning for

Europe grew, for the great artists she was sure she would find there.

Amy, who believed their performances at Newport were a turning point, moved their dancing school to the elegant Windsor Hotel on Fifth Avenue. She rented a suite for them and the big ballroom for the afternoons they had classes. Most of the children they taught were from the socially elect. Amy was fascinated by this location: the Windsor had housed President McKinley, the Astors, and the Vanderbilts.

Lenora, still bored with teaching, was delighted when Justin McCarthy, the poet-playwright, suggested a joint recital of *The Rubáiyát*. By now she had done these verses so often she felt they were her personal property, and McCarthy was even better known than Nevin.

The poet-playwright divided the program into three acts, and the recital began to the sound of harps and amid the perfume of flowers.

Lenora stood as motionless as a Greek statue while the poet-playwright's reading seeped into her, took shape, her shape. Then the harps rose in volume and she danced. She assumed a mournful paganism and bore an ancient cup as McCarthy read:

> *So when at last the angel of the drink*
> *Of darkness finds you by the river-brink,*
> *And, proffering his Cup, invites your Soul*
> *Forth to your lips to quaff it—do not shrink.*

There was a long pause, and then she seemed to tear the cup away from huge, celestial hands. Lifting it to her lips, she swayed emotionally, and suddenly the first act was over. She was unaware that her dress, shorter than was the custom, which she had trimmed before going on—unknown to Mama —had caused some agitation in an audience composed mainly of matrons. Under the spell of the verses, she felt dedicated. And for the second act she wore a longer, more conventional costume and sought to move with a controlled eloquence.

Yet when she began the final act in a thin, gray drapery, revealing bare arms and legs, hitherto not seen in such a setting, there was a hurried stirring in the audience. She heard seats banging, coughs of disapproval, but she refused to lose her concentration. Her mood altered from pessimism to wonder as the words demanded:

> *Ah Love! Could you and I with Fate conspire*
> *To grasp this sorry Scheme of Things entire,*

> *Would not we shatter it to bits—and then*
> *Re-mould it nearer to the Heart's Desire!*

Nothing mattered now to Lenora but to remain in tune with the words, to have her arms white and soft and possessed, to dance with taste, and to look beautiful. But someone giggled at her solemnity—derisively, and it was macabre to Lenora. She did not feel like a gargoyle. They should enjoy her dancing as much as she did. Yet shaken for an instant, it did matter to her, and she hated the audience with a sudden ferocity. Then it was as if the incident had never occurred as she was entranced by the enormity of the poet's design as the reading concluded:

> *And when Yourself with silver foot shall pass*
> *Among the Guests Star-scattered on the Grass,*
> *And in your joyous errand reach the spot*
> *Where I made One—turn down an empty Glass!*

Her body took on a sad contour. Her head bent lower, and she pressed her cheek against the roses in the center of the stage. She turned down an empty glass, slowly, gently. For a long moment she was motionless, and then she jumped hurriedly to her feet to take a bow.

To her surprise, there were boos amid the applause. Justin McCarthy looked distressed as she passed him, going off stage, but no one told her about the people who had left before the end of her performance.

Mama was careful to channel into her dressing room only those who had admired the recital, and thus Lenora was shocked by the adverse criticism that appeared in the press. One article in particular infuriated her, although in a curious manner it was gratifying also. She read:

The celebration of the great Persian poet's birthday at the Lyceum Theater bids fair to result in the splitting up of New York society. Little did Khayyám know when he died one thousand years ago that the deferred obsequies and funeral ceremonies would produce such a disaster. It was all on account of Lenora Malcolm. Lenora is a Chicago production, lithe, athletic and beautiful, so beautiful in fact, that Phil Armour of her native town, connoisseur in high art and food products, said as he looked at her, "She is as sweet as one of them beech nut hams." Can adulation go further?

This was not true, she thought bitterly, her dancing was not athletic and had nothing to do with Chicago. She asked, "Is this widely read?"

Mama said, "It doesn't matter."

It did to Lenora as she jumped a paragraph and read:

It was no fault of Mr. McCarthy's that certain society women got up and left the theater. It may be said on the highest possible authority that Mr. M'Carthy was properly garbed and conducted himself in every respect as an elocutionist and a gentleman should. Notwithstanding this, a matron rose, and giving a horrified look at Miss Malcolm's beautiful bare legs, unobscured by stockings, left the house. She was followed by a bunch of vestals and within five minutes as many as forty had withdrawn. It was the Malcolm's lack of costume that caused all the trouble.

"Oh, Mama, why can't they take me seriously?"

"Those that stayed were appreciative, dear."

Lenora went on reading, having to prove that to herself. She smiled as she read: "What matters is that most of those who left were fat. Not one of them could compete with Miss Malcolm."

Mama assured her, "You were modest and unassuming."

Lenora said, "This is more honest reporting."

Mama said, "You were an oasis in an ugly, drab city."

Just as Mama had convinced Lenora that this furor was all in her favor, that it would create a demand for more performances, a batch of new reviews came in. They were so sarcastic Lenora could not read them through, but kept repeating individual phrases in an angry frenzy, "*Rawboned*, am I? *An ostrich on one leg, a stork, a freak of nature*, am I? And here they say, '*Malcolm, the lanky Californian, is trying to teach us something magnificent, but her legs are bad, ungraceful.*'" Pacing up and down the studio, Lenora shouted, "Fools! Fat, fat fools! I'll show them whether I dare go on with my work!"

Mama and the rest of the family agreed with Lenora but begged her to be tactful. Amy had lost several pupils as a result of the recital, and she was having trouble meeting the enormous rent of the Windsor Hotel.

The next day was St. Patrick's Day, and like good Irish-Americans the Malcolms decorated their studio in green, and Lenora tried to finish their class quickly so they could watch the parade outside on Fifth Avenue. Amy was afraid to rush their class as Lenora suggested, for as always it included the children of socially prominent people. Amy insisted they receive the full time, to Lenora's disgust.

This was just not her day, Lenora decided. She could hear the St. Patrick's Day parade going by, and she felt very Irish at this moment.

Amy was in the middle of a musical accompaniment while Lenora was demonstrating a jig, an Irish one that her Grandma had taught her, keeping in time with the marchers outside—although a jig was considered vulgar—when one of the pupil's maids, who had been waiting for her charge in an adjoining apartment, rushed in and shouted, "Fire! The hotel is on fire!" It was the middle of the afternoon, and for a moment Amy thought this was a joke of Lenora's to end the class early. Then the ballroom was split with the crackling, sinister sounds of fire. Almost without thinking, but with one voice, Lenora and Amy calmed the children, saying this was part of the St. Patrick's Day celebration. Lenora gathered the children into a tight group with Amy's help. Heavy smoke began pouring in, breathing became difficult, but Lenora said, "Don't rush, we're going to play a game." She was as quiet as she knew how, although inside she had a great urge to flee. Amy sat down at the piano even as the smoke and heat increased, while Lenora marshaled the children into a neat double line and led them out of the building to the music of Amy's march.

The Forty-sixth Street portion of the Windsor Hotel was a mass of flame, and Lenora, counting the children, was terrified. Louise Wright and Alice Latham were missing. The police were busy preserving the fire lines, ordering everyone to keep back, and Lenora, deaf to the official commands, broke through the fire lines, eluding the guards who tried to drag her back, and ran into the burning hotel. She found the two eight-year-old girls huddled in a corner of the vast ballroom, blinded and panic-stricken by the huge waves of smoke. Lenora grabbed the sobbing girls and dragged them after her. Never had she run faster, never was she more grateful for the years of practicing that had made her so fit. The lobby was on fire now, and it licked at their heels. When Lenora emerged from the hotel, a child on each arm, a great cheer went up.

She knelt and thanked God. She felt sick inside, seeing the residents of the hotel jumping madly, hopelessly from windows seven, eight stories high. Guests were cremated before her eyes, and several died on the sidewalk in front of her. She thought she would faint. Then a fireman was holding her, taking her pulse, and congratulating her.

Lenora and Amy, who were still in their dancing costumes, were taken to another hotel. The next morning there were feature articles in all the New York newspapers, calling Lenora and Amy Malcolm the heroines of the terrible Windsor Hotel fire, one of the worst in the history of New York. There were over seventy dead, but thanks to the Malcolm girls, the press chorused, no one child had been harmed. Lenora, because of her dash back into the hotel, was the center of many interviews.

Lenora told the reporters mournfully, "We were only able to save what we were wearing. We lost all our properties, including wardrobes for artistic use as well as for everyday wear. I even lost the costumes in which I appeared to illustrate Justin M'Carthy's lecture on Omar Khayyám at the Lyceum Theater on Tuesday. The fire ruined our school, just as it was flourishing."

The reporters reminded her, "You did save thirty children."

"We did, didn't we?" Lenora gave the reporters her most appealing smile. "My sister Amy was wonderful. She kept playing, even when the flames were leaping around our heads. But, oh, our lovely costumes!"

Lenora was certain now they would take the city by storm. Many of the mothers were grateful to the Malcolms for saving their children, and as a reward and to show that they really appreciated art they arranged what was supposed to be a magnificent recital at the Lyceum Theater.

This became almost as great a disaster as the destruction of their costumes. There had been no public demand for her dancing, as she had expected, although she was still being acclaimed as the heroine of the tragic Windsor Hotel fire. So, to stir public interest Lenora announced before the recital that the Malcolms were leaving America for England, implying that this departure was because of America's indifference to "her art," and the sentiment of the press shifted.

Lenora did not expect this. She was dreadfully upset by the sarcastic review of what she assumed would be a tremendously praised recital.

. . . Under the patronage of 67 society women from the inner ranks of New York an impressive function was held yesterday. Miss Lenora Malcolm was assisted by her sister, Miss Amy Malcolm and a large Mama in a blue

gown as she distributed stropes from Ovid. They gave
for the first time in New York some idyls from Theocritus and Birn, done into dance under the name of "The
Happier Age of Gold."

Miss Malcolm has recently had the misfortune to lose
her wardrobe in the Windsor Hotel fire, which probably
accounts for and excuses the fact that her sole costume
for yesterday's dance was a species of surgical bandage
of gauze and satin of the hue of raspberry ice, and with
streamers of various lengths, which floated merrily or
mournfully as the dancer illustrated the burial of Adonis
and the bridal of Helen.

Miss Malcolm's melancholy sister, Amy, read extracts
from Ovid and Theocritus as an accompaniment to the
writhings and painful leaps and hops of Miss Malcolm,
while a concealed orchestra discoursed doleful music,
and the audience of tortured souls gazed at each other
and blushed or giggled, according to their individual
form of nervousness.

When the final dance was finished there was a sigh of
relief that it was over and that Miss Malcolm's bandages
had not fallen off, as they threatened to during the entire
show. Then the audience of 67 solemnly filed upon the
stage to kiss Miss Malcolm, her Mama, and her sister,
and to wish them success in introducing "The Happier
Age of Gold" to London drawing rooms.

Miss Malcolm has fully determined on this reckless
course, which is sad, considering we are at peace with
England at present.

The other article which infuriated Lenora was in a smart
gossip sheet. They had her approach completely wrong, she
thought bitterly, they had pictures of her in two especially
silly poses. And she hated the captions underneath:

"How I love my friends, the Vanderbilts!"

"Isn't Mrs. Highuppe kind to throw these flowers?"

The article was called: *Lenora Malcolm, New York's Society Dancer*.

Miss Malcolm is not a professional dancer, don't make
any mistakes on that score. She isn't a gaudy, giddy
young thing who trips through Broadway burlesque. She
is a society dancer, pure and simple, much too pure for
the professional stage.

Miss Malcolm holds forth in such ultra-fashionable
places as Sherry's, the Waldorf-Astoria. She spurns

Broadway with a large, thick spurn. Miss Malcolm is 'patronized' of course; there are certain women in society who pat her kindly on the back, say a good word for her to their friends who are getting up entertainments, and even, sometimes, engage her themselves.

Yet if Miss Malcolm were to take dinner every night of the week with Mrs. Astor, or go out driving every Saturday morning with Mrs. Vanderbilt, it would not make her more expert at manipulating her feet.

Actually, she is an excellent descriptive dancer; she portrays things with her arms and feet just as Paderewski does with his fingers. She is very, very classic and horribly afraid of becoming anything but absolutely and painfully refined.

Lenora thought, the sooner we are out of such an intolerant country the better. With the money from the recital she booked passage for England. Then she felt triumphant, sure that life in the arts would start in earnest. She felt even more triumphant when Archer decided not to go with them; he wanted to remain in New York so he could continue his acting career. She would be the leader of three women embarking on such a daring venture, for she was certain now that she was both a leader and a woman.

Amy did not agree that Lenora should be the leader, but she said nothing for the moment, waiting for the proper time to assume the leadership of the family. Mama, who was equally critical of Lenora's assertion of womanhood, warned Lenora not to be so expectant.

"I am not," said Lenora, "but I am not mad either."

"But you must go easy, rest more," said Mama.

"We have all of eternity to rest."

"You are overwrought, leaving America."

"No, no, I am going to like London better than anything on earth." Lenora was positive she was prepared for the future, that she would pull together the corners of the earth with her momentum.

But Mama, crossing an ocean she had not expected to cross, was thinking: God be with my children, God give them mercy, they are fine, healthy children. But where is Lenora? Where is my girl?

BOOK THREE

15

Thus the future begins for Lenora in London. The future becomes the stretch of her desire, the pace of her energy, the quest for a Promethean vigor and boldness, and an infinite number of magnificent possibilities. The future is where she has not been before. Where her dreams have not been tested yet. It is a city with a heritage as different as Blake and Byron, Herrick and Pope, Milton and Rossetti, and a host more. Now, with exuberance, she imagines a future as glorious as this past. She tells herself this is a future which must last forever; she has put so much time and energy into the dream; it is lovely and must not spoil. She is young, just turned twenty-one. She is certain this dream can never die.

The future was also supposed to be dancing in the drawing rooms of Berkeley Square, but the fashionable to whom she had been recommended by her patrons in New York were out of London for the summer, and the arts were at a standstill. The future became the effort to capture the look and feel of London.

A few days after their arrival in London the Malcolms found suitable rooms near Berkeley Square. Mama developed a severe headache, thinking of the expense, but Lenora said such feelings were inartistic, while Amy made the choice, decisively. Amy had put aside some money without telling anyone and was not the least bit embarrassed when the others discovered this, saying, "Somebody has to be practical." Near the rooms which Amy rented—rashly thought Mama—was aristocratic Grosvenor Square and Mayfair, pleasant Hyde Park and lovely Kensington Gardens. Amy said, "Miracles can be performed here." This would be a charming life, Amy thought. While the Berkeley Square neighborhood was not creative, its fine houses suggested a passage into another world for her, one which was secure and comfortable.

The neighborhood was wonderful to Lenora, for they were within walking distance of much of historical London. She went around the city on a torrent of emotion, concentrating on the art galleries and histrical sites with the eager curiosity of the born explorer. She was disappointed that everything in London seemed brown and yellow—even the sky; that women's skirts trailed in the dust and mud of the pavements, the clothes just as silly as in America, girls her age wearing shirtwaists to their necks and dressed in skirts to the ankles. But London itself teemed with history, and it would have taken a dozen eyes to see everything she wanted to see.

Mama trotted at her heels. Mama tried to look erect, to find hope in everything. She told herself she must not disappoint her children. But she felt bedeviled; her feet ached in the tight, high-buttoned shoes, and there was disquieting news from home. A letter had come from Aunt Jessie, hysterical and tear-stained, saying that Grandpop was dying, yet Mama could not tell the girls. They would want her to go home, and whatever happened, she could not leave them. She busied herself cooking, dressmaking, repairing her worn pocketbook which was the family bank, and fought against the slowly tightening pressure around her heart with the joy of rendering service.

But Lenora was asking, "Mama, why do you look so sad?"

"I wish you wouldn't talk like that."

"I haven't seen you smile for days."

"It is a long story, and you haven't much time."

"You ought to trust me," Lenora said with unexpected intensity.

"I do."

"Not always. Mama, why haven't you married again?"

Surprised by this question, Mama did not reply, thinking: yes, I have yearned, as deeply as you, Lenora, I had other chances to marry but they dribbled away, like the years, for I had none of the subservience that most men require, oh, I could be a wild growth, too, but the world would say that in a middle-aged woman that is second childhood, and now, no one wants to marry me, and yet I must not wail, it is my own choice, my own big beautiful choice, but can I truly love and live through my children, through Lenora?

"You did not keep me from marrying. No one did."

"I hope I haven't hurt you by what I said."

"Some choices are necessities," said Mama, thinking of her-

self and unable to turn herself inside out, even for Lenora.
Memories of her father revived, and in a marvelous instant he
lost the shadow of death. Grandpop had not been an artist,
but not one for rules either, and he had had a gift for happiness. She had loved him, not as she loved her children, at the
summit of her emotion, but quietly, privately. Suddenly
Mama felt guilty, for she had not seen him for such a long
time, while his old age had been a twilight half-life, yet he had
never complained. But if her departure had been cruel to him,
it would be worse, she thought, to impose such burdens on
Lenora.

"Are you ill?" asked Lenora. Mama's face seemed to have
shrunk.

"Good heavens, do I look that bad? It's these clothes. They
are a threat to health and sanity." Mama struggled out of her
black muslin dress, black purposely so the worn spots would
not show, but she had only begun to undress. There was a
flannel petticoat, whalebone corsets, a corset waist, and this
was less than any woman her age dared to wear. As she
discarded them on the four-poster she shared with her
daughters some of her nervousness vanished. But nothing
could remove the overwhelming tiredness from Mama. And in
the unromantic privacy of the chilly bathroom, where she did
not have to sing old songs to sound cheerful, she wept for her
dying father.

For Lenora however, this was the season of the emerging
artist. She discovered the British Museum. All at once the
cold ashes of the past were heated with a new fire.

The museum was within walking distance, and for days
Lenora hurried along Oxford Street and into Bloomsbury,
entering the generously spaced building through the massive
Ionic colonnade which she came to love. Forty-four columns,
she counted all of them, filled her with a new purpose. She
remembered every step of the way, for now she was carrying
a dream. The great reading room with its large dome of glass
and iron became as holy to Lenora as a cathedral. She studied
the famous Elgin Marbles and fell in love with these sculptures from the Parthenon. She read with a patience new to her
that since the Greeks had built the Parthenon at the time
when Athenian art had reached its noblest harmonies, these
marbles represented the zenith of Greek sculptural art. Then
these sculptures took on an almost unbearable reality. She fell
in love with the Hellenic freedom of the body, their perfection
of line. She found that in their dances the legs did have to
dominate but that the entire body contributed to the expression. Their perfect bodies had nothing to do with keeping fit,

with over-developed muscles, with anatomy lessons, or with handsome savages in loincloths. They were the results of going to the source, to nature.

When Lenora was able to slip into the Elgin Room without anyone else being there, she stood the way the Greek figures stood, turned her head the way their heads turned, lifted her arms and legs the way they lifted. But she was not certain she owned the same fibre. Several times, as she lacked the ease the figures possessed, she discarded her shoes but quickly realized there was far more to dancing in her bare feet than doing it.

When Mama warned her not to imitate, she said, "I'm not. It's not the forms, the surfaces I want, but the reasons. I don't want to live the same as the Greeks, I want to learn what they learned, to use it in my dancing, but I am so lumpy."

Here now, was another Lenora, was another growing up, thought Mama, and she wondered: how many Lenoras will my child become?

Lenora said, "The sculpture is wonderful, but I am a clod."

Lenora looked so tragic in her reversal from vanity to humility that Mama, despite her own burden of grief, had to smile, but Lenora was elsewhere already, holding out her bare arms as if they were marble, engrossed in them with a solitary intentness, loving them with a brooding self-love because that gave them the greatest meaning.

But the future, which was the core of their lives, changed abruptly. The future suddenly lay abandoned, gathering dust, as they ran out of money. Their residence in Berkeley Square ended suddenly with the door locked against them for nonpayment of rent. They almost lost their luggage too, until Lenora climbed in the back window, claiming she was the most agile, basking in the excitement, although Mama wished she was not so reckless and Amy thought it undignified. But Lenora was a quiet shadowy figure climbing through the window, and she handed the luggage to Amy and Mama with a sense of accomplishment.

When Lenora discovered that Mama had taken a job as a parlor-maid so they could afford other rooms in respectable Berkeley Square, she felt responsible and she begged Mama to quit. When Mama refused, Lenora invited a man right off the street into their flat. The man never got in, never even got close to Lenora, but the ruse worked—Lenora threatened to do it again, to go even further—and so Mama quit. Moreover, Lenora learned that one of the potential patrons to whom she had been referred had returned to London for the first social function of the Court and was giving an affair that required entertainment.

Lenora paused on the threshold of the home on Berkeley Square which she had selected, stricken by her own audacity. But a few minutes later, ushered inside by the butler, Lenora announced to Lady Bountiful that she had regards from the Astors and Vanderbilts and spoke as if they were old friends.

It was a game naming her *Lady Bountiful;* Lenora could not think of the marchioness any other way, for this tall stately lady had to be benevolent.

Lady Bountiful seemed pleased to meet her. The marchioness thought: what a poetic-looking young creature! And so properly recommended!

Lenora said, "Our friends in America tell me that no one in England is more interested in art than you."

"I like nice things."

"So do I. In fact, I am staying at the Royal Palace," said Lenora, giving the name of one of London's most fashionable hotels. "I just thought I would drop by and give you regards from the duchess. I danced for her in New York, this past April."

"How nice. You dance in a refined manner?"

"Of course."

"Could you give a cultured recital?"

"I think so . . . except . . . well . . . ?"

"What is it, child?"

"I understand the importance of your entertainment, and I would like it to be worthy of you."

"You are attractive."

"I will need costumes to match." Lenora assumed this would provoke some money, but Lady Bountiful sent her to a good dressmaker, who was willing to give credit, since the marchioness had recommended the American.

Lenora thought she looked beautiful at Lady Bountiful's "entertainment," and she gave the elegant audience a full and elevated program. The applause was casual, and cool. Lenora heard such remarks as: "She holds a pose well." "She must dance because of religious reasons." "What a charming expression!" "And what a strange costume!"

Lenora thought them Philistines when no one noticed that she had caught the imprint of the Greeks and their superb sense of bone structure.

Lady Bountiful was satisfied. A soothing sense of righteous fatigue settled over her guests, and Lenora got other offers to dance in fashionable drawing rooms.

Lenora accepted these offers, but only from a sense of duty. Many times now she danced in costumes and in a style which were an outgrowth of her Greek studies. She believed she was on the verge of an art revolution, for she was dancing in the flowing diaphanous robes of the Greeks. But no one seemed to care. No one reproached her, no one mocked her, but no one seemed impressed either.

Lenora, unable to repress her feelings, suddenly was blurting out her dissatisfaction to Mama, saying, "Society, I am afraid, will always find the artist and self-expression strange and difficult."

"They applaud your dancing."

"Not really. Not with their hearts. I come to them with my art, my new art, and they tell me the only art which counts is the art *that was, that is past, that is dead.* They tell me that all the best paintings have been painted, all the best poetry has been written, all the best dances have been danced, and there is nothing left for us to create."

"You are trying to find the origins of emotion, and perhaps that affronts them. Perhaps emotion is easier for them to experience when it is secondhand."

"They are alive only with the past, the dead generations. I must dance for the artists, for those who have the imagination to appreciate me. I must, Mama, must!"

When Lenora discovered that Pat Campbell lived nearby, with a large garden outside her drawing room, she was elated. She decided to dance for this artist and chose a mild evening when this celebrated actress would be home. She informed Amy, her reluctant accomplice in these plans, "Our senses are most deeply affected by the darkness, it is ideal for the imagination." Lenora wore the white diaphanous robes of the Greeks, which were made more striking by the darkness.

They slipped unseen through the iron gate and silently approached the distinguished-looking house. Lenora whispered, "Don't overrecite, Amy, this could mean a good deal."

Amy began to recite their old reliable, *The Rubáiyát.* A window jarred open. Amy's voice swelled. Lenora grew taut and focused intently as if on stage. A minute later they heard footsteps approaching on the gravel path.

Amy, her mission done, vanished into the shrubbery as they had agreed, while Lenora danced across the garden, feeling frightened that she might be misunderstood, yet having to be in motion, driven and driving, and wondering how Prometheus could have endured being bound a day, let alone a lifetime. She danced with all her grace and newly acquired knowledge as she saw someone tall, dark, hurrying toward her.

Pat Campbell was confused. Born of an Italian mother and an English father; born in India out of a super-abundance of romance; born again as the star of *The Second Mrs. Tanqueray*, greatest theatrical success of the decade, she was prepared to be scathing. The recitation had been dreadful, and if this actress assumed she would attract her interest this way, stupid, stupid woman! Pat Campbell was determined to extinguish this intruder with a word. But although this dancing was strange, almost incredible, it was not stupid. Instead of insulting Lenora, Pat Campbell paused, thinking in a flash—it was no fun thinking any other way—this young dancer illuminated space charmingly, when you became accustomed to her style, for then she possessed the intrinsic grace of natural phenomenon.

Pat Campbell said, however, "Why are you dancing here?"

Lenora said, "Why not?"

"Your slippers are soaking wet." Lenora had stopped dancing, and Pat Campbell, Pat Cat to many, sensed pretension, and that always infuriated her.

"My sandals are Greek style." Lenora wavered, afraid that this artist was going to be unimpressed also.

"And I do not understand your costume."

Lenora could overlook many things, but not criticism of her work. She flared, "Can you stop people from misunderstanding you?"

Pat Campbell, priding herself on her own frankness, said, "No."

"Neither can I. But I will not be corseted to extinction, or walk with mincing steps, or dance with heavy stockings, whatever people say. Would you?"

"I am not a dancer."

"You move like one."

For a moment Pat Cat looked ferocious. Then she said, "You have a perfectly scandalous manner. Wonderful! But you cannot dance in the garden."

"It is far more natural than a rug."

"I can hardly visualize you in a middy blouse or bloomers, but it is cold out here." Pat Cat settled into benevolence of a determined sort and led Lenora into her parlor. Her voice grew vibrant, irresistible, wanting to conquer yet construct. "You are devilishly pretty, and such enchanting arms."

Pat Campbell's parlor was comforting, they were fellow conspirators now, and even as Lenora's independence animated the room, she listened to Pat Campbell as if conquered by her fabulous spirit, willing too, if necessary, to be the protégé of such a superior spirit.

This gave Pat Campbell the feeling that she was the heroine, which she could never resist, and she was intrigued by Lenora's spirit. When Lenora said, "I will not change my art, not for anyone," Pat Cat replied, "Yes, yes, you are incurable. Fine! You must be conjurer, fire-eater all in one."

"But an artist too?"

"That is when you become the greatest artist. But your greatest asset is that you are not a deferential girl. The charm of your fragile mobility is, really, an illusion." Lenora started to protest that she was mobile, and Pat Cat went right over her with pyrotechnic rapidity. "You are not fragile at all. Oh, you are lovely, young, but not tender, not really. You may lack the typical blown-up nineteenth-century bosom, but you do not lack strength." She smiled, delighted that she had startled Lenora with her frankness. "And don't let your hair hang down. It is not worthy of you. You are taking refuge in looking girlish. You must learn to use those passionate eyes of yours. Then you won't have to be insufficiently clad."

By now Lenora had penetrated Pat Campbell's heart, if only briefly, but that was enough, for the actress was keyed up, remembering her own triumphs and carried away by the ones she was creating for Lenora. By saying whatever came into her mind, instinctively, she was witty sometimes; she was never witty when she deliberated.

"You must hold up your head too, so you do not spoil your good looks."

Lenora sat even straighter then. Ugliness, awkwardness, any physical disorder upset Pat Campbell, and she studied Lenora until the latter's walk was as unique and dramatic as her own.

Next, Pat Campbell suggested a new costume, and when Lenora changed the subject, irritably, she realized it was because of a lack of money. Suddenly then, Pat Campbell said, "It is all a matter of taste. When I started in the theater, I had two pounds ten and thought it a great fortune."

Lenora said, "But it must have been a very exciting time."

"It was a vast risk. Just as I started to make my way in the theater, my health broke down, I lost my voice, my husband was in Africa, prospecting and not finding the fortune he was after, and I was not much older than you are, with two children, practically babies, to worry about, and no income but what I could earn in a theater which did not give a damn about me."

"Then suddenly you were a success."

"Not at all. I was in many plays before anyone considered me a decent actress." Pat Campbell had a need to strike deeply now, feeling Lenora's vitality, which seemed so much like her own. "Just before I got the role of Paula Tanqueray in *The Second Mrs. Tanqueray*, one of the most successful roles of our time, I had been a failure. Not only was my previous play harshly reviewed, the producers said it was my fault, my voice was weak, my gestures ineffective, and that nothing I did got over the footlights."

"But you are so theatrical."

"Oh, now? Yes. They say I would shame the devil."

"You have a richness of heart."

"And you have an instinct for flattery . . . Don't blush, child, it is very useful, and you should use it. But be willful too. Half the careers which go wrong are destroyed by too much amiability. You are a young barbarian, and you should remain that way."

"I wish others felt that."

"I will introduce you to others myself."

"How can I thank you?" Lenora looked surprised and ecstatic, almost sincerely ecstatic. "You are a magician."

"Wasn't that the reason you were dancing in my garden?" Pat Cat's dark, vivid eyes twinkled. "Why else would you dance in a wet, chilly garden? It was really quite droll. And by the way, who was reciting?"

"My sister."

"She has the voice of an auctioneer. She does not recite, she breathes."

"She is a philosopher," explained Lenora.

"So I received something I did not bargain for with your art, free thought and progress. But you are more effective without the recitation."

A profound instinct kept Lenora from answering now.

"In any event, I want you to dance for some friends of mine, who helped me when I was struggling."

16

Pat Campbell, determined to prove she was right about Lenora, gave a tea in her home at which Lenora was the only performer. All the guests were presumed to be creative in the arts, and Lenora felt part of a chosen group. When she finished the regular portion of her program, she improvised an encore in what she announced as "my Greek manner."

The audience seemed impressed. Pat Campbell, proud and victorious, introduced her to the fine-featured, middle-aged John Gray, whose bearing seemed to Lenora the precise representation of the artist. Pat Campbell said, "John, I told you the dancing would not depress you."

"Stella, you get your way in everything," he said, but so gently, she could not be offended.

"John, isn't Lenora devilishly pretty!"

"Lovely." He made a gracious little bow.

"Now remember, my dears, don't be solemn," said Pat Campbell, and then she was gone and Lenora expected John Gray to follow.

Instead, he said, "Your Greek dance was performed as if you truly loved it. Hellenism is a state of being, and you captured that."

Lenora tried to use her eyes as Pat Campbell had advised, even as she thought a man such as John Gray would never fall in love with a woman who was merely beautiful. She must have culture, must be able to pursue ideas to their ultimate conclusions, yet she must look incandescent—as if set afire by his words. She spoke about her visits to the British Museum, the art galleries, that she needed aid or she would become fat with just facts.

"You fat? Hardly." His vanity was touched by her awareness of his immense knowledge, he was amused by her impudence, and she was damnably pretty and really had no need to be clever. "Miss Malcolm, may I see you home? Of course, we need not go yet."

She wanted to go. With John Gray she felt able to travel anywhere. The skill with which he spoke of art, his awareness of her creative energy, how could she do better, or even half so well?

The leisurely drive home confirmed her feelings. No wonder she had been attracted to him, she thought. How different he was from the empty society folk; here, at last, was the kind of man she had expected to meet in London. He spoke about music, painting, and literature with an erudition that encompassed the universe. He was a renowned art critic and painter. She adored his grave eyes, his charming smile, and his fine mustache.

She told Mama, "He knows practically everybody, even Ellen Terry," and she did not wish to sound impressed, yet this made her a link in the chain which preserved the past, and Mama was impressed also.

John Gray invited her to view an exhibition in which were some of his paintings. She noticed that although the poses were different the faces were the same: oval-shaped, beautiful, and unreal.

She sighed. It was confusing. She lifted her cheek toward him, and she wished for an instant he was less cool. He did not meet her halfway, but said, "You must chisel your clay harder, then you will have your own style, you will become a perfectly shaped figure," and she had no quarrel with such a design, yet to achieve this, she thought—I should be caressed.

"How interesting," she said.

"But it takes a long time to find your own style, sometimes a lifetime."

"I respect the thought, but I am a dancer. I should be at my best now, not when I am fifty or sixty, when I will be too old to dance."

"Miss Malcolm, all the arts are related. You must feel that way about your dancing. Nature does not change, it is ourselves who must change." He led her into the Italian wing of the art gallery and discoursed on the Renaissance. He revered Michelangelo, Leonardo, and Raphael; he declared that these giants owed much to the Greeks. Parading his knowledge of art, Lenora realized he was paying her a great compliment.

The next few days he took Lenora for drives through Hyde Park, showed her through art galleries, but always, wherever they went, he related it to the culture of other centuries. John actually, thought Lenora, was courting her through Greek civilization, the Roman Empire, and into the Middle Ages. It was an interesting world; it was also very far away and safe.

Then, in response to her request, he gathered about them a group of other artists. Late into the night at his flat they drank sherry or coffee, smoked—even some of the women, which was quite advanced—and ate lightly, for John believed gorging dulled the brain. Most of all they talked eloquently, but always about yesterday, and always, Lenora noted with regret, only talked. But when Neville Bardon joined these discussions she was sure they would alter. Neville was erudite too, a dilettante who had inherited a sizable income, but he was just a few years older than she was, although he wore a slight Vandyke to make himself look older.

Neville was very British, and often she had trouble with his accent, but he loved nature, and he took her for many walks through Hyde Park. When they paused to rest and sat, Neville, unlike John, was still in constant ferment. Suddenly he was saying, "Moralizing is one form of immorality." Or inspired by ambition, he would announce, "What is wanted in the world of art is a spirit and faith that will keep our talent forever young."

This went on for weeks while Lenora waited for Neville to kiss her, but he acted as if she were destined for a loftier life than the mere vulgarity of earthly love, and that left her even more discontented.

Lenora however, was still resolved to be a thinker as well as a dancer, and so she continued to see both Neville and John. She worked in her studio most of the time, still stimulated by the Greeks and the British Museum, but her heart continued to fly around London with her suitors. Neville suggested poetry for her to dance to; John gave her books to study, so she could feed on his erudition. But neither of them pursued her the way she desired to be pursued. John always treated her with a grave politeness, while Neville, although tenderness itself, never even kissed her.

Only the thought of the other aroused them to any show of excitement.

Then Neville said of John's work, "What wonderful lines, what wonderful colors—if he could only paint!"

"I dare say," said the usually even-tempered John about Neville, "he is really a civil fellow, but his taste in art is quite juvenile."

Neville promised to introduce her to a producer he knew; John said he would have her dance for Ellen Terry, when the latter returned from America.

Not one, however, to wait for things to happen, Lenora took matters into her own hands and gave a private recital for her friends. She invited Pat Campbell, who could not come, but at her instigation John and Neville, determined to outdo the other, spurred many of their friends into coming. This became a veritable *Who's Who* of artistic London. Even Amy was impressed, while Mama was jubilant and sure that the last great hurdle was about to be cleared, and Lenora bathed in the air as if it were gold. She served tea in flowing Greek robes, and then she danced for all of these celebrated guests; the bearded one, the calculating one, the intense one, and the somber one. The life of artistic London enveloped Lenora, and she danced buoyantly, as if the dance were all, while her distinguished audience stared at her, quietly, almost detached, as if she were a picture in a gallery.

John said quite loudly, so his praise could be heard by everybody, "She is lovely, a little wood nymph."

Neville, to show that he was a man of action as well as an appreciator, introduced her to "my good friend, Frank Benson, one of the best of our actor-managers," and declared, "Isn't she beautiful!"

"Indeed, she is," said Frank Benson, "a real pre-Raphaelite beauty."

Now there was so much to win, Lenora almost exploded with excitement. She neglected her suitors for the next few minutes, so she could cultivate Frank Benson.

John looked the offended patrician, the first time she had seen him in such a guise, but Neville was pleased that his aid was proving successful.

Lenora asked Benson, "You are a devotee of dancing?"

"Not at all. But your performance, visually, was very nice indeed. Your poses possessed genuine beauty."

Benson had been a beauty himself, Lenora had heard, and though just past forty, he was growing in importance as a manager. He was about to produce a repertory of Shakespeare at Irving's famed Lyceum Theater, which could establish him as the most vital dramatic force in all of England.

Benson asked Lenora, "Have you had any experience in Shakespeare?"

"Not exactly." In this uncertain moment Lenora remembered that Neville had said that Shakespeare was Benson's universe.

He asked, "Have you had any experience at all in the theater?"

Feeling that none of Daly had been a felicitous experience and certainly did not compare with Benson, she said wistfully, "No, not really, although under the proper auspices I am sure I would find it stimulating."

"I am frightfully sorry, Miss Malcolm, but . . ."

"I have danced with Ethelbert Nevin, and I have done Omar Khayyám with Justin M'Carthy."

"Justin? An old friend of mine!"

"We gave a number of recitals together. They were exceedingly well received. If I had known you were a friend of Justin's, I would have brought along some of the notices."

"Not the least bit necessary, really. You have the essential grace that Shakespeare requires. I will be delighted to audition you."

"Wonderful," Neville said afterward. His face was almost against Lenora's, but not quite. "You will be happy with Benson. He is an Oxford graduate, a real gentleman, and a damned industrious man. He has done Shakespeare in the provinces, London, and at Stratford-on-Avon."

Lenora was delighted, too, for once more there was the familiar discrepancy between expenses and income. Although the recital had been a success—much of artistic London had attended, Mama said, and many had been impressed—no other engagements had been offered.

The audition itself was held at the theater before Benson, Neville, and the usual cleaning women. Lenora sought to imagine herself Ariel, her heart set on dancing this role, but she felt enervated before she began. Benson and Neville were whispering in the pit, and she was sure they were critical. The cleaning women were distracting as they dusted the seats. She could not feel any immortal imprints engraved on this stage, although Henry Irving, Ellen Terry, and Edwin Booth had trod these boards. She was as void of emotion as the empty house which yawned before her. Three years had swept by since she had auditioned the same way for Daly, and he was dead now, before his time, tragically, his theater empire in ruins, and she felt just as dead, inhabiting her body without meaning. Benson had said, "Dance a few pretty steps?" What was pretty, and how many breaths did it take? How fervently she would have sought to be pretty a year or two ago, but now she longed for much more. Suddenly she did not know how to start.

The Grieg began as she had suggested. It seemed to fit the aerial murmurs of Shakespeare, and some of her confidence returned. Fine for the purposes of now, she thought, and she danced, seeking to be Ariel although she did not feel like Ariel. The feeling, insistent in her, that in the years since Daly she had achieved nothing was intolerable suddenly. She halted, unable to bear this. No one said anything. No one ever did, she thought, the English were so damned polite. She whispered, "Chopin, please."

The accompanist nodded; the elderly, wispy pianist, far from the best, far from the prominence he had desired thirty years ago, found music which she liked. He was accustomed to changing at a moment's notice, to the hallucinations of artists who thought they could sing or dance to anything.

She forgot Ariel now. She forgot Daly, Benson, Neville. She had come to the end of a phase and was starting a new one. Lenora stood straight, and then moved forward as the Greek statuary had suggested, to understand nature as they had—from the source.

Neville whispered to Benson, "She is lovely."

"Lovely. But not theater."

"She is such a beautiful figure on stage, tender, palpable . . ."

"But not for the theater." Benson refused to argue. His face turned toward the stage and assumed a boyish charm as he halted her. She paused, feeling lost, and he told her that it was fine, charming, and enough.

Waiting for her to dress, Benson said to Neville, "I do not wish to be blunt, but what is your role in this situation?"

"Frank, sometimes, really, you have the tact of a water buffalo."

"And this girl, she is quite certain she is going to be magnificent some day, and she has the drive of a water buffalo."

"How absurd!"

"Or I dare say, she is going to convert you. She is a bit of an evangelist, you know, with this exaltation of the Greeks."

Having evaluated this treason properly, Neville became calm and said, "You can see that she is an artist. What have you got against her?"

"Nothing, as an artist in the proper framework. Or as a woman, either, only you insist on treating her as an elf, as if her sensuality is chaste, which fits *The Tempest*, but not Miss Malcolm. You may think she is a kitten, but she is more apt to grow into a tigress, mark my words."

"First you call her a water buffalo, then a tigress. You are quite a study, old man. You have been doing too much *Hamlet*."

"I also have a sense of proportion."

"Then you are not using her?"

Benson's face took on an expression that Neville disliked, a quiet sureness. He said, "At her studio we were surrounded by frightfully intellectual people who can appreciate her sort of thing, but in the theater . . . the critics will make a shambles of her."

"You mean you have nothing for Miss Malcolm?"

"Nothing that she really wants. What do you want?"

Neville felt impotent, and so he was indignant. "There is no comparison between the two situations."

"Miss Malcolm desires to improve her situation, but do you? Do you really find her quite acceptable?"

This was no compliment and was not intended as one, yet Neville could not deny the implication. However he applauded Lenora's dancing, it was true she was of shabby parentage. Lenora had boasted, seeking to match Neville's socially elect family, that her father had been president of the Academy of Arts in San Francisco, when Neville doubted there was such an institution. And while he thought Mama meant well, he felt her scholarship quite ragged, she preferred

Shelley to Swinburne, and she hardly hid her wish for an explanation of his intentions toward Lenora. And there were other injudicious matters. Anxious as Neville was to enthrone Lenora as his symbol of beauty, she was creating complications. Her refusal to wear dresses to her toes as everyone else did was embarrassing. While he regarded this as an innocent bit of nonsense on her part, it caused others to doubt her virtue. Friends of his family who had seen him with Lenora— oh, they tolerated her dancing since she had danced in a number of fashionable drawing rooms—but they thought that as a companion she exceeded the boundaries of modesty.

Benson asked Neville, "Have you introduced her to your family?"

Upset by this probing, Neville muttered, "My feelings in this are not vital, but her career is. Aren't you giving her any chance?"

"To dance, yes. But to wreck a production, no."

From the moment Benson said to Lenora, "It was charming," she was sure he was indifferent to her art. She was not surprised when he gave her one of the smallest roles in *Henry V*. She sensed from Neville's abashed countenance that she had not been considered appropriate for Shakespeare. She did not hate Benson for this new disappointment; she thought him stuffy but still more cultured than Daly.

Lenora was annoyed most at herself for having been excited to so little purpose, yet, as always, in performance she sought to wash over the stage with all her energy. The few moments she danced alone on the stage in *Henry V*, however, were painfully cruel. It were as if God taunted her by opening his hand and allowed her to dance upon it, for a far too brief instant, and then closed it tight, so tight she could not even squirm.

The Lyceum audience was swank and a triumph for Benson. Neville said to Lenora, whose irritation was obvious, "You do not run away from such opportunities," but she had to run away from this. She agreed with critic Max Beerbohm, who wrote in the *Saturday Review*:

. . . as a branch of university cricket, the whole performance was, indeed, beyond praise. But, as a form of acting, Benson's production of "Henry the Fifth" was not impressive. He must, really, break himself and his company of his fatal cricketing habit.

When she was glad she had not been mentioned in any of the reviews, her role was so tiny, and she made no effort to

continue with Benson, Neville was offended. From then on
Neville practiced his courtship by mail.

John was gratified that Neville's aid had proven futile, as he
had expected. He promised Lenora a recital at the gallery
where he exhibited, to be given as soon as his good friend
Ellen Terry returned from her farewell American tour. He
assured her it would make her name known throughout England. And he asked Lenora to pose for him.

She hurried to his studio, repeating to herself that a woman
must live, wanting to be willing, but afraid, even in her anticipation. She could imagine John chanting a measure of love as
he embraced her. But what else, she was not sure, except
whatever happened—it must be with importance, it must not
be casual, it must wrap her endearingly in joy.

John, however, was so circumspect it struck her as the
greatest violation of all.

Mama asked, finding Lenora irritable after a number of
posings, "No luck?"

"What do you mean?"

"When a man sees you as often as Gray does, he must be
quite serious."

"He is too serious," burst out Lenora, "and I don't care, I
don't care!"

But Lenora did care, thought Mama, and it left both of
them unsettled. Mama awoke every morning now, tense and
rigid, expecting bad news about Grandpop—the last she had
heard he had been in a coma for days—or about Lenora,
fearful that her daughter would give herself to a man who
seemed determined never to marry. Mama had learned that
John Gray had lived many years with his ailing mother, and
the pattern seemed obvious.

Lenora, tired of waiting for John's promised help, arranged
a special matinee at old St. George's Hall of "The Happier
Age of Gold," featuring the idyls of Theocritus. When Mama
said this was essentially the same program Lenora had done in
New York, she retorted, "I am not doing it the same way.
When you play Chopin, play it purely, without ornamenting
it." Mama looked unhappy and Lenora kissed her. "I'm going
to dance without any scenery at all."

Mama protested, "That's impossible."

"If I think so, yes. But I do not have to think so."

"Lenora, the audiences have to be comfortable also."

"They were comfortable in Greece without scenery. The
audiences here are spoiled by too much scenery and not
enough inner feelings."

"Henry Irving, who uses more scenery than any other actor, is England's most famous actor."

"His pictorial effects are amazing, but they go to see him, not a piece of wood. And even with a bare stage, there will be plenty for you to do."

Mama was quiet, and in her mind something moved painfully, something sharper than grief, something almost like a declaration of war. Her peace of mind depended on being a mother, respected and cherished and listened to as a mother. She recalled all the years that the total passion of her being, whatever else had happened, had focused on her children. Now was she going to be thrown aside? Was that inevitable? But she must not complain; Lenora would say that was tiresome.

Lenora draped the walls of the stage with blue velvet curtains, but otherwise the stage was bare. She began the recital with Mama at the piano. She looked through the curtain into the audience and was disappointed that there was no sign of Pat Campbell, but she saw John, Neville, and Benson.

As she danced downstage she repeated to herself: it is not difficult to hold an audience by yourself, all you have to do is just go out and pause and then dance a little, and then she had to smile at her own naïveté.

She imagined herself in a Greek temple. She felt the lofty reach of the Parthenon, and her arms lifted with such a reach. And now she danced as if the dance was all, as if nothing else had been put by, as if this were a very loving day, a day to be remembered with joy.

There was a great silence when Lenora finished. The audience seemed asleep, or bewildered. She came forward, wondering whether to bow, and there was a smattering of applause. Her long, flowing tunic threw shadows about her. She wore nothing else, neither jewel nor flower. She stood still, a few steps away from the silent audience, and then she raised her head defiantly. And suddenly, abruptly, there was an upheaval in the audience.

A tall, matronly, exuberant woman had risen at the rear of the hall, and Lenora trembled, recognizing Ellen Terry. The famous actress was crying out with all the urgency of her rich, vibrant voice, "Do you realize what you are looking at? Do you understand that this is the most incomparably beautiful dancing in the world? Do you appreciate what this woman is doing for you? Bringing back the lost beauty of the old world of art!"

John, sitting beside Ellen Terry, rose excitedly and applauded loudly.

Ellen Terry plunged on, "Do you realize that she has shed our fears, our humiliations, our defeats!"

As long as she lived, Lenora would remember this. Everyone was around her now, John, Neville, Benson, but she had eyes only for Ellen Terry. Fair and lovely she was indeed, thought Lenora, but more the queen than the princess now, in her fifties, stately, a touch of gray in her light hair. And witty too, as Lenora had expected, but never a word of malice in a malicious profession but the divine voice that made everyone fall in love with her, made all of them feel they must be at their best.

Ellen Terry said, "John, my dear, told me how lovely you were, but I would not have believed it unless I had seen it. There is an inner feeling in you that is deeper than your movements, yet it is your movements too."

Impossible to contain herself, yet Lenora did somehow.

Neville said, "Miss Terry, I am glad Gray had the good taste to bring you."

Lenora, who had hoped for a duel at the very least between Neville and John, was thinking—so much of love was shadow boxing.

Benson remarked, "Perfect, quite quite perfect."

Lenora found her voice then, reminding him, "You did not feel that way a few weeks ago when I wanted to dance Puck."

Ellen Terry said, "A nice role, but for a child."

Benson said, "For a child like Miss Terry. It was her first great role."

Ellen Terry said, "I was thirteen when I played it. But why compare? It is like saying a lily is prettier than a rose."

Lenora persisted however, still directing her fire at Benson, "I would have profaned the character?"

"My dear," smiled Benson, "you might have ennobled it. You might also be another one of my errors of judgment."

Ellen Terry said, "And now, Lenora, you want to take the shoes and stockings off the world of dancers?"

"Isn't that the most natural way to dance!" exclaimed Lenora. Now, she felt, she was under oath to the Greeks.

"I dare say," said Ellen Terry. "It is also more natural not to wear corsets, or tied-in waists, but everybody does, even dancers, except you."

And Mama, who before the recital had worried so, was amazed, and yet not amazed. There had been a new sculptural beauty in Lenora's dancing. There had been moments when Lenora had held the attention with complete authority. But it was risky to stay so high pitched, and Lenora was pitched as high as the stars, and no one could remain so high without falling sometimes, sometimes dreadfully hard. So Mama said, feeling like a little grain of sand among huge boulders, "Praise is fine, but too much can be suffocating."

Ellen Terry, who thought Mama's face a kind nice one, but aged before its time by too much anxiety and work, agreed in part, and added a favorite saying, "I think we all know that imagination, intelligence, and industry are all indispensable to the artist, but of these three, the greatest is, without doubt, imagination, and your daughter certainly has that."

John said, "As Ellen is the painter's actress, Lenora will become the painter's dancer."

"She will need more than that," said Mama, seeking to retain some balance amid the extravagances of the theater.

Ellen Terry, with her mischievousness, could not resist asking, "Are you good friends?"

"The best," Mama said wryly. "We are such close friends that unfortunately we can say all sorts of rude, truthful things to each other."

"Does she listen to you, Mrs. Malcolm?" asked Ellen Terry.

"Sometimes."

"Perhaps," said Ellen Terry, "she should listen only to herself."

They talked performing for an hour then, and a century of English acting stretched out before Lenora. They were like laughing children, putting their memories to happy use, thought Lenora.

They were like peacocks, thought Mama, with absolutely nothing put by. Her mind was crowded with patched clothes and unfulfilled hopes, and Lenora might be all these things, but they were remembering because remembering was better than middle age.

Lenora expanded in the heat of their attention. Never, never again must she be dissatisfied or discouraged, she told herself, however the rest of the world ridiculed her. These artists were right: art must be all!

So Lenora kept repeating to herself what Ellen Terry had said:

"Do you understand that this is the most incomparably beautiful dancing in the world? Do you appreciate what this woman is doing for you? Bringing back the lost beauty of the old world of art!"

It might not be quite true yet, but she would make it true. Lenora knew that never in her life would she feel more dedicated to her destiny, or more encouraged by the choice of her dedication.

17

Now there was intense activity among the Malcolms. Not only were the old dances revived, but new dances were rehearsed by Lenora to music hitherto not attempted, Gluck, Mozart, Schumann, while Mama went through these musical accompaniments with a renewed, although sometimes puzzled fervor, and Amy planned new lessons for her pupils.

Lenora seldom left the studio, keeping a sharp outlook for managers; Mama practiced regularly now and mended costumes; Amy studied the different theaters in London so she could select the best one for a series of special recitals. The next day, every day from then on, became the instant many wondrous things were to happen. But nothing happened. The month which rolled into nothingness failed to transform the eager Lenora from a drawing-room dancer into a concert star, as she had expected. It seemed as if there was not a management in all of London which had any use for her kind of dancing.

The tide of Lenora's feeling altered. No longer feeling admired or exalted, she kicked angrily at the floor of the studio as she rehearsed.

Mama warned, "At this rate, dear, you will wear yourself out."

"Thanks," she muttered, and danced harder.

Mama said, "If only you did not have to go at such a furious pace!"

If, oh so many things, and suddenly anyone who did not believe in her was the enemy. Lenora halted, very tired in this moment of despair. She stared at the floor underfoot, thinking: she had stumbled over it, scraped it, and slipped on it, but never, it seemed at this dire moment, had she elevated it. A thousand different steps, dust and aching muscles and endless sweat, and had she gained any ground? Yet the laudatory words continued to echo in her ears, but she told herself this was an illusion, she was in love with artists still out of reach.

Mama said, "Perhaps they are involved in their own problems."

Soon after Lenora learned that Pat Campbell had lost her husband in the Boer War and in an effort to forget this sorrow had plunged into a new play and was seeing no one, not even close friends. John assured Lenora that Ellen Terry had fidelity, but suddenly she was unavailable too, lost in her own troubles. John added that Terry was quite disturbed at the prospect of ending her long partnership with Irving, which had been the foundation of her professional existence. John said, "Irving is ill, and Terry does not wish to desert him. She never deserts anyone, and she is incapable of resentment," mildly rebuking Lenora, who was full of resentment just now. "So Terry has gone into seclusion while seeking to come to a decision."

Benson was touring the provinces, Neville was out of town, and Lenora wondered aloud as some of her anger abated, "Was their praise a mockery?"

"Of course not," said John, "but that is how actors talk."

"I thought they really liked my dancing."

"Indeed, everyone adored it. Ellen thought it a miracle. But what I would consider an exaggeration, is a normal gesture for actors. I think it illogical to raise my voice, and to them that is perfectly normal."

Yet it was John who saved the aftermath from becoming a total failure. Lenora decided to go to Paris, hearing that concerts cost much less there and that audiences were far more appreciative, and John, who was visiting Paris soon, promised to introduce her to the city which he knew thoroughly.

When Lenora mentioned Paris to Mama, she was disappointed, for Mama was not sympathetic as she expected. Lenora thought Mama was becoming too easily frightened since the force of Ellen Terry's enthusiasm had worn off.

Mama had received a sad letter from Aunt Jessie: Grandpop, after lingering for a long, torturing time, had died. The severity of the letter was a laceration, and many of the harsh phrases remained painfully in Mama's mind, such as the last portion of the letter.

. . . your lack of success is quite typical of such expeditions as yours. In your preoccupation with Lenora and her phantoms, you have lost touch with the family. Yet, to judge from what you have written us, you still need support, and your character is obviously not suited for such a foreign climate.

It has been evident from the start that Lenora has a restless, injudicious foot, but it was your early indulgences which encouraged her discontent with her surroundings. And has Lenora shown any sign of becoming another Elssler? No, alas, and I submit to you, that your headstrong daughter has had ample time to prove herself. She may be a born wayfarer, but my dear Lena, you are not. I am writing this to clear the air, for if you return to your senses, to America, you may yet give our mother some of the happiness which you deprived our father of through your aimless wanderings.

Otherwise, although I am not given to predictions, it is apparent that you will all come to a distressing end, no matter how I try to protect you.

Mama thought bitterly: I will never see any of them again. She was caught with an overwhelming desire to see her mother, for the years were running out on her mother, who was seventy-one. Lenora was rehearsing feverishly again in the studio, and Mama asked, abruptly this time, "Don't you ever get tired?"

"Why should I get tired?"

"You have been working day after day." A tender grief seized Mama, and—— No, it was not a sacrifice, she assured herself, but she could not tell Lenora about Grandpop, it was not fair.

Lenora went on rehearsing as if Prometheus had handed her the sacred fire from heaven.

Mama said unexpectedly, "I think we ought to return to America."

"Are you serious?" Shocked, Lenora stopped practicing.

"You have had some success in England, and so you will be better received at home now. Try one more year in America and then——"

"A year? Why, that is an absolute eternity. It isn't even worth considering. Remember the dreadful way they reviewed me."

"I don't want to be selfish, but a child's place is with her family," Mama said quietly, although her heart was full of grief.

"I am not a child!"

"Have you no regard for your family?"

Lenora said resentfully, "Aunt Jessie has been writing you again."

The deception came hard but Mama managed to say, "No." I must be fair, reflected Mama, she is still young, but the young can be too impulsive, too self-centered. How odd, that the very traits which are virtues when she dances—her daring, her lawlessness, her originality—are now so annoying. But Mama made a great effort to hide her increasing pain and said gently, "Aunt Jessie can be difficult, but don't you want see your family again?"

"Naturally. But America is impoverished artistically. You know this." Lenora returned to her rehearsing with a flourish.

Deeply as Mama loved her parents, to be in San Francisco while Lenora was in Paris was impossible, but if they journeyed to Paris now, they would become a little shabbier, a little more disillusioned, and as Aunt Jessie said—and for once she agreed with her—what about their characters?

Lenora said, "If you want to go back to San Francisco with Amy, I could manage quite well by myself."

"Now look, dear, let us not be so challenging."

"One more week of walking down Piccadilly or listening to the speeches in Hyde Park—oh, I know every tree in the park —and all I will be good for is a music hall." The last thought filled Lenora with horror and she strode off.

Mama returned to the last letter from Aunt Jessie. It revived other memories of Grandpop, his faith in Lenora—he would have been the first to insist that Lenora have her way. So Mama sought to practice a decent worldliness. Mama told Amy about Grandpop, believing that her older daughter was better able to cope with the sad news, and asked Amy if she would return to San Francisco to comfort Grandma? In such a situation Mama believed a woman was necessary, and moreover, Archer was struggling to create an acting career in New York, and she hadn't the heart to ask him. Amy accepted the news and the assignment with dogged fortitude and agreed to keep the news of the death away from Lenora, although she thought that silly.

The arrangements for Amy's departure were completed quickly, the excuse being that she was returning to America to recreate her school. Amy's strong-willed manner, often as overwhelming as Lenora's, was convincing. Her decisiveness had a cool, composed quality. She made it plain that, although she cared for Lenora, she did not think Lenora clever about some things. She said that Lenora was often vague in her theories, but she expressed this only within the family. Amy still possessed the same pride in being a Malcolm, the same obstinate faith in self that baffled others. She was sure she could manage Lenora, if ever allowed a fair try.

They were saying good-by to Amy at the dock, when the pain of parting engulfed Mama. Torn by anguish, she was bewildered, her mind riveted to Amy, her heart to Lenora, and she detested such distinctions. Mama burst into tears, sobbing as if her heart would break. It was so rarely that she cried, Lenora and Amy were shocked.

Lenora threw her arms around Mama's thin body. They

clung together until Mama grew calmer. Lenora asked, "How have I hurt you?"

"Never mind." But Mama began to sob again.

Amy said, "You see, this is what always happens. We always end up hurting each other more than anyone else."

"What did I do?" asked Lenora, able to be truculent with Amy.

"What haven't you done?"

"Please," said Mama, "I am not angry at either of you."

"Is it because I want to go to Paris?"

"No," said Mama.

Amy said, "You never think of pleasing Mama, only yourself."

"I don't please you, Mama?" repeated Lenora, surprised at this accusation.

Mama lowered her eyes in embarrassment, and Amy said, "Lenora, I am not leaving to teach dancing." She went over Mama's efforts to hush her. "I am going to San Francisco to see Grandma, who is all alone now."

"She is not alone!" cried Lenora. "There is Aunt Jessie, Grandpop?" Lenora halted, feeling betrayed by the expression on their faces, feeling all the wonderful moments the family had shared, and now Mama's silence was profane.

Then Mama whispered, sobbing again, "I didn't want to spoil anything."

Lenora knew the answer now but even so she had to ask. "Grandpop? What's the matter with Grandpop? Is he dead?"

Mama nodded, and life seemed to ebb from her face.

"Someone had to know, and I am the older," Amy said. "You were being spared too, for the sake of your talent."

"I will not go to Paris," declared Lenora, sensing a deep recoil, almost contempt in Amy. I am being placed in a false position, she thought, I would give way to Mama if Mama were right. And a fear of hurting Mama swept through Lenora. "I don't want to go anywhere without you, Mama. Poor Grandpop, I can't believe that we will never see him again."

Amy said, "You do not have to say this."

Lenora said, "But Mama told you, not me. Why didn't she tell me?"

"Perhaps I'm braver. You always seem so sure of yourself, but people who are really brave do not have to push so."

Lenora stood a minute without replying and then, a humbling sense of apology, of having wronged, of guilt grew in Lenora and she burst into a torrent of words, rushing on breathlessly, reshaping some of the most crucial moments of her existence: "Oh, yes, I have been an enormous success? I

stood on the stage in Chicago, New York, London, and I
looked confident enough to embrace the universe, to capture
the audience no matter how its attention shifted, but it was
Mama's face that was in front of me, wherever she sat. Yes, I
am very aggressive, you tell me, Amy, and so stubborn, but
when no one knocks on our door I say to myself—no one will
come, no one really cares for my dancing. Certainly it is
easier to look triumphant, to act as if everything will happen
as I wish. If I look as frightened as I feel, nobody will watch
me. Of course I have cultivated the witty, the artists, but who
else has shown any interest in my art? Except, except Mama,
Mama . . . !" Lenora halted, crying tears of self-crucifixion.

"Darling, don't say any more," whispered Mama. "Whatever you have to do, you have to do. You are right for
yourself, and that is important, more important than pleasing
others, especially if you want to rise above the ordinary."

Lenora embraced Mama with all her passion.

Mama suddenly knew her duty. "Yes, darling, you are right
about yourself. You must go to Paris, and I must go with
you."

"I might have been wrong," said Amy. "Good-by."

Mama kissed her, then Lenora. Mama said, "Come back
soon, dear."

"Soon," repeated Lenora, with all her affection now.

"And tell Grandma, dear," Mama said proudly, "that Lenora has danced for Ellen Terry and Pat Campbell, and is
sure to be a success."

"I will," said Amy, smiling through her tears.

Arm in arm, crying, and then drying their wet cheeks again
and again, Mama and Lenora stood watching Amy long after
she had vanished in the fading dusk, seeing Grandpop also in
the shadow of the ocean liner.

Mama said, "I am sure Amy understands now."

"Yes, and after all," said Lenora, "the earth is round, and
we will all come together again some day. Archer, too."

Mama felt her still damp cheeks. "Dear me, we have been
serious, haven't we?" She tried to make her voice cheerful and
reassuring, as Grandpop would have desired, as he would
have said, "Sensible."

18

Here is Paris. Here now are auspicious portents of the future, and many signs of a genius and a passion seldom found elsewhere. Paris is a city which inspires Lenora to explore her own insight and enthusiasm. It is a spirit where for years the arts have converged and flourished. The light is pure and clear much of the time and splendid for painting, the language lends itself to literature, and many seem willing to encourage dancing, although few comprehend it. This is 1900, the year of the Exposition Universelle. This is also a year in which Sarah Bernhardt, at the height of her fame, is starring in *L'Aiglon*. It is also the year in which Pablo Picasso, aged nineteen and unknown, visits Paris for the first time. It is the moment when many are reading D'Annunzio's *La Gioconda*, and Rodin is sixty and is having his first one-man show.

Here Lenora is positive she will conceive new dances, and a new importance. She is determined that nothing will disillusion her, nothing suppress her. She is sworn to success.

Hurrying into such an inspiring world, Lenora and Mama were filled with a fresh burst of courage. The day of arrival was clear, the Paris sky was a bright blue, and they felt as if they had been transformed overnight. Even the hectic and disorderly railroad station seemed gay and exciting.

Lenora rented a flat on a narrow, crooked street, and the rent was far less than London. It seemed an absurdly low price to Lenora, but the concierge assumed they were artists —no other Americans would live sans bed, bowls, and curtains. Lenora did not mind that they had to sleep on the floor. They were within walking distance of the noble Pantheon, the learned Sorbonne, the lovely Luxembourg Gardens. On a clear day, standing on the roof of their room, on their tiptoes, they could see the gleaming magnificence of Notre Dame, the imposing masonry of the Louvre. As the rent was less than Mama had expected, Mama relaxed and was even willing to sleep on the floor, especially since it was temporary and Lenora was closer to her than she had been for a long time.

John was due in Paris within a week, and while Lenora waited for him, she came to a vital decision. She decided not to give any recitals in Paris until she was properly prepared. By properly prepared, she meant more education and more and better personal inspiration—determined now to find a love and a patron who would inspire her fully. Until then, she would survive by teaching, although she felt that was standing still and better suited to Amy. She was certain now that her art needed the stimulation of a genius, that then, but only then, love and inspiration would go hand in hand.

So while Lenora taught an occasional morning and several afternoons a week, just enough to support themselves, she spent the rest of her time in search of love and inspiration. She was even willing to give John another chance to become this genius, and while she waited for him—his visit to Paris had been delayed a few days—she searched the city itself for inspiration.

Paris as a way of life was a kind of genius in itself, she felt, and she was stimulated constantly. It was delightful to look at the donkeys harnessed to the two-wheeled carts piled high with vegetables and red gooseberries. She wondered how on earth the girls in the felt slippers and in the leather-covered sabots could walk, but they did, often with grace. She felt an affinity with the bearded arguers at the sidewalk cafés, eloquent on a bottle of *vin ordinaire,* and after she sampled that she talked dancing by the hours with a chestnut tree in the Luxembourg Gardens.

But she was happiest when she visited the Louvre with Mama. Lenora could not speak French yet, but in the Louvre art seemed to speak with one voice, the voice that knew all languages and the still unborn ones.

Lenora and Mama visited the Louvre day after day. Lenora behaved as if it were a temple. Here were the subtle Etruscan antiques, the perfect Tanagra figures. Much of the time the Malcolms were the only ones in this section of the Louvre, and then Lenora, advancing from her experiences in the British Museum, danced with a new sense of beauty. This elated Mama, for it was as if Lenora and the young women of the Tanagra figures recognized each other as of the same blood. Mama's irritation and fatigue vanished, everything seemed significant, and she felt that would have made Grandpop content.

Lenora, even as she rejoiced in the inspiration of the Tanagra figures, was restless again, feeling there was still so much to learn, that she needed the sagacity of the archaeologist as well as the instinct of the artist. "Apollo is especially important," she cried. "Sometimes the gods themselves dance, and he is of the first rank." Impulsive again, Lenora had her shoes off, loving the feel of the stone under her feet.

Mama was swept with a deep feeling of hope. Mama wanted to shout bravo.

Lenora had no thought of prettiness in mind, and no desire for pastels, but suddenly white was the exact tone she desired. White to her was the soul before man was blemished by experience; white was the beginning—the beginning was the real womb, the first universal womb.

The Roman sculpture bored Lenora. The statue of Augustus, supposed to depict majesty, was too literal and cold for her. But her conversation, which, staring at the Roman art, had become loud and critical, suddenly hushed. How long she stared at the beauty of the Greek statues she had no way of telling, but she knew she would love these originals as long as she lived. She felt beauty in every inch of the Venus of Milo, but it was the monumental Victory of Samothrace she felt the most.

This armless but powerful figure was an astonishing expression of movement, reflected Lenora. It was irresistible, the ideal. It was as basic to nature as the wave was to the sea. This was not decoration, not ritual, but was mind and spirit in equilibrium. It had an almost perfect simplicity, a simplicity that was organic to nature.

She longed to applaud, but it would have been sacrilegious. But she thrust her body forward as one with the Victory of Samothrace and sought to imagine what the sculptor must have felt, celebrating this naval victory. She felt the same harmony. This was a new beginning, where the soul and body were equal.

John arrived in Paris and became her escort. He said he could stay only several weeks, but when he saw her every day, she assumed he would display the passion and genius he knew so much about. This was Paris, she thought, and they could be free. She waited eagerly for John to make the first gesture, and as usual he was courtly, intellectual, but no more.

Seeking to provoke him into at least one amorous gesture, she said, "I wish I could tell the demimondaines from the smart women parading on the Champs Elysées, what fascinating tales they must know!" And he did not reply. "John," she said. "Do you really think the demimondaines hold the spark until it burns off their fingers? Do they really have no rights by law? It seems to me they should have the greatest interest in morality. Don't you think so?"

"That depends," he said, and changed the subject.

She was exasperated. She wanted to shake him. Yet the

next instant she thought he was the most interesting man in the world, for he was discussing art in such a moving, devout way it gave her an exquisite sense of intimacy.

She told Mama, who grew alarmed by the frequency of his visits, "I like him very much, but I am not exactly engaged to him."

If Lenora had not been her daughter, Mama would have found this charming. Lenora's disinterest in marriage would have been less vital to Mama, who had no wish to play the watchdog, but Lenora was twenty-two although she admitted only to twenty, and Mama felt it was time Lenora became serious about settling down. Mama still believed in female freedom, in theory, but emotionally, when it came to her own daughter, it was impossible to remain philosophical. One day Lenora desired to be a *femme fatale,* the next she was innocent and virginal, then suddenly she was in a turmoil or incalculable. How passionate was she, wondered Mama. Was Lenora's body the servant or the master? There was an impatience and restlessness in Lenora now which was more than a need for freedom, for discovery.

Settling down was the last thing Lenora desired at this moment. As she sat in a café in the Latin Quarter with John, she yearned to join the boisterous group at the adjoining table, singing. Ah, it is good to be alive, to be young, to love, but John looked uncomfortable in this free and easy atmosphere.

He was more relaxed when they went to the Exposition Universelle to view the art exhibits. Lenora was bored until she saw the sculpture of Rodin. Attracted by the robust yet amorous strength of his sculpture, she lost her heart to him at once. Several times she slipped into the Rodin exhibit without John, for it was evident he felt much of it was immodest.

Lenora discovered that others agreed with John. One afternoon she was staring at Rodin's figures, wishing she could convey his intensity and sense of motion in a dance, when suddenly the derision of his critics was too much for her. They were sneering, "Look at his bones, like broken rock, and people do not squat that way!" and furious, she shouted at them, "Idiots, he is a genius!"

Someone whispered, "Her accent is unmistakably American."

Lenora prepared to make a speech, but the crowd dissolved before her fury. They must be blind, she thought. This stone was pressed out from experience, was the essence of experience, in many ways their experience. Suddenly an intensity of feeling possessed Lenora which was different from anything she had ever known. Beyond reason, she was filled with an irresistible impulse to experience his heat. Then she felt confused, and unresolved.

John had to return to London, and so he decided to introduce her to a friend of his, Henri Morisse. Before doing so John explained, "Morisse is a man of great talent. He is recognized as one of the leaders of the new school, but he confines himself almost entirely to pictures of jockeys and ballet girls, which does not appeal to what he calls my antiquated taste."

"I detest ballet."

"Suppose he flatters you? Suppose he wants to paint you?"

"Then why are you introducing him to me?"

"Morisse knows many artists, most of them well known, who can help you."

"Does he know Rodin?"

"Probably." John paused, for in this instant her face was as radiant as he had ever seen it. Yet she was only twenty-two, while Rodin was sixty, even older than himself, with the instincts of a satyr—if a somewhat senile one—so it was said.

John changed the subject, and the day he was departing he introduced her to Morisse with an obvious warning to his friend to be the gentleman. Lenora was annoyed by John's prudence, but it was difficult to say good-by to him. She wondered, does he really care for me, will he really miss me, and she moved closer to him and asked, "Have you liked being with me?"

His expression softened, and he said gently, "I have loved it."

"Will I see you again?"

"I don't know. It depends."

"I don't think I'll ever see you again."

He did not answer.

"It's terrible to say good-by."

He said, "You will succeed. In Paris exoticism is virtually a religion, and you will appeal to many for that reason."

"Why don't you stay, John?"

"And return to London next year and paint English pictures with a bad French accent? No, Lenora, that would be pointless."

"You are not cross with me, with my staying?"

"Of course not. You are young, but I am——"

"You are young in heart," she said vehemently.

"If I were twenty years younger I would test that. But now,

you would become bored with being magnanimous." John held her tightly, as if he would never let her go, and then he kissed her gently and was gone, so quickly she did not even have time to say good-by.

19

Lenora was not lonely for long. Henri Morisse became her constant companion, attentive, gallant, and apparently quite pleased with her. But he, too, was not the genius she was seeking. He was tall, youthful, with a dark, sharp-featured attractiveness, but she could predict his behavior without effort. He was completely constant: a man who was deeply sensitive about his charm, but cynical about love and art. He thought her quite pretty, but not the *volupté* which fitted his ideal of sensuousness.

Henri was also amused by the passion with which she pursued what she called "self-expression." He was struck with the intensity with which Lenora consulted the wine lists and thought that droll. He favored absinthe, which he considered a man's drink, but she had to sample them all, even though she preferred champagne. She also preferred his attentions to none at all, although she had no desire to yield to him. She had no difficulty keeping him at a distance, and he introduced her to other artists who became her admirers. The most intriguing were Pierre Alençon, also youthful, attractive, and a promising painter; the short, bald dramatist, Marcel Roncourt; and the dashing Edmond de Grenelle, who composed songs. Mama thought there was safety in numbers, while Lenora was sure they were all in love with her. Even as she saw all of them often, she kept thinking of Rodin, how his sculpture manifested such a strong personality, such a deep comprehension of nature and energy.

She continued to slip into the Rodin exhibit to view his art. She went alone, not wanting to be caught in the transports of passion which his work evoked. She associated, with the quick exaggerated imagination of the virgin, the most ravishing and insatiable abandonment to this artist. Never could she content herself with pebbles or grains of sand, she assured herself, when such a massive rock of a genius was available. Often she had to lean against the walls of the exhibit to contain her emotion. She felt they shared the awareness of the beauty of the naked body which had been the genius of the Greeks, that here truly was an artist who understood the statuary of antiquity.

Yet Morisse, who knew Rodin, was discouraging. Morisse told her that work was Rodin's sole absorption, and recognition for his work. And her other escorts thought her "too young" for Rodin.

Still thinking of her desire for Rodin, she declared, "It is foolish to be reasonable when it is fashionable to be insane."

It was a popular saying of the moment, and Morisse embraced her, calling her "our great philosopher," while de Grenelle cried "Bravo!" and Roncourt insisted her emphasis was wrong, that "It is the fashionable who are insane!"

"You want to be a genius," said Pierre Alençon. "You will have to have a very sad history."

Lenora danced Chopin then, seeking to be simple and spare in her art, to be perfect in stature and yet delicate in content.

Roncourt murmured, "I cannot imagine anything more perfect."

"This is Parisian?" asked a puzzled, not altogether pleased Morisse.

"No, it is not Parisian," she shouted in her newly learned French.

Pierre Alençon asked, "This is easy to do?"

"No," she said, "it is sad, like . . ."

"Like pain," filled in Roncourt, smiling wanly. "And big enough to shatter the Théâtre Municipale and the Moulin Rouge."

"You are bizarre," said de Grenelle, almost as bewildered as Morisse. "Lenora, you never kick? Turn somersaults? Stand on your toes?"

"Never! This is not a divertissement. This comes from within."

"Some will not like you," said de Grenelle.

Morisse said, "I must introduce you to Eugène Carrière. He is a great painter, and he will understand you."

"And he is a close friend of Rodin," remarked Pierre Alençon, slyly, she felt, but how could she tell this gallant, sweet, but really such an immature boy what a fire consumed her for the passion of a mature man?

Since Carrière was widely admired by his colleagues, although he was still living, Lenora assumed he would reside in an obsequious neighborhood.

Instead, Morisse led her to a poor, very hilly section of Montmartre. They walked up many flights of steep, winding, narrow stairs. The studio was in one of the highest parts of

Paris, and even from a stairway window Lenora could see much of the city. A blue haze covered Paris, and the sunlight danced from roof to roof.

Carrière's flat was modest, but his rooms were large. Lenora's impression was of a region where time had no meaning. She felt in a world where no one ever raised his voice. She saw canvases leaning against the walls, new canvases done during the past year, canvases touched up again and again. Morisse, not cynical for once, identified some of Carrière's most famous portraits: Verlaine, Daudet, Rodin, Goncourt, and many lovely paintings of children. "Carrière's children," said Morisse.

Lenora stared at a portrait of a child. "How beautiful," she whispered. The background was dark, almost indifferent, but the face gleamed with a singular tenderness.

Morisse was no longer the sophisticated, superior artist as he explained that Carrière's studies of mother and child were famous, that poverty had forced him to use his own family as models. "He considers that a blessing," said Morisse, "for he never paints anyone he does not esteem. He says it is absurd to paint what you do not like. I think, too, why other artists regard him so warmly is that Carrière is completely without the need for self-aggrandizement. His work is the other extreme from Rodin, yet he loves Rodin's art with a devotion most artists save only for their own work."

Suddenly a chunky-faced, middle-aged man, just past fifty, with brown hair, a brown mustache, and an enormous forehead stood before them, bowing and apologizing for keeping them waiting.

Morisse said, "Eugène, this is Lenora Malcolm."

Carrière smiled at her gently.

Lenora looked so innocent, she seemed like another of Carrière's children. She also remembered to look her very best.

"Charming!" exclaimed Carrière, and asked Morisse if she were a student for his art class.

Morisse said, "Lenora is a dancer who uses the sky and sea and air for inspiration."

"You must be an exceptional spirit," said Carrière, without any attempt to flatter.

Almost every time Lenora danced, she felt she grew a little. But now she felt like nothing; to move for the great Carrière meant to move in perfect harmony; she was afraid she could not live up to their praise; yet she had to finish what she had begun. She glanced at his many canvases of mother and child and sought to capture their reflection. She bowed her head and her emotion was childlike. She moved forward, hesitantly at first. Then she felt true to the tone of his paintings. Before Carrière, she imagined herself before a Greek temple; she danced as simply as she knew how, yet with all the depths of understanding she had reached these past few months.

When Lenora finished, Carrière smiled with a wonderful sweetness and said in a very low voice, which Lenora had to strain to hear, that such beauty and inspiration would always be welcome.

From then on Carrière's studio became her chapel of beauty. Many days she opened his door as if it were the golden door of morning and intently watched him paint. The colors gradually fading out until only the morning blue was left, and then that became the background and nothing was distinct except the faces, only the faces gave light. There was an exquisite tenderness in the way he painted. Hushed prayers seemed to rise from his faces, particularly those of the children.

Lenora danced for him often now. But gradually, as de Grenelle promised to arrange a recital for his prominent friends and nothing happened, as Rodin seemed further away than ever, she grew melancholy.

One morning Carrière saw her gloom and said, "I have written introductions for Rodin. I will write one for you. That will bring the artists."

"No one will come," she said with a pessimism she seldom allowed herself.

"Everyone will come. I will say that you are incomparable. I will say that for the sake of the Third Republic, we must support you."

"Thank you." She asked abruptly, "Does Rodin live far away?"

"In a different world."

"I mean . . . does he have a studio in Paris?"

"Yes. He is there almost all of the time." Carrière gave her the address.

Many weary minutes passed before Lenora decided how to use this address. When she did, however, it was swiftly. She was grateful that Carrière did not offer her any advice.

Early the next morning Lenora prepared for her visit to Rodin. It was a clear, lovely, auspicious day. It was a mad, fabulous, marvelous day. She felt truly beautiful; she was full of a blissful determination. It was a day she was sure would put all other days to shame. There was something in her face that Mama had never seen before, but Lenora did not tell

Mama that today, come what may, she was resolved to know love. She dressed her thick brown hair in Grecian style. She put on a simple white dress over her scanty tunic.

Today was going to be a kind of wedding day, she thought. Mama asked, "Where are you going, dear?"

"Out." She regained some presence of mind. "For a walk."

"Are you getting so dressed up for the Carrières?"

"I'm going to see a friend," and hurried out before she gave herself away.

She arrived at Rodin's studio looking her most compelling. There would be no ring, no wedding ceremony, Lenora decided—Rodin was a freethinker, as she was—and she possessed nothing in the world but grace and beauty and talent and a willingness to give herself to the great moments. She was certain this was an arrangement which would work admirably.

Lenora entered Rodin's spacious studio and was surprised by what she saw. She expected a tall, massive man who would be extraordinarily picturesque, about forty, but here was a man of sixty, with a gray beard like a grandfather's, and his skin was wrinkled—like folds of stone. And he was stocky, almost squat, and he moved without any grace.

"You are a friend of Carrière's?" he said, repeating her awkward French.

Lenora nodded and sought to slow up her emotions. She noticed he had a massive head despite his disappointing stature, which seemed a true indication of genius.

Rodin was accustomed to pretty girls visiting him and fawning on him. His mouth took on the look of a sensualist.

Lenora took a deep breath to relax, but her body became even more tense as she stepped closer to him and announced, "I am Lenora Malcolm, the dancer." Now she felt his equal.

This made no impression on his mind. He looked at her blankly, as if this time he did not understand her clumsy French. He put on his glasses to examine her more closely, and Lenora became aware that he was nearsighted. His beard was quite heavy, down to his chest. For a moment he was like an indifferent peasant to her; he had been toiling bare-armed, while the light lasted. There were sketches everywhere and more nudes than Lenora had ever seen. Then she realized that nudes were an ordinary sight to Rodin and that she must dance for him. She approached him and assumed a dancing pose. Rodin was captivated; he was almost always immediately captivated by youth. He began to sketch her. He seemed huge now in his linen smock.

He was drawing her, she thought, with his personal vision.

Feeling just as original, she said, "My dancing is my own, I am my own choreographer."

This time, understanding her French, he stared at her as if that were a masterpiece of understatement. He was enticed by her grace, which the absence of the usual coquetry made even more inviting. He was fascinated by her naturalness. The truth in her, whatever she was, now shone through.

Lenora stepped out of her dress. Rodin blinked, the scanty dress costume was not what he expected. She was in motion, yet not. She hung between her virginal past and the uncertain future. He moved close to her, as if to put his hands on her, and she backed away, dancing with the tide of her blood. He paused, then resumed sketching her. She was still over-wrought, and she moved with a wide-legged, exaggerated stride, thinking he was the challenge to her love, but would he bring her love? Although she was dancing for the God of her choice, underneath lay a world not easy to explore. To dance this way, was not only to dance. But she saw Rodin smile, and that was belittling, and suddenly Lenora was furious and dancing as if the world would come to an end if she did not dance. Even as she improvised, she imagined herself in the grip of an uncontrollable sexual excitement.

Finished, she said, "I take my art from nature too."

Rodin's eyes gleamed as he approached her.

She thought, he was an *exalté,* as Carrière had said. In a few moments her tunic would be off, and she would be following him without will, without conscious movement, the antic-ipation of passion in itself a pleasure, but all at once, even as her flesh quivered at the thought of his genius, the pressure of his intention was too strong against her soft flesh.

"I am not stone," she whispered. "I am a virgin."

It must not be too quick, she prayed. Didn't he hear what she said?

"I am a virgin," she repeated. Be gentle, she prayed.

If Rodin heard her, he gave no sign. She felt the pressure of his intention increase. She felt demoralized and filled with a strange nausea which she could not explain. Her ecstatic dream was being eclipsed by the harshness of realism. Who is he? A genius, yes, but what am I to him? Lenora felt frantic, waiting for Rodin to say he loved her, worshiped her, that she was his destiny. He loved the virgin white marble of her body, and even if he had not heard her admission, he should know instinctively she was a virgin. She held her hand against his cheek, and he pressed her back without a word, without any tenderness she could translate into love, and she pulled away from him. She felt numb and weak. Didn't he know there had to be a heroism about love, that he had to value her offering or it was nothing—and it could not be nothing.

Rodin did not pursue her. It was not in his conception of time and work. At his age he was uncomplicated about women, love was a natural physical urge to be experienced and satisfied, on a take and to-be-taken basis. He was not angry, but he was annoyed since she had offered herself voluntarily. He was not accustomed to having an attack become a retreat.

Lenora took another deep breath, as if to explain herself and at the same time take into consideration his views. But she could not put her feelings into words. Rodin was not the love of which she had dreamed—certainly his intensity was no myth, and he had hands like Prometheus—but this encounter had been so clumsy and painful. She mumbled, "I'm sorry." Her eyes filled with tears.

He said, "Do not feel sorry. You are young and beautiful. Can you say I am young and beautiful? And I lost my patience a long time ago."

"I am sorry for myself, not for you."

"A man with patience will come along, my beautiful one."

But she stared at him as if love were unreal and wondered —what now, what now? It had seemed so easy, and it had become so difficult.

Rodin's bewilderment lasted a moment more, and then his expression became mellow and earthy. It seemed to say—how droll! And in a quick motion he was working on the clay that had occupied him when she had entered, now with a new intensity, to make up for the loss of time.

Lenora stood by her window that evening, naked and alone, and thought: how stupid I was, how adolescent, and I such a freethinker. She felt tragic and ashamed that she had fled before the stimulation of this genius. Now the unsatisfied passion in Lenora pleaded with the cold stars for satisfaction and relief. But it was too late, much too late.

"Are you ill?" Mama appeared at the door separating their rooms. For a moment they stood opposite each other, Lenora by the dark window, Mama by the open door. Even in the darkness Mama's concern was evident.

"I'm all right." Lenora almost added, I can get along without you now, I am a woman, but she did not.

"If it is a man, he is not worth wasting any regret on. Believe me."

Lenora had not said anything to Mama about Rodin, and she had no intention of starting now. She said, "I have many

concerts to arrange. Carrière is going to write a special introduction, de Grenelle is going to invite his friends, and Roncourt is going to speak on the art of the Greeks."

"Fine, fine, but you must be very tired."

Lenora was not listening. She was weary of being Mama's
child.

Mama vanished from the doorway as Lenora went to bed.
But Lenora could not fall asleep, tossing between her sheets in
combat with life until dawn. The urgent pressure of Rodin
was upon her body all night. She felt she had faced one of the
tests of her life, of the heroic life, and had failed.

20

The search for a genius whose love would inspire her having
been fruitless, Lenora resumed her recitals, this time in her
studio for the artists and the potential patrons. Her life became one of constant rehearsals, of dance steps and emotions
learned, of feeling abused when she was unable to express the
emotion within her.

It was also a time when she stopped teaching, when, determined not to display cowardice—still unhappy about her failure with Rodin—she moved out of the small Left Bank studio
and rented a large studio on the Right Bank. Large enough to
hold a whole town, Mama teased, to hide her apprehensions
that they might be expanding too fast. But Lenora's recitals
filled this enormous studio, for she came to be regarded as
novel, bizarre, intriguing, her boldness a sensation, especially
the increasing scantiness of her costume. Carrière introduced
her to other fine artists; the well-connected de Grenelle invited
potential patrons to her recitals; Roncourt, Alençon, and Morisse continued to surround her with their casual courtship.

Lenora told herself that while love might still be delayed or
elusive, recognition was arriving with almost acceptable speed.
But there was still the constant race between income and
expenses. No enlightened manager offered her any recitals or
concert tours. The studio audiences, with the exception of her
coterie of artists, was a repetition of the London drawing
rooms. The only new opportunities she got were to appear in
the salons of the Faubourg St.-Germain, considered an honor,
but which added to her sense of discouragement. She felt she
was standing still. Often, as she searched for new ways to

express the growing range of emotion within her, and her feeling was so much greater than her resources, she was sad.

When it came to love she should be recklessly emotional, she reflected, but dancing was such hard work, seeking to make emotion come alive with a gesture. When it came to dancing there were days when the world seemed illiterate. There were no books to go to for what she desired, no one was dancing the way she had to dance, and to imitate was impossible. It meant pursuing her craft beyond sleep and comfort, making her body a dancer's body, making her mind a philosopher's mind, making her heart a God's heart. It meant many difficulties.

No one, however, lived more purposefully. If Lenora allowed herself no luxuries, she spared herself no necessities, and dancing was the first necessity. Recitals, patrons, artists, they seemed necessities: a lover, she was not certain, though more than ever she regretted her flight from Rodin. Her dancing, which had been experimental, was gaining definite form. She settled on a natural white costume which would stress the beauty of her body rather than hide it. She also decided that her background should be severe, without any scenery, except for flowers and drapes. Wherever possible, she suggested simplicity. "It is truer to nature," she told Mama, who was not in total agreement with such radical innovations in staging.

Their income remained uncertain; the recitals sometimes paid for themselves but seldom for anything else. Archer wrote that he was getting more vital roles in the New York theater but that it was impossible to help them. Lenora did not expect aid, but Mama did, when holding off the concierge for back rent became difficult. Amy, reading flattering notices which were appearing in America about Lenora, was certain Lenora needed her to complete this success and planned to return to Europe. Grandma was living with Aunt Jessie now and thought Amy's place was with her mother and sister, especially since they were doing so well.

But none of Lenora's wealthy patrons wanted to go as far or as fast as she did. Time pushed by so swiftly that suddenly she found herself in Paris several years and still dancing only in her studio and in drawing rooms, despite much praise and controversy. The concert stage which was her ambition was still denied her.

Her deepest regret remained her failure with Rodin. She was certain now, looking back, that if she had allowed him to take her, a great dance work would have emerged. In retrospect Rodin was not too old or too clumsy, and she was disgusted by the way she had handled this situation. And as she became disgusted with herself for having failed him, she also grew disgusted with her present life and the limitations it imposed upon her art.

She spoke of arranging her own concert tour, and Mama warned, "We can't afford to rent a theater, costumes, and scenery."

"You can make the costumes, and we will dispense with the scenery."

"We still have to rent the theater and advertise."

"We are not destitute."

"A few hundred francs to our name?" Mama was upset. Lenora recalled every detail of her dancing, and none about money.

Where, when, Lenora wondered somberly, would society need art as bread?

Mama, stricken by Lenora's sadness, was swept with a wave of protectiveness and said, "Your dancing now is sculpture in motion."

"But what am I? Where am I going? What have I accomplished?"

"To dance, to discover, to create is in itself a great deliverance. Continue to follow nature, as the Greeks did, and you will be appreciated. It will just take a little longer."

"When I talk about the Greeks, they act as if I am absurd." Lenora stared out the window of their studio with a fragile melancholy. "I will go to Greece," Lenora said with sudden defiance.

Mama was shocked. Mama said, "That's impossible."

"Nothing is impossible. And I'll stifle if I stay here."

"You need a good manager, one with vision and imagination." Lenora was not listening, lost in her own thoughts. Mama, frightened by the prospect of suddenly and impulsively dashing off to Greece—and Lenora was just resentful enough about her career to do that—decided something fresh had to be done about Lenora's career. Lenora is too proud to seek a manager, thought Mama, but I cannot afford to be. Lenora is living on the adoration of her artists, but actually they are a small, unimportant coterie.

Mama sought out Loie Fuller. Loie Fuller was the most celebrated American dancer in Europe. The serpentine dancer, born in an Illinois tavern, had achieved popular success in Paris on the concert stage and at the Folies-Bergère, and Mama heard that Loie Fuller also managed other dancers and sometimes gave combined recitals. Mama obtained an interview with Loie Fuller, who was staying at a Paris hotel, and showed the dancer-manager Lenora's notices. The money-minded Loie Fuller was especially impressed by an article which had appeared in an American paper.

. . . Miss Malcolm has made an unique success in Paris. She dances without stays of any kind, and all Paris thinks she is fascinating. The very best people in the city have taken her up, and she has appeared in the most impenetrable drawing rooms of the Faubourg St.-Germain, into which many rich Americans have striven in vain to enter. Miss Malcolm has appeared in the drawing rooms of the Countess Greffuhle, the Countess de Trobriand, the Baroness de Muhlens, the Princess de Polignac, the Count D'Uzes, Paul Clemenceau's, and many other aristocratic houses.

Miss Malcolm's notices were encouraging, admitted Loie Fuller, and her dancing had a novelty that might prove profitable. The renowned serpentine dancer agreed to talk to Lenora about a possible tour under her management.

Performance time was approaching when Lenora arrived backstage to meet Loie Fuller. Lenora was amazed by Loie's nonchalance. The serpentine dancer's recital was less than an hour away, yet she looked bored.

Loie Fuller was pudgy, and only when she smiled, her white teeth shining and her blue eyes widening in her heavy face, was she pretty. She seemed tired and far older than the thirty-two she gave as her age. Her legs were thick; she perspired even when she did not move. She wore a long gray diaphanous robe which was cumbersome and made her look shapeless.

Yet when she danced, a few minutes later, clothed with layers of gauze, her movements were lovely and exciting. Lenora was enraptured. Forgotten was the aging, bored, uninspiring woman who had come on late, whose delay had stimulated the audience instead of irritating them as Lenora had expected.

Lenora admitted to Mama that Loie Fuller was an unusual dancer.

"A true dancer," said Mama, wanting Lenora to avail herself of Loie Fuller's sponsorship.

"A true dancer," repeated Lenora, desiring to make Mama happy. But this is not Lenora Malcolm, thought the younger dancer, much as she respected Loie Fuller now, and how can she find me intriguing when I am so different?

Lenora came into her audition for Loie with a curious hauteur. She wore a transparent robe and depended on self and simplicity and hardly any color or light. Loie gave a gasp as Lenora began. Loie was shocked by the scanty robe, then she grew absorbed as Lenora's arms rose as if to embrace the heavens. She applauded as spontaneously as Lenora had danced, and said, "I will sponsor your tour, when you are ready. Meet me in Berlin, next week."

Lenora assumed she would be ready the instant she met Loie in Berlin. She hurried there the next week as Loie had suggested, sure she was dispensing with the drawing rooms forever. It was without Mama; no Mamas were allowed; Loie was the Mama. It was the first time Lenora had gone anywhere without Mama, despite her feeling of womanhood, and she was confused. Mama had radiated encouragement for so long, it was like living without half her faith. But saying good-by, Mama had said, "No regrets, dear," to make Lenora brave, and had turned away before she showed the pain of parting.

Once Lenora was in Berlin, Loie puzzled her. Loie beckoned Lenora to come close with a warmth that seemed far more exotic than maternal. A group of lovely-looking girls, in their early twenties, sat at Loie's feet, as if in a harem. Loie introduced these girls, who were part of her dancing troupe, with a possessive pride.

Now was the time to slip away, thought Lenora, for Loie would not notice, she was so absorbed in one of the girls who was dressed like a man, but Loie was talking about the concerts Lenora would give in Vienna.

"Vienna? You said I would start in Berlin."

"Darling, you are very talented, but you need more study and practice."

Aghast, Lenora again wanted to flee, but Loie was drawing her close, as if to possess her completely, as if all of beauty dwelt in her group.

How odd it was, thought Lenora. Loie told the press that Lenora Malcolm was ill, instead of not ready as Loie believed, and everyone was accepting that. "Not quite ready for the concert stage, darling," Loie told Lenora. "But in Vienna are some of the most magnificent drawing rooms in the world."

"I have sponsors in Paris and all the drawing rooms I want."

"The sponsors I get will encourage you to explore all phases of your Grecian dancing." Loie made reservations for her troupe, including Lenora, in one of Vienna's finest hotels. She gave Lenora a smile of deepest tenderness, but when she went to embrace Lenora the latter backed away.

That evening Lenora wrote Mama to join her in Vienna.

When Loie, her troupe, and Lenora arrived in Vienna, Loie got busy organizing concerts for Lenora in Viennese drawing rooms. The most vital potential patron was the Princess Metternich, the ruler of artistic Vienna. Past sixty, the Princess Metternich was gray-haired, ugly, with one of the sharpest tongues in Europe, and an enormous reputation as a patron, having greatly aided Wagner, Liszt, and Loie Fuller.

Loie told the princess that this new protégé of hers could become one of the important dancers, and the princess asked, "How can I be of value?"

"If you become one of her sponsors."

"You are certain she will become an important artist?"

"Oh yes, I can always recognize talent."

The princess promised to attend the first Viennese recital of Miss Lenora Malcolm, and so a fashionable audience was assured. Such a large audience, that Loie had to rent a hall, although it was against Lenora's taste, for she thought it ugly.

Loie, after noting with satisfaction that the most fashionable people in Vienna were filling the hall, went backstage to see Lenora. Loie was shocked by Lenora's scanty costume, but Lenora thought the idea of dancing for a drawing-room audience quite tiresome, and if Loie could keep an audience waiting, so could she. If they would not be startled by the presence of her genius, they would be startled by other things, vital things.

When the curtain rose, Lenora eased forward until she seemed about to embrace the surprised audience. And as she danced all the meaning of Schubert seemed within reach. She danced with a simplicity that was magical.

Loie, despite her anger, found it magical too. She forgave the fancied slights, even the pain of having been embarrassed.

The applause was sparse. Lenora bowed coldly and retired. Loie hurried backstage to fetch Lenora, for Princess Metternich wished to speak to the young dancer, and got a new shock. Lenora was still in her scanty robe, resting. Lenora appreciated the princess' interest, but she had to rest. The princess was amused by this impudence and came into the dressing room in person.

The princess said, "Your performance was interesting."

Lenora accepted this casually, ignoring the imperial bearing.

Loie rushed on to say, "The princess was a close friend of Wagner and Liszt. She was responsible for the French production of *Tannhäuser*."

The princess said, "Richard Wagner was responsible. I just sponsored the performance."

Lenora adored Wagner. She grew animated and inquired, "Was he grateful?"

"He did not have to be. It was enough that I could help his genius."

"Yes," said Lenora, "That must be so!"

"But Liszt was appreciative of aid and profuse with his thanks."

"Loie has been lovely to me." But not always clever, thought Lenora.

The princess said, "I found quite a bit of novelty in your work. What do you call it?"

"Dancing."

"Oh!" The princess' fierce eyes narrowed. "When I was your age Fanny Elssler was our guest. My grandparents, Chancellor Prince Metternich and his wife, were very fond of her. They admired not only her unsurpassable art but her exquisite manners."

Lenora stood up and made a curtsy, as graceful as she knew how. The princess barely acknowledged this, however, and departed soon after, showing no further interest in Lenora. Loie went with her, to appease her.

Lenora had just finished dressing when Mama arrived backstage. Neither of them were demonstrative, but they were happy to be reunited, and then Mama had news. Mama had invited an important concert manager to see Lenora dance but had kept it a secret so Lenora would not get nervous. And now, having seen Lenora dance, the manager wanted to meet her.

An excited Lenora expected the manager to be tall and imposing. Instead, Victor Lothar was chunky, short, with black bushy hair and a forehead that was almost as square as it was broad. He did not declare that she was magnificent as she also expected, but said, "This hall you danced in is too large, and not theatrical enough."

"Even when I danced 'The Blue Danube'?"

"Especially when you danced 'The Blue Danube.' But we could remedy that. You should dance in an intimate theater, small and charming, where you could give the feeling of reaching out and touching your audience."

"No, no! I must dance where many can see me, in a magnificent theater like the Théâtre Sarah-Bernhardt in Paris."

"That is foolish," he stated emphatically.

"You know the Théâtre Sarah-Bernhardt?"

"Of course. It is an immense barn. It has seventeen hundred seats. You would be lost in it."

"It is the theater of Sarah Bernhardt."

"It is a good theater, for her. She is old."

"Old?" Lenora was shocked to hear such sacrilege about an idol.

"Almost sixty now, and she is better off where she can still create an illusion, as long as the audience is not too near her. But you are young, pretty, and should be close to your audience."

"You do not understand artists. Sarah Bernhardt is a genius." She motioned to the door, dismissing him, but he ignored that.

He said, "I manage artists throughout Europe, but mainly in Germany and Vienna. I am Viennese."

Still affronted by what she considered his lack of taste, she said, "You sound more like a butcher."

He smiled and answered, "That is what Brahms said."

"Did you know Brahms?" She was interested in spite of her effort to appear blasé.

"I studied the cello with him. He said I butchered it."

"Did you?"

"Yes. So instead of becoming a third-rate cellist, I became a first-rate manager." He enumerated a list of the artists he managed, and she had to admit it was impressive.

In a sudden change of mind she asked, "Could I make my debut in Berlin?"

"In Budapest . . . if we agree on terms." Victor Lothar went on to explain, for she looked dismayed at the thought of Budapest. "You see, Miss Malcolm, Budapest is far enough away that if you are a failure, the rest of Europe—Paris, London, Berlin, the important concert cities—will not hear about it. But Budapest is also large enough so that if you should be a success, the rest of Europe can be made to hear. And the Hungarians are very emotional, they may very well like your dancing."

Lenora knew she should be offended, but after all, he had known the great Brahms, and he did speak with authority. She asked, "Were you a friend of Brahms?"

"When I gave up the cello—yes."

"Do you think I should dance to Brahms?"

"No. If you go to Budapest, Liszt would be preferable, and some Chopin." Victor Lothar calmly examined her, particularly her hands and feet. He was far more casual than she wanted her discoverer to be, and his terms were not as grand as she had expected, but they were terms. She remembered Loie Fuller, but there was no contract and Loie's girls disturbed her and the serpentine dancer seemed more interested in society than in art, and Mama was nodding vehemently to accept.

Mama was tremendously excited, her cheeks as pink and bright as a young girl. Mama liked Victor Lothar, his calmness, his preference for calling things by their right names.

"Very well," said Lenora, "if I can choose my own numbers."

"Very well," said Victor Lothar, "if I can choose the theaters, write the publicity, and arrange the bookings."

Lenora waited until Loie was asleep and then slipped out of the hotel. She left a note for Loie: "Budapest has guaranteed me fifteen thousand francs to appear there. Cannot refuse. Thanks for everything. You have been very kind. Lenora."

Lenora sent a cable to Amy, who was now in New York teaching dancing, although she had to borrow the money for the cable from Lothar. She wrote Amy that she was being guaranteed twenty thousand francs to appear in Budapest and that Amy should join her there as soon as possible. She did not tell her sister how to raise the money to get to Budapest; she was positive that Amy, as a Malcolm, could manage that.

Not even a thousand francs had been guaranteed, but Lenora had to depart with a grand splash. Nothing had been guaranteed by Lothar, except a percentage of the profits—if there were any, but Lenora was certain this debut would be a triumph. They were on the train to Budapest before Loie Fuller knew that Lenora and Mama were gone.

BOOK FOUR

21

Now Lenora felt there was so much to experience. She fell in love with Budapest's dramatic location on the Danube, with its romantic legends, with its Arabian Night's atmosphere. Here atmosphere was all, atmosphere was a dedication to the senses, to whirling czardas and the intoxication of the unexpected. The spirited czardas were scarcely music, but sheer passion. They were the dances of her blood, its extravagances and its fancies. They made her want to dance with her whole self, to sway as if in an enormous wind. Her flesh lost its cool pure definitions: one moment she was drifting with a languorous tenderness, the next she was driven with an incredible vitality.

She poured these feelings into her dancing, and her recitals were acclaimed at once. Victor Lothar's taste was right. The week's engagement was lengthened to several because of the popular demand. The small theater was jammed nightly with smart audiences: journalists, army officers, theater folk, and the chic of the *demimonde*. Lenora was proud this was a recognized theater and not a music hall; this added to her growing respect for Victor. A long time ago she had vowed never to dance in anything as cheap as a music hall, and this theater was historic and tasteful.

Lenora felt she could not do without love now, and it gave her dancing a more striking quality. She was still delicate in appearance, but she had lost her pre-Raphaelite youthfulness. There was a mixture of the profane as well as the sacred in her dancing now. She stood in front of her audiences, stretch-

ing her white arms above her head, and she was embracing
them also. She was touching them with her passionate
longing, with all of her amazing sincerity, and the ecstatic
Hungarian audiences took her to their heart. When they
shouted for more! more! she danced until her bones ached.
She danced as if in the grip of a tremendous personal experience, and yet she was improvising. Step by step they followed her in the audience, beating their hands in time, with as
deep a need as hers.

Then even this was not sufficient for Lenora. She required
more outlets for the passion mounting within her. When Victor lengthened her engagement she began to cater to the
patriotic desires of the populace. At the start of the second
week, when the crowd stamped for more! more! her music
became the national music of Hungary. And when she appeared for her first encore, waving the national flag of a
Hungary that felt itself imprisoned by the vise of the Austrian
Hapsburg Empire, there was a deep silence. This was sacred
to her audience. And as she danced as an act of sacrifice and
seemed to die by inches, then to come to glorious life at the
end, on the darkened stage she was saying: in the midst of
death, life persists, in the midst of lies, truth persists.

Never, never again would she be content with less.

The patriotic Hungarians rose as one when she finished,
exalted by her feeling, and she came down front, as humble as
she had been tempestuous. The applause lasted for many minutes. Flowers were strewn at her feet.

How beautiful she looks, thought Mama, and so inspiring.
Lenora was without make-up, without ornaments, without
tricks, except perhaps the greatest trick of all, her amazing
sincerity.

Even Victor was impressed, although he was Viennese and
a veteran of the concert wars, and after this performance he
wanted her to meet a good friend of his, the Austrian journalist, Adam Steyr. Lenora was still in her dressing gown, thinking ruefully that there were no men in Budapest who fitted the
romantic tone of the city, certain that this Adam Steyr was
not worth changing for, and suddenly she wished she had.

As Victor introduced the Austrian journalist, Adam bent
low, kissed her hand, and whispered, "You are quite an impossible artist. Quite impossible to achieve on stage the feeling
you sought, and yet you did, somehow. When you danced
your final encore it was almost more than I could endure."

"Thank you."

"You were like a shaft of light coming out of a dark night."

Delight filled her as she stared at him. Their eyes met, and already she felt lost. His eyes were blue, like deep pools which seemed to reflect her own beauty. He was fair, with blond hair, and a perfectly groomed blond mustache. Adam Steyr was handsome in a masculine aesthetic way in spite of being rather short. It obviously relieved him of any doubts about himself, and she liked that and his air of mature certainty. She was fascinated by his fair coloring, so rare in Budapest, and then remembered, Adam was Austrian.

Lenora accepted his invitation to dinner. She always ate lightly before a recital, but somehow tonight, although she should have been very hungry, she pushed all the food away. Adam spoke French and German fluently; he represented a Viennese newspaper in Hungary; she was most interested in the fact that he was translating Byron's *Don Juan* into German.

Don Juan it must be. Don Juan was her ideal. Don Juan it became.

She accepted his invitation to hear him read his translation of the first canto, which he had completed just a few days ago. She was not giving a performance the following evening; she only gave four a week because of the demands her dancing made upon her body.

It was exciting to hear him read. It was almost like a performance, she thought, as he paced up and down his hotel suite. Reciting Don Juan's feverish search for love, he reminded Lenora of a proud, preening bird of paradise despite his shortness. She liked that, disliking men who went about with downcast eyes. He read with such eloquence that she ached with desire for him.

He is wonderful, she thought. She applauded loudly when he finished, remarking on how magnificently he had read, and he replied that it was because Lenora Malcolm had inspired him. He is irresistible, she decided, a genius, artistic at heart whatever his profession.

Every night, then, they saw each other. Performances began at seven in Budapest, and the evening was young when she finished. They had dinner in his hotel suite, and then he read to her from Byron's *Don Juan,* usually the more amorous portions.

Lenora did not explain to Mama where she went after her performances, and Mama did not ask.

Mama had no wish to erect a wall around Lenora, but she was apprehensive about Adam Steyr. She thought that he was in love with the sound of his own voice, that his ability to be exhilarated by Lenora's dancing was a kind of skill, that actually Adam was interested in her art only because Lenora was the new sensation. It was also evident to Mama there were disturbing emotions ripping at her daughter. Lenora had frequent outbursts of anger at trivial things now, and they came more often despite her success. Not that she feared Lenora would sin, Mama assured herself in the debate which went on so much within her, but Lenora's dancing now required a rigorous discipline which demanded almost constant mortification of the other emotions. Most of the time now, when the performance ended, Mama simply said, "Good, Lenora," and watched Adam, who watched Lenora.

"It is good, sometimes," said Lenora, and wished Mama would not look so much like a watchdog these days.

One night during the middle of her engagement, just as Lenora was afraid he would remain Adam Steyr, he was Don Juan. Someone had warned her that he was dangerous, a notorious gallant, and now she saw him in a new aspect, an even more intriguing aspect, and he seemed to sense this. He said it was extraordinary, she would have made a perfect model for Byron's heroines, and a moment later he was kissing Lenora's hand, her arm, her neck, her shoulder, as if love was everything. He did not kiss her on the lips. Then suddenly he was Adam again, saying he might not be healthy for her dancing. And she was very upset, and craving, craved even more. She could hardly wait any longer.

After he departed there was insomnia, nervous exhaustion, depressed spirits. Never had Lenora felt more miserable.

Then one evening he was Don Juan again, and he went almost as far as she desired. He kissed her arm, her neck, her shoulder again, but not her lips, although he was all ardor. His fair skin was bright as he held her closely, and she prepared to collapse into a soft heap. They almost took flight then, without another word. But when she remembered the performance the following evening, she plaintively said it was impossible. He looked furious, but he did not argue.

The next night he failed to call, and the next, and Lenora gave several unhappy performances. The public did not notice; by now she was an accepted sensation, but she felt even more miserable than before. It was dreadful enough to be a fool about love, to do stupid things, but to fail in her dancing, there was nothing which justified that. She was overwhelmed with harsh confusions.

Lenora was just about to bury her pride and send him a note, when he called. It was her final performance of this engagement, and the theater was completely sold out in advance. Mama was bursting with pride, and suddenly, abruptly, Lenora shushed her. "Please, it is all very grand," and it was now, for Adam stood in the doorway. Lenora sent Mama out to see if everyone was seated; until then she was not ready. Mama gave Adam a critical glance and departed with an expression of distrust.

Then Adam was Don Juan once more, the Don Juan she loved, as he handed her a bouquet of roses and said, "Lovely, lovely Lenora, I do not flatter you when I say you have made the season here."

There was a tumult in her heart, but she sat still.

"I am sorry. I am a fool. I have made it ugly." He turned to go.

"No, no!" How many times had she thought of him these last few days: a thousand!

His blue eyes lit up. "You must believe me, Lenora, it is not wickedness, it is what we are."

"For myself, I do not mind, but . . ."

"Would you suspend the laws of nature?" He held out his arms.

Lenora wavered a moment and then came into them, and he was not arguing any more, but kissing her, everywhere but on the lips. She reached up and kissed him, squarely on his lips. He was startled, for this instant now pleased, as if an essential initiative had been stolen from him and he had become an imitation male, and was she the kind of woman he desired?

Sensing his annoyance, she said, "You are a perfect Don Juan."

Appeased, he said, "And you are the perfect artist. We will find somewhere to stay."

"Yes." She said it quickly before she changed her mind.

"We will be so happy."

"We will do wonderful things together. My dancing will be even more exciting, you see."

"Lenora, I will force nothing on you."

It was a fortunate audience at that performance. Lenora looked like a virgin at the birth of the world when she began, and then she became transformed and took on the passionate heat of the Magyars. Her final number was one of fulfillment, and she danced with a passion she had not thought herself capable of, discovering that she owned new ways of expressing her emotion, that dancing was not yesterday or tomorrow but now. Tonight she was not forcing her way through space;

space seemed to be lifting her. But she refused to dance many encores, wishing to save herself for him, although the packed theater did not want her to halt.

Afterward she told Mama that she was going to a party and might not be home until very late, and she vanished with Don Juan. He led her out the rear of the theater, evading everyone else with a practiced skill.

The night was dark and chilly, and she lost track of time and place, although she sensed it was very late and that they were far away from Budapest when they reached their destination.

The brawny innkeeper was not surprised to be awakened at this hour. Don Juan was an old friend, and the innkeeper led them into a rambling inn smothered with ivy, low-roofed, quaint, and private.

In her honor, bowed the innkeeper, they had the Empire Lodge.

It was enormous, and there was much ornamentation, a large French chandelier which gave no light but which was quite decorative, massive gilt-edged furniture which seemed to serve no purpose except the sensual, and a huge bed with a frilly pink canopy.

Then she was absorbed by his arms. Don Juan was direct and certain. There were no words; she uttered a gasp of surprise, and then, flesh against flesh, she felt incredible and foolish and wonderful and truly in love.

Afterward he promised her the world. His lips closed over hers, full and firm and a trifle moist. In the quivering darkness she felt proud that upon this bed she had touched immensity. She could hear Don Juan breathing violently. She stretched out her legs, nothing in the world as smooth, as far-reaching as her legs, and he had fallen asleep.

Lenora was still awake when the sun came in the next morning. In the daylight the horizon was within view, and she had a moment of feeling she had forgotten Mama, or betrayed her, and then that seemed silly. Don Juan was even more handsome now, if a little vain. Awake, he was pressing her down to deep caverns hitherto undared.

When he left their room a little later Lenora heard him tell the innkeeper, "We are going to be your guests a while longer."

"How much longer?" Lenora asked, when he returned.

"What, darling?" He was not really listening to her.

"Will we leave this afternoon, Adam?"

"I adore you." His hand encountered her breasts, and she was amazed how easy it was. Fear was really such an abstract idea, and she was thinking you can live with an emotion all your life and never understand it.

"I adore you," he said each time he wooed her.

Love was his instinctive means of expression, she realized the next few days. He had not learned it, it had come of itself, of his nature. He loved with an astonishing rapidity, yet with the naïveté of a child, as if it were his right, yet also with a skill which was an art.

Lenora slept close to him all the next night and the next, and when she awoke she lay back and thought, aren't we mad! But instead of being satiated, she was on the increase. It was almost too much, this beauty and ecstasy, and she wondered why she had waited so long.

22

Mama waited too, waited day after day in the now dreary hotel suite, chiding herself for not having found an excuse to remain with Lenora the night of the farewell performance. She had liked Budapest at first, because it had liked Lenora, but that had turned to distrust. The wild czardas had become a kind of debauchery. How she wished Raskowski the fiddler, whose romantic music was the feature of the dining room, would stop playing. His sensuous music mocked her and kept reminding her of lust and libertines. She felt shabby, resentful, and dreadfully concerned. Just as the music lied, Lenora had lied and, worse, had vanished without a word, and there was not a thing she could do about it. Mama had not thought she would worry so, only Lenora had been guilty of an enormously rash deed. The enterprising Victor Lothar had arranged concerts throughout Hungary, more were being planned elsewhere; indeed, everything Lenora had yearned for seemed about to happen. But where was Lenora?

Mama felt the habits of a lifetime disintegrating. How could she speak intimately to Lenora of what was already too intimate to be known?

And now Amy, who had arrived from America during

Lenora's absence and in response to Lenora's cable, to share Lenora's success, stood beside her like a shadow. Amy was even angrier than Mama at what Lenora was jeopardizing. Amy said, "She must be mad to risk this opportunity."

"She is in love," said Mama. "I think."

"What can we do about it?"

There was nothing to do but wait. The days passed with Mama a prey to many gloomy fancies. It was almost a week later when Lenora burst in, glowing with beauty and ecstasy. Mama's first impulse was to say, "Thank God," then she caught hold of herself. She was facing a dilemma: she thought, mothers are supposed to love the things their children love, yet I find myself hating what she loves.

Lenora could hardly believe it was Mama she was seeing— Mama looked so pallid, thin, aged. And strange, with a sadness which was not like Mama. Her behavior had been foolish, ugly; she could read the verdict in Mama's eyes. She longed to sing witty, romantic songs. To sing "let the punishment fit the crime"; no—she had not reflected; she had possessed a compulsion to be exultant, to defy, to go headlong, and had done so, but why was Mama so troubled? Wanting to love as she felt loved, Lenora greeted Amy with joy and affection. But Amy acted as if she had been immaculately conceived and regarded Lenora as lurid and far too emotional.

There was a moment of awkward silence. They could hear the insistent rhythm of the zimbalon, Hungary's favorite musical instrument.

Lenora asked, "You love me, don't you, Mama?"

Mama said warily, "I love all my family."

"You want me to be happy, don't you?"

"I want you to do what is right."

Amy said, "To run off as you did? Without a word? Was it that vital?"

Lenora had nothing against her older sister, but Amy was almost spinsterish now, and she retorted intensely, "It was the highest expression of the world around us." How could they lecture her like a wayward child when she felt like a goddess!

Yet even now Amy was asking, "And where on earth have you been?"

"Paradise," said Lenora, lightly yet ecstatically.

"Should we tell that to Lothar when he talks of canceling your recitals next week because you haven't even rehearsed your new programs?"

"I don't have to, now. I'm doing a different program. A different kind of Chopin, the music he wrote that was born of love."

Lenora had altered, reflected Mama. Even a week ago, with all her new Hungarian recklessness, Lenora had retained some of the quality of innocence, but today her emotion was not chaste. Lenora no longer seemed her daughter, but a mystery, and Mama feared that Lenora did not need her any more.

Lenora said to Mama, as calmly as announcing the next number on her program, "I am in love with Adam."

What was gone was gone, but Mama's head did not clear. She knew she must not be prudish or scornful, yet Lenora's eyes were so radiant at the mention of love that Mama's pain grew.

Amy asked, "You spent the week with him?"

"You prefer that we keep everything the same?" Lenora was prepared to burst instantly into argument.

Mama said, "We prefer that you have a career of your own choosing."

Lenora said, "Then you should help me."

Amy said, "And that will satisfy you? That will be worth risking your future?"

"I will see him again, as often as I want, and no one will halt me."

"Suppose he does not want to marry you?" asked Mama.

"I may not want to marry him." Mama's throat ached, and she could not go on, but there was no compromise in Lenora. "Can't you see how happy I am?"

Amy said, "I can see that the chances of failure have increased."

"That's not so," said Lenora, as if failure now was impossible.

Mama whispered, "You think you will be able to deceive everyone?"

Lenora gave her mother an affectionate but exasperated glance. "I do not intend to deceive anyone. You really ought to help us, not hinder us. That will make it easier for all of you, yourself as well."

Amy said, "It will ruin your career."

"If anything, it will nourish my career. I understand so much more now." Lenora stood adorning herself with new gestures, as if she had found a new genius, a new sunlight, and a new temperament. Amy stared at Lenora as if the latter was totally incapable of comprehending the practical world, but it was Mama's somber silence that provoked Lenora and caused her to exclaim, "Do you want me to banish love?"

"No," Mama replied sadly, "but I can't talk to you. As far as you are concerned I might as well be talking Latin."

"Go ahead, Mama," laughed Lenora. "I'll learn Latin."

Mama stared unhappily out the window. She had imagined a love for Lenora which would be tender and poetic, which, most of all, would be blessed with dignity and constancy. It was the way love had to be for her; the absence of these qualities had been why her husband had failed her. She had never expected a child of hers to become one of those individualists whose intensity could not be forced to compromise. But it was evident that Lenora's passion had become a conversion. We stand at opposite ends of the world, thought Mama, and I have only a secondary place in her heart, and in this metamorphosis I cannot influence her. Mama looked so helpless and melancholy that Lenora put an arm around her and was shocked when Mama began to weep. As they clung together, Mama sobbed with a lost and overwhelming sadness.

Lenora suddenly looked very young. She said, "Mama, you have been the courageous one in the family. You brought us up to be enlightened, free."

Amy reminded, "But to run off without a word. That was cruel."

"Why are you so moralistic? Haven't you ever been in love?"

Amy did not reply. She had just as many lovely dreams as Lenora, but who else found them lovely? Which Don Juan?

Lenora asked, "Is it so awful to be in love?"

Mama could not discuss it now. Words were useless. To be in love was wonderful, if it were true love, but all that she had labored for seemed so blindly, stupidly, wantonly jeopardized.

Lenora said, "I am not going to be a fugitive from love."

Amy said, "You could be more cautious."

"Cautious! Cautious!" shouted Lenora. "What is that but a watchdog. I will not be afraid. I will not!"

"Hush," said Mama, "I'm tired," and thought Lenora must have been born intoxicated. Mama had no resistance when Amy suggested they take a month's vacation in Switzerland.

At the train Mama longed to cry, Lenora be happy, have a rich wonderful life, darling, it is better to have love than not know it at all, I can see past my nose, but please be cautious, darling, for love can be quite unreasonable. Mama said nothing as her eyes grew heavy with tears. All she could see was a child running away from Aunt Jessie, from provincial living, very small but very defiant, panting as if having raced a hundred miles, but not yielding, never yielding. In some ways Lenora had not changed, yet in some ways she no longer knew her daughter.

So Lenora arranged for a continuation of her idyllic romance with Don Juan. She forgot only one thing: to listen to him. He objected to the hours she had to give to rehearsing, to her engagements elsewhere in Hungary which he could not join. He resented Lothar, accusing the impresario of trying to separate them, although the latter was his friend and approved of their affair and had not interfered in any way. The impresario had attributed her disappearance to temperament, and to Lothar the performer without temperament, the capacity to feel intensely, magnificently, was not an artist, and so Lothar accepted Lenora's behavior as one of the inevitable hazards of his profession. But Don Juan acted as if every instant Lenora was away from him was immoral, especially at this moment in their lives. To him nothing came before love, his love.

Lenora promised Don Juan that when she returned from these new engagements he would have all of her, and that it would be heavenly, and forever. They spent several lovely but brief evenings together, and then she left for the more primitive parts of Hungary. She was certain that the nights she experienced his love would give birth to masterpieces. She thought of herself and Don Juan as a team.

There was a new boldness in her dancing. She gave her Magyar public, who were highly emotional, such a sense of fulfillment she was hailed everywhere she danced, although there was apprehension that the more civilized countries of Europe might be shocked by her freeness.

When she came back to Budapest she had several free weeks before her next engagement—Lothar was still undecided about what would be the wisest next step, Berlin, Vienna, Munich, Brussels, or Paris—and she resolved to make the most of every moment. Don Juan seemed agreeable. His blue eyes glowed as he said, "Darling, there hasn't been any life here in Budapest since you left. I haven't been able to translate a single line." He awakened her to another aspect of love, and then she lived in a voluptuous languor, which was tinged with a sadness that this might never be enjoyed so fully again.

And when she began to rehearse again, he resented each second it took her away from him. He had ample time; his work for his Viennese newspaper was of a leisurely nature, demanding only that he remain close to Budapest for the time being. They had their first quarrel, and it upset her. She could forgive him for mixing champagne with claret, although it spoiled the champagne in her opinion; she could ignore the rings he wore, she wore none; but for him not to be overwhelmed by her art was a calamity. She was deeply hurt. But she tried to compromise. For his sake she appeared to modify her passion for her art. She rehearsed less and less. Yet she realized she could never accept an existence in which she was not creative. She wondered if he knew this and would it break his heart.

She was his passion; he told her so every few minutes. He kept her fully informed on the state of his affections. He knew he had a gift for inspiring love. He expected as much from her as his due.

Then he took her to the inn along the Danube where they had first known love. An orchestra played outside their room, peasants danced in the courtyard, there was a moon at their window, and he said that when she married him, within a month he hoped, he would transfer to Vienna, his native town, and settle there.

Startled, she said, "Adam, are you really serious?"

"Of course. You are just what I want a wife to be."

Lenora did not know what to say. She believed so many lives were ruined by marriage, and she did not wish to be solemn about it. "But what about my dancing?"

"You will be my wife. That is the life nature selected for you."

Don Juan was too happy to hurt, she thought, as he renewed their intimacy with fresh vigor. That evening she entered their bedroom in a new manner. She wore a small red scarf around her neck. It was all she wore. Then she danced a bacchanal. He could not keep away from her; he swept her into his arms as if he were Lord Byron himself. So she could not dance, so that she did not want to dance. He made love to her with an argumentative intensity.

It seemed as if all was perfect, but several days later there was a new quarrel. He ordered her to move into his hotel suite, until he returned to Vienna, and she reminded him, "I have concerts next week. In Berlin, probably, or Paris," which was her wish, although Lothar was still indefinite about her next engagement.

Adam said, irate, "An Austrian woman's career is by her husband's side."

"I'm Irish-American."

"But your mother did marry. She is a lady. Almost too much, sometimes."

"Adam, I am not very much of a lady."

"I did not say that."

"It is true. I don't want to be anything but a dancer."

"Darling, women are God's most beautiful creation, but they are at their best when they follow their natural calling of wife and mother. Do not compete with men. When you compete, you forfeit what we value the most, your femininity. You know that."

"I know that you are just as severe about women as the Germans you like to criticize, that you believe we should be interested only in *Kirche, Küche, und Kinder*."

"Lenora, don't you want a family?"

"Naturally. But when I have children, I want them my way."

"You want to usher in a new era."

"Adam, strength makes its own rules. You did, when you met me."

"I love you. I still do." At this moment he was full of tireless energy. "But you love only your own legs."

"My legs are not the legs of others. I am bound to them."

"For an intelligent woman, you are sometimes naïve. Your dancing is charming, but as a future, let us not be foolish. Only peasants in Austria and Hungary go about with bare legs and bare feet."

"That's not fair."

"Darling, have I no influence on you?"

"Of course. But no one has the right to change another person's life."

"You are tired. You will feel differently tomorrow," he insisted. He assembled all the appropriate gestures, and she met him halfway, but he was unusually thoughtful the rest of the evening.

The following day Adam offered as a compromise to introduce her to the *maître de ballet* of the Royal Opera Company. It struck her as a dismal suggestion and she hated it, but she forced a smile as she declined. She was swollen with an unpleasant ache; he was somber with repressed fury, and he grew stiff and formal.

At the railroad station the next day Adam was so grim he was a stranger. He waited for Lenora to give in, but she did not give in. So he remained grim, oh how grim, she thought, and her heart was like a wilderness. She stumbled on to the train. She slumped into her compartment and cried as if her heart would break.

Victor sat down beside her and said quietly, "He is not that unusual a man."

"He is a fine journalist," she said with a flash of defiance.

"No, Lenora, he will lose all his contacts when he loses his looks, when he grows fat, like an ox."

"I love him."

"You love the illusions he created."

She could not agree. She could not make him less or think their love less because she had lost him. Although her love had grown from passion, she felt she had lost him because of principle. She had failed, she thought; she had made the wrong choice. Don Juan had behaved according to his own nature, but romance was not enough hereafter. Somewhere there must be a lover who could respect her dancing and principles, yet understand her heart. She must search among the many men of genius who had been drawn to her art.

She was unable, however, to forge her heart into a hard core as she wished. She was feverish, then chilly on the train.

Victor Lothar, with a faith she had not expected, took her to Salzburg and assumed responsibility for her recovery. He said he was arranging concerts in Germany, but a depressed Lenora did not believe him.

Lenora did not believe anything; she did not like the world, herself, anything. Turned inward, stripped of faith, self-castigated, her illness became a need for purification. The doctor said her illness was nothing serious, nothing to be diagnosed medically, nothing but accumulated fatigue and heartbreak.

Despising everything in her misery and humiliation, she ignored the doctor. She felt dimly that she had danced on the rooftops of the world, but the fall had been so far, so hard— no, never, never again. And Lenora drifted into a strange world which had no time or boundaries, and sometimes she lay as if dead. She spoke not a word for many grieving days, and then slowly, awkwardly, she came out of the cold of the grave. She felt a gentle hand on her forehead, the first thing she had felt in many days, the first touch she could endure in such a long time. It was not to be explained, but she felt better. Mama was caressing her. Lenora prepared herself for scorn, but there was no scorn.

Victor was saying, "Ah, your patient is improving."

Mama smiled patiently and said, "She'll get better now."

In the days which followed all of Mama's deep affection was concentrated on Lenora. Recovery became a great happiness, for Lenora and Mama and Amy were reconciled. It was Mama who chose Lenora's dancing costumes and washed them, who told her what a wonderful manager Victor Lothar was, and Amy agreed.

"But you are my manager," Lenora said to Mama as she gathered strength.

"I am your claque, dear," replied Mama. "Victor is your impresario. He has a sixth sense about audiences. He has arranged a series of concerts in Germany. You will give your first new recital in Munich."

Lenora was disappointed; she had expected Berlin, a world capital, to be next.

Lothar said, "Munich is the key to Europe's attention. But I can delay your opening there if you are not ready."

He was a sly dog. Of course she was ready. Yet for a terrible moment Lenora felt like a masquerader as she put on her studio costume. Then she began practicing. It was difficult at first, but it was with a new intensity.

23

Lenora adored Munich at once. The home-grown *Gemütlichkeit* of the city was an intoxicating draught which made her drunk with life. She exulted in the miles of magnificent art galleries, in the vigor of the inhabitants, in their worship of all the arts. On all the earth there seemed no city better fitted to be a grand audience.

A week after her arrival she looked very pretty once more, and slim and rested and shining brightly. In the morning she took a pot of steaming hot coffee, huge rolls, and eggs past counting, yet by eleven she was eating sausage, and at noon she was selecting a dinner which would have finished her elsewhere. Halfway through the afternoon she found it essential to have a snack of cold meat and more coffee, as if that were necessary to go on, and always an enormous supper, and even then she had to eat before going to bed.

A whole week Lenora forgot all else as she walked, talked, ate, drank, absorbing the cultivation of her senses. It was the best cure for Adam. She no longer cried when she thought about the loss of their divine love. She assured herself that he was just a memory, although there were moments when she yearned intensely for him. But each time this yearning became

almost unbearable, she threw herself deeply into the life of
Munich and into preparation for her debut.

All the famous artists of Munich were in attendance: Kaul-
bach, Munch, Samberger, Meister. They expected tricks, to
be startled.

Lenora employed no tricks. She wore a soft gray tunic
severe in its simplicity. The drapery was so slight that the
outlines of her figure could be seen clearly. There was no
stage, not even a platform. A square space like the area before a Greek temple was carpeted for her bare feet, was the
whole of her apparatus, the rest was Lenora Malcolm.

The music was Gluck, Chopin, and Mozart. She stood motionless in front of the audience for what seemed an eternity
to Mama, and then, just as the audience could not wait any
longer, she eased forward like an angel moving out of heaven.
With never an abrupt movement, with never a sharp or ugly
angle, she danced as if it were the gospel. She danced as if
this were the birth of creation. She was music and poetry and
motion, and she was combining them into an image of beauty
which possessed her entire soul. The tunic was even more
noticeably transparent now, and everyone focused on her.

When Lenora finished there was a demonstration which
Mama had never seen before. The audience rose as one,
shouted, laughed, and sang:

"Die gottliche, heilige Lenora."

"The divine, and sainted Lenora," translated Victor Lothar.

The audience repeated that praise, the old ladies waved
little lace handkerchiefs in harmony with her, the young
women said did you see how she balanced, most wonderful
balancer you ever saw, and the men young and old felt as if
she had made love to each one of them, while the artists said
she was the poetry which grew out of the earth. And Lenora
stood looking innocent and lovely, and Mama was so happy
again she wanted to cry, while Amy was proud that they were
all Malcolms. Such a storm of emotion blew through the
audience it seemed as if the evening would never end.

From then on Munich was her patron saint. The enraptured populace said she must dance in Munich forever. What
the first-night audience called her in all seriousness and with
all its eloquence became the toast of the city.

"Die gottliche, heilige Lenora."

The few who disagreed with this judgment were shouted
down by her admirers. The initial recital stretched into a
dozen. The critics said she was *"wunderschön."* Hans Plout,
the romantic Teuton painter with the spirit of an antique
Greek, did a poetic portrait of her.

Looking for new worlds to conquer, Lenora danced next for the students. She became the epitome of artistic freedom. They loved her from the start, and they became her favorite audience; they were young and impulsive as she was. She made much less money dancing for them, but she did not care. When she felt their adoration nothing seemed out of reach; their devoted words were dancing words. And she loved them all and preferred no one. Not even Don Juan, she told herself; she belonged to a different species, to the strong and the free. Now she believed that it had been out of pure generosity she had given herself to him.

She was positive now that Victor had been right when he had said, before her Munich debut, "Munich is the artistic center of Europe. If you make a success here, you will make it everywhere."

Vienna was Lenora's next triumph. She danced for the Emperor Franz Josef, and her dancing was more circumspect for the Emperor. She wore a heavier costume and danced none of the revolutionary numbers she had done in Hungary —but once again her dancing spoke across the gulf of time and space. The Emperor led the applause for "The Malcolm," and the court joined in.

There were romantic stories linking Lenora with the Grand Duke Ferdinand, which were untrue, although Ferdinand did admire her beauty, but this pleased Lothar, for these rumors were useful publicity. What was most acclaimed was when she danced "The Blue Danube." Then she could do no wrong. There were no street demonstrations, which she missed, but full houses greeted every performance.

Then Adam wrote her, asking to see her in Vienna. She agreed, although Mama was upset and sought to dissuade her. "There is nothing to worry about," she told Mama, amused that this troubled Mama. Budapest and her passion for Adam seemed ages ago. Nonetheless her heart quickened as Adam approached, and she had a moment of apprehension—would he find her just as lovely? He was still handsome, but there were deep circles under his eyes and he was thinner. He took her hands, kissed them, and said, "You know how I feel." His pressure on her hands increased.

She smiled to show that she was friendly, but not slavish.

He embraced her resolutely, as if nothing amiss had happened. For one brief evening it was almost the same. Almost, for though he was tender and charming she realized she no longer loved him. Don Juan had never appeared so elegant, yet so virile, but she had altered. She was determined that from now on her lover had to be a genius, a changer of worlds, art worlds, the most special kind of a Don Juan.

After a highly charged evening she said she had to go on to Berlin.

Don Juan said sadly, "Darling, you wound me."

"I have an audience waiting for me."

"You are afraid that staying here, with me, will hurt your career."

"Afraid?" She said with sudden vigor, "I am not afraid of anything!"

He thought for a moment, then said, "It must be someone in your company."

"I am the company."

"What about your manager, your orchestra leader, the musicians!" It was incredible to an expert like himself that it could be otherwise. Don Juan knew that all women in the theater were ambitious, that many of them, almost all, possessed lovers. It was beyond his belief that the battle for success could be won any other way, as she was insisting.

She said, "It is really none of your business, but as I told you, there is no one."

He refused to believe her. He repeated, "Americans spoil their women."

He was so petulant that she wanted to spank him. Yet it was true we were really one, her mind ran on, but there was no way to go back; no—no way at all. But it had been wonderful when everything had meant *I love you*.

He said, "I am the only one you can rely on. These Germans, these painters, are totally undependable."

This was vulgar, untrue, and she did not answer.

They stared at each other sadly. It had been too much, their beauty and happiness. He took her to her hotel and talked about nothing at all.

Berlin was determined to outdo Vienna and Munich. But Mama feared Lothar was too ambitious, hiring a prominent theater for Lenora to dance with the Philharmonic Orchestra. Lothar replied that Berlin was Lenora's greatest opportunity, the heart of the musical world, and that Berliners would not be impressed unless Lenora danced in an important house.

Mama had to admit that Lothar was clever. A story appeared, inspired by him, which said that the Emperor Franz Josef wanted "The Malcolm" to be the court dancer at the Hofburg Theater in Vienna. Lothar also let it be known that she would dance in a tunic more transparent than ever and that Munich was begging her to return. There was a great rush for tickets; opening night sold out quickly.

The night of the Berlin opening came too fast for Lenora, however, for she felt unprepared for the excitement that had been aroused. But Lothar was not nervous, saying she would succeed if she danced as she had in Munich and Vienna, while Mama said she must express her inner convictions.

Nonetheless, Lenora's nervousness remained. The recital began very late. The audience grew quite restless—Berlin audiences were not accustomed to waiting—and could hardly contain itself. She came forward so quietly the audience was not conscious of her movements. Lenora had sipped champagne before coming on, and that was as stimulating as Munich's bracing air, and the nervousness was gone now. No one could explain it, but as she danced the audience felt full of love and grace. She knit them to her with a look, a turn of her head, the lift of her arms. To an audience preoccupied with squabbles and indigestion, she stated truths that could be accepted without question. In lives where all else was uncertain, she became the stable faith, became beauty in everything. There was beauty in her music, in her movements, in her simplicity, in the world she created on stage.

Several critics wrote that Lenora Malcolm had learned only the beginnings of her art, another condemned her scanty costume, another declared it was sacrilegious to dance to Chopin and Mozart. But the final encore, "The Blue Danube," drowned out the critics. Berliners, usually regarded as cold, who considered Munich *Gemütlichkeit* as weak and effeminate, who were proud of their military strength, cheered her with immense warmth.

At the end of a month of packed houses there was talk of building a theater just for "The Malcolm." Arguments about her raged fiercely, fanned by Lothar, who made certain that each rumor reached the press immediately. The Kaiser had her give a court performance, was seen to applaud her, and this was reported on the front page. Even the American press said: "Lenora Malcolm's poetic dancing has divided the Fatherland into two camps. The most talked of girl in Europe is the California dancer, she of the bare feet that have either scandalized or delighted so many thousands of spectators."

What was regarded as even more audacious was the talk of raising $250,000 for a temple of art to be built in the Greek style just for her dancing. Lenora felt supreme, for the Emperor was reputed to have written her, "You must return to

Vienna. You can dance when you will and come and go as you please. Do not refuse this chance to brighten the declining years of a lonesome old man."

This was followed by a report which said, "Wilhelm II learned of these negotiations, and he has sent an emissary to prevent Miss Malcolm from signing with the Emperor Franz Josef. He has said, 'Whatever value the Emperor sets on your services, I am willing to meet. In my country you will be identified with the great artists of the world, your fame will be spread everywhere.'"

The artists of Munich took a hand in this argument and wrote, "Do not restrict your art by selling it to royalty. Stay with us, who first appreciated you. We understand your art. We will immortalize you in famous paintings. We will make up for you in worship what you will lose in cash."

The Berlin press retorted proudly, "Already, some of the $250,000 for the Greek Temple of Art has been subscribed."

Lenora waited for construction to start on this temple, for despite the press exaggerations, there was a contest between Berlin and Vienna over her. She had no wish to be a court dancer, but a Greek Temple of Art would be wonderful. But no temple was forthcoming, and Lenora grew impatient and irritable. Mama was advising her to be patient; Lothar was delighted with the large audiences she was still attracting; Amy was talking about opening a school; but when Archer wrote her from New York that their rightful home was Greece, she was suddenly inspired again, she had to be inspired now, she had to have constant excitement now. Greece became a wonderful idea.

She was sure Greece would appreciate her art and inspire it to greater heights. She was also bored and in desperate need of a change. For in spite of the Germans' adoration of her, it was evident that *Kirche, Küche, und Kinder* also persisted in Germany. It was a rich country, and yet that was a delusion, she thought. They could not afford her except as an entertainer. Suddenly the entire business reeked of excellencies. Just as suddenly she felt that Archer had read her mind: they belonged in Greece.

And since she did not believe in hesitating she decided to go to Greece without further thought, although she was in the middle of her engagement in Berlin and was still playing to profitable houses.

She cabled Archer to meet them in Athens, at the foot of the Parthenon, as if it were her idea now. He would be free of the crassness of the commercial theater, she added. He could even create a School of Acting there, she advised him, the cable several pages long now, while Amy could create a School of Dancing, Mama would help him and Amy, and she would establish the performing center that would give the fullest expression to all their dreams.

After she sent the cable to Archer she told Mama and Amy, "We must go to Greece," and before they could question this she announced to the press that the entire Malcolm family was establishing a Greek Temple of Art in Athens. That was all. The decision was made. Lenora was delighted with her show of resolution and resolved to stay a year, or perhaps forever.

Mama objected, thinking that Greece was a legend and it would be a pity if it lost the air of mystery and beauty it held for them now, but she was overruled.

Amy wanted to go to Greece also, but she resented Lenora's assumption of authority. She protested and Lenora said, her love for the Greeks now the most powerful passion of her being, "If ever there was a time when art went hand in hand with life, it was in Athens. All the arts were placed on equal footing with living. We have to recapture that." And Amy found herself agreeing, although some resentment remained.

Lothar was shocked. "You are at the top of your career. I have engagements for all over Europe!"

"They can wait," Lenora said with genuine unconcern. "I have to return to the Greeks."

"You are so involved with lofty matters, you cannot see what is under your nose."

"Victor, you will defend me when I am away."

"How will I explain it?"

"Don't. Victor, will I have enough money to take my family?"

"I think so. But you will have nothing left."

"Will I have enough for a year?"

"You always make me give in to your wishes. You are insatiable. Lenora, are you not celebrated enough?"

"The Greeks are elevated people, even now. They will help me establish my Temple of Art. They will be delighted that I am restoring the glory that was Greece."

"You cannot be certain."

"It is a battle, in any case."

"Lenora, when will you grow up?"

"It isn't that. I'm approaching twenty-five, and yet there is so much I haven't done. Oh, I know that Germany and Hungary and Austria have been wonderful, and I appreciate all that, but here they still have a false conception of the importance of dancing. They accept it as long as it is entertainment but it should be far more to them. Dancing should be a guide to understanding the inner and outer meanings of nature, of themselves. Dancing should be their religion. As it was to the ancient Greeks. And in Athens I will be able to feel that way and live that way."

"You will not find that in Athens," he said skeptically.

There was a long silence as they sipped their liqueurs. He wondered, what does Lenora really want? She thought, he is a decent man, but he worries too much, especially about commercial matters and what people will say and other unessentials.

He asked, "How long do you really think you will be gone?"

"For as long as it is necessary."

He was quiet then out of a sense of helplessness.

24

Thus the future begins again for Lenora in Greece. The future is again the stretch of her desire, the splendor of her energy, the quest for a Promethean fire, and an infinite number of magnificent possibilities.

This is a future where her dreams have borne her many times, a world with a galaxy of heroes as inspiring as Homer and Phidias, Apollo and Plato, and a host more. Long ago, it seems such a vast time now, Mama has inoculated her with the glory that is Greece. She is resolved to be Promethean indeed, the supreme rebel, never to be shaken, never to submit, never to feel conquered, whatever the scorn. Now she intends to dance before the Parthenon, at the Theater of Dionysus, throughout ancient and modern Greece. This is the temple she wishes to inhabit the rest of her life. She knows the future is just beyond the horizon, that the extent of her intensity has not deceived her.

The day after the Malcolms' arrival in Brindisi, Italy, a warm summer day, Lenora found a suitable conveyance for their journey to Greece, a small ship familiar with the Ionian Sea. Lenora was determined that their voyage should follow the route of the Odyssey.

Mama was upset, afraid of the danger and hardship, but

Lenora said that was unhellenic and sealed the decision with another payment to the ship's captain. Mama could not add what they both knew, that the Odyssey had taken ten years; it would have been a betrayal of what she herself had taught Lenora. Her voice cracked with anxiety, however, as she said, "There is a regular Venice-Brindisi-Constantinople steamer which stops at Piraeus, the seaport of Athens. It is quicker, costs less." Mama was sure; she had checked with her Baedeker. "I'm sure that it is the better boat."

"Pull yourself together, Mama," said Lenora, "we've made our choice." She went on hurriedly, before a wavering Amy could join forces with Mama, "The other way would be too easy, and it was Homer himself who said rocky Ithaca was the most important entrance to Greece."

What to Lenora was the power and the glory had become something very different to Mama. By now it had become to her a desperate, imprudent pilgrimage that never seemed to have an end. Why couldn't Lenora remain in Europe—to Mama, Greece was not Europe—and continue her triumphs? Why couldn't Lenora ever be satisfied? Was she truly insatiable? Since they had left Berlin a month ago it had been one pension after another, endlessly moving, endlessly packing. It was even worse than when they had possessed no money, no fame. Pale, exhausted, often miserable, Mama busied herself with the Baedeker, learning fares, hotel rates, sites of historical interest, and tried to gather fresh energy from the memory of the victories. Lenora had graduated with honor from the school of the artist, and yet, now, all she wanted was to dance before the Parthenon. Or was that all, Mama wondered.

Mama could endure living in bare studios where the only furniture was the mattress on which they slept; she could endure the uncertainty—it was as natural to her as the weather; she could even endure the traveling, even though she was utterly tired of it . . . but she could not accept the growing remoteness of Lenora. She could not justify this with any of Lenora's high motives. Lenora had drifted away from her love into the keeping of a secret self, a wild strange self, thought Mama. It was almost unbearable to Mama. She could not touch this self, yet it choked her. It was essential to Mama to encourage, to believe in, to serve, to give: these were her expressions of love. Without these things she felt useless, yet Lenora had become so self-sufficient she seldom wanted any of these things from Mama now.

Mama was still in the pension in Brindisi when it came time to sail. She had packed for hours, and now she was too exhausted to move. She sat on the bed waiting, not certain what for, and Lenora entered.

Lenora was shocked. Mama, without her enthusiasm, seemed to have shrunken. Her dress was dowdy suddenly, obviously neglected. Her feet were misshapen in the stupid, unhealthy shoes which she insisted on wearing instead of Lenora's beloved sandals. She sat like an old woman, her legs apart, dangling. Her face was gray and drab. Lenora asked, frightened, "Mama, what is wrong?"

"I have to go home. Back home to San Francisco."

Lenora sat down beside Mama, concerned. She noticed that Mama's hands were trembling, that Mama had been hurrying, fussing, although everything was done. Mama always hurried when she was upset, and was talking about inconsequential things which meant that she was thinking about matters of great consequence to her. Lenora asked, "Are you afraid of Greece?" unable to touch Mama, although she felt she should.

Mama said, "It is too large an undertaking."

Lenora realized that very much depended on what she said, that there was grief and disappointment in Mama that was not easy to erase. She asked, "What do you want?"

"To stay in one place for a while."

"I need a better foundation for my art."

A sense of doom spread in Mama, a sense that Lenora was growing more reckless rather than less. Mama said, "You want life to conform to your ideals, but that is unrealistic."

"Is it more realistic to wait for life to give us what we want? And get nothing! Whatever we want, we must take."

"What is wrong with staying here for a while then? Italy will expose you to the bloom of great art. As much as Greece, won't it?"

"I shouldn't have to explain to you, Mama," said Lenora, with a sudden feeling of grievance. How loyal she used to be, how blind.

In her quietest voice Mama said, "I don't want to exasperate you, but give one place a real chance. Don't be capricious. Stay in Berlin another year, or Vienna. Then if you are still restless, unhappy . . ."

"I am not unhappy," Lenora said sharply. "I have to go to Greece."

"I shall miss you," Mama said.

"You really intend to go back to San Francisco?"

"I have no choice. But why are you so amazed?"

"Do you want me to go back to San Francisco too?"

"I want you to do what you have to do."

"But San Francisco is home, not Greece, not Athens?"

"What is home? At least, this will be the last time I have to pack."

It was like a death, and it was not to be endured. As Mama moved away, to alter the address on her luggage, Lenora cried, "Don't be an idiot!"

Mama paused, shocked.

"Even when I was a child I worshiped the Greeks. Before I could even read, you took me on the Odyssey by reading it to me, by believing in it, in the Greece of Apollo and Dionysus and Ulysses. Thanks to you, I grew up living with these gods. After that could I ever worship any other gods?"

Mama was flushed and tearful, and Lenora was relentless.

"Was teaching that to me a mistake? When I earned some money it was inevitable that I go to Greece, to the Parnassus you discovered for us. If anybody understands ancient Greece, you do. Or do you want me to be a music-hall entertainer, pleasing people with tricks? To obey each rule, so my work will have no relevance? Or should I obey my training, my teacher?"

Mama said, bewildered, "You can get along without me."

"I can get along without love, but who wants to?" Lenora stroked Mama's gray hair, her wrinkled hands. "Why is it we have never said to each other: 'I love you'? Why is it considered silly for a daughter to say that to a mother, once she is grown, or for a mother to say that to a daughter? Should we stay in such a conventional world, as if we must be neutral to each other?"

Mama said, "We are defeated by our own fears. And ourselves."

"And sometimes by others. And sometimes we get too familiar, we take each other for granted. And now," said Lenora, "you are telling me I can't worship any of the gods you gave me in the first place."

They burst into laughter, they had been so solemn. Surely, there would be no more difficulties or misunderstandings. They laughed long and it hurt. Mama wondered if all reconciliations had to be so terrible and wonderful. They decided that her impulse to return to San Francisco should be just their secret, and Lenora asked as they left the pension, "Am I chasing my tail?"

"Definitely not!" Mama was prepared to challenge anyone who thought such a ridiculous thought.

Lenora, the navigator too, ordered the captain of the small ship to sail directly for the island of Ithaca, although the surly sailor was reluctant. He asserted this route was dangerous, but Lenora insisted they had to follow the route of the Odyssey, although the scowling captain had never heard of the Odyssey and thought them mad. He added that Ithaca was rocky and that it was impractical to voyage in such uncertain waters with a party of tourists, all of them ladies.

"We have come all the way from San Francisco," said Lenora, annoyed at the implication that they were the weaker sex. In a few chosen words, about a thousand, Lenora exclaimed: had they not read the *Odyssey*, tirelessly! She added more gold drachmas to the agreed fee. This raised the total to far more than the captain earned in five ordinary voyages, and so against his better judgment he headed on to the stormy Ionian Sea, thinking he was in the hands of maniacs.

One hour out from Brindisi and Lenora had to struggle to keep from turning green. The ship which was picturesque at a distance was filthy inside. The cabin where she had expected to recline in comfort swarmed with vermin and had a hideous odor. It was safer to be on deck, and that was not safe either. The wind grew stronger, the sea grew choppier. They were all uneasy now, even Lenora. Mama sought to find consolation in her Baedeker, and Lenora's need for her faith. Lenora looked for grace and courage by remembering Ulysses. And Amy, poor girl, was ignoble; she got seasick.

The weather grew worse minute by minute, not better, as Lenora assured them it would. Each minute became like an hour, and each hour was like an eternity to Mama. Even Lenora grew concerned as the assault of the sea pressed in upon them, ugly, shattering, as everything became gray and green. It was as if the gods were furious at them for daring to follow the path of Ulysses. They were soaked to the skin; the boat's speed slowed. It was difficult to tell whether the worried captain had anything under control, yet Lenora could not ask him to turn back.

Mama said, "If we don't make land before dark, we're lost."

Lenora did not seem to hear her. Lenora said, "I love Greece," although the heavy waves drenched her in a constant rush now. Then she had no breath at all. The entire boat vibrated from the impact of the waves. It was all Lenora could do to hold on. The captain turned toward land, any land, and no one objected. When they put into Preveza just as darkness fell, there were no complaints. Preveza was a gray, drab Turkish port some miles above Ithaca, but they were too tired to do anything but rest. Yet when the surly captain refused to go on to Ithaca the next day, although the sea was calmer, Lenora felt betrayed.

The only ship they could hire was a tiny sloop. Its captain

was elderly, sorrowful, and desperately in need of money, hardly the man to pass them into the land of milk and honey, but he was a Greek—they discovered that the captain of the previous ship had been only an Albanian. Everyone ached from yesterday's voyage, but they were ashamed to turn back.

Now their travels had no order, and yet the strongest order. They went not by the map, but by their emotion. Whatever they yearned for, they visited. Sappho's rock was first, although it was far from Athens and off their route. Lenora felt this was the heart of Greece, and she climbed on to the promontory from which the poetess had flung herself. She danced a moment, to the spirit of the poetess. She felt so exalted she envied herself, although the climb was so arduous she forgot the quotations she had memorized and a massage would have been welcome.

After a whole day spent visiting Homeric Ithaca, viewing many places described in the *Odyssey*, they felt content. They set sail across the gulf for Missolonghi, where Byron had died and their next important destination, and the wind changed. They were blown west, back into the Ionian Sea, then north, back to Preveza, back to where none of them wanted to go. Then the wind changed once more and they were blown east, past Preveza, which they did not like anyhow, and on to the mainland of Greece, many rocky miles from Missolonghi.

The Malcolms had never heard of Karavassara, a tiny peasant Greek village, but Lenora told Mama, when the latter complained about the vagaries of the wind, "It is fate." Karavassara was a primitive, half-ruined village, but this did not trouble Lenora. She felt triumphant when she saw the tall Greek men in their native costumes, their donkeys, black goats, and acropolis—the last a mass of ruins but still dominant on a hill that overlooked the village.

History lived in the villagers as they welcomed the Malcolms. History lived in the Malcolms now too, and even Mama and Amy felt happy and free. The villagers, the men in short skirts and the women in long, bowed before them with a graceful simplicity. It was meeting like a family, sharing like a family, living and sharing a history. It was everyone joining hands, led by Lenora, and dancing with a Dionysiac abandon.

A little girl brought flowers and presented them to Lenora, and they became a garland upon her head. The whole village gathered around the Malcolms, and several little boys handed them clusters of grapes to eat.

Lenora could not bear this inability to communicate, and she fondled the faces of the children to express her love. She put up her hands to the sky to give thanks. She wanted to discard her clothes for the classic peplum and chlamys, but there were no such clothes in Karavassara, no stores of any kind. She wanted to talk to them, but she knew only a few words of Greek and the villagers knew nothing else.

Then a young man stepped forward. Andreas Sathinsius knew some English, had a little education, and was a shepherd who liked to read and talk. Andreas was lean, about twenty, dark, with eyes like black olives, and had the start of a mustache. He was precious at once to Lenora, and she named him Sophocles. It fitted his appearance and was much easier to pronounce. She appointed him their guide and interpreter, which made him quite proud.

Flurried but full of joy, Andreas "Sophocles" Sathinsius did not know what to make of the Malcolms. The old woman did not behave like a parent. Mama's joking with her daughters, her dancing with them, was foreign to his experience. And they liked each other, talked as if it were completely spontaneous, and he could not anticipate their next thought. They were difficult to keep up with, but they included him in their intimacy and assumed he was a well of information. And they laughed so much, when he knew laughter was a brief pleasure, always followed by some sorrow. Their quick friendship moved him, and he liked his new name. It had a fine sound the way they said it, especially their leader Lenora, who made it sound like a proclamation. So this bronze youth, his skin moist with nervousness but aglow with vitality, led them to what was the nearest thing to a hotel in Karavassara.

He isn't quite what I had in mind, Lenora reflected. He looks more like a peasant than an artist, but he is handsome and willing.

He won't disturb me, thought Amy.

He is an attractive thing with eyes that would appeal to many girls, thought Mama, but he needs a mother—his mouth is good but cruelty has tightened it.

The hotel turned out to be the one hut in the village large enough for the Malcolms. Their bed was the stone floor. When they grew so tired that the stone was of no concern, the pests made the night hideous. They were given insect powder, but the vermin seemed to thrive on it. There were no windows, yet it became very cold, and then they were given rugs which they draped on the stone floor; they draped other rugs over themselves and lay with their feet to the fire in a semicircle, with their host, wife, and seven children at the other end of the semicircle. But they told themselves they must be content, they were in their beloved Greece.

They were up very early—Mama had not slept at all and

Amy and Lenora very little—and Sophocles hired a wagon to take them on to Stratos, the next stop on the way to Athens. There were no railroads, they were tired of the sea, and Sophocles was glad to join their great adventure, to be with these at-ease people. A new and wonderful wave of friendship washed over him. Lenora, who walked like a goddess in his eyes, said they had two years to study and dance; they seemed so privileged, so ordained by fate for happiness; they refused to talk soberly, as if there would never be a day of reckoning; and they did not act with any sense of superiority. But they had some odd ideas, he thought, such as believing it was noble to be a shepherd. He told Lenora, "The land is too rough."

She asked, "What about farming?"

"It is even rougher for that, although most of us do farm. But I do not like it. When I am a little boy, I hold the horses of the richest man in the district, the baron."

"Then you decided you wanted to be rich?"

"I guess so—— No!" They were artists, weren't they?

"What about your parents?"

"They are dead."

"What did you want to be?"

"A farmer, but the land is too rocky. God does not like the Greeks."

Lenora thought the Greeks had been the most blessed by God, they had been the greatest artists, whose passion for beauty and truth had remained a permanent miracle. She said, "Don't you feel proud of being a Greek? Doesn't being one of the great race of Homer exalt you?"

He squirmed. He would be content with money, happiness, but who knew what happiness was? He said, "Yes. But it will take great luck."

"And a belief in the essential things."

Sophocles did not want to make any mistakes, and he did want to get to Athens, and a ruthlessness, born of panic, pushed him, and so he answered as he thought she wanted him to answer. He remembered what she had said when she had landed, and he repeated, "I am dedicated." He did not say to what.

A little later Lenora, an undaunted daughter of desire, led them out of Karavassara as the natives turned out to cheer their cavalcade. The natives escorted them to the outskirts, singing and dancing, and then the road got too rocky and steep for such festivity and barely wide enough for their wagon. Sophocles had hired a Greek wagon owner, with a tomato-red face, who was tremendously proud of his donkeys, his cursing, his gypsy indifference to the elements; and Lenora named him Aeneas because his name was unpronounceable and because he paused at every tavern for raki, the native wine

The raki was impregnated with resin, which at first made it quite unpalatable to the Malcolms, but after a few drinks it scarcely interfered with their drinking, and the fraternal feeling was magnificent. Everyone but Mama walked, for the wagon was filled with their luggage and several crates of grapes which Aeneas was carrying just in case these mad Americans failed to pay him properly. Mama traded insults with Aeneas and sat on a crate of grapes and to kill the taste of raki began to nibble on the grapes. The combination was like a lighted match, and as the precious juice oozed over her, Mama imagined herself Dionysus. When Aeneas begged her to stop nibbling on the grapes or there would be no profit left, she said to Lenora, "Tell him to go to hell . . . no, I mean Hades." Then she told him herself.

Aeneas retorted that she was making a cesspool of his grapes, and she yelled, "I don't want any grapes!" Mama had eaten pounds and pounds, and anyway, this wagon was riding like an elevator, and she was nobly wild, going round and round, but not mad. When the cart broke down a mile or so farther on—there were no guideposts on this road—and the country was without any signs of civilization, miles from any life, Aeneas refused to go on unless properly recompensed. The gold drachmas which followed would have paid for a dozen of his wagons, but now Mama rode proudly on one of the donkeys, while Aeneas rode on the other donkey, his long feet scraping the ground, and Sophocles, Lenora, and Amy continued to walk. By now they were exhausted but no one would admit that.

"Tired, not a wee bit," giggled Mama. "I'm not a rabbit." She was the one who insisted on stopping at the next inn for another drop of raki. She could keep up with this long-eared Aeneas, she declared. And the raki went just right with the bounce of the donkey whom she called Plato, saying his eyes were so profound. "Always remember," Mama volunteered, unable to stop talking now, "we must never waste wine."

So they moved on toward Stratos and Agrinion and Missolonghi, where Byron had died. Lenora was in the mood of Byron now, but Mama sat triumphantly upon this mass of culture, this Plato, this erudition, this Peloponnesian donkey, and now she rattled with Homeric laughter. "Drunk, not at all, I told you I am not a rabbit." Mama thought them cowards, wanting to take the boat to Patras and then the train to Athens.

"Have you no will to dare, to experiment!" Mama cried, mimicking her daughters. "Anybody can take a boat or a train, but we are the Malcolms!" She was an individualist too. Good God, did she feel like an individualist! She could be as Greek as anyone. And it was nice to be the prima donna for a change. When Mama left Aeneas at Missolonghi, they cursed each other with loud affection; she wanted to kiss him and the lovely beautiful hairy Peloponnesian donkey, her Plato, and "Why not!" she declared. "Do I have anything better to do!"

Aeneas stood at attention then, saying good-by, swearing eternal devotion. Such a mad, mad lady, Mama, but no rabbit, no rabbit indeed, and not really old.

Mama said afterward, "Did you ever see anything more beautiful than his bow! Do you know, I think he really liked me." She smiled. "What's the matter, Lenora?" Her daughter was so solemn.

"I was thinking of Byron."

"Ah, Byron, he was a professional liberator . . . and is he thinking of you?" Mama felt high enough to fly. She was having such a wonderful, happy, uninhibited time she wished it would never end. She was having so much fun, for a change, she knew it must not end.

25

Lenora was even more intoxicated, arriving at the foot of the Acropolis in Athens a few days later and climbing up toward the Parthenon.

Climbing through the barriers of air and time, through the borders of the new Athens and into the old, the very thought made Lenora ecstatic. Climbing past the Theater of Dionysus, although it was off the main route but Lenora insisted on it, Lenora led, climbing up and past the Areopagus where the apostle Paul had addressed the Athenians in the spirit of Jesus, where Orestes was reputed to have obtained absolution for the murder of his mother Clytemnestra. Climbing through the Beule Gate, past the sanctuaries of Pan and Apollo, climbing past the natives gazing at them with indifferent eyes, Lenora fitted her fancies to every resolute footstep.

Her heart overflowed with emotion, and she wanted to make love to every stone. Climbing past the Temple of Nike, the Goddess of Victory, past where Pericles and Phidias had stood and planned, Lenora cried for those laggards, Mama, Archer, and Amy, to hurry. Climbing through the lovely Propylaea, that wonder of approaches, that stood so greatly on the stern rocky slope before the Parthenon, Lenora was far ahead of the others, running, dancing, ahead of even the wiry, lean, mountain-trained Sophocles. Her energy was immense, for she was climbing with the spirit of love. Climbing on to the Acropolis itself, she danced with worship toward the Parthenon. She stood upon this promontory as if to climb into the sky itself and pierce a multitude of hearts. She resolved there must be no going back.

Archer knelt on the ground in silent prayer; Mama was too exhausted to kneel; Amy said the stone was too hard for her knees; Sophocles sat down in companionable silence. By now he thought them quite mad, yet to guide anyone else would have been sacrilege.

Lenora said, "Although the Parthenon is smaller than I expected, it towers above Athens with an astonishing arch."

Amy said, "But it is so shattered." Amy was disappointed.

Lenora said, "It is still supreme. It dominates the entire country, and not by accident. This is the Greek way of stating they could create what was just as wonderful as the sea and the mountains, both of which frame the Parthenon with a remarkable beauty. So it is in ruins. It was built in triumph, as the quintessence of hope." Now they were all listening as Lenora desired. "Each stone was placed with loving care, each stone is an expression of man's faith in himself, in his own capacity to create beauty and harmony. There is not an ounce of spare flesh on the Parthenon, on this skeleton that has so much of the life force. Someone wrote, Byron perhaps, but I am not sure, that 'though the Parthenon is in ruins, literally broken down and cast down, it is not in despair.' Whatever happens, we must never despair."

Archer said, "I always thought the Parthenon and Acropolis were the same, but now I see that the Parthenon stands upon the Acropolis, which is really a rocky plateau that rises above Athens."

Lenora said, "Yet the Parthenon is the center of the Acropolis, and the Acropolis is the center of Athens, and Athens is the center of Greece, our center." She vowed to create a dance worthy of this temple.

The family joined Lenora's vow to stay in Greece.

Mama's prayer was to love each other better and more

serenely, to be content and steadfast, and not to crave the impossible. And to the hope that Lenora, sometimes at least, would follow the smaller light of discretion. Yet none of them, ever, must feel ashamed.

That evening the family also vowed to erect a Temple of Art as worthy as the Parthenon, and obtained a pension within walking distance of it. The rooms were large, the rates reasonable, but Mama developed a skin rash, for she could not elude the pests which shared their pension. Mama could not complain, that would have been unworthy of their vows, and the view was exquisite.

Archer, usually the most stable of the Malcolms, was the one who threatened to betray their vows. Overjoyed as he was to be reunited with his family, all of whom seemed to have thrived except Mama, who had become too thin, he wanted to open a School of Acting at once, which meant opening a commonplace studio. But Lenora insisted they must find a place at the foot of the Parthenon and if that was not suitable —and it was not, as the authorities informed them emphatically—they must find a site as inspiring as the Parthenon. Lenora also was disappointed when Archer did not want to wait until they were outfitted in the clothes of the ancient Greeks. In many ways she felt closer to Archer than to anyone else, in spite of their long separation, for he was a performing artist like herself and kind and understanding about her art, but now she wondered if he was hardy enough to withstand the rigors of being a Hellene.

Lenora told him to be patient, while she searched for the garments of classic Greece in order that they could immerse themselves in this new existence. None of these garments were available except in the museums, so she had to have them made to order.

When they were finished, everyone, even a protesting Mama and a startled Sophocles, had to put on these clothes. Sophocles pretended they were a noble gesture, although as an ex-shepherd he felt they were ridiculous.

Lenora almost divorced Archer from the family when he declared that the peplum, tunic, and chlamys would hinder his acting. She disagreed, saying that with his splendid voice and understanding, plus these inspiring clothes, he would be able to exercise his genius for Greek classic theater. He gave in, overwhelmed by her arguments, although he began to wonder whether he had been wise to put the idea of coming to Greece in her impulsive mind.

Mama was more outspoken, annoyed and uncomfortable with these clothes, especially when the peplum kept falling off her shoulder. She asked Lenora, "How the devil does this thing go on?" and Lenora showed her, but the peplum kept slipping. Mama's sandals were also picking up dirt and pebbles, although Lenora assured Mama that she would become accustomed to such minor inconveniences. But when Mama was finally tied and tucked in, she said, "Very original, dear, really very original."

Lenora wondered why Mama had become so sarcastic, for Mama looked impressive in the peplum, chlamys, and the fillets for the hair. The hair was vital. Led by Lenora, the family, disregarding the discomfort of wearing unaccustomed clothes, marched down to the historic Bay of Salamis and in memory of this famous Greek victory cut their hair and threw it into the water as a gift of homage. Mama protested violently, but Lenora said that long hair was transitory and that Mama exaggerated its value. So Mama's lovely long hair, grown carefully over many years, went into the bay also.

Mama won one victory. After a few days at the pension even Lenora could not ignore the bad drinking water, the chilly nights. Lenora agreed to move into the comfortable Hôtel de la Minerve with its central heating, lifts, and baths. Lenora rationalized that it was for Mama's sake and because it was named after her favorite goddess, but she looked forward to the comfort. But the management refused to give her a suite at first because of what they called "her strange barbaric garb." Lenora reminded them that these costumes were the glory that had been Greece, and she wanted an expensive suite, and the press were flocking around this "New Maid of Athens," and finally the Malcolms were able to move into the hotel to everyone's secret relief.

The press took pictures of Lenora posing as Thaïs and captioned it:

"The American girl who made Athens gasp by wearing classic Grecian costumes in the streets and to the theaters."

Lenora's perspective actually was far more intense. For her this was the season of the maturing artist. She felt part Homer, part Athene. The Acropolis and Parthenon were always within view, and as the days passed they became even more her major focus. No impression, however, surpassed the first time she was at the Parthenon alone. She stood before the Doric columns and felt she was absorbing their harmony. Within her grew the feeling that no emotion must be held back, that here she would find her dance; and what had gone before, with all its learning and triumphs, was just a beginning.

So the early days of Athens were filled with a need to be

inspired. Lenora instilled patience in Archer—he had no choice in the matter, for she refused to start their Temple of Art until she found the perfect location and so far that had evaded her. And much of Athens was not inspiring. Many of the natives wore conventional clothes; the city itself was more French than Greek; most of the famous art was in the British Museum and the Louvre, which shocked her.

Then Lenora came into the ruins of the Theater of Dionysus, once the center of the dramatic art of Greece, and though it was a collection of ruins, all about her was the emotion of the temple, and she was inspired again. She shouted this to Sophocles, who had guided her here, and he looked confused.

She said, annoyed, "Doesn't this . . . your heritage . . . exalt you? The genius of your people is here, isn't it?"

"I don't know. I never thought about it."

"What do you want to be?"

Sophocles searched for something to say, something appropriate.

"A shepherd?"

"No." He said that with force.

"A holder of rich men's horses?"

Sophocles looked away in embarrassment.

"A poet, or perhaps a dancer?"

"It would be gracious of you to teach me." That should appeal to her, and that would give them plenty of time together.

Lenora was surprised. She had been taunting him, irritated at his matter-of-fact attitude, but dancing was not a bauble to be shone carelessly and then tossed aside. She said, prepared to cut him down with devastating irony, "You think it is easy to be a dancer?"

"I think it is very hard."

"But if you echo my feet?"

"I wouldn't do that." He had learned that she detested imitation above all else. "But you are inspiring."

"Really? And there is something inspiring about dancing, life and love and death in your body, and the eyes of the world on you. Never to have to conceal your feelings, but always express—oh, it is quite wonderful to be a dancer, resolute, dedicated, and black and blue, even as you adore your own shadow, are full of self-love, and married only to yourself. Is that why you want to be a dancer?"

This was a side of Lenora which he had not seen before, and he did not wish to sound foolish, so he did not say anything.

"Or that frightens you?" she asked, expecting him to lie.

"I am frightened already." If he was, he was also handsome with his black hair, dark face, shiny eyes, and intense manner, as attractive as Don Juan, saying, "I will do anything you ask, unless you think my wanting to be a dancer is a dream and I am mad."

They did not practice dancing then, but she taught him other arts, to sing, to recite, to give her his hand, to whet her appetite and his. And sometimes, he thought, to exasperate him, for she kept him at a distance even as she taught him. And occasionally she moved so that his body felt her movement. It stirred him, but he did not know how to respond. She did arouse his desire, even as he told himself that to pursue Lenora Malcolm, already famous, was foolhardy. Yet the quality of his service altered. Now his days were the days of youth. It was the first time he had felt like a youth, and as she tutored him in the past he felt as headstrong and giddy as she. Each day he gained a little knowledge and lost a little of the native charm which had attracted her. She was unlike any woman he had ever seen, and Sophocles felt bewitched. He debated how to embrace her even as he felt that was an impossibility, that she was merely being kind. But tomorrow became his only thought, and in his dreams he saw her naked, and felt damned as his yearnings grew. Worse, he could not tell how she really felt.

Lenora could not tell either: he lacked so many of the things she desired in a man. Despite his birth, she realized he was alien to much of the Greece she worshiped, that he was not destined to be one of the immortals, however she instructed him; and she had no intention of teaching him to dance, for he had not shown any special gift or interest. But the constant talk of Venus, or Dionysus, the constant stimulation of the open air and his dark charm made her very restless. He became nature incarnate. She had not known any man so primitive in his roots. It caused her to magnify his good looks. She referred to this often in her mind, to give herself a *raison d'être*, yet something within her kept saying not yet. She knew by now that Sophocles was not that rare and desired love, a genius who would inspire her, however she rationalized. So she wavered, torn between craving and possible disillusionment, and continued to see him daily.

Lenora also continued to search for a site for her temple, and when she found Kopanas, a hill some miles outside of Athens, but almost as high as the Acropolis which they could see from the top of Kopanas, she insisted on buying several acres at the peak—inspired by this happy coincidence. She informed her family, "We will build our temple, school, and home here."

Mama thought this land so inhospitable it was immoral. To reach the top, where Lenora intended to build the temple, Mama had to push through dense, waist-high weeds. The ground seemed mostly stone. She was sure Lenora had paid far more for the land than it was worth. But when Mama suggested a far more suitable site would be Kolonos, where the original Sophocles and Plato had lived, where they would be a short walk away from the center of Athens and living would be far more comfortable, Lenora said this was cowardice. Mama sighed wearily and gave in, although for a moment Archer seemed on the verge of supporting her.

A jubilant Lenora was full of tomorrow. At Kopanas the moon would be like a dancing girl; she would constantly face the Acropolis and lift herself toward heaven. They would live there forever. She told Archer and Amy, the practical ones, to hurry with the building of the temple and not to worry about the expense. She felt content, almost totally content.

26

A few days later Lenora gave a huge party to celebrate the purchase of Kopanas and announced that everyone was welcome. The entire family, even a reluctant Mama and a hesitant Archer, arrived at noon with the avowed intention of permanently establishing itself at Kopanas after the party. The sun was warm and the air was clear and Lenora was positive that their real inspiration could only start after they settled here. But only Amy actually agreed with Lenora.

The party was friendly, and the life of Greece swarmed about Lenora. By late afternoon she felt she had danced a hundred miles and that the natives possessed a Herculean thirst which she sought to keep up with as they toasted their new friends, the Malcolms, with a holy fervor.

Mama grew cold when the sun was gone, but Lenora said it was too splendid a party to halt for such a poor reason, although a tired Sophocles and a bored Archer agreed with Mama.

Lenora felt on the verge of something tremendous, felt face to face with the universe here at Kopanas, felt wedded to earth and sky. She experienced such a sense of resolution and exaltation it struck her as sacrilege to leave this hilltop. But when she stopped dancing and night fell she began to shiver. She found herself forced to accept the goat-hair cape which Sophocles had brought along out of his greater experience with the country weather, and she had to move into the spruce-bough hut that the previous owners of the land had built for themselves. It was hardly her choice of a temple, and it was crowded with Mama, Amy, Archer, and Sophocles alongside of her, but the mood of the fete was still on her, and she grew eloquent again describing the perfect world they were going to create here.

Mama asked, "What about the cost?"

"When the funds run out, I'll dance." Lenora was certain, however, although Mama was not, that their funds would last a long time. She could face the great truths, it was the small details she despised. But by midnight it was too cold for even Lenora to sleep. Twisting uncomfortably on the hard ground, Lenora realized that the distinction of her inspiration and hospitality were not sufficient to confine the hardships of the countryside. They were supposed to sleep on the ground, but it was brutally hard and frost had frozen it. The goat hides were warm but not warm enough as the cold seeped underneath them. There were the usual bugs which seemed to be everywhere in Greece, and they ignored the insect powder— as usual—that Mama sprinkled over the hill. It was difficult to tell which was worse, the vermin or the smell of the powder. Then just as Lenora found a spot that was almost bearable the sheep dogs began to howl in the hills, hideously.

Lenora was leaning against a huge rock on top of the hill, when Sophocles joined her. He seemed even more like a modern Apollo with his new assurance. He pretended to be surprised to see her. He acted as if it were quite by accident he had found her here, although it wasn't. She moved close to him; his flesh was warm. Suddenly he was her strength. Don Juan was remote now; she saw Don Juan in this bronze Greek. Yet as she pressed closer, ardent and impulsive, she was wondering whether he was a genuine Hellene or just a poetaster not of her faith.

He fumbled for her, his urgency eloquent, his hands impatient for her.

"Wait," she whispered, just as all seemed open to him. There was a pause, and she pulled free.

"What is wrong?" He was confused, angry.

"I hear someone coming. Stay where you are, talk about Homer or Kopanas, but talk."

They were discussing Ulysses, with Lenora providing most

of the talk when Mama wandered in front of them. Mama
moved as if in a stupor. She had to slake her thirst, but she
could not find a drop of water. Everyone was up by now, no
one had been able to sleep soundly, and so the search for
water began. They were still searching without success when
the sun arose.

They sought the shepherds who had shown them this spot,
and they were told, "You never asked about water. On Kopanas there is nothing like it."

Mama asked incredulously, "There are no springs in the
neighborhood?"

"No. But most of the springs are unsafe, anyway."

Amy announced, suddenly craving some attention, too, "I'll
dig a well. It will be our well of wisdom. It will nourish us,
cleanse us, inspire us, it will . . ." Amy threatened to surpass
Lenora's romanticism until Lenora changed the subject.

While the others retreated to Athens and the *Hôtel de la
Minerve*, Amy remained at Kopanas and supervised the creation of a well. She dug downward through the stubborn rocks
until it appeared she would come out at the other side of the
world. When even Lenora expressed concern about the speed
with which money was vanishing down the well, Amy said,
"You must not be timid." After digging many days there was
still no sign of water. Amy said this was their time of trial and
danger. Amy was not discouraged, however. She knew she
could be a discoverer and a leader also. Amy went on digging,
on and on.

Archer, unable to wait any longer, started a School of
Acting in a studio in Athens, although Lenora felt that was a
betrayal of their Temple of Art.

Lenora continued to think herself in love with dark eyes.
Many evenings now she climbed the Acropolis with
Sophocles. Mama thought this might be serious, but she had
pride. So Mama remained wordless and did the shabby, dull
details that no one admired but which kept the family together.

One night on the Acropolis, one night warmer than usual,
Sophocles swore that he would love Lenora ". . . till death
do us part."

The next night he told her how beautiful she looked against
the Parthenon and said it in haste, as if it were spontaneous.
His quick embrace was fierce, imperative. There was no place
here for unlocking all the emotion within them. So in the
depths of the night while everyone was sleeping he led her to
a dark part of the town. It still seemed spontaneous, as she
adored. But when they arrived at the room he was so much

at home in it, she knew he had not been spontaneous and uncalculating as he pretended. Suddenly she did not feel she was his "one and only love" as he swore. She wrenched free from his grasp. He begged her forgiveness, and she said, "There is nothing to forgive," but also, there was not enough to love.

The next afternoon they went walking in the hills; they sat in the sun reading Euripides; then all at once he knelt before her, asking her to marry him, now, immediately, whenever she desired. He looked tragic. He made it plain this was a life-and-death issue. He declared that they were superior souls of the same stamp—Lenora could hear herself talking now—destined to adore each other. He seized her hand and planted burning kisses upon it. He declared he would go to her mother at once.

"No," she said.

"No?" He looked bewildered. After all he had promised. "Don't you love me?"

"That is not the question."

"I will not be poor for long, and you have said yourself that I have learned much from my ancestors."

Yes, thought Lenora, he looks more like an Apollo than ever with his tall, dark, handsome urgency, but that is an illusion. Unlike her ideal, he did not scorn the world's lies. It made Lenora very sad. Young, but already a faithful follower of the drachma, he had lost his initial charm even as he remained attractive. When they strolled along Homer or Hermes streets he caught none of the daring of those heroes. He repeated that he must speak to her mother, and finally she said, "Whatever you feel you must not go to my mother!"

"It is the custom in Greece."

"I know the customs, the bad ones too. I know also that most people wish in their hearts they could abolish the custom of marriage."

"Didn't you ever love me?"

"It is for the sake of our love I tell you these things. It is safer not to marry the man you love. Then it has a chance to endure."

"You are tired of me."

Lenora grew angry at his insistence on thinking nothing but the worst. "I love you," she said, and felt she did, even as she pulled away from his embrace. "But feelings change. People fall in love believing sincerely that they will never change, but love and marriage are not the same thing. To have to see the same person every day, to have to pretend adoration when you do not feel it, to face the inevitability of seeing unhappiness come, no—marriage is not worth it."

"You are foolish. No one, not even an ignorant shepherd boy like myself, will listen to such a philosophy."

"You are neither ignorant nor a shepherd boy now." But it was odd, she thought: although she was older he was far more set in his ways. And though she would be the one blamed, for that was custom also, she cared far less for what people said. Someday she would possess that rare and desired lover, a genius of a man; then she would not care about anything else at all.

Sophocles left her at the hotel, saying, "I am not disheartened, I have no other love." He could not believe that she could love him, yet not marry him in the manner which was customary. She had taught him that they were equals, and now he believed it. The trouble was, he reflected, she was not truly a Greek girl. All the Greek girls he knew thought it bad taste to disobey their men. But she was so swollen with ecstatic brotherhood, she made his life miserable. Once they were wed, he would put a stop to this.

While Lenora waited for Sophocles to become a Homeric Greek and for Amy to find water at Kopanas—there was still no trace of water at Kopanas where Amy was still supervising the digging with feverish energy—Mama told her, "I have learned that the land at Kopanas is dry calcareous soil, that in such soil there is never any water."

Lenora said, "We will find it."

"I just told you . . . there isn't any to find."

"We would be bound with shame if we gave up now."

"You might feel ashamed, dear, but I'm leaving."

"You promised!"

"I promised nothing!"

"If you could only feel and see Greece as I do."

"I see it with your eyes, but I feel it with my skin."

"I cannot stop you if you wish to leave," said Lenora, with one of her sudden changes of mood which were becoming frequent. "You are your own liberator and your own jailer. I thought Greece would introduce you to many wonders, the very air tingles with inspiration, but if you are tired?"

"Lenora, I am not tired!"

"You think that if we just survive, we should be satisfied?"

Mama paused and reflected, I am a stranger to Lenora in so many ways now. Lenora does not know that I am a hardy perennial too, even if I cannot propitiate her with any more sacrifices. Then Mama was annoyed at herself for this display of self-pity and weakness. She had been too hard on Lenora: Lenora must know she understood her dancing. Mama said, "I know you want to transform dancing into a serious, profound art."

"That is why I came to Greece. I am not copying figures from Greek sculpture, I am studying them. And in studying them, I am learning how to study nature. In nature it is natural to move spontaneously, instinctively. But when we become civilized we inhibit our natural impulses, and ignore the universe around us. The Greeks were smarter, they were always aware of the universe, and to express this awareness, they danced."

They looked at each other across the years, recalling the early enthusiasms, San Francisco and other discouragements and how they had conquered them, recalling Daly, and he had said, "This is not for the stage," but Ellen Terry, whom Daly had admired enormously, had called it "the most beutiful dancing in the world."

Lenora said, "I have to stay here. I must learn to be an inspired dancer, as the Greeks were inspired artists." And Mama reacted as Lenora expected. Mama remained, bound by pride and all the years of memory and aspiration. No, it was not being patient or good, as Lenora said. It was something she could not help, as inevitable as life and death and insecurity.

But the temple of Kopanas remained elusive as Amy failed to find water, although she reported regularly that the well was progressing and that she expected to strike water at any moment. Lenora, just as regularly, gave Amy money to go on and searched for her inspiration elsewhere. Sophocles had taken a job with an importer, and she seldom saw him now. She pretended it did not matter, but she was disappointed by his apparent indifference.

To prepare for her first Greek recital she visited the ancient Theater of Bacchus and danced there as the Greeks of long ago had danced, a riotous dance. Other times she danced the measured step of those who had worshiped at the Parthenon. Still other times she danced at the foot of Mount Pentelicus. And still other times Lenora came to the oracle at Delphi, now in ruins, and moved with a slow, processional pace. And there were the patterns she followed in the hills, when she was nature personified, her companions Pan and Silenus, when she danced with complete abandon.

Much of this went into her first Greek recital, and it was acclaimed, especially when she did her encores draped in the blue and white flag of Greece. Mama was jubilant when Lenora was requested to repeat this for the King. Lenora saw Sophocles standing in the wings during this command performance and sensed that he had not given up the chase. He had been busy earning money so he could support her, but he had no chance to talk to her, for afterward she was told the King wanted to see her. The King praised her, but she was disappointed, for he said nothing about subsidizing her temple, which she felt was his national duty.

So Lenora announced that she was going to build her own temple at Kopanas without any outside aid but that it would remain free to all Greeks who worshiped beauty. To Lenora, her funds were limitless. But when she wired Lothar for money, he replied there was none left. She was indignant. She wired back, demanding to know where the money had gone, and Lothar informed her that she had spent it on Greece—particularly her well at Kopanas.

Lenora went to her bank in Athens and was told that she had a small balance, enough for about another week at the present rate of withdrawals, and that was all. Lenora was irate: why hadn't they told her sooner? She knew money did not last forever, but who wanted it to! It was the well which was dry, not her art. She had earned one fortune, she would earn another.

Lenora exchanged more wires with Lothar in Berlin, who informed her that now she was overdrawn, now she had to return. They spent the next few days arguing about this, by wire, which she sent him collect, even as she lived in a damn-the-expense style with growing defiance and fell deeper into debt. Just as it seemed impossible to solve this impasse Lothar wired that he could get her an engagement at Bayreuth. Cosima Wagner herself, the widow and cultural heiress of Richard Wagner, one of Lenora's idols, wanted Lenora to dance the "Bacchanale" in *Tannhäuser*. No American artist had ever performed at Bayreuth, added Lothar, the invitation was an enormous honor. So Lenora agreed to dance at Bayreuth, if an advance was forthcoming. An advance was, out of the pocket of Lothar.

Archer was relieved to leave Greece. He wanted to return to modern clothes, to New York, where he was sure he could star in character leads. He vowed to never again wear the peplum, tunic, and chlamys, it had interfered so with his acting, a vow he intended to keep.

Amy decided to return to Berlin to teach privately and to investigate the possibilities of opening a school.

Mama was accompanying Lenora to Bayreuth, since she needed a rest, and Bayreuth was located in beautiful, peaceful country.

And Lenora assumed that Sophocles was remaining in Greece. For a moment she envied him. She walked to where she and Sophocles almost had known love. Then, thinking of how she could revolutionize the ballet at Bayreuth, she forgot the pain and grief of leaving Greece. Now the future rushed in, and the need for change, and suddenly she felt inspired by Bayreuth, and she could not wait to leave.

Lenora had stayed five months in Greece, but now it seemed a year.

Yet at the railroad station a few days later Lenora said she would never forget Greece. There was a crowd at the station, and she threw kisses to all of them, turned to join Mama, Amy, and Archer, and saw Sophocles standing before her. Sophocles looked so romantic, his dark eyes glowing, and everybody was talking about loving everybody else, and suddenly she yearned for him. Why hadn't he come sooner? A day, a week ago? Sounding angry although she did not want to, she asked, "What do you want?"

He winced, said awkwardly, "I came . . . came . . ." He had come to ask to go with her, or to beg her to stay, but he was young, so young in the ways of the world despite the money he had earned, money to provide for her, and he lacked the courage to express his yearnings.

She said, "Good-by."

He did not want to take her seriously, but he was confused. He stood uncertainly and murmured "good-by" obediently, too obediently for Lenora, but he was also overwhelmed by the magnificence of the public farewell, and it made him feel insignificant. His eyes filled; hers did too. He had given some of her life wings. That was real, that was worth remembering.

A mist brooded over the Parthenon, like her tears. There was snow on Mount Pentelicus and Mount Olympus as the Malcolms passed these peaks on their way out of Greece. Lenora remembered what the Greek philosopher Heraclitus had said: "There is nothing permanent in the world but change."

It was strange. Change had become home.

BOOK FIVE

27

You are Lenora Malcolm. Your dream is still original and splendid. There is no risk of oblivion now. On the continent you are one of the most widely known of Americans. Your dancing and your personal life have seen to that.

Budapest has called you "fantastic."

Munich has called you "the divine, the sainted Lenora."

Athens has acclaimed you as her daughter.

And Berlin insists that it is your home.

Yet you still provoke ridicule. There are critics who sneer at your pursuit of beauty, who claim you are flat-footed and pretentious, who call you a freak. But you say criticism does not matter. You walk with an open, free stride. You are Lenora Malcolm. You are becoming so well known that nothing else is necessary. You are even excellent box office. But you are an artist among artists. You are Lenora Malcolm who never wanted to be anybody else. The dream has no horizons now. You are becoming a way of life.

So after what had become a millennium in Greece, and many lovely pictures of Lenora posing before the Parthenon —which had managed to find their way back to Paris and Berlin and New York, thanks to Lenora's awareness of their publicity value—Lenora settled in Bayreuth. She was determined once more to be loved, to live at the top of her emotion, to find as much *Gemütlichkeit* in Bayreuth as she had found in Munich.

Mama sought to share Lenora's adoration of this small provincial town in the Franconia hills of Bavaria, but from the start she disliked Bayreuth. She could not abide the tourists who overran the town. She felt that while the tourists pretended to listen to Wagner with religious yearning, actually the music gave them a sensuous response. This struck Mama as false, as accepting the passion of Wagner as a substitute for their own. Then Lenora lodged her in an expensive hotel which was crowded and uncomfortable, and she was too close to the memory of poverty to accept the exorbitant prices with equanimity. To Mama all the items were too high. Everything about Bayreuth became money-grabbing to Mama.

Mama was also upset by Lenora's evident preference for other company. It was as if her daughter found her ancient, and Mama was mortified. She grew very lonesome. She was stricken with self-pity, which hitherto she had scorned as weakness. She became envious of Lenora's youth and energy. She felt that Lenora, the visionary, was losing her vision when it came to Mama. And she was so tired of Lenora's constant projecting toward the ultimate, wherever Lenora was.

Yet they loved each other. Mama repeated that to herself, to put her own mind at rest. But when Lenora ordered her to wear what Lenora was wearing, a Greek robe of cream-colored silk and a pair of Greek gold sandals, Mama refused. Lenora desired to look like a bacchante, which fitted her role in *Tannhäuser,* but Mama felt absurd in such a costume.

This offended Lenora. It was as if Mama was betraying her. She stopped discussing her plans with Mama.

Gradually everything came to displease Mama. When Lenora proposed taking her to visit Frau Cosima Wagner, Richard Wagner's widow and the ruler of Bayreuth, Mama pleaded a headache and remained in the hotel. Pale and feverish, she did not argue when Lenora suggested a vacation.

Lenora kissed Mama with a show of affection, but soon after Mama joined Amy in Berlin, where Amy was teaching.

Lenora felt delightfully free now. She rented a rural retreat and furnished it as a sanctuary for poetry and beauty. There was always open house; everyone was welcome, as long as they were artists, or witty, beauty-loving people. Beauty was absolute and all that mattered.

Thus, the first days of Bayreuth, as with the first days of Athens, were the best yet. She was within walking distance of the Villa Wahnfried, the home of Cosima Wagner and the tomb of Richard Wagner. She loved the broad streets, the picturesque view from the Festival Theater which overlooked Bayreuth. Lenora saw Bayreuth as the perfect German community, the epitome of German romanticism. She was disappointed in the tourists, who were often loud and vulgar, but she enjoyed the way they gaped at her. Everyone was talking

about the audacity of the barefoot Lenora Malcolm, dressed
in Greek robes, and stared at her as she drove about the town
in an elegant carriage.

Frau Cosima, sympathetic to her aspirations, regarded her
as half nymph, half *Wunderkind*. After a few minutes of
earnest conversation Frau Cosima seemed to Lenora noble,
sensitive, and a fellow worshiper of beauty. Frau Cosima
blushed at Lenora's seminudity, but she applauded when Lenora said, "I have adored German philosophy all my life, and
now that I am twenty-two I am giving my art, which that
philosophy has broadened, to Germany!" She had just passed
her twenty-sixth birthday, but she was so happy she hardly
felt twenty. She was the feature of the festival this year.

But when she came on for her first rehearsals of
Tannhäuser she felt very unhappy. It seemed impossible to
combine the cool clarity of the Greeks with the heated sensuality of Wagner. Caught between these opposites, she hated
herself for being afraid she could not bridge the worlds of the
Grecian Venus and the Germanic Venus. So Lenora sought to
be ecstatic yet profound, but Wagner's music was full of
spells, incantations, and tricks, and she abhorred tricks. As
Lenora wrestled through these difficult days Villa Wahnfried
became her refuge. It was like a medieval court, and in its
sumptuous ritual Frau Cosima was the empress.

Frau Cosima assured Lenora that she would be pleasing in
performance and prayed that Lenora would wear sufficient
clothes and be the box-office attraction she expected. Lenora
did not wish to be just pleasing; she hungered to express the
voluptuous longings of Tannhäuser. So utterly did she desire
this, she practiced with a new frenzy. Yet much was lacking.
She knew that herself, no matter how much Frau Cosima
praised her. She could not express love when she did not feel
love.

Troubled, disconsolate, uncertain, and passionately craving
love—for *Tannhäuser* was flooded with it—she decided there
was only one remedy: she must find a lover to inspire her.
That should not be difficult, she reflected, there were so many
geniuses and near-geniuses in Bayreuth for the music festival.

She surveyed the field carefully. She became friendly with
Weingartner, Humperdinck, Mottl, and Richter, all famous
musicians, with the eminent Wagnerite Bernard Shaw. After
her failure with Sophocles she was determined that her inspiration be of the highest intellectual order. She also became
friendly with King Ferdinand of Bulgaria, the Grand Duke of
Hesse, but she knew love with them would be insufficiently

intellectual. She thought of Siegfried Wagner, he was the closest tie to the great Richard Wagner, but he was intent on being a businessman, and that depressed her.

Her choice became Otto Harz, music historian and biographer. Otto was a younger version of Rodin: stocky, with a massive head and a vast forehead, old enough to be experienced and young enough to be vital. And he was the most erudite man she had ever met.

Lenora invited Otto to her retreat to discuss *Tannhäuser*— he was an authority on Wagner's music—and she was delighted when he accepted. It was after a long and arduous rehearsal of *Tannhäuser*, an early summer evening, and the weather was warm. She wore her most sensuous robe, light and transparent. She put the music of *Tannhäuser* on her gramophone, and as the music swelled with passion she expected him to lift her to a towering summit of emotion.

Instead, he strode up and down her studio, ignoring the music, talking at great length about the intensity of his conscience, of the rich sadness of his life, that the critics failed to understand him. He treated Lenora to champagne, which he borrowed from her. He declared his devotion to their mutual greatness and to the magnificent work he was writing. He said no one had ever given him a sense of glory like Lenora and that he treasured this. He seemed on the verge of a grand pronouncement, and she leaned toward him, radiant and vulnerable, and he spoke earnestly about the temptations that had assailed Saint Augustine, he was writing a critical study of the author of the famed *Confessiones*, and how his hero had been most magnificent when resisting the temptations, and that his book must capture this.

Lenora felt miserable. Otto must see how expectant she was, how yearning and exposed. Then, just as she felt worn out from waiting, he came close. He seemed about to consummate the long-desired contact, but seeing her glowing eyes and eager mouth, he said, "It would be profane."

"In Bayreuth?"

"Anywhere!"

"But how could it be profane when Bayreuth is dedicated to love?"

"You are very sensitive, Lenora. You are a genuine romanticist." He smiled to make certain she knew this was a compliment. "You are the most beautiful and inspiring creature in the entire festival."

She stood so that he could see all of her vibrant body

through her sheer robes. She was almost naked but not quite, yet her naked self was close.

He did not come any closer, but his sonorous voice became an amorous opera in itself. Subtle and caressing now, it lingered over her with such a voluptuous allure, she felt she belonged totally to him. He spoke of her as a goddess who had triumphed. He repeated that she had the genius to arouse the adulation of a genius.

She was certain now that their spirits were fused in anguish and exaltation. But when he finished speaking, although his words embraced her and she felt possessed, she was exhausted. When he was gone, after a brief farewell, she felt sick from craving, yet craved him even more.

She could not sleep for craving him, his words, this constant excitation of her senses which was becoming a constant aphrodisiac.

She could not concentrate on rehearsals. Just before the opening of *Tannhäuser,* afraid she would be unable to dance in such a chaotic state, she resolved to bring matters to a head. She decorated her studio with flowers whose sensuous scent was overwhelming. She wore a robe of the sheerest white silk. When he arrived to discuss his newest section on Saint Augustine with her, she led him into her studio. He looked at her sternly. She grew pink as a little child, a feeling she detested, but she said gently, "I am as interested in Saint Augustine as you are, Otto."

He stood at the door of her studio as if to depart.

"I really do want to discuss him, Otto."

"You do not have to beg."

"I am not begging," she said in exasperation.

"It cannot be helped. I am bound to cause my friends distress, for I reside in the pure mountain air of philosophy. Lenora, you know that I do not care about myself as a human being, but this book must not be lost." Not for any reason, he thought. This prodigally sensual Lenora must not be tempted too far, must not test him too far, or he would lose her as his inspiration. "It doesn't matter what we are, it is only our work that counts."

She did not reply.

Feeling noble, he turned his back on her and started away.

"Otto," she called.

This time he did not reply. He stood as if in renunciation.

"Otto," she repeated. Still he was motionless, and her tension grew. Perhaps she was not fit for his courage and wisdom, yet lately she had endured as much as Saint Augustine, and more. "Your feeling is noble."

"Yes, it is poignant and true." Inspired, he exerted his sensuous speech upon her once more. He felt even stronger than Saint Augustine as he deliberately invited Lenora to tempt him, yet refused her.

Gradually, however, in the days that passed, Lenora transferred the yearnings he aroused to the role of Venus. As she rehearsed she explored the new desires Otto had awakened in her. She became a Teutonic Venus, heavier, more voluptuous, in an intense and anguished craving for fulfillment. It was bewildering and wonderful. One moment she felt transported with desire, the next tortured with frustration.

The day she prepared for her first performance of *Tannhäuser,* to the most crowded house of the season, she was overflowing with emotion. She put on her most revealing, most daring robe. She felt transfigured, a true Venus, about to dance a passionate bacchanal. Yet she prepared herself gravely, saying she must also dance renunciation, like Otto and his Saint Augustine.

Frau Cosima was shocked when she saw Lenora's near-naked appearance. She ordered Lenora to put on more clothes, and Lenora refused, saying, "When you see a dancer you don't want to see clothes, you want to see the body."

Frau Cosima's face grew gaunt. She said, "Child, you make a bad joke."

"Do you want an understudy to dance it, without rehearsal?"

"But to see almost all of your legs, your shoulders, your bosom?"

"You have to be Venus to dance the 'Venusberg Music.' "

The stage manager was calling for Lenora, every one of the 1450 seats were filled to see "The Malcolm." Frau Cosima hurriedly compromised; she unfastened her shawl and threw it over Lenora's shoulders to cover the latter's half-exposed breasts. But Lenora discarded the shawl in the wings. She came on in her scanty robe. A gasp rose from the audience. Never before had a dancer appeared at Bayreuth so nearly naked, yet she looked Venus, she was Venus, she was the erotic dreams of Tannhäuser. Her frustrations from her near affair with Otto made her perfect for the "Bacchanale." She thrust her pent-up longing for him into her dancing. Her fertile years of dancing were also her lovers. She danced with the symmetry of the Parthenon, with the intensity of Rodin. She danced with her beautiful bare arms lifted high, with all her rapture. Was it wrong to long for love, her body seemed to say. A sin to be free? To be the voice of love in the wilderness?

The audience gave Lenora an ovation usually given only to tenors, and unheard of for a dancer. In the wings even the stolid stage hands were watching and applauding. The opera had come to sensuous life because of Lenora. The audience wanted to be where she was, off on the whirlwind.

28

Lenora's dance triumph in *Tannhäuser* brought renewed requests to dance throughout Germany. But she said no, that to do anything else now would be sacrilege, that all else in Germany was music hall alongside Bayreuth.

Frau Cosima beamed at her with a saturnine beatification and looked very wise. Siegfried praised her in his pontifical manner, sounding as infallible as his father, and stated in his best Herr Wagner tones that he would write in a special ballet just for her in his next grand opera.

But when Otto arrived at her retreat after the opening of *Tannhäuser* she was stretched out on her chaise longue like Venus. He told her how nobly she had danced, how she had conveyed suffering passion and enlightenment.

"You saw me dance?" There had been no trace of him at the opening.

"I always see you dance, wherever I am."

She wanted to fall at his feet and beg his forgiveness, but that would have been uncomfortable. Moreover, she longed for homage also. So with a languid gesture she sank back against the silk cushions and waited.

"Lenora, you could be overwhelming."

Her eyes blurred with tears. She felt a sudden quickening of her senses.

"But you should spend more time making yourself spiritual."

She did not know whether to be ashamed or angry.

"Then you would complete the act of destiny. Then with your art mankind would know the pain of greatness. You would be another Saint Augustine."

"I tried." She felt so parched emotionally, she wanted to beg for mercy.

"To sacrifice oneself is to grow great." He was on his knees, his hands clasped to hers in prayer.

"Is sacrifice what you really want from me?"

"It is what the world wants. Follow the path I have marked, and you will be the foremost." She wondered aloud how could she match his heroic spirit, and he stared at her with renewed fire. He enlarged his theme to a sermon about the ineffectual flesh and the joy of renunciation.

He seemed about to embrace her, finally. It was very romantic and sad. He eased toward her and then just as subtly eased away from her. He stared at her as if he were taking a picture of her for all eternity. She wanted to give of herself until the pain of desire was out of her, to drown in his emotions, to love, love, love. But Otto looked like Cain now. He gripped her fiercely with his gaze and then abruptly tore himself away. Her heart felt about to burst, and he left her with the image of her sacrifice and his.

The next day Otto went on a lecture tour of Germany. His subject was Saint Augustine and the triumph of renunciation.

It was intolerable that she spend the evenings alone; however, she wanted to follow Otto's precepts. Lenora gave frequent parties after the performances of *Tannhäuser,* and though the pleasure from them vanished almost immediately, it was less painful than being alone. And while she was gay, she felt gay; while she was adored, she felt adored. Her retreat was furnished with luxurious couches, the revels were loud and late, often until dawn; Lenora dressed in robes which were exciting, dramatic; her talk was provocative and full of enigmatic laughter.

At the Festival Theater the audiences continued to acclaim her, and she remained the sensation of *Tannhäuser,* but there were no new roles to dance. Lenora offered her art for the *Ring,* and Siegfried said she was a miracle in *Tannhäuser* and could not find any place for her ardor elsewhere. Neither Siegfried nor Frau Cosima told Lenora how distressed they had been when the main publicity in the American newspapers had been about "the American dancer," that there had been no mention of their enormous ballet company, the most enormous in all of Europe. Moreover, they believed that Lenora regarded Bayreuth as a preparation for work, not a goal in itself.

Then the festival came to an end, and Frau Cosima gave an enormous supper to which the entire personnel was invited.

After much effort Lenora got a moment alone with Frau Cosima. Frau Cosima was sitting austere and silent; she was almost too austere for Lenora. For a moment Lenora longed to smash down Frau Cosima's walls, so that Frau Cosima would not be unapproachable, so that Frau Cosima would do one impulsive thing, just once!

The stern dark face that was Frau Cosima turned toward Lenora and said, "I think I know what you have come to ask me, mademoiselle. My severity, you can be certain, comes from my sympathy. You dance divinely, but others will have to be satisfied with their own poor tastes and talents."

"I don't want to talk about myself. I want to speak to you about creating a school for children in Bayreuth. Oh, not just to train them to dance, but to give them the heritage of beauty to which they are entitled."

"It is impractical."

"Here in Bayreuth? Where you have the greatest resources in the world? Think of the children you could inspire, encourage, who would adore you!"

Frau Cosima was silent. A protective court formed around her.

Lenora was exasperated at being unable to reach Frau Cosima. Impulsively now she was on fire with a desire to fight for what had become the greatest of causes—youth! What could be finer than to set youth against decrepitude, the future against the past! Yet the circle around Frau Cosima was discussing plans to raise a million marks in order to build a new theater. Everybody seemed so tedious.

Lenora wrote Mama and Amy in Berlin that she had to see them at once, and when they arrived in Bayreuth she explained the urgency. "You must help me establish a school. For children. That will be our Temple of Art." She rushed into Mama's arms, her face shining.

And Mama, who had resolved to be casual, to climb back each step at a time or not at all, if necessary, was joined irresistibly to her in this instant.

Lenora rushed on, "We will develop gifted children in no time at all."

Mama said, "I find children fascinating. It is the adults who complicate things."

Amy said, "What about the business details?"

Lenora said, "You handle the money."

Amy was irritated until Lenora added that Amy would be a partner and supervise all instruction. Teaching was deeply rooted in Amy; she desired active sharing, not submission.

Amy raised no more questions about the school, while Mama thought, if Lenora could only have the strength and patience to wait for the right man and not have to throw all of herself into every romantic situation. If Lenora could only compromise sometimes, or learn that love—even when it was living with all her senses aroused to the highest pitch, as if every instant of it was unforgettable—was seldom decisive and often a waste.

Mama and Amy had agreed fully with Lenora on the wisdom of opening a school in Berlin when Otto came back to Bayreuth. Once again he appeared to be reaching out to her, but there was no physical intimacy between them. Otto remained the fanatical, disquieting visionary; he was still transfigured with his own renunciation, his own suffering. He was certain it would bring her the same bliss. But once again he lit her with a blazing desire. When it came time to part it was more than Lenora could endure. She pressed toward him, to swallow and to be swallowed up, to yield and to be yielded to, and he withdrew and cried, "What insanity is this?"

"It is not. It is . . ." She could not say what she felt.

"It would be madness," he said. "It would ruin everything."

"Is there no alternative?" she asked.

"No. But it has been beautiful," he assured her. "I will remember your heavenly inspiration all my life." Then, as he said good-by, for the first and only time, he kissed her.

29

In a few days Lenora found an ideal location for her school, a large mansion in Grunewald, a suburb southwest of Berlin. She had to pay what Lothar regarded as an exorbitant sum for the building and the grounds, but she insisted it was worth the expenditure.

"Grunewald means green woods," she told him. "Royal green woods."

Lothar knew that. What he did not know was her ultimate intention.

"I am offering my school to Germany."

"For nothing?" His impresario instincts were shocked.

"For their good. Victor, I need your help."

He pointed at her body, said, "That is your help."

"I need your great gift of enthusiasm. Tell them what we

know, that to dance is to live, that Grunewald is the answer to the Philistines."

"Here—in Berlin?"

"Berlin is an enlightened city."

"Berlin is Babylon, with Prussian trimmings. The music and art are only a kind of fat to hide the bones of militarism."

But there was no dissuading Lenora. Her eyes shone with a holy light as she continued to denounce the Philistines while Lothar reluctantly agreed to prepare the announcement of the opening of her school. To improve his disposition and her bank account, which was depleted by the demands of the school, she resumed her recitals. She kept them down to four matinees a week, although there was a demand for more. She said that more would exhaust her.

It was a treasured day when the school was ready at Grunewald. Lenora could hardly contain herself as she and Mama and Amy went there for the opening. The school was the fulfillment of one of her most precious dreams. She wanted to dance all the way.

Amy loved the neighborhood; it was one of the most fashionable suburbs of Berlin. This was one of the best of Lenora's dreams, she thought, one she could follow a long way.

There were tears in Mama's eyes. They had come so far, she reflected. She was proud of her daughters. Here, between the three of them, Mama vowed, life would blossom with lovely children.

Stately Ionic columns stood before the entrance. Just within the front door was a bust of Schiller and his poem to the muse of the dance. The main dancing hall ran the length of the mansion, and over the floor was spread a blue carpet. A grand piano, almost hidden beneath flowers, was in a corner to furnish the best music for the pupils. Mama caressed the piano. She had imagined a piano like this for Chopin or Liszt, but not for Lena Malcolm, a shy unknown piano teacher. This piano must have been fabulously expensive, and they must have all lost their senses, and yet the truth was, Mama told herself, this was the spirit of Lenora and the measure of her span.

The school was arranged to accept fifteen children. The classrooms contained fifteen desks, there were fifteen charming beds, and a dining room simply but tastefully designed to seat comfortably fifteen little girls and their teachers. Mama thought better quarters would have been impossible to find. All of the school was flooded with light and air. From the great ballroom to the neat sleeping quarters was the same spotless order. "A noble idea," said Mama. "It must work."

"We are here," said Lenora. "Didn't Aunt Jessie say, ten years ago, that was impossible!" Lenora's arms rose as if to embrace the universe.

No one could move in this manner and not look ridiculous but Lenora, thought Mama. Lenora is manifestly transported, and nothing will deter her. Of all the changing things this child has become the most changing and mysterious. This child has avoided monotony as if it were a plague and at the same time has grown, gone away, returned, and gone away again with an inexhaustible yearning for change. Yet each time she has returned to me, no matter where she has gone or to whom. In truth, what is my daughter but an American who has gone in search of the far places; what is her constant changing but a function of her energy and a need to experience *the now?*

Lenora's rules for admission were printed widely. They stated:

"All that Miss Malcolm requires is that the children who come to her shall be between the ages of six and twelve, and that their parents must agree that the children remain under her tutelage until they are twenty. They must be normal physically and mentally, note the word is normal, not perfect or exceptional.

The support of the school comes out of Miss Malcolm's private fortune, and not even a child of a millionaire can pay tuition, if it is fortunate enough to win her approval. The school is absolutely free, and all the children will be clothed, fed, and educated from childhood to maturity without money or price.

No performance by the school will be given for money. Nor can money buy Miss Malcolm's services as a teacher.

Yet Miss Malcolm will supervise all the instructions, personally and individually, and will be supported by Miss Amy Malcolm, Mrs. Lena Malcolm, other teachers, and a trained nurse.

The child will be allowed one day a month at home with his or her family and about five weeks' vacation in summer. There are no restrictions as to race, creed, or social position.

Only one thing is preferred: youth. 'You cannot teach them,' Miss Malcolm maintains, 'after childhood is past. Dancing requires the plastic body and mind. Dancing is an expression of life and must begin with life's beginning.'

Applicants will be welcome at the Grunewald Academy, Trauden Strasse, Grunewald. Miss Malcolm will receive them on Tuesday and Friday, from 2 to 4 and 6 to 8 P.M. respectively."

Such a crowd gathered before the school the police had to be called out to restore order, and the street in front of the mansion had to be closed to all traffic. The applicants wanted to see Lenora first, to congratulate her on choosing their child. Lenora was surrounded in the hallway by parents and children. To catch her breath and to bring order out of this chaos, Lenora announced that the selecting would take place in the ballroom. In an instant the ballroom was jammed, its beautiful floor scratched, several precious statues broken, the crowd coming at her like a cavalry charge.

The worst catastrophe was Lenora's costume. She had worn her long floating coat of blue crepe de Chine, but in the rush to reach her, to clutch at this *gottliche* Lenora, as if the very touch would make them acceptable, they had torn the crepe de Chine, and half of it was gone.

Mama, however, restored order and led Lenora in front of the assembled parents and children. The applause was tremendous. This made the selecting of the fifteen girls even more difficult. They all seemed to love her, and she loved them too. She repeated that in English and German. The children crowded closer, all sizes and shapes and sorts. Lenora longed to take them all, but there were many times fifteen in front of her. Lenora held up her hand for them to wait, knowing that if they embraced her, all judgment would vanish. She said, "What the world needs, my friends, is more love."

"But what good will that do!" cried one mother. "I know my child is a born dancer!"

Another mother declared, "What has love to do with dancing?"

Another said, "My child is beautiful enough."

A fourth said, "Look at my daughter's soul."

A cynic said, "Children fed and clothed without strings. I don't believe it."

Then there was the belligerent mother who insisted that her young darling came straight from nature.

After the more insistent applicants were weeded out, Lenora sought to be logical. But every time a child appealed to her, she was lost: she wanted to adopt this child at once. Finally, Amy decided to use energy and other physical things as a test. Amy ordered the children to walk across the room. Some sought to dance, some tried to walk like ladies, stiff and proper, some marched like soldiers, and a few, the minority, were natural.

They took the children who walked best, but Lenora also chose a child who was as ethereal as an angel, another because she felt sorry for a frail six-year-old and thought good food would help this child. She also found herself taking several four-year-olds, although it was against the stated regulations, desiring to mother them. She made certain that some of the girls were daughters of German peasants and artisans; she selected two girls solely because they were robust. Half believing in phrenology, she also chose several girls because she liked the shape of their heads. The pretentious parents she avoided as the plague. Lenora chose another child because of her faunlike run, another because of her impudence, another who seemed life-intoxicated.

Here the auditions, such as they were, stopped. Amy ushered out those who had not been chosen. Then Lenora served champagne to the parents of the chosen, to celebrate the happy event. Lenora took several heavy draughts. Suddenly she was afraid. But this was unworthy of her ideals; the champagne revived her; now she felt like a soldier in a battle.

The champagne loosened Mama's tongue. She and a few of the mothers whose children had been accepted made speeches of mutual admiration. But some of the mothers were hysterical when they had to say good-by to their children, and most of the leave-takings were difficult.

Soon after the school began in earnest. Mama made it warm and lovable; Amy made it efficient; Lenora made it inspirational. Mama also had passionate fits of neatness, as a counterweight to Lenora's untidiness. She tried to make the children understand the benefits of cleanliness without feeling guilty. She encouraged them to snuggle within her warmth, while at the same time she enforced certain rules.

Lenora's first major chore consisted of changing the clothes of the children. They arrived wearing many petticoats, clodlike shoes, which struck her as madness. She told Mama and Amy, "In these clothes the children are trussed fowls. We'll make them free." The children were put in simple tunics of Lenora's designing. They resembled a Greek tunic, styled for comfort and freedom. They were a dainty blue, with a touch of pink added by Mama. Sandals were supplied for the house, while they were given commodious shoes for the street, fitted correctly to the foot, and blue and white cloaks and capes to match. The children were taught to be proud of their costumes.

Within a few days most of the children were very happy. When the parents came to see them at the end of the first week, the parents were the outsiders. The children, except for a few, acknowledged their parents briefly and then rushed off to the more exciting activities of the school.

Amy assured the parents, "It is not unusual for children to act this way." She sore a one-piece dress, because fitted clothes disturbed her essential center of gravity. Amy, a small woman with a pert face and a little-girl voice, looked like a timid field mouse and had a will of iron. She added, "Our dancing is for use, for learning how to live."

Amy believed in rules, and she established them firmly. At seven each morning a musical bell awoke the children, and they were marched quickly to the showers. After they were rubbed dry and dressed to the sound of music, they combined singing with breathing exercises. Breakfast consisted of milk, fruit, cereals, and hot cocoa for those children who were chilled. The rest of the morning was devoted to history, languages, literature, singing, and drama. Lunch came at noon and stressed fruit and green vegetables, but no meat or candy. The next hour was devoted to walks through the woods and to play in the gardens. Tea was served at three, and then the last hours of the afternoon were devoted exclusively to dancing—outdoors when the weather permitted. The afternoon dancing session was the most popular part of the day, for this was when Lenora led. Supper was served at six, then the children occupied themselves with games. At eight in the evening all the children retired.

Special teachers took care of the morning sessions, there was a nurse on the grounds, but the heart of the school remained the dancing.

Lenora told the children with ferocity, "Thou art the chosen. Your movements must grow out of nature." She illustrated with great intensity.

During these periods of emotional excitement, Lenora wore Greek robes draped high over one shoulder, leaving her other arm bare, and was adored by the children who regarded her as a goddess. When visitors asked them, "Don't you miss your mothers?" most of them replied, "Lenora is our mother, our art mother," and felt a bit divine themselves. Several of the older girls stated, much as Lenora did, "Art mothers are more important to the world than physical mothers. Even cats and dogs have physical mothers, but only artists have art mothers."

When visitors objected, claiming this was a manipulated attitude, Lenora retorted, "It is time the children learned the truth."

And when there was public grumbling about this, and Mama warned Lenora against feeling freer than she was, Lenora replied, "It is the truth, and I will keep on teaching them

what I feel." Lenora rushed on with greater abandon, leading
the children in singing:

"Dancing is the foundation of life. I prefer death to a life
without dancing. Dancing is the soul of the universe."

The child who disobeyed was not punished. Instead, Lenora
said, "I am not angry," and looked so sad the disobedient
child usually ended in tears.

Amy complained to Mama that this was a poor, uncertain
way to discipline children, and Mama said, "Lenora is a great
artist, and one of her best works of art is herself. Admitted,
she poses sometimes. Can you say her poses are untrue to her
character or emotion?"

"No. But we must have a method, an order to our discipline."

"Amy, dear, she will be off on another tour soon, and then
we can modify some of her more romantic ideals."

"She swears she will never leave the children."

Mama smiled patiently. "With Lenora, never is a short
time. You know how soon we will need more money to keep
the school going." Mama, however, was not alarmed; since
the birth of the school she had gained a new vitality.

Little by little Amy was able to assert herself in the dancing
classes. When Lenora had a matinee in Berlin, or was delayed
—which was often—Amy took advantage of the lovely autumn weather and gave the children their dancing lessons in
the woods. The air's tang was invigorating, and Amy spoke
earnestly to the children, and they seemed to understand the
fineness of dancing in the open air, so that when they came to
dance on the stage they must always imagine they were in the
open air. Amy felt closer to Lenora then. Although Amy
lacked Lenora's grandeur, she possessed an astonishing force
of her own. When the children danced as she suggested she
was extremely pleased. When no one was looking she rewarded them with kisses and books.

Lenora had no intention of leaving her children, but gradually, after a month of matinees, her audiences began to dwin-
dle. Yet she was offended when Lothar said, "If you want to
keep your school in existence, you will have to tour, and I can
get your school very well known by having you dance in St.
Petersburg, the home of the ballet."

Lenora repeated, "I will not leave my children."

But when Lothar said, "You are afraid to tour in Russia,
afraid of what the ballet masters there will say about you,"
she was angry.

"Oh!" she cried out. "They think themselves unusual, but

they have not created anything original. Ballet is a hang-over from the past."

Alternately goading and warning her, Lothar said, "I hear that Russian women are the most supple in the world, and—"

"Gymnasts," she growled. She still had no intention of touring Russia, but when a creditor threatened to padlock her school she borrowed money from Lothar to avert such a disaster and agreed to go to Russia.

Archer had obtained several good roles in America, but no starring ones, and she would not have asked him for money in any case. And suddenly, after not having missed him for a long time, the thought of going to mysterious, remote Russia made her miss her brother very much. She was uneasy as she said good-by to Mama, Amy, and the children. Several of the children cried. It made Lenora uncomfortable, surly. She longed to rejoice with the children, and already she was bound by responsibility.

Then Lothar said she should have a maid, and she did not want a maid. A maid would get in the way if she fell in love, and she could always hire one in St. Petersburg. But she mentioned none of this when Lothar asked, with shocked surprise, "Why do you want to go alone?"

Instead, she flared, "Because I am not getting soft. Because all I need is myself, my art, and my blue curtains."

Although Lothar said nothing more there was a touch of apprehension in him at the thought of her traveling alone which she could not forget. Crossing the border between Germany and Russia, alone, it had become a matter of pride now. She felt she was traveling into yesterday.

30

Lenora's first week in Russia was to be forever stamped on her memory as the week split into two emotions: one of terror and one of triumph. Of what happened in St. Petersburg this week of January 22, 1905, she was always to have the most vivid recollection.

Lenora expected Russia, in all its brilliance and majesty, to be waiting for her at the railway station. She knew that as the first dancer to dance in her bare feet she was a historic curiosity in toe-shod Russia. But it was far past midnight when she reached St. Petersburg, the Warsaw Station was lonely and desolate and empty except for a special-guard regiment posted outside the station, and suddenly she sensed a harshness and constraint in the air. Shaken by this display of military might, she felt naked standing in the center of the station, even though she was surrounded by her impressive luggage. She was told that she could go to her hotel, but there were no conveyances to be found.

How long Lenora stood there she could not tell, but when she heard an English voice it was as if from another world. Brian Pomeroy introduced himself as a correspondent for a London newspaper. He knew her name without an introduction. He pointed to her trunks on which was blazoned in large gold letters: LENORA MALCOLM. He knew who Lenora Malcolm was, that she was dancing in St. Petersburg, and that he intended to see her dance.

Brian was tall, slim, with a face a little too thin to be handsome, and his eyes were worried. He was not calm in spite of his quiet voice, but he seemed to know the city thoroughly. His ability to communicate was a comfort, and he understood her problem at once. He said he would be honored if she shared his carriage. He ignored the show of military force, as if the ominous guard about the station was an everyday occurrence.

He did not tell Lenora that after what had happened this Sunday many expected all of Russia to burst into revolution. God knows, he thought, she was not prepared for such violence. He noticed she was hatless, although the night was so cold it numbed the flesh, that her coat was thin and without fur. And that she wore sandals, as advertised, which might be comfortable for traveling, but which were utterly impossible in the below-zero weather of this night. He thought her feet large, and perhaps that was why she danced in her bare feet and not just to create a commotion. He liked her ankles, which were lovely and well shaped, but thought her legs heavy for a dancer, although he was pleased that they were not knotted like those of the ballerinas he knew. Her face was ruddy and healthy-looking, almost English, he decided, in its show of vigor. She was larger than any of the ballerinas who performed in the Imperial Ballet, and he wondered if she would shock them as much as they would shock her.

The contrast could be most amusing, and disastrous. Didn't she know how different she was? Certainly to judge from her manner and appearance Lenora Malcolm was no longer a girl or an innocent.

Lenora liked Brian at once. Her manner grew more

assured. To have an attractive man escort her was worth some discomfort. She considered it one of the more interesting forms of flattery.

And yet, when they were outside, sitting in the carriage he had hired, her apprehensions came back to haunt her. The ballet was a stupid confectioner's dream, she was positive, but would any of the Russians agree with her? Lothar had insisted she would conquer—aye, to conquer, that was the challenge she could never resist, but what then? This was not a new world, but an older, darker, colder one. Never had she felt such gloom, such cold, such an immensity of snow and ice. These soldiers, giants as befitted those belonging to the Imperial Guard, standing with fixed bayonets about the station, made her feel as if these bayonets were pointing at her heart. She knew that Russia was at war with Japan, but she had not expected the symptoms to penetrate as far from the battlefields as St. Petersburg.

Brian wrapped her in furs; only the tip of her nose showed, but she continued to freeze. Even before they started her arms and legs were so cold they felt like sticks of ice. She had a horrible moment of dread, afraid she would never have any feeling in her body, afraid she would never be able to dance again. No, no—that was unthinkable. Such a possibility did not exist, and if it did it would be intolerable. No, she indeed, rooted to the earth, gathering her strength and sustenance from the good good earth, would dance always, as long as she drew breath.

But to draw breath came hard. The air was raw and terrible. Breathing was no longer the most natural thing she could do, but spitting ice. The wind that swept through the city swept through her. The night was strangely quiet and strangely black.

St. Petersburg was a city of the dead. What had Gogol written and Tolstoi and Dostoyevsky, and she realized how little she knew about Imperial Russia, Great Russia, Terrible Russia, Barbaric Russia, Russia at War.

Her dread grew as the carriage wheeled slowly off the main avenue and turned down a back street. Brian did not explain, and she did not ask.

Lenora sank into a corner of the carriage, all sense of adventure gone, her teeth chattering violently. The snow drove more pitilessly with each passing moment.

Brian whispered that it was a bad storm but nothing compared to what the streets of St. Petersburg had seen earlier that day.

"What storm?" she mumbled between frozen lips.

"I saw them go down," he said, shivering.

"Who went down?"

He could not seem to open his lips.

Down the back street they went, down what was hardly a street, through snowdrifts and snowbanks as high as houses, through an indistinct immensity as terrifying as death. She felt perched in space, a frozen figment of her own imagination. She tried to reassure herself by thinking this was someone's home, there were houses and children and warm hearths just beyond the driving snow, but what terrified her the most was the possibility that this might not be true. The streets of St. Petersburg were the dreariest she had ever seen. The cold was so biting now it seemed to come from the North Pole.

They were near the hotel of Mechailoff Street when she heard the sound of many feet in the snow. The coachman sat up abruptly. He had to halt, their way blocked. They could not turn the corner into Mechailoff Street as a procession approached. At first it was just a blurred shape, then gradually Lenora saw people dragging things by hand.

The people were also marching, she thought, but no, marching was not it; they were being dragged along by forces stronger than themselves.

Brian cursed, the driver cringed against his seat, and she saw that it was an immense mass funeral. Her horror grew as she saw many crude coffins laid upon lumber sledges and being dragged by hand. Most horrifying of all were the corpses of those too poor to afford a closed coffin, which were spread out on a pile of boards. There were no horses to pull the sledges, nor the usual priest ahead of the mass funeral. There were men and women prostrate in the snow, exhausted from the pulling, unable to go another step, yet to remain motionless meant death. Vicious gusts drove many of the coffins into the huge snowdrifts on the sides of the street. She wanted to help them, and Brian said it was useless—there were too many of them and they were beyond help. The women were covered with shawls which furnished no protection at all, and the funeral column had to halt when the wind swept most fiercely, the mourners cowering in the doorways and then making their way behind the funeral until the next blast drove them to a new shelter.

Then a sound rose that Lenora was never to forget. The mourners seemed possessed. They sobbed as one, with a melancholy she had never heard before. Their anguish had a sense of hopelessness that stung like a laceration. It was constant now, and obscene with pain. Brian whispered, "They are weeping for their loved ones shot down. It was horrible."

She said, "What happened?"

"They have to bury their dead now or not have them buried at all."

"Why won't the government allow them to be buried normally?" Suddenly this seemed to Lenora the greatest blessing life could bestow.

The mourners were gone except for those who had collapsed in the snowdrifts, or who had been dragged into doorways to rest or die. Brian ordered the driver to move on, and when Brian mastered his shivering he explained, "The government is afraid that a mass funeral, done openly, will explode into a public demonstration. The government prefers to throw them through the ice, as it did yesterday. Those who did not die in the streets in front of the Winter Palace, died in the Neva, shoved through the ice."

The wailing had blended into the shriek of the wind. Lenora was about to shout back, it cannot be true, this was a nightmare, when Cossacks came trotting down the street. They wore bashlyks which protected their heads from the piercing wind. They carried carbines slung across their shoulders, and their stirrups were covered with felt and straw to keep off the cold. Despite the hour this vigorous, alert cavalcade was a magnificent sight. Their colonel checked Lenora and Brian's visas and warned them this was no time to be on the streets of St. Petersburg. He was a cultured man who spoke excellent English, but in this moment Lenora hated him with a murderous rage which mounted as Brian told her what happened yesterday.

She forgot her frostbitten arms and legs, the fear that she would never dance again. When they reached her hotel she insisted he join her for a drink. Her suite was lavish, in Imperial gold, a small replica of the ballroom of the Winter Palace, but she could not get the wailing out of her mind. She had never heard a story which shook her more as Brian went on.

"It started innocently enough with a strike by workers who wanted an eight-hour day and better wages. They decided to present a petition for better working conditions to the Czar himself, believing that as their Little Father, once he knew the truth, he would redress their grievances.

"But when Czar Nicholas refused to see them, they set out on a pilgrimage to his Winter Palace. It was Sunday morning, they were unarmed, they were sure the Czar would listen to them. The workmen brought their wives and children along to show their peaceful intentions, and Father Gopon, a liberal priest, marched at their head carrying the largest crucifix I ever saw. They looked as if they were on a Sunday picnic.

They were determined about only one thing—they wanted to see the Czar. They did not know that the Czar had left the Winter Palace for Tsarskoe-Selo, some miles from St. Petersburg, because he was afraid to meet them. He had placed between them and himself fifty thousand soldiers under the command of Grand Duke Vladimir.

"I had heard rumors that the parade would be met with force, but I could not believe it, even when the marchers were ordered to halt by the Ismailovsky Guards, the Czar's favorite regiment. An order to disperse was ignored; I doubt anybody but the first few rows of marchers heard it, and they were too hemmed in by those behind them to move anywhere but forward.

"At the same time I could see the cold faces of the guard regiment, proud that they were the Czar's favorites, proud that nothing could move them, but proud that they were Russians too, I thought. They will not shoot their own people, I told myself, especially since they are in no danger themselves.

"But when another order to disperse was ignored, when the people shouted to the Imperial Guard, 'Brothers, we are not Japanese, do not brutalize us,' a volley rang out, as if the soldiers took this as a taunt rather than as a plea for mercy, and men, women, and children fell in bloody heaps. Oddly enough, this seemed to encourage the soldiers and another volley rang out. Many women were shot in the back as they tried to escape. I saw children with smashed thighs, crushed skulls. Splashes of blood stained the snow, and the Cossacks charged to clear the square, to carry out the order to disperse. Then, and only then, did the crowd cry out in pain and rage: 'Give us *Konstitutsia! Konstitutsia!*'

"I saw the grand duke, who had ordered this massacre, standing on the high pedestal before the Winter Palace, but his face was gray, as if only now he realized the consequences of his act. In front of him was the statue commemorating the defeat of Napoleon, growing red with blood as dying petitioners tried to grab it to keep from collapsing into the snow and frozen death. Bloody ikons were everywhere, and more corpses than I could count.

"I ran then, for the Cossacks, still on the move, were not being selective. I ran also, to file my story, which I sent out with a friend of mine on the Warsaw train, hidden in his boots to elude the censorship.

"And soon the world will know this has been a day of unspeakable horror in St. Petersburg, and nothing will happen. Oh, there will be some protests, but that will be all.

One of the reasons your train was so late was that strikers tore up part of the Warsaw and Baltic Railroad in protest, but that will only make the oppression worse. The government will put St. Petersburg under a state of siege and use that as an excuse to throw into prison anyone they dislike. It is as if the Russian people have jumped into an everlasting deep hole, a bloody, bloody hole."

Brian Pomeroy halted, looking tense, defeated, sad.

There was circulation in Lenora's arms and legs now, but she stiffened with a feeling of outrage, as if this attack had been made upon herself; she found herself in this moment fiercely in conflict with the authorities here.

Brian reminded her that it was almost dawn, and he had work to do. Anything could still happen, and he had to be on the scene, but he agreed to come to her Russian debut as her guest—if there was a debut. He had heard that all the theaters had been closed, to prevent crowds from assembling, but perhaps in a few days—perhaps everything would be back to normal, or should he say abnormal, he smiled cynically.

They shook hands and said good-by almost formally. They looked at each other for a moment more with a troubled and unhappy expression, as if there was something else to say. But neither could express it. Whatever communion they had felt this bloody night had vanished with the coming of the sun. Lenora had a disappointed, confused sense of the night being incomplete if he left this way, and then he was gone.

The snow had stopped. The sky was clear now. The sun was a crimson glow of fire. But it was impossible to fall asleep that morning.

Tossing, tossing, tossing, Lenora roamed in these nightmarish hours down the bloody, snow-covered streets of St. Petersburg. She saw herself one step ahead of a Cossack with a huge saber, about to chop off her legs, one slippery step ahead, fleeing, slipping, falling into the frozen night. Her dreams, relived in this half-awake, half-asleep state, were a constant battle to retrace the midnight journey, to find the bloody tracks and erase them. But the tracks were lost in the huge labyrinth of her chaotic dreams.

31

All that next long day troops marched past the hotel. Nothing was open, neither theater nor ballet nor restaurant. No one came to see her, not Lothar's representative in St. Petersburg, not even Brian. Lenora wept by her window, feeling she was in a bitter exile. She was warned to keep off the streets, on which she could be shot at. Rumors prevailed and wiped out all sense of security: rumors that revolution was spreading over Russia; rumors that thousands were in jail and that thousands more had been slain.

And Lenora, who felt herself the rare, fine artist, the sensitive, certain artist, the artist who admitted no weakness, could not rid herself of bewilderment and doubt. She was assailed with the uncertainty of solitude and loneliness, which she hated. It inhabited the walls of the hotel, the numb and chilling vacancy of the streets. She felt without friends, without hope, which was even worse, and in a silent world, as forlorn as she had ever felt.

And why did her toes ache so!

She lifted her foot quickly from the floor, but the cold was not there; it was in her bones, her flesh, her blood. She tried the simple movements of standing, walking, and running, but the pain did not go away. If anything, it got worse. It was as if her legs had lost the better part of their feeling. When she touched them there was only pain. She had not exercised strenuously, yet she felt helpless and idiotic. Here she was in the stronghold of the ballet, and there was no rapture. She felt heavy and anxious instead of exuberant.

What if this ache would never go away?

Suddenly, furiously, Lenora beat her legs against the floor.

Oh, darling, darling legs! Why don't I feel a current of blood?

She could not find words for her doubt and bewilderment. She wiped the tears off her cheeks. She tried a new step, but the ache remained.

She gathered what strength she had left to control her emotions, and ordered a hot bath, the hottest available. So hot that she thought she could not endure it, and she almost fainted from the heat and steam, but she held on to the sides of the bathtub, swearing she would never let go until blood

and strength came back to her legs. Her face colored; she felt
waterlogged; but gradually her legs became part of her again.

When she was able to stand without pain, then walk and
run a little, she felt as if a miracle had come to pass. She slept
a little, hurried over her breakfast, and when Brian came
through the door the next morning she ran to greet him,
relieved, almost gay, although some of the ache had returned
to her legs. But if she could dance again she could endure
anything. "What is happening outside?"

"St. Petersburg has been placed in a state of siege. Many
think revolution is imminent. Some say it will be as terrible as
the French revolution, but I don't believe it. I think the government is merely using that as an excuse to throw more
people in jail."

When she asked about those shot down, their survivors, he
changed the subject. She was surprised at his fear, for she was
sure it was that. Thus, although she had intended to suggest
love, her estimate of him went down. No one she cared about
could be less than herself. She said, "Can't you do something
about it?"

"I have to consider how the government will react when
they learn what I have reported," he said.

"You are not a Russian citizen. I would tell them to go to
hell."

"And get bloody well kicked out of here."

"Fine."

"It is different for you. They will forgive your criticism.
You are an artist. They will say you are bound to be illogical,
that you merely want to attract attention, that every artist is
allowed a certain amount of foolishness."

Lenora was shocked. Brian sounded as if he believed this
slander too. There was a silence, and then she spoke quietly
but intensely. "When I was a child I was taught that the artist
should strive for perfection. But when I looked around me, I
saw no perfection. When I said this people laughed at me—I
was a child, I was making funny remarks, I was a female, and
who ever heard of a female having ideas? It was unnatural,
they said. But what men saw, I saw. What you saw the other
night, I saw. Should I cut off that half of life? Should I say
there is no perfection, and never will be? Should I dance, so
disillusioned, and yet expect to display perfection on stage?
Should I worry about what people will say? If I did I would
have stopped dancing long ago. I would not be here, I would
not be Lenora Malcolm. But for better or worse, I am Lenora
Malcolm. I am arrogant, they say, and proud, and dogmatic,
and poppycock, and dance only when the spirit moves me.

Do you know how many thousands of years I have studied and practiced to become a dancer? Lenora Malcolm with her vanity, her dreams, wants perfection, but what right does she have to expect that? As long as there are no fatal consequences to her, to those she loves, why should she care? Nothing really shines the way it should, there is no perfection, that is the way it is, accept it, resign yourself to it, but whatever happens, don't attempt to reach perfection, that childhood fancy, that——"

"I'm sorry, Lenora, I——".

"No. I must try to make the world a better place, silly or stupid or whatever that might be. So my children, and I will have children, will not hate me when they grow up. So when I dance perfection, when I dance Chopin and Schubert and even Beethoven and Bach some day, I will not dance a lie."

They heard the crunch-crunch of hoofs on the snow, and they hurried to the window. Three special-guard regiments rode by: the Preobrajensky Guards in their brilliant gold uniforms; the Pavolosky Guards in their striking bronze helmets, catching the sun as they passed; and the Czarina's personal regiment, all in black. Brian said, "Just the same, wherever you go, make sure you have your visa, your American one." Then he followed the soldiers, for where the soldiers were there would be news.

The next day, however, the city seemed to have resumed some of its normal appearance. Lenora noticed, though, that the inhabitants were nervous, sullen, and she was still advised to stay indoors. A fine, damp snow was falling again, and only occasionally did she hear troops clatter by. Lothar's representative in St. Petersburg informed her that the ballet would open first, as befitted its Imperial patronage, and then the theaters, and that her debut might be permitted within a week, provided law and order prevailed.

In the memories in which she took refuge the mourners she had seen became the world for her, and she had to explore it. It was not just sympathy that accounted for this immersion. It was anger, and what came from her nature, her inheritance, from Mama's teachings, from the way the Malcolms had grown up. And so Lenora sought the core of her recital in Blake and his *Auguries of Innocence,* in his:

> *"To see a World in a Grain of Sand*
> *And a Heaven in a Wild Flower,*
> *Hold Infinity in the palm of your hand*
> *And Eternity in an hour."*

She pondered these lines, thinking how she should tell their story. How lovely these words were, and true, and she began to feel the dance movements that would express them. She went back to the time she had been a little girl. That had been a good time, a time of innocence, and now she was far away from these feelings. Yet she was still beautiful. Staring into her mirror, she knew that in this, at least, she had not altered. And when she felt sad she caught the heart of her program: the Chopin who was the sad, sentimental spirit of Poland, also oppressed by the Czar. Suddenly she was full of her old zest, although there was still some ache in her legs. She stopped dancing only when she saw Brian at the door with tickets for the ballet. She embraced him and shouted how good it was to see him.

"Yes," he said, looking flustered and backing away. "They gave me tickets for a box where you will have a perfect view of the ballet."

"I detest ballet," she said.

"They want you to be their special guest."

"That is really insulting." But she agreed to come, and she was not insulted but delighted, yet still determined not to be won over, however they cajoled her.

At the Marinsky Theater she was offended when she heard that she had come to St. Petersburg to join the Imperial Ballet. For an instant she almost shouted that down, but Brian said, "No one really believes that."

"Bravo! You have put an end to all rumors!"

Brian sighed deeply. "It is not true. Isn't that enough?"

"No one here will understand my dancing." She hummed a few measures of a Chopin waltz, then said abruptly, "This audience does not deserve to understand." Brian tried to assure her that they would, but she waved that aside. Lenora had made up her mind that she would be misunderstood, and she took a morbid relish in the thought.

Lenora, of course, had not the slightest intention of being misunderstood. But as she sat in the opulent Marinsky Theater, which did not resemble a temple in any way, it awakened the memories of all the ballets she had detested. The Marinsky had many tiers, and the gilding and crimson brocade draperies were as lavish as any she had ever seen, and as conventional. She recalled the ballet lessons in San Francisco, and tonight, in the Marinsky, although the curtain had not yet risen, she had the same horrible feeling of a rope closing around her.

Depressed and unhappy, she glanced at Brian sitting quietly by her side with his faultless grooming. She wanted to feel an immense wave of love and tenderness for him, but he was not her lover, or a lover; there was nothing of Don Juan or Otto in him. Yet he served her emotional purposes, and for the moment that was sufficient.

The last time Lenora had seen *Giselle* had been years ago. She had a strong feeling this was the same production. It possessed the same empty gestures and marble postures of the other *Giselle*. But the Russians had been lavish about it. There were tons of scenery, expensive and spectacular. To Lenora, after what she had seen on the streets of St. Petersburg a few nights before, this was an ugly and deliberate evasion, an anachronism, everything in the best taste of a hundred years ago. There was not the slightest suggestion of feeling. It struck her that no expense had been spared to make the dancing dull. But what offended her even more were the costumes, which greatly hampered any ease of movement. The dancers wore tight corsets, packets of voluminous tarlatans which started at the waistline and came to far below the knee, and headdresses and wigs so ornamented and huge they were grotesque. This was a seamstresses' holiday, she thought, but where was the intensity, the inspiration? No one was without stockings, and then the performances . . . Oh God! she cried to herself. He is not a dancer, he is an acrobat. She got so angry she became dizzy and her legs shook. This was absurd. She had not seen such uninspired dancing since she had left Augustin Daly. The dancers were saying absolutely nothing at all. None of them were of the sacred few. Even when a ballerina commanded the stage there was no inspiration for Lenora. She struck Lenora as a technician, not an artist. Her dancing was fireworks—it startled but it had no meaning. Lenora wearied of her at once. What difference did it make how many pirouettes she did! But the ballerina went on spinning, all the quicker, justifying her technique by a few extra turns on her points.

Lenora was feeling miserable when a frail-looking ballerina danced onto the stage. The huge Marinsky dwarfed her. It pained Lenora to see this very thin young woman, who looked as if she needed feeding, so exposed. She waited for an extension of the tedium of the program, but this ballerina made no effort to command attention by fireworks or by outdoing the acrobatics of the others. In spite of her frailness, or perhaps because of it, this dancer moved with a delicacy that was astonishing.

Brian whispered, "It is Anna Pavlova, first soloist."

Pavlova's expressive face seemed to merge with the expressiveness of her body so that the whole became a single instrument.

Pavlova, Lenora thought, had a style of her own, even with the limitations of the conventional ballet. Pavlova danced across the stage and made the improbable probable. Pavlova stood on her toes and distracted Lenora from the stilted language of the ballet by the loveliness of her motion. There seemed no weight to her as she left the earth. Lenora forgot her anger at the ballet; the dancer had become more vital than the technique.

Lenora heard people in the next box whispering that Pavlova was not dancing with the music, that Pavlova was forcing the music to follow her, and Lenora shushed them with a peremptory, "Quiet!"

In such a moment Lenora could not restrain herself. The instant the ballet ended she hurried backstage, Brian trailing her, Brian forgotten, the need to have a man in attendance forgotten, everything forgotten in this instant but the vision of loveliness on stage. Generous, magnanimously generous, Lenora swept into Pavlova's dressing room, past her maid, dresser, past the admirers, and threw her arms around the ballerina. Lenora, taller and heavier, threatened to overwhelm the frail ballerina, and for a moment Pavlova was startled, not certain whether this was an assault or a wooing.

Then someone shouted, "It is the American," and Pavlova smiled in acknowledgment of this tribute.

The next few minutes passed in a babble of bad French; Lenora with her American accent, Pavlova with her Russian accent. Lenora paced up and down in a whirl of wordless ecstasy, for her French was totally inadequate to express what she felt. She was filled with love and praise. She was sure Pavlova had the same fire she had, even if they did express the sacred flame differently.

Pavlova stared at this strange American and wondered how such a tall and thickset young woman could be light and lifting on stage. Pavlova was puzzled also by the confident charm, the enormous sincerity—it was so enormous it could hardly be true—and yet the American was not praising anyone else. Indeed, the American seemed uncomfortable when other dancers came into the conversation and grew angry when the ballets themselves were praised. For a moment Pavlova thought the American would explode, her face became so ruddy when the production of *Giselle* was lauded.

Champagne was served and soothed the momentary irritation, although Pavlova said nothing about Lenora's dancing.

Nothing at all; no, we are not competitors, Lenora wanted to shout in her face, suddenly sorry that she had been so generous with praise, then just as sorry that she had this moment of spite.

Saying good-by, Lenora gave Pavlova a final affectionate embrace and received a polite bow in return. Lenora knew most ballerinas hated other ballerinas and only masked their hostility with superficial politeness. But Pavlova was a genius, Pavlova should be above such pettiness, Pavlova had no need of such jealousy. She caught Pavlova smiling slyly to her maid. This ballerina was as skeptical as all the others, thought Lenora; this ballerina will hope and expect me to fail.

It was almost more than Lenora could endure. She swelled with a great need to justify herself, and then she was furious at herself for feeling this. Pavlova, all of them, were not lovers she had to win. How could she tell Pavlova that she did not care for what Pavlova danced, even though she did care for Pavlova. To be less than generous was to be less than life itself. But it was a great strain not to lose her temper. She found herself saying to herself: you cannot allow me to be less than myself. You know my all-or-nothing spirit. They must see and feel more than a pale sweet face. I must be one with mother earth, whatever their scorn. My dancing must be life lived extraordinarily. Give me strength to dance like a goddess, I must not half give, half receive.

Lenora rushed out of the dressing room even faster than she had entered. Brian was waiting for her, but she was not waiting for him. She was too angry to maintain even the illusion of courtship.

The moment she felt anything, she thought, she felt too much.

The day of her debut she saw no one. By now the massacre was buried in the past and order had settled over St. Petersburg, and it seemed incredible that anything as harsh and malevolent as the massacre had occurred. But Lenora could not forget; she vowed she would never forget. She was nervous, irritable, and resentful. Although the city seemed cowed into submissiveness there was a tension underneath, and this added to her urge to rebel, to shock.

Self-communion, however, did not serve her well this day. Her legs still had a touch of numbness, and though she bathed them again, massaged them, and there was life in them again, she did not trust them. She did not trust anything, except her own heart, and even that was not charged with communication today. She wanted each dance tonight to be as if it were a first. But how to combine nature and the joy and vigor of living with what she had to express about the mourners, it was too difficult, too much of a struggle; she conquered one imperfection, and a dozen others sprouted and were ludicrous and upsetting. She began to feel it was impossible to dance precisely as she felt, to embrace Russia's pain as well as pleasure.

And when she lay in bed for several hours before going to the theater, missing Mama, Amy, even Archer, surprised by this sudden nostalgia, for she had come alone to Russia of her own choice, her loneliness was like a death. Tears came to her eyes. Tears for herself, for what Mama had written: "Russia must be very exciting."

Mama's letter made her loneliness worse. The letter was full of Mama's characteristic hope and enthusiasm. Be brave, be vigorous, it said.

It reminded her how Mama's letters were always for Lenora, for her core, for her dreams, for never taking No, for never taking less than the best.

Yet, reflected Lenora, Mama was tired and aging and must be missing her also, even more painfully. But Mama was writing about the children, how much they were improving, and so was the school, and would she please be careful, the Berlin newspapers said St. Petersburg was quiet now, but Lenora could be so impulsive.

The letter caused Lenora to recall even more vividly Mama's teaching them, encouraging them, transforming them into beings greater than herself. Needing Mama, Lenora became doubly aware of Mama's life-giving essence. Mama would never admit discouragement, whatever her doubts, but always threw herself with impetuousness and generosity into anyone who needed encouragement, provided the *anyone* had a vestige of talent. Lenora was crying now, missing her even more. How could she replace the irreplaceable!

Lenora was still trembling when a maid arrived to give her a final body massage, but all her feelings had come to a focus, thanks to Mama. The maid came highly recommended by Lothar's representative in St. Petersburg, but she spoke a poor French, her square features were like a stone face, her middle-aged drabness chilled Lenora. Lenora found it unnerving in this moment of intense feeling to be touched physically, especially by one so uninspiring, and to feel on her legs the pressure of strange hands, and more tears came to her eyes. She wanted to tell the Russian maid that her tears were not from fear or self-pity but for others not so fortunate, perhaps for the maid's own family and friends. For once, however,

Lenora could not tell someone else what was in her heart. It would have to wait until she faced her audience, and then several things would happen:

Pavlova, Diaghilev, Fokine, the grand dukes would say: ". . . so she skips about the stage, runs and turns, is that dancing?"

Or, she hoped, cry out: ". . . this is the essence of our life and she is the experience thereof and the constant reminder. She is the extraordinary life lived extraordinarily."

After another full body massage the maid wrapped Lenora in blankets and had her carried to a waiting carriage. Lenora remained blanketed to keep all her muscles warm, but as they drove to the theater she saw fires in the distance. She was told they were the bivouac fires where infantrymen slept with stacked rifles. It almost broke her mood.

The theater was simpler and smaller than the Marinsky, for Lothar had selected it to fit the intimate simplicity of her dancing. She realized he had been wise, that this theater was far more suitable for her art than the Marinsky. Much of the audience was in full dress and evening gown, a world of wealth, fashion, and art, the most influential and sophisticated in Russia, and it had come to jeer—who ever heard of an American who could dance? Or a barefoot dancer who was artistic? Others came to be shocked; to dance barefooted was not in good taste. And as Pavlova had said, the American was much too tall and thickset, an absurd body for a dancer.

Good enough she might not be, she thought, but great enough she must be.

So she made them wait. When Lothar's representative warned her to take the Chopin "Funeral March" off her program, because it might offend the aristocratic audience, she refused. "I cannot change my program for anybody," she said decisively. Not even for the Czar himself, she meant. "I have promised to dance Chopin, and the "Funeral March" is one of his finest compositions."

The burly, dark manager tried to argue with her, shouting, "Are you out of your mind?" and she shut the door in his face. Did he really think she would change now!

The audience, expecting the introductory flare of an orchestra, was startled when she appeared before the simple blue curtains without a sound. They were disappointed too, for there was nothing extraordinary or odd about her appearance, except her remarkable simplicity. Her arms hung at her sides, her whole attitude suggested extreme attention, reflection, waiting. Her costume was a soft, diaphanous Greek robe, also simple in the extreme, of a lovely, quiet gray. Then the audience gasped. The American was in her bare feet, and her legs were uncovered. This was shocking, or heroic, the audience was not sure which. But still Lenora did not move. She waited quietly as the music began. A marvelous stillness prevailed; the audience found itself listening as she was listening. Then she turned as if with the roll of the earth. Lenora was propelled by the certitude of her feeling. She was positive they sat in front of her with their unbelief, trusting it to destroy her—as they had destroyed the marchers, and now she swept across the stage feeling born reckless.

Brian, trying to understand the truth of this experience, was spellbound, enslaved by the contrast she created, by the fascination of her feeling. She was much too reckless to be loved, but it was startling—her feeling was the only feeling possible at this moment. Strange, and very exciting, as everything about her demanded feel, feel, feel!

How long the American stood motionless by the blue curtain Pavlova could not tell. Not very long, a few seconds perhaps, but suddenly the ballerina felt a strange sensation down her backbone. The music seemed to fill the American to overflowing. The lightly clad figure leapt forward with the freest, most abandoned gesture imaginable and began to dance. No, it was not dancing, Pavlova told herself, it was beyond any such formality. Pavlova, who had come to sneer, was startled. The American depended on none of the usual things which gave a dancer security, such as technique, specific choreography, beautiful scenery, a phenomenal balance, prodigious virtuosity—and yet she was enchanting. The American was dancing across the stage to her own secret music. It was not even Chopin actually, thought Pavlova, although that was the music that was being played. The beat of the music was heavy by comparison with the American. It was unbelievable that this should be the case, but Lenora Malcolm was existing in obvious defiance of the laws of gravity. She was not making her way through space; space was bowing humbly and getting out of her way. As she lifted herself about the stage, the stage took on some of her lightness; when she reached toward the audience, the audience took on her emotion. Pavlova no longer found it difficult to feel the nymph the American was dancing; it was as if the American came first and that the nymphs had been imitating her for years. Yet Pavlova did not understand what Lenora Malcolm was saying, although she knew the American was trying to say something significant. And it did not matter, and Pavlova did not care. It was enough that this dancing was a marvelous expression of feeling and intoxication.

On the stage Lenora felt nothing now but her own pain that there was no love in St. Petersburg, city of massacres, pain for her sweet mother not sharing all this attention, pain for the great searching eyes that looked and saw not, pain for those killed before their time, pain for those silent with so much within them to say.

When she sensed that the audience was completely intent on her, she began to dance Poland struggling, Poland oppressed, Poland free. It was her memorium to the shot-down citizens of St. Petersburg, to all those slain by the Czar's tyranny; it was an inescapable urgency in her. Her movements became ironic, sad, pitiful. She suggested a mournful twilight, a pale Chopin dancing to his death. And as the phrase *dancing to his death* drummed in her, she sought to surpass all that had gone before in her finale. The music was Chopin's "Funeral March," and she was sure even the stupid would comprehend. She appeared in a red tunic, looking tragic and passionate, and as she intended she heard the audience gasp. Full of revolt and intense suffering, she ran across the stage with a fearful concentration. Her hair blew down in disorder, and on her face and body could be felt the marks of grief and doom. Before she was halfway done she knew everyone was looking and listening. The familiar funeral music seemed to pursue her even more then, and she filled the theater with her feeling.

Suddenly, unexpectedly, it was over. The music ended and she stopped, just as abruptly as she had begun. And now an unrehearsed effect took place. Instead of leaving the stage, Lenora paused in the center, lifted her beautiful arms upward, and stood motionless like the Winged Victory of Samothrace.

It was very upsetting to Pavlova, thinking, the American is taking every advantage of the audience's feeling, of the feeling she has aroused, but it is the truth, her truth. Pavlova knew that it was impossible to expect this free dancing to succeed, it was so without form and rules, and so new, and the American had no chance at all, and the audience was standing and cheering, Pavlova with them, and the old, familiar barrier between artist and audience was shattered by a thousand enthusiasts.

When Lenora came out of the stage door of the theater and her admirers still cried bravo and took off their fur coats and spread them over the icy ground in front of her carriage, she felt the equal of Bernhardt and Duse.

Brian was by her side, but she did not want Brian; she wanted a genius, equal to herself. Brian was saying how wonderful she was, and her mind was elsewhere, although she answered him with a simple "Thank you." She stiffened before the rush of pride her thoughts gave her, and she tried to tell herself she was only an instrument, but she did not believe that.

And more praise came toward her in the form of Pavlova, with an invitation to come to a magnificent party that was being given in her honor.

Lenora said, "I am tired."

Pavlova said, "In this cold, naturally. You will come, tomorrow?"

"I'll try." It was like a command performance, and Lenora knew that when she went she would have to be prepared for anything.

32

The following evening, with an unreal ease and audacity, she met the world of ballet face to face. Lenora entered the salon of Pavlova, all in white, in a simple but lovely robe which reached to the floor, its lines as direct and dramatic as those of the Parthenon, and which set her off with a glow of heavenly innocence. She looked like an angel although she felt like a devil, prepared to storm this citadel of the ballet. She could hear the gasp that went up at the sight of her costume, so striking in its simplicity and so startling by contrast with the lavish evening gowns. Ornamentation seemed to mean nothing to her, only the homage that was given to her art mattered. Nobody else looked so dedicated.

The walls of the salon were banked with mirrors, which were framed with gold and which heightened the luster. Flowers were everywhere, and the effect was enchanting.

Pavlova greeted her warmly, everyone spoke an understandable French, considered the language of cultivated people, and introductions followed quickly: the dancers Preobrajenskaya and Kchesinska, the painter Bakst, the dancer-choreographer Fokine, and the man who fitted no category, Diaghilev. Preobrajenskaya and Kchesinska were familiar names to Lenora, but it was Diaghilev who caught her attention, who seemed least impressed with her entrance.

Lenora studied this man who during the last few years had caused a sensation in Russia with his criticism of the ballet. She knew that Sergei Pavlovich Diaghilev had started the famous art review known as *The World of Art*, that he had organized several famous art exhibitions, that he had wanted to be a composer until discouraged by Rimski-Korsakov, and that his energy was said to be phenomenal.

But it was foolish to fear him, to fear any of them, for she was sailing on a flood of triumphant emotion, and none of them could halt her. So she observed his person more critically. A dandy, Lenora decided, intensely interested in his personal appearance, the most carefully groomed man she had ever seen. He carried himself with a sense of absolute superiority. But his head was too large for his body; he could never have been a dancer, she thought. He was tall, almost portly, although a young man somewhere in his early thirties. She did find his face interesting with its small black mustache, his brown hair combed back high which highlighted the white streak in it with a theatrical flair.

Diaghilev looked at her skeptically and said, "I cannot understand your choreography, and neither can Bakst, can you, Léon?"

Bakst said, "Well, it is damned different. No style to it."

Diaghilev said, "Why don't you dance nice simple wholesome things that we don't have to think and worry about?"

At first Lenora thought he was jesting, and then she was not certain. He was arrogant, and she did not know how to take him. She retorted, "It is not nice or wholesome to go against one's genius."

"And of course," Diaghilev said, "you are a genius?"

"A dancer can be the equal of a Duse or a Bernhardt," said Lenora.

"Oh, really!" said Diaghilev, as if he did not believe her.

"An inspired dancer can."

"And you will give birth to inspired dances?"

"No. I leave that to the masters of toe work." What other remark was possible to such stupidity?

There was a pause, and in the pause the gulf of things never to be agreed on loomed large. Pavlova, who had not said anything, now offered Lenora tea from the huge samovar or vodka, whichever the American preferred. Lenora took the vodka, although it was difficult to swallow and made the most normal gesture become dramatic.

Pavlova said, "Now that you have met everyone do you know which is which?"

Lenora said, "Diaghilev is insolence, Bakst is elegance, and Fokine is philosophy."

"And Pavlova?"

"Heavenly."

Pavlova laughed, and said, "You know it is risky, telling us how stupidly we dance."

Lenora replied, "I did not say you were stupid. But your ballets are barren things and do not stretch to experience life."

Pavlova wondered with alarm if the American was mad and sat silent, waiting in vain for an intelligent counterargument to present itself. Finally she said, "Ballet is not such a futile farce to us, to normal people."

"Oh, normal people?" Lenora watched Pavlova composing her thoughts and added, "Are any of us really normal?" She looked at Pavlova with distress. Pavlova, poor Pavlova, had to be theatrical, but her style was sincere enough, and she could be forgiven because she was a genius.

Pavlova said, "Diaghilev thinks we are anything but normal. In that, at least, he does agree with you."

"Diaghilev?" Lenora shrugged, now regarding him with amusement, now seeing a portrait of a dilettante, with features a trifle blurred as if he was still finding himself, yet his expression sensual and cynical and proud.

Diaghilev caught her staring and stared back. "Well . . . ?" He halted and waited for another of her decisive statements. But beside him was Fokine. Diaghilev said to Fokine, "Miss Malcolm is very noble about her dancing."

"Miss Malcolm is wonderful," Fokine said with utter seriousness.

"You are very kind," she said, but he was not kind, but intelligent; she could see that in his eyes. His expression was magnificent, and he reeked of hero worship. "See, Diaghilev, you are not an appreciator."

"That is just what I am, Lenora," said Diaghilev, "I am the best appreciator in the world. Oh, you are fortunate, you dance, Bakst paints, Fokine dances and creates choreography, even Preobrajenskaya and Kchesinska create occasionally in spite of being ballerinas, and certainly Pavlova, but I create nothing, unless, unless . . . Isn't it strange how some legs take naturally to dancing and some legs take to nothing? Mine could not dance if I spent all my life trying to make them, but they know how the steps should be made, they understand without having it explained. And some legs can make lovely movements without knowing how, or understanding why. Some people are just legs. Idiot legs, with everything imbecile about them, and yet when they dance they have moments of perfection, and I, some day, will tell them how to reach that. I, some day, will——" Diaghilev halted abruptly. He was surrendering one of his most precious secrets, and suddenly his face was a mask again and he was being simply clever.

But Fokine's mind came freely to meet Lenora's. He admired her work; he discussed it with an intelligence that astonished and pleased her. He said she was showing the way to break the grip of stultifying tradition. This, then, was happiness and harmony. She wondered what kind of a lover Fokine would make, and she said, "I don't ever want to stop growing."

"You won't," Fokine assured her, but that was nothing to embrace.

"I wish I could be sure."

"I am sure."

"Fokine, you don't really know me."

"I'll never know you better than I do now," Fokine said. She waited for spontaneous combustion to occur, but he went on talking about her art. "Your recital was remarkable. What extraordinary things you said, and with such an extraordinary freedom. It seemed so natural the way you danced, yet in the ballet they tell us such things are unsuitable and impossible."

They were interrupted by Pavlova and Bakst, strolling back from the other rooms, and as the ballerina entered the light Lenora was struck anew by the lack of one memorable feature in the whole of Pavlova. Her body, which had been so lovely on stage, had no distinction now. Her skin was pale, her black hair was without luster, and yet she seemed happy this way.

But Bakst looked tired and bored, Diaghilev detached, and Fokine had been diverted by the famous Kchesinska, the mistress of a grand duke, who was reputed to have everything her own way at the Marinsky.

These strange, disheartening people, thought Lenora. They were suddenly so alike, as if one overpowering attitude had pressed them into the same mold. She was certain now that they did not speak her language, not even Fokine, really. What she found natural they called disgusting, what she found disgusting they called good manners.

Introductions forgotten on the spot; women whose attention was only on the men; laughter tipped with prodigality; champagne, vodka, hands moving frantically yet meaninglessly. And no longer the hush that had been so impressive when she had entered.

She decided they were examples of a dying species. Their welcome to her was distinctly freezing. None of them gave a damn about the poor people shot down, about the lack of freedom. After a few more minutes of what Lenora felt was utter waste, she resolved to depart. Others were leaving now, the party was thinning out; it was not her party as she had expected. Lenora started for the door when Pavlova halted her. She explained there was another party starting, of her closest friends, after the government officials and businessmen departed.

Diaghilev still seemed to regard her with indifference, yet he said, "Are you afraid to stay, Miss Malcolm, are you afraid of the risk?"

Something in Lenora came to life again, something fierce and reckless, something that never allowed her to run from risk. She was an American, and they could drive an American too far. She allowed Pavlova to take her arm and lead her to the fine buffet supper that appeared. Lenora thought, how beautiful is food and drink when it is served with taste, then it establishes amity even among enemies.

It was nearly midnight, the most propitious hour to talk, to become joyous, to agree that art was all, a gentle madness was acceptable, and a subtle bond developed between the artists. How meager and impoverished was the world without art, without congenial friends to pursue splendid truth—her truth, their truth, the truth. Lenora, red-cheeked from vodka, her feet planted firmly on the floor, was prepared to hold all others at bay. Those remaining—Diaghilev, Bakst, Fokine, and a few others—followed her to the table. She became the center of the conversation. At last she felt beautiful, as when she had entered. Her white robe was creased, but she draped it becomingly about herself and felt like a Greek goddess. She was glad she had not brought Brian; Brian was nice, but she longed for more than niceness now. Feeling fabulous, for even Diaghilev was listening attentively to her, she did a parody of a ballerina dying on stage. Her mimicry was effective. Those who were not shocked were hilarious, but several disputants almost came to blows. Pavlova was virtually in a state of collapse, afraid that half of her remaining guests would never talk to her for having invited the American, while the other half would carry the American about on their shoulders.

And Diaghilev, who up to now had seen Lenora Malcolm as a young woman with plain brown hair, prominent buttocks, and aggressive breasts, none of which interested him, was interested in her mimicry. It expressed much of what he thought was wrong with the ballet of the Imperial School. Thus, he provoked her, saying, "How can you know that our ballet is rigid? How can you ignore the five positions? Cast aside the sacred toe shoes, the very sustenance of our dancing, the very symbol of our grace?"

"Because," she declared, "such shoes are cramping and artificial. Because I cast aside all your conventions, the stiff tarlatans, the heavy stockings, all the things that stifle."

Diaghilev said sarcastically, "All things?"

"All things," Lenora said automatically, and went on to say what she had said many times. "I find most ballet dancing ridiculous." Even Pavlova and Fokine looked shocked until she added, "But I exclude individuals such as Pavlova, who is beautiful and ethereal."

Diaghilev said, "You want freedom from discipline, from everything."

Lenora said, "I want truth. Your own great novelist, Dostoyevsky, said, 'The world will be saved only by beauty and suffering.' "

Bakst said, "Yet you claim dancing should be celebration."

"Celebration, indeed!" cried Lenora. "And joy. Revealed, splendid joy!"

"You would make this the best of all possible worlds?" asked Fokine.

"Exactly," said Lenora.

"And social reforms too," said Bakst.

"Yes," said Lenora, "that must be so."

"Good," said Bakst, but his smile became sardonic. "But who enjoys being moral! We were put in the world to enjoy ourselves, not to redeem people. That is why I detest idealism in art, it creates all sorts of illusions. You call goodness a virtue, but in art I call it a menace."

Lenora thought of the mass funeral and said, "Then it is true that no one cares about what happened here in St. Petersburg a week ago?"

There was no reply. Pavlova bore a pained expression; Diaghilev looked angry; Bakst blushed, as if caught in an act of shame.

Then Bakst, determined to regain his emotional position, burst out, "Ugliness arouses the very devil in me. I loathe it, but beauty, I want beauty always around me. I want to assimilate it in every part of my being. Don't you want beautiful people around you, beautiful costumes, colors, tons of lovely things to touch and feel and see!" Bakst was ecstatic, his face radiant with pleasure. "I'm sensuous and I adore it. Now look at you, Lenora. You would make a lovely Cleopatra, if you reduced a little, if you took some of the steam baths for which St. Petersburg is noted."

Lenora knew she should be furious, but it was impossible to be furious at Léon Bakst, with his curly red hair, his lively, laughing eyes that held so little malice.

But Diaghilev, he was the irritation. Diaghilev, she sensed, had to compete and conquer. Diaghilev had the same restlessness she had, but as a lover . . .? Lenora shuddered at the thought. Diaghilev was so obviously without the slightest interest in her as a woman that the very idea was repulsive to her.

Diaghilev said, "Not everyone can run about the stage looking innocent and bewildered."

Fokine said, "I loved her simplicity and artlessness."

Lenora said, "Ballet is an expression of a sentimentality which we must outgrow. And it is full of an unctuous servility."

Diaghilev said, "And you are capricious and childish in your arbitrary condemnation of all things ballet."

Lenora said, "You think that ballet costumes are not absurd?"

Diaghilev had to smile in agreement despite his desire not to.

"And unaesthetic?" said Lenora.

"Very unaesthetic," said Fokine.

"And you would discard all technique?" asked Diaghilev.

Lenora said, outraged, "Do you think my art is just a beautiful accident?"

Pavlova said, "Well, your dancing does not seem to have any connection with technique at all."

Lenora said, "I have a technique, but it does not show."

Pavlova understood, but Diaghilev wanted to know why.

"I hide it so no one will imitate me. As soon as a dancer imitates me, she fails to discover herself, and without self there can be no great art."

Diaghilev asked, as if searching now for something which would give revelation to him, "But for these free dances, as you call them, you choose music full of emotional elements that have no choreographic significance?"

"How can you have choreographic significance without emotion!" she exploded.

"How can you dance with only that!" Diaghilev exploded back.

"I don't. But what I feel, I dance."

"And so, if you have a happy personal life, you dance happiness, if you feel sad . . . you dance sadness. But Anna here, our most inspired dancer, does not allow herself a personal life."

Lenora turned to Pavlova, "You do not allow yourself to feel when you dance?"

Pavlova shrugged, but looked white and vulnerable in this instant.

Lenora cried, "Fantastic!"

Pavlova changed the subject. Pavlova was amazed at Lenora dancing in her bare feet. "I can never find a pair of ballet shoes to suit me, I am always cutting them up so they conform most closely to my arch, but without them—how can you feel any security?"

Lenora replied, "And how can you feel emotionally honest without some improvisation? That would seem to me a false security."

Diaghilev was just devilish enough to sharpen these contrasts, saying, "Every detail of Anna's performance, once established, remains fixed. Anna has spent years and years on this."

The Nevsky Prospect could be seen from the window, but the room darkened. Oh, this world, groaned Lenora, no freedom in it at all. She stared at the admirers crowding around her, and all the young men had the same white teeth and the same white smile and the same high cheekbones, and none of them was a breaker of traditions. The compliments they bestowed upon her were like haunting tunes. They sought to capture her but she was not captured, though there were exceptions. Fokine and Bakst, at least, had their own ideas. Diaghilev, even when she resented that he was neither dancer, director, painter nor composer, had flair. And when Pavlova danced, she forgave much. But what Lenora could not forgive was their avoidance of any mention of Black Sunday, unaware that Diaghilev had protested and so had Bakst and Fokine, and had risked much. No one had mentioned even the Russian-Japanese War, which was being waged at great cost. All she had heard was discussion of pirouettes and entrechats and foutettés which had been performed with prodigious virtuosity and which had nothing to do with self-expression in her opinion, or with the emotions and state of mind of the Russian people.

Upset, Lenora had to give expression to her feelings, and she exploded in a tirade against a government that shot down innocent citizens.

Pavlova replied, "How can we be in arms against a Czar who gives us our position, career, and education?"

And Boris Vilenkov, who up to now had said less than anyone, eased Lenora into a corner where no one else could hear them and explained, "Many of us feel the way you do, but it is not wise to express that, not openly." He had a large Slavic head, with broad cheekbones and wide-set eyes. He glanced around the room, at the others still arguing whether Lenora's dancing was art or insanity. Boris whispered, "Many of us feel that our officers are braver against a defenseless public than against the Japanese. It is said that ammunition may be scarce in the Far East, but it is too plentiful here. In fact, it is said this is the only victory our soldiers have won in a year of fighting."

She asked, "Are you a socialist?"

"I am a Russian."

"But silence is acquiescence."

"Not always. One never knows who is a spy, even here."

"Like Diaghilev?"

"No. Diaghilev hates calm."

"You mean he has threatened to revolt too?" She could not believe that.

"It isn't that. But Diaghilev likes to say, 'We have all of eternity to rest in.' Sergei is at his best in a state of agitation, such as now. He welcomes upheaval, for it gives him a chance to do what he wants. He has no settled political convictions, just a distaste for authority, someone else's authority."

"And you, Boris?"

He took out a paper which he had kept carefully hidden and proudly read it to Lenora: "Today inaugurated revolution in Russia. The Emperor's prestige is irrevocably shattered by the shedding of innocent blood. The Emperor has alienated himself forever from the people."

"Did you write that?" She was prepared to admire his heroism.

"No, alas."

"Still, you do agree with it?"

"Yes. It is by Gorki. It is more courageous than wise."

"Who is always wise?" The thought of Gorki's heroism was inspiring.

"Gorki has been thrown into the secret section of the St. Petersburg fortress for writing this, and so would I be, caught reading this."

Lenora was filled with a sudden joy. A hero was the next best thing to a genius, and had a kind of genius too. She felt released from bondage. She was prepared to be embraced by Boris. But now he seemed more interested in explaining, "It is madness to openly criticize the government."

"You have."

"Secretly."

"Yet you have. And to me, a stranger."

"And a friend."

"How can you be sure?"

"It was in your dancing. But I wanted to warn you. Even you, an American and an artist, could be thrown in jail if the

Czar so ordered. You must be more careful, not express your feelings so openly."

And Lenora, whose body just a moment ago had ached with desire for this handsome, virile man who understood her intimate, personal, courageous art so perfectly, was filled suddenly with physical nausea by his caution.

"What is the matter?" he asked, noticing that she had become very pale.

Lenora glanced at him with annoyance, irritated that she could have anticipated going so far with him so quickly. How could she have believed such a careful man was worthy of her love! Everything about him repulsed her now, especially his fear. She thanked him for his warning and turned to go.

But Fokine and Diaghilev were still arguing over her. Fokine was saying, "She is a naturally inspired dancer who has evolved a form of dancing that suits her own personality," and Diaghilev was saying, "But her dancing has no vocabulary, and some of her interpretations are inaccurate, and worst of all, she insists on trying to express what cannot be expressed—social difficulties and disasters."

Shocked by this, Lenora cried out, "Sooner or later, the senseless slaughter of the poor has to be talked about!"

At first Diaghilev did not answer, standing there looking hard and solid, and then he said, "Lenora, Lenora, talking about the past is not going to solve anything. It is useless, and anyway, since when are you such an expert on our politics? It is really quite preposterous."

She described the mass funeral, detail by detail, and Diaghilev grew white—unable to endure talk of death, unable to accept its inevitability, its sickening inevitability. There was no accomplishment in death, no heroism, and only art gave relief from that dread, had a life beyond the grave. And so, as always, when he detested the conversation, he attacked on another front, saying, "Are all American dancers so forthright?"

"You cannot make dancing with lies."

"Even if that leaves you naked, emotionally?"

"Even if it leaves me completely naked."

"A Cleopatra all bare!" Diaghilev laughed savagely. "With her stomach showing! Could anything be uglier or more vulgar!"

"Or more exciting," said Bakst. "We could paint her stomach a brilliant red or an exotic green, or a——"

Diaghilev dismissed Bakst's idea without even being civil. "Lenora, you have no sense of privacy."

"Art is risk," she said, "and someday I will dance upon the

stage naked, and it will be the greatest art, for in the body is the organization of the universe, God, and man."

"In public?" asked Bakst, intrigued with the thought.

"Of course."

"Naked?" This time Pavlova was shocked.

"Naked means uncovered. I'll uncover the truth and show the design of the universe. Our thrust must come where and when it can, and since my thrust is to show the wholeness of creation, not to cover it, dance this way I must. It is the truest expression of the natural world."

Lenora stood up as if prepared to demonstrate here and now, but no one accepted this challenge, and the conversation became general.

Pavlova said, "You were beautiful and plastic," which was a great compliment for her to give to another dancer.

Diaghilev, escorting her to the door with Fokine and Pavlova, was the greatest surprise of all. She knew by now he liked to control people, especially men, and that he must be completely impossible as a lover, but he was not a mere dilettante—his interest in dancing was a life-time devotion and far more than a flair. He was saying as he helped her on with her coat, "I am a great charmer, they tell me, and of course a charlatan, and of course with great cheek—like you, Lenora —and with no gifts—unlike you—except the ability to organize, which is no gift at all, of course, just energy, but all of us look at death every day, in our mirrors, in ourselves, and sometimes I think you are depraved, making us think of death in your dancing, and yet . . ." He paused, as if to sum up what he really felt, and then plunged on, ". . . though you have no style, no technique, heavy legs, and an athletic body it is right that you dance to music of the first order, that your décor and choreography are all of a piece, and that you regard dancing as a serious art, perhaps the greatest of all arts, our religion." He bowed then, his hand on his heart, for once utterly serious, and added, "For this, Lenora, we should be most grateful."

"But don't rush things," Pavlova warned. "It's not going to be easy to change the world, even in this little select gathering here."

What Fokine said was most important of all. He kissed her hand and, looking into her green eyes, said, "Our dancing will never be the same hereafter. You have shown us how to dance past the period of despair, past the period of exhaustion, and still go on. After seeing you, Lenora, I almost think we should throw away our ballet shoes."

BOOK SIX

33

So Lenora returned home in triumph. Mama was waiting for her, and Amy and the children, who swarmed about her, and there were many arms around her, gentle, affectionate, proud, but the arms she desired the most were absent. Out of the weavings of her blood, out of the triumph—and that it was, for artistic Europe was talking about how she had stormed and captured the citadel of the ballet—there was an increasing desire in her for an Apollo or a Dionysus. The failure of a Brian, a Fokine, a Diaghilev to fulfill this desire gave her a fiercer wanting and made her triumph both wonderful and terrible. Lenora knew she should be happy, for she stood on the pinnacle now, but she was not happy. Never had she felt so beautiful, but instead of making her joyful, it drove her frantic to feel so fair and unrequited. She was so charged with emotion that everything was intense, the children laughing, Mama hugging them, Amy kissing them, the sun on her window in the morning. And all this added to her pain; it was as if she had everything but the one thing she wanted the most.

And as the days passed and spring approached, the season when the self-denials of love were most difficult to bear, Lenora's pain and craving grew. In these days of self-denial she concentrated on the children even as her dreams of a perfect lover expanded and took a fiercer hold on her desires. Lenora assured herself that the children were her natural calling, but she grew tense, nervous, irritable; she found it harder to teach the children lovely movements without pain. Desire shook her so severely now it was almost impossible to be reasonable, to postpone any longer her craving for love, whose absence threatened to destroy her.

Several times she started to express her feelings to Mama and each time halted, deciding that Mama would think them ridiculous. When she was alone in her dressing room, however, there was no limit to her feelings. She stared at her naked body in the mirror and was stirred with a new restlessness. It became impossible to read herself to sleep as Mama suggested. To read anything now was a waste. More and more she measured her naked image in the mirror and wondered who would be her benefactor.

Mama sensed that Lenora was unhappy. Lenora's temper flared over trivial things. Mama proclaimed her a giver of beauty, and Lenora retorted that she wished someone would give her beauty. Lenora's dream life was wild and frenzied. Many times Mama came upon her daughter tossing restlessly, crying out in her sleep, in a turmoil.

When Lenora was invited to dance in Vienna as part of the observance of the centennial of the first performance of Beethoven's *Eroica* Symphony, Mama was greatly gratified. It was just the kind of recognition she desired for her daughter, and she hoped it would divert or ease Lenora's emotional restlessness.

Lenora, feeling triumphant once more, decided to go to Vienna alone, since she was only staying several days. She assured Mama that she would be back in Grunewald by Monday, for she had concerts the following week in Bonn and Cologne and Heidelberg.

The Beethoven centennial was filled with musicians, and Lenora was more nervous than usual. Since Beethoven, however, was everyone's utopia this afternoon, she resolved to dance at least once to his music, although this added to her nervousness. It was the first time she had danced Beethoven in public, and she lacked her usual self-confidence. Then she decided she was being weak, and for her finale she plunged into a movement of the *Eroica,* transcribed for a small orchestra, even as she sensed that the musical purists might be offended, *this was not respectable!* She kept the stage in complete darkness except for a single shaft of light on her. She called on all her native intensity, but instead of conveying the thunder and tempest of the music she suggested a song of passion.

Afterward she realized that the audience had preferred the delicacy of her Chopin to the vitality of her Beethoven, had not been overwhelmed by the *Eroica* as she had desired. The applause for this number had been sporadic. The audience had demanded less encores than usual, certainly less than she had expected.

Lenora was resting in her dressing room after this matinee recital, not even sure she wanted supper, telling herself that the Chopin at least had created bliss, although that did not remove her dissatisfaction, when the maid informed her that someone was examining the stage. This was contrary to her orders. No one was allowed on stage before or after her recitals; it broke her mood, was fatal to her feeling.

It was a man evaluating the dimensions of the stage on which she had danced. Lenora looked angry, but he continued to assume various positions. He did not turn to greet her, nor did he gush that she had been wonderful. He said, "This stage is too small for Beethoven. You should not have danced the *Eroica*."

"And I invited you to say this?" She intended to wither him.

"Does it matter?" he said impatiently. "You were wrong."

"Do you know who I am?"

"Don't be such a fool! Naturally I do. You are a dancer."

"Is that all?"

"Oh, of course not. How ridiculous! You are Lenora Malcolm!"

"Thank you."

"I saw it on the program."

"Really!" Now she was determined to blast him, but he was not listening.

He was looking at her music and shaking his head disparagingly. "Look," he said, "you have no modern music on your program."

"I don't find it inspiring."

"You would if you used the music I wrote for *Peer Gynt* in Oslo, for *Hamlet* at Elsinore, or what I composed for *Antigone* in Athens, which I——"

"I? I? I?" She interrupted sarcastically "Who is I? The Lord God Jehovah himself, or Beethoven, or——"

"Don't be a fool. You know very well who I am."

"But I don't."

"It is just as well. Then you can listen to my criticism without prejudice."

He started to explain why the *Eroica* had been wrong, at least on this stage, and she said, "Now, that's enough!"

They stood facing each other, and then he looked at her sorrowfully, shaking his head with pity.

Lenora said, trying to put together this puzzle, "You wrote

music for *Antigone,* which was done in Athens?" She had heard about this production and its music; both had been experimental, like so much of her own work. "With whom?"

"How typical. With whom. Nothing about the director, the writer, the composer, but with whom?" he said sarcastically. "What great star? And suppose we did not have a star? Not even the Beethoven who wrote *Fidelio.*"

"But you did. I remember now. The composer was the star, he was the one everybody talked about."

He smiled in spite of an obvious effort to appear humble.

Now Lenora knew who he was: Niels Nordahl, composer and pianist. He was Norwegian, son of the great novelist, Svend Nordahl, but Niels was becoming famous for his revolutionary ideas on composing and for his fantastically sensuous music. Unquestionably, she thought, an artist, and perhaps a genius and an Apollo. He was a mature-looking man, though rather short, with a fine, attractive head, large and broad, almost like a Beethoven's. His features were strong, very masculine in their certainty. She liked his dark brown hair, his wide shoulders. She could not dismiss him now, but she could not give in to him either, although that was her impulse.

He said, "You should dance more romantic music, and it will fit your appearance."

"But I don't want romantic music," she replied. "I don't need it."

"You should have romantic music," he insisted. "I have an infallible ear, and I say your dominant mood should be romantic, lovely and poetic."

"No," she said. She was tired of things like "The Blue Danube."

"Oh, I suppose some serious music would be effective, but I repeat——"

"Perhaps it is the stage," she said, having a sudden desire to compromise. "It is too small for Beethoven."

"Of course. Basically you are on the right track. You have the same sense of honesty and simplicity that I have. You do not cater to the box office, you focus on the aesthetics of your art. You won't give in to the Philistines either."

"Never."

"Precisely." He smiled. "You must never dance to obvious music."

"And I did," she said unhappily. This became the worst of offenses, for he looked so critical and she could not argue with him, he was so attractive and interesting. "Perhaps my choice of music was wrong."

"Yes," he said, "when you used the Beethoven." Then

seeing the stricken figure of Lenora, he added, "But your Chopin was lovely. It was the most beautiful dancing I've ever seen."

Suddenly she felt wonderful. Now she could see that he had great gifts: presence, intelligence, and inherited taste. He moved about the stage admiring her setting with the grace of an Apollo. Despite his shortness, he was quite good-looking and obviously more mature than Adam. It was after her recitals that Lenora was in her fiercest state of excitement and when, hitherto, most men had failed her. But Nordahl had the same excitement as he said her choice of Chopin was an act of genius. Discussing her art, he spoke with an intensity that seemed far greater than anyone she had known. "You should dance to Schubert too," he added, "and perhaps even Gluck and Schumann. But some modern music, also. The next step in your art is not Beethoven, but if you must be epic, to dance a heroic Hecuba or Electra, to my music."

Lenora was not sure she could dance to his music, but she adored his taste. All she had ever desired was a man handsome, brilliant, and great enough to prove that he was a genius, and here he was. Lenora was not just falling in love; it was far more than that now. Her appetite for sensation, for the realization of beauty and ecstasy was constantly seeking expansion, for the personality who would arouse to the fullest expression those elements within her. It was a seeking for qualities rather than for persons, for the poetic rather than for just the poet. She felt at this instant he was essential to every emotion of her life. He brought all her feelings into an irresistible focus since he was so much of a poetic, romantic, striving artist himself.

Nordahl was saying, "When you danced the Chopin, you seemed to grow out of the music as a tree grows out of the soil. With lifted arms you seemed to touch the sky."

"Yes," said Lenora, "yes!"

"Then you used movements as a Michelangelo used marble."

Lenora thought he was overpraising her now somewhat, but he did have a genuine feeling for her art. Then her heart grew heavy. She must leave with him, or he might vanish, but would he be willing? Yet if she did not seize this opportunity it might be gone irrevocably; he would slip away from her just as the genius she had waited for so long was within reach. She said, "I'd love to hear your music."

"Some other time."

She was panic-stricken then, and for once did not know what to say.

There was a painful pause, and suddenly he said, "Would you like to see Vienna?"

"I'd be delighted." She had seen Vienna before, but never through his eyes.

The rest was like a dream. Lenora suggested they take a carriage, and Niels hesitated, and she sensed that he had very little money, but when she said she wanted to dance on the rooftops of Vienna, he grew reckless too. He hired the fanciest carriage he could find, although he could not afford any. He did not drive to a restaurant or show her Vienna, and she did not expect him to. Niels did not halt until they reached his rooms on the other side of Vienna, and then he said, "You don't want to go back, do you?"

"No."

He began to laugh, as if they were mad. And they were mad, thought Lenora, and she was laughing too. But Niels grew serious when he said, "Do you love your dancing very much?"

"Yes."

"But you need not have answered. No one should ask about love. It should be taken as given, or not at all."

Perhaps that was not true, she thought, perhaps she represented difficulty, perhaps her love would take him from his friends and career. In this instant she saw herself as dangerous to him, and she moved away from him suddenly and painfully.

"What is wrong?" He peered into her face, anxious all at once.

"It won't be easy."

"I adore you."

"You do like me?" Adore she had heard a thousand times.

"More than anyone I have ever known."

Niels' rooms were large and comfortable and contained many pictures of composers: Chopin, Liszt, Berlioz, Wagner, Brahms. Romantics all, in one way or another, she thought. But she had a profound instinct to say nothing, to allow him to set the pace and mood. She lay perfectly still on his bed and waited for him to come to her. Then he was beside her, the world turned upside down, and nothing was altered, and everything. When she came back to earth and he was still beside her, she knew an exultant and wordless rapture. She felt him close, and she whispered, "I wonder why nature made your skin so soft. It just can't be for the obvious reason to entice me. Nature is so subtle," and she felt deeply that his skin had its own fragrance, it could not be compared to any other skin-flower in the world.

He thought, how wonderful it was that they were meeting for the first time, but she knew she had met him many times before: Niels was precisely what she had always desired in a lover.

They slept around the clock, but it did not matter those first few days. She had scheduled recitals in Bonn and Cologne and Heidelberg, but she forgot about them. Mama did not know where she was, and she could not spoil her mood by informing Mama. Niels was protective now, and she loved it. A week later they were more in love than ever, although Lenora began to worry about Mama. But when Niels continued to make love with passion and authority everything else was blotted out. "We will create lovely things," he said after such triumphs. He lay back with a satisfied sigh, and she told herself that their love would go on forever. "We will accomplish so much together," he assured her, and she nodded and kissed him. Both of them were certain that was true, as each to the other was a revelation.

34

It was a dreadful time for Mama. The wait for Lenora's return seemed endless, Lenora had promised to be back in two days, and as it stretched into a week it was almost unbearable. Mama was unable to feel a moment of peace; it was waiting for her world to be smashed, the world she had built with such care. She wanted to rush off to Vienna, to comb the city, but that was impossible; she did not know where to start

Mama told Lothar to cancel Lenora's performances, although she felt this was a terrible thing to do, and she tried to hide her panic even as it became a kind of terror. Whatever Mama pretended to anyone else, she was shocked that Lenora could vanish with recitals scheduled, and with such utter disdain.

Amy recalled Budapest and Lenora's flight with Adam Steyr and said in her remote, almost aescetic way that Lenora would return, Lenora always did. Amy was full of calculated indifference; it was easier than showing concern.

Mama tried to follow Amy's example, but she was too upset. And when Lenora came across the lawn at Grunewald, some days later, Mama asked angrily, although she was also relieved, "Where were you? What happened?"

"Nothing happened."

"You didn't have an accident? You were not sick?"

"Of course not!" How could Mama be so blind! She had been in so many wonderful places since the last time she had seen her mother.

"You disregarded your engagements without a word."

"I did not feel like dancing these past few days."

"Suppose the audience does not feel like coming the next few weeks?"

"They will come," Lenora said with assurance.

"Not if they don't trust you."

"They trust my inspiration." Now there was so much more to express. "When they see my new program they will be more enthusiastic than ever."

"I wonder. I must have refunded a thousand dollars this past week."

Lenora laughed contemptuously.

Mama flared, "Very amusing! I am so terrified by your disappearance I even think of dragging the Danube, I am certain something horrible has happened to you, and you feel no responsibility, not for the pain you've given me, not for the engagements broken, not for anything, but——"

"I'm in love."

"I could understand what happened in Budapest. Adam had a kind of light Viennese charm, he knew how to bow and kiss your hand and make you feel beautiful. And then, at least, you had no more recitals at the moment, you were young, it was the first time."

"This is the first time. I've never known anyone like Niels before."

"You said that about Adam too."

"Adam was a talented journalist, but Niels is an artist. He's the son of the Norwegian novelist, Svend Nordahl, he's gaining renown in his own right as a composer, we have much in common. He adores Mozart, Beethoven, Chopin, Liszt but I shouldn't have to tell you all this." Lenora halted, angry at herself for allowing anyone to push her into making such a boastful explanation. But Mama was still staring at her as if she were a child. How absurd, Mama was being provincial, forgetting that blithe candor was far more desirable than the usual hypocritical display of virtue. She declared, "Niels will not fail me. We are fundamental to each other."

"I hope so."

"Hope? Do you really?"

Mama flushed, and pride struggled with indignation. It was

as if her ideals had played her false. Mama's mind went back
to a day when she had lain on her side waiting for the unknown, for the bursting forth, and her astonished joy when
this child, even more than the others, had shown such an
awareness of the creative life, and now this child was saying
Touch Me Not! What a happy time then, what pain to recall
it now with Archer acting in New York and Amy totally
involved in the school. Lenora was right; there was no more
hope in her, but a desperate effort to continue the status quo.
Mama said, "Naturally I hope for your happiness." Naturally,
with Lenora stretched out on his bed and the umbilical cord
cut? Anything was possible with Lenora now, and most of the
possibilities were even more appalling, but there was no turning back. Mama went on, "I just want you to wait until you
are sure whatever man you choose is really the man you
love."

Lenora said, "Love can never wait. It is outside ourselves. I
was made to love in a certain way, just as I was made to
suffer in a certain way."

Mama gazed helplessly at Lenora. She was suffering too,
but who cared about her suffering?

Lenora said, "All you are interested in is preserving my
reputation."

At that Mama could not help smiling, but so savagely it
was like a sword.

Lenora said, "Actually, I consider myself extremely moral,
because in all my relations with Niels I am doing only what is
beautiful." Mama shuddered, expecting sexual confidences,
which was too much to endure, and was silent. They had
started out with such fine ideals, but this was not what she had
wanted her daughter to be. Lenora went on, "Though, in your
terms, I am not chaste, I always look upon an alliance as a
oneness, and so I am faithful, far more faithful than most
married couples. I keep myself entirely for the man I choose."

Mama said, sighing, "Some people want their children to be
more famous. I think I want you to be less."

"That won't get me married any sooner."

"I didn't say that," Mama said angrily.

"It is what you are thinking," Lenora said with a take-it-or-
leave-it gesture. "So make your choice, for I am not giving up
Niels."

"I have to give in," Mama said hastily. "If anybody has to
give in, it is me. But I wish you would realize that quickly as
you give love, it does matter. So few women are free to
choose, but you are. You are one of the most celebrated

women in Europe, your art has become a byword. It is certainly not essential that you give yourself so quickly, without any promise for the future, like a streetwalker."

"And you," Lenora said rudely, "you chose my father."

Mama flushed, feeling shamefaced and apologetic, as if she had sold herself piece by piece to her husband, although in truth it had been quite different and she had been the first freethinker in the family.

"Did you love my father?"

"When I married him. But that's not the point. I want you to have the best."

"I will. By God, I will!" Marriage struck Lenora as ridiculous, but love was a deadly serious business. Mama could not find an answer, for there was an assurance in Lenora that was impregnable.

Nordahl became for Mama the Norwegian Liszt, although there was no physical resemblance, a very clever composer but romantically utterly undependable. And she was critical of his shortness and thought him too stocky to be attractive, thinking he was almost too masculine for a musician, but Lenora continued to insist that Niels was the most inspiring man she had ever met.

Lenora had complete confidence in herself now, and, having made up her mind, nothing was swaying her. For all her love and determination, however, she did not want to live in Vienna, but this was not easy to change.

In Vienna, Niels felt, he was in the presence of the great masters, Mozart, Schubert, Beethoven, Brahms. And to Niels this was a vital advantage. Music was not the same in Berlin, he argued, not as deeply rooted. Lenora replied that he would have more opportunities to hear his music in Berlin, for Berlin had more symphony orchestras than any other city in the world, and that she would use her influence to help him obtain these opportunities. Although Niels was irritated by the implication that he needed anyone's help he was gratified by her generosity.

Inevitably, as if it had been his decision from the start, Niels found himself sharing the fine house Lenora rented in a fashionable section of Berlin. It was shielded from prying eyes by large trees, and Niels agreed that it was idyllic and wondered if this mansion didn't cost far more than they could afford. Lenora answered that he should not trouble himself with such mundane matters, he must concentrate only on composing.

Each night when she greeted him she wore flowing Grecian

robes with exquisite crepe shawls and sought to be inspiring. She agreed that it was wise for an artist to be Spartan when it came to things of the flesh, and with her usual unconcern about the cost of things insisted on having a lavishly stocked table at whose side stood a silver champagne cooler and caviar and roast duck and lobster, whatever he preferred.

Love shook her each time they were together. She thought, looking at him when he was in one of his intoxicated bursts of creativity, of Beethoven's inspired magnificence.

This evening they were lying on a low divan by the ceiling-high windows and looking out upon Berlin. This had become her studio and was dimly lit, with furnishings striking in their simplicity. It was the instant after love, and she leaned back, feeling as lofty as the lofty ceiling. Everything seemed reconcilable, and she felt lucid in a rare way. She whispered, "When will you compose music for me?"

He fondled her hair and said, "Where do you want me to start?"

"Where Mozart started."

"But my music is modern."

"What about Wagner?" she suggested.

"Too fortissimo." Niels was annoyed; he wanted to be Nordahl and nobody else. "What do you think of this theme?" He hurried to her piano to show her.

She said it was delicate and lovely, but it was the following evening before he finished it. They were exhausted from this continuous creating, but neither dared admit that; it would have been unromantic.

The song was too brief for her to dance to, yet it made them very happy. They were so pleased with this work that Niels decided to compose a musical suite just for her. It became their absorbing passion the next few weeks. Lothar was unhappy that Lenora gave only matinee performances now, so she could be free to be with Niels each evening, but she disregarded Lothar's warning that the enthusiasm of the audiences might not last much longer and that gossip about her and Niels could be harmful. All that mattered was Niels. She desired nothing else. It was enough to be close to him, to feel her pulse stir as he approached, to create with him, to know that he was what he looked: an artist and a genius.

Niels was positive that the suite of dances he composed for her would strongly advance her dancing, but his music disappointed Lenora. He thought it would heighten her ethereal, romantic quality, but to Lenora this suite sounded like Debussy, and she did not care for Debussy.

Niels' music, if it had to sound like anyone else's, she

thought, should sound like Wagner or Mozart or Chopin or Strauss.

Niels sensed her recoil, for although she said this suite was charming she made no effort to dance to it. Offended, he said, "It offends you."

"It is true, so how can it offend?"

"Lenora, we must not lie, especially to each other."

"Why should we? Ever?" But still she lay on a divan, not moving, even after he played the suite a second time, although when he played Chopin or Strauss she danced spontaneously. He turned to depart, and it evoked distress in her as he had hoped. She cried out, "You don't want me to dance to what I don't feel. I must be utterly ruthless when it comes to my art, and I want you to be, also. I don't want you to agree with me, if you can't."

"Of course." He picked up his score, still angry at her unwillingness to dance to it but deciding to stay a little while longer, at least until he said a few things that were on his mind. "Your dancing is not always appropriate for others. Sometimes your dancing does gush too much."

"Perhaps."

"Now you are offended."

"I am not." But a slow flush spread up her temples, and she was miserable over the way the discussion was going.

"I want to protect you, Lenora."

"I don't need protection!" Then she wished she had held her tongue, he looked so wounded. She hurried to say, "You must always tell me the truth, whatever the circumstances."

"Love doesn't always flourish on it," he warned.

"Lying is worse. Once you don't trust a person, it is like living on quicksand. It creates doubt, suspicion, which can torture you to death. Tell me, Niels, what do you really think of my art?"

"Darling, do you really want my opinion?"

"Certainly." Suddenly she was not certain. To retreat, however, was impossible, and she said automatically, "Go on, what don't you like about my dancing?"

"It isn't that." Niels spoke with the utmost care now. "But while watching you it is wise to suspend one's ordinary critical faculties, for you do not create the clear, precise image, but the lush, exuberant, sense-drunk one. There is very little that is subtle in your dancing, but a need to hurl the whole of experience at us. Your dancing does not fit any academic definitions—it is a veritable deluge of intensity."

"And you would prefer the clear, precise, cold image?"

"I didn't say that. When you have a romantic emotion,

your style is perfect for that. Then you make every instant of life important to us, the audience. You make us feel the agitation and grandeur and anguish of it."

"It is what I feel."

"Yes, when your dancing is at its best, you are like a seed splitting open with birth pushing out and clutching at existence and your movements so perfectly expressive of that, of the rapture of birth, that I am overwhelmed with an impossible grace, feel that I can conquer the universe, and ache with life."

She kissed him passionately, convinced that they had captured the rhythm of the world's heart. But suddenly she asked, "Do you always tell the truth?'

He looked startled, but he answered quickly, "Almost always. Do you?"

It was her turn to laugh and say, "Isn't that obvious?"

So they had another bottle of champagne, this time to truth, and again the instant of love came and passed, came and passed, and then there was silence, as if they had left all earthly cares. But when they came back to reality he said, as serious as she had ever heard him, "Lenora, without question you are an Elizabethan, with a capacity for passion that would terrify most men. Love literally spills out of you, and when I am close to you it spills on me and I cannot control myself."

"Neither can I," she whispered.

"But I like the risk. And that you do not measure love. For you, love is not just a giving or a taking, it is a total involvement, a willingness—no, a need to leave nothing unfelt. It is, like you, all or nothing. And sometimes, a great danger. Lenora, what will we do when we are apart?"

"I miss you even before you are gone."

"So do I, but I have a career."

"And I?" she asked intensely.

Niels did not answer. How to tell her that even lovely flowers were often useless? He looked stern and paced the length of her studio, as if to go, yet unable to, deep in indecision, regrets, and self-pity. She did not speak, sensing his desire to quarrel, to blame her for the doubts now assailing him. She lay on her couch, apparently allowing him to make up his own mind. But gradually the shawl that had been covering her slipped down until her body was exposed in all its sensuousness except for a tantalizing portion, and with a subtle twist of her waist she seemed to incline toward him, and yet she had not moved. She looked like a figure out of Rubens as she stretched full length, as if to go to sleep just as she was. Then she rolled completely on her back and seemed to hang in space. His pacing stopped, and he had to cover her nakedness, he had to plunge whatever the consequences.

Niels did not leave that night, or the next, and she was insatiable and insinuating and irresistible, and he did not know which of the three troubled him the most. There were still times when he could not contain his inner doubts, and his pacing resumed, knowing he must depart, must return to his composing, and yet he could not leave the voluptuous figure on the couch.

Thus, even though he took possession of her, now he began to feel it was at her command—that she led and he followed —and it infuriated him; he who had had such self-control; he who had lived only for music, composing, change.

He said abruptly, after one especially amorous night, "I didn't know your legs were so long," meaning, I did not know you were so insatiable and eager. She started to protest, but he went on, very seriously, "Lenora, you cannot afford to offend these rich Berliners. Your school has become so expensive you cannot exist without their support. But they will withdraw it as soon as they find out about us."

"They have," she replied, and smiled to show that she did not care.

"Suppose you should become pregnant?"

"You have a prejudice against that?"

"You cannot defy all the conventions. You have taught yourself to be both woman and artist, but the woman can destroy the artist."

She felt torn open. She could be pregnant; she had had a suspicion of that for several weeks now, but she could not tell Niels. Mama was talking about visiting Archer, who had come to Paris to act, and she was indifferent to Mama, Archer, and Amy, to everybody but Niels, and she wondered if that sufficed. The more he was absent from his work, the more restive he became. She thought it inspiring for Niels to feel so intensely, yet as their love lengthened she sensed it no longer made him indifferent to everything else.

She leaned affectionately into his arms as a kind of rebuttal, and he went on complaining about how his art was suffering. It bored her suddenly and struck her as vulgar. But he was ignoring her wishes. He was going on as if she had to listen to him whether she wanted to or not. She fell asleep, as a child would, while he was saying, ". . . you are too demanding."

Niels was gone when she awoke. From then on their love was never the same two nights running. There were still nights when he could not live without her, when he was the one demanding all or nothing, but even then his love was implacable. More often he was resentful that it had diverted him from his work. Then, feeling debauched, he almost hated her, and yet without her, he was even more irritable. He wanted to study, compose, reflect; pleasure he needed in ardent but small, controlled doses, while she still craved it all the time. She began to feel they had a most sophisticated marriage; they fought and made up many times now. He was still pleased that she worshiped the ground he walked on, even as he pretended that was of no consequence. He was less happy with her ideas: Lenora seemed out to save the world, and he did not know whether he could stand it.

His dance suite was praised when she used it as an overture to her program, but she continued to refuse to dance to it. No one asked him to compose music, for he was willing to do this only on his own terms, which meant complete control, and this added to his irritability. She arranged a tour of Germany in conjunction with his music, hoping that would restore his amiability, but when he learned that her dancing was given top billing he was furious. He did not blame her, he said, it was the fault of selfish managers such as Lothar. He decided to supervise her, but she could not accept anyone's supervision. It was her turn to be upset. Much as she loved him, this was too much!

So they no longer flattered each other, and Lenora knew it was quite preposterous but Niels thought he knew as much about dancing as she, and yet she had absolute trust in him— as a genius. Her love was far more than a mood, it was a way of life. This led to another effort to restore their love. Nothing else mattered, she repeated to herself.

She made a bridal bower of her studio, surrounding her divans with white lilies and hanging magnificent clusters of ivy over her windows. Then, with all this beauty, he complained about her taste.

Until this moment Lenora had been certain they were reconciled. But now she felt shaken. She continued to smile, but she was not amused.

Niels was not amused either. A reporter was outside, asking confirmation of their marriage. Niels blamed this rumor on her, although it was just as much of a surprise to her. He threw the reviews between them which made his music a footnote to her dancing.

Lenora began to cry She had not meant to; she never cried, but it was as if he had struck her, and that was humiliating. He was compassionate suddenly, for her show of weakness made him feel stronger. He said, "This is a crystallization. We really want the same thing, beauty. But you must listen to me more, and then we will have no more failures."

Listen in obedience, she thought, but she said nothing.

"I do love you, Lenora, but I express it differently."

She nodded, unable to trust her voice.

He forgave her, and her penance became an almost total putting of herself in his hands. They started a joint tour of Germany, but it quickly became a long-sustained quarrel. When they returned to Berlin he seemed to dictate to her even in her sleep; she lost days, then weeks from her dancing. Lenora found herself having no plans but his plans, no future but his, and heartache. He took to dropping in on her without notice, coming and going to suit himself. Yet he continued to adore her dancing—he said that often, particularly after they had just quarreled, to show that he had quarreled objectively.

No one knew. Lenora was too proud to admit that her idyll was having unhappy days. What hurt her most was when, after an especially bitter quarrel, he said, "After all, a thing like a love affair only happens ten or twelve times in a person's life."

When Mama finally decided to visit Archer in Paris, Lenora did not even see her off. Lenora had gone away suddenly for a weekend with Niels, saying nothing to anyone, it had been his impulse, and Mama had been too hurt to wait. Mama was homesick for San Francisco, and now, in a curious way, Archer was home. Nearly sick from constant crying, Mama told Amy that she was going for just a few weeks, although she planned to stay away for good.

Several days later Lenora, returning to Berlin with Niels, heard of Mama's departure. In a moment of need she cried, "Why?" and Amy replied coldly, "You must allow Mama her conscience," and Lenora wondered why her sister had got so righteous; they had started out with the same ideals.

Lenora, who knew now that she was pregnant, who wanted Mama for the first time in months, who had been unable to tell Niels or anyone else, said nothing. She became as chilly and reserved as Amy. She had expected this to be the supreme happiness of her life, and there was no one with whom to celebrate it. She held her clenched fists beneath her flowing robes, which hid her swelling stomach. There was the sound of Niels' excitement over a sonata he had just completed, and I must be self-controlled, she thought.

When you are loved by an artist, she told herself, you

cannot be sure he wants to be a father. But this child, she prayed, must be a genius.

As she prayed she began to feel beautiful once more. She grew proud and happy that she was going to be a mother, proud too of the father. She knew she must go to the Scandinavian land that had given birth to Niels, where she was certain she would nourish his seed.

A few days later Lenora journeyed by herself to the Norwegian city of Trondheim, where Niels had been born, although he had not been there for many years and he no longer had any family living there.

35

The wind swept upon Lenora with a joyous turbulence. This was wind swarming with life, with a happy wildness. It was like confetti scattering over her at a gaily furious carnival. This invigorating air reminded Lenora of what she desired her child to become. Trondheim was as picturesque as she had anticipated, and she sat on the elevated sun porch of the hotel and hoped that her child would have as much reckless exuberance as the wind whistling around her.

Then her mood altered, and she became very lonesome. She had been reading Swinburne in the hope this romantic would revive lovely memories of Niels, but his lyrics were full of grief and of being forsaken. Suddenly the land and sky seemed too vast and inhuman for her to find any comfort in it. She felt like a pygmy before the immensity of nature. Now she was sorry that she had come to this Norwegian city by herself. She felt cut off from Niels, from all that mattered.

A month to go before the baby came, the doctor had said. As she thought of that, of Niels, she felt a rising tide of emotion within her. She remembered Niels as she had seen him the last time he had come to her.

When Niels found out about their child he arrived in Trondheim in a blinding rain, soaked through and through, and furious at Lenora for not telling him. But she was exalted by his tenderness, once he forgave her for keeping him in ignorance, and she hugged that to her heart. He was also ardent again, although not with an unwearied devotion. After the rain stopped he went into the woods back of his birthplace to compose—he said the city was too full of the eighteenth and nineteenth century to be inspiring—and he returned hours later greatly shaken by the melodies he had conceived. Strange, she thought, all she could feel was the child within her, and he was treating that as a minor act of creation, although he was proud that the seed was his. She begged him to stay in Trondheim with her, and he said the wind made his eyes burn and that the city bored him.

No man, Lenora decided, ever really understood what went on in the body and mind of a pregnant woman. His tenderness, however, when he spoke about their child, remained eloquent. He was considerate, for he said, as he was about to leave for Vienna, "Lenora, you must not worry about your weight, and don't be afraid. Your sole absorption must be on the child, and then he will be born healthy." She nodded, even while her thoughts flowed furiously. He was still the most attractive man she had known, and she rejoiced that she bore the harvest of their beauty. She told herself this was enough.

Yet he could not stay with her, he explained, when she repeated this request. "What shall I do with the idle days, the useless days?" he cried. And when she did not answer, he said he would miss her dreadfully. She nodded, and he kissed her passionately and then was gone.

Now there came a time of pain. The bitter truth was that her dancing made birth more difficult. Dancing had hardened her stomach muscles, when she had thought dancing would help; instead her body ached more and more as birth approached.

She awoke one dawn when the pain came at her with such a fury she was afraid it would crush her insides. It seemed to have a sinister intention to rip out this life, to smash and destroy her. It was a miracle to Lenora how she lived through this torment. She spent many hours hating herself, feeling ill-starred and hopeless. And when the birth pangs increased until an uncontrollable rush of anguish gripped her and made her writhe on the couch, she did not care what her end would be. The brutality of a universe that made such cruelty common filled her with a despair that was overwhelming. Life runs too passionately through me, she thought, my body is too weak, nature is indifferent, no one cares about me.

Lenora longed to bestride the world and shout of the beauty of birth like an honorable artist, but now she could not even identify herself with Prometheus. She had such a chaos in her. She felt about to give birth to a whirling nebula, about to explode with anguish. How strange it seemed to hold such a tremendous thing as a new life within her! What invisible forces swarmed through her like a prophetic storm? She was bloated with an ominous dread that this child would inherit her anguish. She was too proud, too stricken to call for help, but she felt she was falling into an abyss far deeper than her womb.

When Mama arrived it was a blessing. Lenora, choked with gratitude, was unable to speak. She had been telling herself that it was finished between them, she had thrown Mama over, and here was Mama calm and smiling.

Mama had heard about the impending birth from an alarmed Amy, who could not leave the school and children. Mama had rushed here from Paris: Mama did not permit herself to think of the past; she knew that Lenora needed her, and she pretended that was enough.

Mama sat down by her trembling daughter. Lenora was half crazy with pain, and she thought it was her time to die, but she managed a smile. Then Lenora felt herself drowning, please, dear God, stop the pain, and a piteous cry rose to her lips. So it happened a million million times, she thought, and she wondered why a child should wish to poke its little head into such a world. How had Mama had three? Then she heard a cry of defiance, and a little boy was breathing by her side.

Afterward a wonderful light pervaded the room. Lenora was filled with tenderness, naming him Dion, after Dionysus, for she saw her dancing as Dionysian. She thought, this small, lovely blossom appearing in the midst of an often harsh world is a reminder of the existence of hope; it is not sensible to expect such a fragile blossom to survive in this overpowering universe, but reason is not everything; here is hope and faith. This blossom, pushing outward, is determined there will be a world to receive it. So easily bruised, so small, yet its appearance says gently but firmly that despair has lasted long enough.

But Lenora never forgot the torment she had endured during childbirth. It made Dion and the first dancing steps she took doubly precious. She had wondered many times during the anguish of birth whether she would ever be able to dance again, and now, with Mama watching her, she was about to make the attempt. It was some weeks after the birth of Dion, and Lenora walked alongside the River Nid, which circled Trondheim. She had to be close to water now, but as she walked by the river there was a doubt inside of her shattering to bits the peace of the day: it was too soon to return to dancing, too difficult. Many objections assailed her.

Mama asked, "How do you feel?"

"Fine." No matter how she felt, it must be fine.

"Dion is a splendid name." Mama smiled, and for the first time in months Lenora felt Mama's approval.

That relaxed Lenora, and she took her first dancing step. It was a simple motion, but pain went through her like the stab of a knife but she did not halt. Gradually she was able to stand straight as she danced. Then she danced in Mama's direction, weak but triumphant. Always triumphant, it was unthinkable to be anything else.

36

Triumph indeed; Lenora assumed that from now on triumph would follow triumph as surely as day followed day. When her return to dancing was greeted with adulation she accepted that as inevitable. When Eleonora Duse came backstage after one of her Berlin recitals to express her delight with Lenora's art, Lenora was pleased but not surprised.

Lenora opened the door for the famous Italian actress, and her first impression was an odd one. She had always pictured Duse with beautiful dark hair, magnificent eyes, and a nobly romantic appearance framed by a striking black velvet dress with antique lace and lovely diamonds—that had been the way the actress had seemed on stage. But now Duse looked like anything but a great actress; her dress was dowdy, she was thin and sallow, her hair was tinged with gray, her features were very sad, and there were no diamonds or lace. Yet it was remarkable: the instant Duse spoke or moved the entire impression was striking. Then Lenora saw expressive dark eyes, a sensitive face, changing with each remark, a mouth mobile and lovely, and beautifully sensuous hands.

As if to show that her real interest was Lenora and not herself, Duse said, "You were like a painting."

"Not quite real?" asked Lenora, prepared to be argumentative.

"Too real, almost," Duse said sadly. "But then that would be presumptuous. Your dancing is something to be divined, not proved. You have wonderful instinctive gestures. I had to come back and tell you."

Lenora, with all her assurance, wanted to fling herself down on her knees before Duse. Nothing could inspire her more.

Duse was one of her idols. Duse's face was passionately sincere, and Lenora thought this praise was as difficult to counterfeit as it was to reject, and she was not stone. When Duse continued to praise her, she felt transfigured.

It became a friendship stronger than any that had gone before. It was spring—and Dion was growing into a beautiful baby—and Lenora fell in love with motoring, with flashing about the countryside at a risky twenty, thirty miles an hour. Duse was as restless as Lenora, and Niels was away almost all the time now, lecturing throughout Germany on composing, and so motoring became their joint passion the next few weeks.

Lenora felt dashing in the long motoring robe, styled like a flowing Grecian gown, in the huge soft felt hat, and the magnificent flowing scarf which she swung about her neck with bravado. She took Dion often, although Mama was against it, but she said it was good for the baby: the breathless intoxication of the wind in their faces, the rush of the scenery past, the speed and movement and excitement. Then even Duse's pallid cheeks became flushed, and she almost lost her constant air of tragedy and left behind the Gabrieles, Cesares, Marios all constantly on the simmer and ready at an instant to come to a boil for the great, the incomparable Duse, fixing their melting dark eyes on her and purring solicitations, few of which she believed. For Duse knew her correct age, which was forty-seven, and in her mirror she was not magnificent or beautiful, but in the auto, rushing, rushing, so much could be forgotten. Lenora Malcolm was right; Lenora Malcolm was, she repeated, *"veramente simpatica"*; they felt godlike in their conquest of space.

Even the danger made their hearts beat more wildly, and there was danger on these primitive German roads. Their chauffeur was skillful, especially at changing tires and quick repairs, but the large open auto was rickety, often shook insanely, and dust caked their faces. And when they drove through the romantic German countryside, particularly at night, the people they preferred to avoid faded out of sight and mind, and there seemed nothing ahead but a canopy of stars. Underlying the intoxication of the motoring was Lenora's decision to dance an entire program of Niels' music, certain that would help and please him, although they had just quarreled again.

In Lenora's opinion it had been for the stupidest of reasons. A few days before she had met Duse, Niels had come backstage in a fury. She had managed to smile, but panic had descended upon her. She had never seen him so angry, and she had seen him quite angry the past few months.

Niels held up a newspaper as if it were a knife sticking out of him and read from it: "Lenora Malcolm, the renowned dancer, is said to have married Niels Nordahl, the brilliant Norwegian composer."

That was it, the pursuer felt pursued, the conqueror conquered. Lenora laughed, to show how absurd she thought these rumors were, and he assumed she was laughing at him. He stormed out before she could say another word.

So now, although Duse thought Lenora was being too reckless, she made a platform out of her next recital. When Lenora finished dancing, she came down to the footlights, asked the audience to remain, and then gave a diatribe denouncing marriage, to show Niels how she felt. She was in her favorite tunic, and she wore a crown of myrtle and bore a lily in her hand, to look her most innocent, but the Berlin police were not appeased. The next day they prohibited her from appearing in public in this costume, claiming it was indecent because much of her body was visible. But Lenora believed this censorship was because she had dared to have a child without marriage and had said so publicly.

It was Mama's conscience that was troubled, that was a mixture of anger, confusion, and forced self-justification. Much as she wanted to rebuke Lenora, she could not, she knew it would be ignored. Yet Mama was also offended by the righteousness of supporters of the school who came to her and said Lenora should marry, must marry, for the sake of the children in the school. Then Mama said to them, "I can recall when you used to cross the street just to be seen saying hello to the famous dancer, Lenora Malcolm." Nonetheless, many came to regard the American as wicked, especially when she continued to be seen with Nordahl, feeling that she had become an anarchist and that if her ideas were accepted it would be the end of *Kultur*. Others felt she was not fit to associate with children, even if she was giving them a free education and a beautiful body, and they withdrew their support of the school at Grunewald.

That did not trouble Lenora even when Amy pointed out, "You are spending far more money than you are earning."

Lenora's face was radiant. She had just returned from a wonderful drive in her auto, and she had forgotten about money. "Oh, really," she said, "can't that wait?"

Amy's ironic look said that was impossible.

Lenora was annoyed. Amy, who was just as much for freedom as she was but who hid that for business reasons, was saying Lenora ought to apologize for her remarks against marriage, and Lenora blurted out, "You save for me. Why should I save when I have so much to spend?"

From then on Amy began to plan a paid school while Lenora regarded the uproar over her remarks quite ridiculous, but typical of a Berlin that bristled with warlike things. She refused to heed Lothar when he added his word of caution. Lenora, to show her disdain for the Prussian authority and anyone who tried to confine her, did not apologize for her previous comments or agree to confine her remarks just to dancing. The next time she danced, she stated, as a kind of encore, "Berlin is a tasteless city, except for its interest in music."

Almost everyone withdrew their support now, and Amy decided to move the school to Düsseldorf, although much money had been put into Grunewald.

Lenora was happy again, however, for Niels had returned as she had expected, convinced now that she did not want to trap him and indignant over the unfair way she was being criticized. Then she had asked him if she could dance an entire program of his music, and he was pleased with her development of taste.

Niels became charming and courtly. He was excited in a way Lenora had not seen for months. His eyes sparkled, and he was extravagantly interested in her dancing; he said she was splendid and courageous to dance to his modern music. He assured her that she would make a genius out of any composer with the discernment to use her wonderful presence. He even laughed, and she had not heard him laugh for a long time.

The concert was arranged for Oslo, since he was Norwegian and their son was half-Norwegian, and she thought this was a wonderful gesture. Niels would have preferred Vienna, he thought Oslo rather drab musically, but Lenora was allowing him to supervise the entire program—a rare honor—but because it was his music, and he resolved to be content although some irritation remained.

Then Lenora took Dion with her, hoping their child would inspire Niels. It was his first real exposure to his son, and it put him in a curious frame of mind. He thought the baby very healthy but distracting, and he could not afford that, not with this marvelous opportunity about to occur. And he loathed maternal women and he wondered if this was a side of Lenora he had missed, and anybody could have a child, although Dion was an unusually attractive one. It was almost incongruous that this peaceful, smiling infant could belong to him and the tempestuous Lenora. Lenora asked, "Do you like Dion?" and how fatuous could she be, he wondered. Of course he did, but he would not be prodded into saying so. He said, "We must rehearse. The concert is only several days off."

Lenora, who had planned a quiet domestic dinner spent discussing future plans, was upset. She said, "You know I seldom need rehearsing."

"This is new music for you, that you have never danced before."

"I know it. Almost as well as you do."

"But we have to make some changes. Your dancing still isn't idyllic enough."

She said unhappily, "I've got a headache."

He had never seen her behave like this before. Suddenly Lenora was like all the females from which he had hitherto separated her. He said grimly, "You had better go to bed. I'll work out the dynamics myself."

The next day, however, when she agreed to rehearse under his supervision and conducting, he was a different person. Despite her apprehensions—she never allowed anyone to direct her dancing—it almost satisfied Niels. He said "very nice," and that she would improve in dress rehearsal.

Nothing more was said by either, but Lenora realized that the dress rehearsal would have to contain the quality of a performance, that would be the only way she could dance romantically enough to satisfy Niels.

It was a great strain on her, but the dress rehearsal went so well he fervently embraced her and said her dancing was a miracle, she shed divine energy, had caught almost all the pastoral beauty of the finale, and she replied, "Darling, since Wagner, believe me, nothing has been composed to equal your tone poems."

Niels frowned. Pleased as he was with her appreciation and some of her interpretation, she still lacked understanding. His music was far more lyrical than Wagner's. Everyone who knew music in Scandinavia said he was the inevitable successor to Norway's first nationalist composer, Richard Nordraak, and her most recent, Edvard Grieg.

And much of artistic Oslo came to Lenora's recital of Niels' music. They rose to their feet as he took his place at the conductor's desk, and suddenly, greatly moved by the ovation he had received, she sought to be heroic, it seemed so appropriate for the mood of the audience. She created an atmosphere of excitement that aroused the audience to a frenzy. They forgot the music, the conductor; all that seemed important was this ecstatic, valiant figure on stage. At the end of the recital the entire audience surged toward her, wanting to embrace her as she had embraced them. When she calmed them down with a lift of her arms, she pointed to Niels and shouted bravo as she applauded him. The audience followed her example, but the bravos were loudest for her. Then she brought him on stage, to share the continuing applause. But when they took their bows she felt his hand tighten on hers until she thought it would crush all life out of her.

And in her dressing room, when they were finally alone and she turned to congratulate him, she was shocked by his appearance. Instead of smiling happily he was staring at her with such an expression of anguish it was almost unbearable. He said, "You promise to dance to my music, and you make it your music."

"Niels, it was our music."

"No, you made it *your* music. You had to be the star."

"I had to dance what I felt."

"What *you* felt, not what I felt."

She went to kiss him affectionately, as if to say what did that matter, but he pulled away from her. His anger and anguish, if anything, were worse.

He said, "You're very clever. You pretend to express my music and end up exploiting it for your own advantage."

Lenora was astonished. "But, Niels, that's just what I did not do."

"Then your art is only a series of accidental confessions. But my art is deliberate, honest."

"You want me to be dumb?"

"Dancers are dumb anyway. I compose idyllic, romantic music, and you dance it fortissimo, like Wagner."

"Wagner? You should be delighted with the comparison. When Wagner composed for the stage he kept the music subservient to the action on stage."

Niels lost his temper now, for he hated being compared to anyone else, especially Wagner, and he shouted, "You want *Tannhäuser*? You want inflated operas, exaggerated emotions, dead ideas. It's no wonder. You are a feminine artist, you women who can only absorb art as you absorb men. But the masculine artist absorbs life itself, and life derives from the new material he turns into art. I can't expect that you would understand this, however."

"Niels!" This was sacrilege. Lenora was shocked by his prejudice.

"You women, trying to be artists, make me sick!"

"I'm Lenora Malcolm, not women, not like anybody else!"

"Wonderful! But you are all alike. All you women!"

"All of what?" Lenora said furiously. "I'm not one of anything. I'm myself, that's who I am. But you are so extreme. The trouble with you is you don't understand women."

"Oh, yes I do! I understand the whole damned lot of you! You are more interested in having us breed your children than in creating great art."

Lenora could not reply, looking at him sadly. She thought he was proud, arrogant, believing most of all in his own greatness, in the supreme importance of what he was doing, in the vast superiority of his music to anyone else's, in the obligation of others to help him, admire him, and support him, and yet she still loved him. For he was also inspiring, exciting, attractive, with a passion for perfection that was often marked with genius.

Lenora was jolted back to the present when he canceled their reservation at the hotel. When she asked why, he replied that she regarded his music as merchandise.

"You're mad!"

"The truth hurts, doesn't it? You had no more awareness of what my music meant than that flimsy robe you are so proud of wearing. My music, which is different than anyone else's in the world, and a ballerina could do it better."

And Lenora, who had thought she could share everything with Niels, could not share this. What had he said about women? A wave of nausea choked her. He was flaying her for crimes she had not committed. But she said as he strode to the door, "I'll see you later."

Niels laughed, and something in it, bitter and sinister, struck her like a slap in the face. "I must go," he said. "I must go to where my music is appreciated." Then he was gone, still in a rage.

Lenora returned to Berlin with Dion, and when she told Duse what had happened in Oslo, Duse said, "Believe me, he is mad, it is the nature of genius."

"He hasn't come back."

"It is the nature of suffering." Duse sought to be consoling. "Suffering enriches art. Women are born to suffer, and sacrifice."

"If he were truly in love with me there would have been no blame."

"That is when there is the most," Duse said with a melancholy air.

By now Lenora was aware that Duse was in love with suffering, but Lenora was not; Lenora was in love with love.

The next day she heard that Niels had gone on to Vienna. Duse said it was fate, repeating that this was the nature of suffering, but Lenora could not be resigned. Duse regarded her as a saint in misfortune, enmeshed by a web of circumstances that could trap the most knowing woman, but Lenora felt in a fever which bordered on delirium. And Duse insisted on talking about renunciation. Oh God! she did not want renunciation, she wanted love. Duse was advising her to wait, and she could not wait. Duse was declaring it was best to leave things as they were, and that made her feel hopeless. Suddenly Lenora wanted to go to Moscow. There had been arrangements for such a trip pending for weeks with Lothar, who had been waiting for her to assent to terms, and that was real, that was all that was real. Lenora told Lothar she was prepared to dance in Moscow, the sooner the better.

That evening there was a knock on her door. Lenora was rigid yet tense, sure it was Niels and then not sure, feeling triumphant and feeling tormented, and then she opened the door. It was not Niels. It was Anthony, a bit actor in Duse's company. Anthony was dapper, dark, and graceful. He had a message from Duse; the actress was returning to Italy and wanted Lenora to accompany her, but Lenora's mind was elsewhere.

Anthony would not quarrel with her, would not question her art; Anthony acted only because it was the easiest way to make a living.

And so thinking, I am Lenora Malcolm and it would be simple to take Anthony to Moscow as my personal manager and who is to say I cannot, she held out her hand for him to enter. Anthony kissed her hand, and when he saw the invitation in her eyes he whispered gallantly, "I had to come."

But that evening, for a terrible moment, his body seemed the very same body she missed so much. Then she was full of despair, but Anthony was laughing and Niels seldom laughed; he was drawing her close as if she were the only thing that mattered in his life. She felt his heart pounding, and she realized he was young, younger than she, and she said to herself, Niels is the last man I take seriously.

After that there was nothing but plans for Moscow, but she knew this journey was different. When she had fallen in love with Niels, she had had dreams that it would be forever, but she was certain that she and Anthony would not die together.

Lenora stopped off at Grunewald to leave Dion there. It

was like a lovely garden, and too beautiful to endure. Amy
had not yet moved to Düsseldorf, finding it heartbreaking to
relinquish this school which, not so long ago, she and Mama
and Lenora had found so splendid and adventurous. But Lenora was not to be distracted by such concerns. Lenora left
for Moscow before anything could be discussed, with Anthony obvious in her entourage as her personal manager, leaving the six-month-old Dion with Mama and Amy in such a
way they felt merely like two nursemaids.

37

Where was she going? What lay ahead? Did they really desire
her dancing? Lenora stood in the wings of the Moscow
theater, about to start her first recital there, and all these
doubts spun through her mind.

It was several weeks later, and so far none of this romantic
flight with Anthony had been the idyl she had anticipated.
The days had been tedious and boring. She had wasted most
of the evenings, unable to practice, dreaming of Niels with a
voluptuous sadness, unable to forget him in spite of Anthony.
Their love had not become magnificent, although Anthony
had remained a pretty and charming boy. She had read him
the Song of Solomon, certain that would inspire him, and he
had fallen asleep after their moment of love. There had been
a distressing letter from Amy in Berlin, which had added to
her sadness. Mama had caught a chill and seemed so exhausted by it that even the disciplined Amy was worried.
Mama was in bed and Amy was nursing her and Dion was
fine but missing Lenora, while Mama was saying that the
moment she got better she was returning to America.

Lenora's heart was heavy. The last of the day's heavy snow
lay over Moscow like a depressing blanket, and she peered
through the stage curtains and that was another sorrow. The
theater was less than half full, despite her success in St. Petersburg. It was so cold, even in the theater, that she wore a
heavy fur coat over her dancing tunic. The stage, which she
had tried out behind the curtains, was like ice, and yet for the
opening number she planned to lie on the floor. Then there
were other resentments and doubts. Lenora was shocked by
the posters in front of the theater which were of a ballerina in
the middle of a pirouette. And beneath this horror, which she

was sure had been done deliberately to provoke her, was the tiny announcement: "Lenora Malcolm, American dancer." When she questioned this publicity, so obnoxious to her, controlling her temper with difficulty, the manager of the theater shrugged and said, "That is all we have in Russia, ballet dancers, and it doesn't matter, as long as we have your name here, and spelled correctly." She realized then that Anthony was not even a good personal manager, and she felt anxious and alone, and if it were not for the distant manipulations of Lothar she would be in desperate straits indeed.

And now Anthony stood beside her—although she had forbidden that, no one must disturb her concentration before a recital—and he was saying, "I would not dance Chopin tonight. The Russians will consider it unpatriotic."

"No."

"Lenora, the risk . . ."

"I said no!" He started to caress her, and she moved away. He had no real awareness of her dancing, that it was not a profession but a religion. Knowing then that if she lingered any longer she would be lost, she nodded to the conductor to begin—although she did not trust this second-rate orchestra, another of Anthony's errors—and the lights went down and she appeared before the curtain and there was uncertain applause. How dull this audience was, she thought, and slowly and softly she approached them. She came downstage until she could almost touch them, but the audience and stage was so cold it was as if she had to learn to dance all over again. Anger prodded her, and suddenly she rose from the floor, although the music asked for a sustained pause. Then she danced two Chopin polonaises which were called "Poland Enchained" and "Poland Resurrected." They had been the dances which had won St. Petersburg, but Moscow did not respond. At the end of the first half of the program there was fitful applause.

Despondent, Lenora lay motionless in her dressing room during the intermission while her maid undressed and bathed her. Lenora's body was soaked with perspiration, and the maid sponged her with many thick towels. There was a sharp pain in her back from the icy floor and the drafts in the theater, but after her body was dry she donned a fresh tunic and sipped some champagne and felt somewhat revived.

She was opening the second half of her program with the "Venusberg Music" from *Tannhäuser*—as a tribute to Nordahl—and before the curtain rose she spoke to the audience about her interpretation. She said they must add their imagination and intensity to hers. But even this did not seem to go well. The audience shifted restlessly, and there were even a few boos. She saw Anthony watching her and thought he was not the one concerned. She was, and perhaps Mama, and certainly Niels, and now the "Venusberg Music" became precious. Putting aside politics, she was dancing for him, dancing love requited and unrequited. Lenora seemed to come out of a sea of emotion, to embrace the audience with an overwhelming joy. Their faces took on the appearance of Niels; she was dancing for a hundred Niels. There was love in everything now, in her arms, in the music, in her intensity. The audience did not stir restlessly any more, but watched intently, their disdain forgotten, all forgotten but the blossoming of love before them. When she finished her final number, "The Elysian Fields," she pointed to the sky and gallery with an ecstatic glow, and the whole audience stood up and applauded and the gallery shouted "Bravo!"

Her first encore was the "March Slav," and this time the audience stayed standing while she danced, as if the spirit of Russia danced before them. Her second encore was from the *Symphonie Pathétique*, and now a wave of patriotism swept the audience.

The curtains parted again and again, and Lenora stopped counting after the tenth call. They turned up the lights in the audience, made longer and longer waits between the calls, and still the crowd cheered and refused to allow her to halt. Then the orchestra conductor turned out the lights so he and his men could go home, but students from the gallery rushed onto the stage, dragged out the piano, and lit candles so they could see Lenora. A pianist was found in the audience, and the encores became one improvisation after another. Finally, however, it was even more than Lenora could dance, and when after the tenth encore the enthusiasm was still unabated she asked for a candle, and when they gave it to her, she ordered all the other candles put out. Then she asked, "What is the Russian for good night?" And when she was told she went into the darkness carrying her lighted candle and wished those still applauding a fervent *"Dobroi Nochie."*

Yet even now, past midnight, the theater unlit and icy cold, the enthusiasm did not lessen. Stanislavsky, the Russian actor-director, stood in front of her with an ecstatic expression on his face. "Miss Malcolm . . . !" His voice quivered with emotion. "Never, but never, have I seen a dancer express so perfectly and vividly the inner life. Miss Malcolm, upon my honor, it is a great triumph."

Stanislavsky towered over her with his unusual height. He had splendid, large features, wavy hair, an artistic carriage, and he stirred Lenora at once. She was certain he was intelligent and idealistic.

Lenora, without hesitating, discussed art, literature, music, and the theater with him. When she and Stanislavsky got into the auto she had hired she ignored Anthony, who had gone on to the hotel and was waiting for her there, and asked Stanislavsky to show her Moscow. They had an animated dinner at the famous Hermitage Restaurant. Stanislavsky was so gentle, so thoughtful, so erudite she wanted it to never end, wanted to go for a ride in the dawn air, wanted to continue this wonderfully lively, witty, clever conversation in her borrowed fur coat and heavy Russian moujik cap. But with the coming of the dawn Stanislavsky became self-conscious. He suddenly recalled he had a rehearsal this afternoon. He agreed that the dawn was beautiful and added, "But we must not be indiscreet."

My dear, she wanted to retort, let us stop pretending. But they had just met, and she did not want to offend him. So she said, "Yes, we must be honest with each other."

Five minutes later he was gone with the promise to return that evening.

Anthony was more primitive when she found him at the hotel, sitting in a huge chair, dressed in one of her kimonos and in a vile humor, with a splitting headache. And when she told him that Moscow was too cold and lonely for him and that he should return to Berlin where she would meet him several weeks later, he revealed a talent for acting he had not hitherto shown. His face went through an entire scale of forlorn, tragic expressions. There was the constant chorus, "Lenora, *mia*, I love you."

But she no longer cared for him. She agreed it was sad, disappointing, even disillusioning and absurd, but that fact remained. She appealed to Anthony to be civilized, but Anthony, in a fever of jealousy, broke several chairs before she was able to calm him.

"In any case," she assured him, "our love has been worth it."

The strange thing was that Lenora could not, however hard she thought, place her finger on the moment when her desire for Anthony had ended. She lay in bed, after Anthony had departed, trying to sleep, but thinking one second, I am in love with Niels, and the next, I accept Anthony. Acceptance, however, is not love, but Anthony does not know that, he is too insensitive and that is why he does not inspire love. And now he will think I am leaving him for Stanislavsky. All the Anthonys don't know they are the ones who cheat me. Men,

men, the limited unimaginative men who cannot give me what I need. . . . Lenora was frightened as she imagined dozens of men passing her, each giving her a kiss on her mouth which she accepted. No, no, she cried, she must not accept again—she must only love. Acceptance would ruin her, would blunt her reach and inspiration, would waste her body, would trample on all the gods in her mind. But what if she weakened, if her strength and inspiration were exhausted in this search, this unending search. If people could only understand this hunger for a great love which almost drove her frantic. Would it never be satisfied? Then she thought of Stanislavsky, and she was filled with hope again.

In some ways Lenora was right about Stanislavsky: he was civilized. He led those in Moscow supporting the remainder of her recitals, and that assured her continued triumph. He spoke an excellent French, and they had no difficulty talking to each other. But he refused the champagne she adored; he said it muddled his senses. He was a hearty eater, but he never overate; he said too much weight hindered him as an actor. Despite his culture, his taste was so severe and uncompromising there were moments when the impatient Lenora saw him as a Puritan. Yet she was certain their friendship would proceed on normal lines. She rented a car; she had two chauffeurs, so one would always be on call. And Stanislavsky enjoyed driving about Moscow and showing her the sights.

She did not seem to stir him otherwise, and so after her last recital in Moscow she invited him to her suite for a farewell party. He was startled to find no one else there; he had expected at least a dozen other people. He thought it was time to go home, but he was intrigued. Lenora was sensuously attractive, and she carried herself with unusual grace. She wore a perfume which was subtle yet penetrating. She pressed against him. He wanted to embrace her, the thought of not embracing her gave him physical pain.

She could feel the warmth of his body, his desire was indisputable—his acting and her dancing grew out of the same inner creative feeling, and he was so tall and interesting—yet suddenly he retreated in obvious distress.

Lenora was amazed. He understood her in a way Niels had not; he should be the perfect lover, but when she suggested love he sat down on the couch and said gloomily, "I am married. It is impossible."

"I don't want to take you away from your wife. What we have is different from what she has."

"It isn't that. I don't want to involve you in an offensive situation."

"We can still be friends."

"Not that way." He was almost choking as he apologized. "I shouldn't have led you on." He gazed at her sadly, desiring her lovely body, vital and voluptuous, wishing it did not hurt so to reject it, to be practical.

"Let's drink, friend," she said gaily.

The vodka, which he preferred, did not alter his gloomy demeanor. He grew more somber. He said, "I am dedicated to the theater, but you need a man who could love you all the time. Forgive me, it is my fault, I am sorry."

"My dear Stanislavsky," she smiled, "I don't insist."

By now the memory of Niels left her numb. When she thought clearly about him, she realized they had yielded to each other because they had been creating each other in their own image. Other times, however, she decided Duse had been right about their separation: it had been fate.

And Moscow had not been a waste. While she was riding in an open carriage to the railroad station—it was one of the few mild winter afternoons in the city and Stanislavsky was escorting her—several persons recognized her. One, a ballet student at the Imperial School, ran after the carriage. The young woman, hardly more than eighteen, reached the carriage when it paused at an intersection and frightened Lenora by leaping up the steps. For a moment Lenora thought the young woman intended violence. Before Lenora could cry out, however, the ballet student threw a bouquet of flowers at her and shouted, "To Lenora, our sister in art!"

Lenora had been thinking of Stanislavsky and feeling a little sorry for herself, but this tribute drove everything else out of her mind. She leaned out and threw a kiss to the ballet student, to everyone within reach.

38

You are Mama Malcolm. Your fondest dreams have come true. Your daughter is crowned with more praise and profit than you have ever imagined. There is no risk of oblivion now; whatever happens your daughter will always be remembered. She has become one of the world's best-known artists. But for you the world has become dark and cold. Your daughter says criticism does not matter, she takes great pride in doing just what she pleases, and you are weary of what she pleases, of her damn-the-consequences behavior. Yet you know she is possessed with an inspiration that inspires others, her audiences feel that her emotion is their emotion. You have shouted to her many times to be brave; you have lived to see her name a byword. And now you feel lost. Her future is out of your hands. There is no need for her to depend upon you for anything.

So Mama had no bouquets for the returning Lenora. A memory book shredded into jagged pieces . . . a string of broken promises . . . a strange man's face appearing suddenly at the window of Lenora's bedroom. These were the things Mama remembered when Lenora came back from Moscow. To make matters worse, Anthony demanded a hand in the running of the school, as Lenora's personal manager, until Amy threw him out. But this was not the end of Mama's distress. Although Anthony finally had gone back to Rome, and Lenora looked relieved, now there was Romain. When Mama asked where this stocky, brown-haired man came from —he was almost a physical duplicate of Niels, but little else— Lenora replied airily, "From the moon."

"Another personal manager?"

"Oh, no!" Lenora was not making that mistake again. "Lothar is handling my recitals, and no one else."

"Then what does this man do?"

Lenora smiled. "He is sweet and kind and understanding." Lenora did not add what she was thinking: and so I accepted him, but that is not love; I am still waiting for that great love. "He is fun to be with, interesting, he is . . . well, just Romain. My affection for him is genuine. I admit he hasn't much depth, but he gives me happiness, I love him in a way, he . . ."

Mama did not listen to the rest. An aimless wind blew through her, and she was chilled. She had been out of bed a week now, and she could not retreat to it again, for it was no retreat any longer. Spring was in full bloom, Grunewald never looked lovelier, and she was stricken with a dreadful depression. Men will ruin her, Mama cried to herself, I will not suffer this, she is incurable. Mama said suddenly, "I'm leaving. I mean it. No one is changing my mind." Her words came out in a torrent so Lenora had to hear at least once, at least now. "And it isn't a question of forgiveness. I can't help it, Lenora. I suppose it is the way I was made. But you can't be monogamous."

Lenora, thinking that although she still loved Mama, Mama had her tiresome moments, fussing over them as if they were still children, retorted, "That is stupid. It has nothing to do with being monogamous. It has nothing to do with being a woman, it is what we are as individuals. I can no longer deny myself . . . I did for years and I suffered for it. I love only one man at a time, and I should not have to explain that to you. When I was a child I thought as a child, but I haven't been a child for a long time."

"Don't you take love seriously, or motherhood?"

"Please, don't you preach to me, you are not so easy to live with."

"Lenora?" No, she could not suffer this.

"You insist on forgiving me all the time, when I don't want forgiveness."

Mama cried, "That is not the issue. You prefer to be free and irresponsible, free to make love to whomever you prefer at the moment. Well, I won't interfere, hereafter. I won't be here."

"It's that loathsome publicity that bothers you."

"No, Lenora, it is you. I no longer have any real place in your life, and it is time we recognized that." But how would she bear it?

"You need amusement, Mama."

"No. Perhaps when I am away I will care less. You will care less, in any event, as soon as you meet new people, a new lover!" It was out although she had not intended to say it.

"Gossip. Don't you know that treasures of imagination and intelligence are wasted in inventing rumors and scandals of all kinds?"

"I am not concerned about rumors, I am concerned about you and me." Mama looked old and gaunt. She started to pack, and this time Lenora made no effort to halt her. And Mama, unable to think the worst of her daughter even in this bitter moment, thought, it is simply the force of Lenora's creative instinct that even if her career depended on her doing without me, she would orphan herself without a moment's hesitation, and that is necessary for the artist.

Lenora leaned back on her luxurious couch and searched for the right thing to say. Anthony had been stupid, and Romain was not a genius, but disapproval of them was moral rubbish. She wished to embrace Mama, but in the midst of such a discussion Mama might be offended. She quoted Plutarch: "To find fault is easy, to do better is difficult."

Mama said, "You don't understand me at all."

"Do you understand me?"

"I know that you are promiscuous, and that is a waste. You are throwing yourself away."

"Really?" There was a startling nakedness in Lenora's eyes as she prodded Mama to continue.

"And it isn't the morality of it that troubles me, as you think," said Mama, almost at a whisper, "or that I think you are rotten and dirty and stupid. But I am your mother . . . !" This came out in a piteous cry, and she murmured, "If you were really in love I'd do anything I could to make it work. Only you are not, you are promiscuous, and I can't stand that!"

Lenora sighed. "Promiscuous is just a word. If ever I find a man who satisfies me in the way I need, I will stay with him." How could she tell Mama that Niels left her, not she Niels, and ever since she had been searching for a new Niels, and that the greatest thing in life was to discover herself, and discovering perfect love was part of discovering oneself, and to the extent she did, she could say, I have lived, and you have to do that at a price. She said proudly, "I am not promiscuous. I have never loved more than one man at a time. That you can believe. And you know I have never lied to you. Have I?"

"I believe . . . you."

"And that my love is real?"

Mama was silent.

"You don't believe that?" Lenora was shocked.

"It's no use," Mama said sadly. She looked out on the lawn at Grunewald. The sun had risen high, it was a beautiful day, and she was trespassing, she felt that whatever Lenora said. And now she was talking to herself as much as to Lenora. "I feel so alone, no matter what you say. Maybe I am the stupid one, the selfish one, maybe I should have left you long ago. After Budapest, when I felt I should."

"Were you ashamed of me then?"

"It doesn't matter. But if ever you really need me, I will come back, if you ask me to. Now you don't need me."

Mama was sounding just like Duse. Lenora wondered: did all middle-aged women live in renunciation?

"Remember this," said Mama, "I always want you to be happy. I live for your happiness."

"Romain will make me happy."

"Perhaps."

"You don't believe this either."

"I'm not sure. But I do know you must have heightened feelings, and I cannot give you that. When you were a child, when you were growing up, when we first came to Europe my faith fed you, perhaps even inspired you, but now that isn't necessary. Perhaps you are right, perhaps you need a Romain, but . . ." Mama wept, full of pity for herself, for the heaven they had no longer. Lenora embraced her and begged her to stay, but Mama could not stay. There were only words now, words which apologized for past mistakes and accomplished nothing.

Lenora was attentive the rest of Mama's stay at Grunewald, the way she used to be. There were no more recriminations. Amy, deciding to move the school to Düsseldorf, agreed with Mama's decision. The one time Amy started to criticize Lenora to Mama, Mama said, "Lenora is sincere. You may not agree with her, but she is sincere."

"Don't misunderstand me," Amy replied. "I don't deny her ability, but . . ."

"Lenora is a law unto herself," said Mama. "We must recognize that."

Farewells came hard, however, and Mama could hardly breathe saying good-by. It was a kind of death, and she felt forsaken. This was the end of her road and her dream. Motherhood was over, and she thought, now the world will see me as a silent woman, prim, conventional, disloyal, when I tried so often to be loyal even when I no longer had faith, I tried not to complain although I hated the lonesomeness when Lenora was away, I hated the bare studios, the sleeping on the floor, the voyage to Greece, the peplum and chlamys and the cutting of my lovely, long-grown hair, I hated the constant moving, a dozen different residences without ever feeling at home, but Lenora was such a lovely child, such a beautiful young woman, and now she is too heavy but I cannot tell her, she is no longer a model of virginal innocence though she still dances it and behaves as if each lover is the first, and it is impossible to be motherly and benign. Where, oh where, is my Lenora?

Mama arrived in New York several weeks later, but she did not remain with Archer, who had returned from Paris to act on Broadway. Although he was doing well playing character leads she went on to San Francisco. Perhaps there the ache would be less: this break must be as clean as an amputation. But the ache did not lessen. When Mama got off the train at San Francisco she could not recall Jessie's address. Her sister was waiting for her, however, having been notified by Archer. The once striking Jessie was stout, plain, looking twenty years older; Mama felt a hundred.

In Europe a troubled Lenora began to dream with a frequency that upset her. There was one dream in particular which was quite disturbing and which occurred repeatedly.

She was standing on a huge stage, but she could not dance. The stage had no boundaries but seemed as vast as the Pacific and there was nothing else. Music started, but she could not move. She could not recall how the piece began, or who it was by, or what it was about. The audience was jeering at her, and Mama would tell her how it started, Mama knew, and where was Mama?

Awake suddenly, Lenora sprang out of bed, ignoring Romain who lay in a deep sleep, unaware of her nightmare. A soundless scream rose to her lips as she realized Mama was many weeks away. What had Mama said: "Home is where we go when everything else shuts us out." -

Lenora cried for the remainder of the night, longing for Mama, for Mama's genius for love. For the first time she gave Mama credit for genius.

The moving of the school to Düsseldorf seemed a success— Dion and the children adored the change, the novelty—and Lenora was due to dance in Paris soon, and even Lothar thought there would be no difficulties there.

But Lenora knew now that she had never planned, even in her imagination, to be apart from Mama. Her wish to see Mama, now that Mama was gone, beat at her like a hammer. And suddenly Lenora decided to tour America, as soon as it could be arranged, without Romain.

39

So this summer, still yearning for Mama, Lenora left for an extensive tour of America, leaving Romain to shift for himself and Dion and the school in the care of Amy. But to her surprise and disappointment Mama had not remained with Archer as she had expected, but had gone on to San Francisco.

Mama's absence was painful, and Lenora, as always when unhappy, went to the best hotel. She wondered if Mama's months apart had separated them irrevocably, and that added to her irritation, although she had scant time to brood. The instant Lenora came out to the drawing room of her large, lavish suite she was surrounded by reporters. She told the press, which regarded her as the latest curiosity of the hour, that she had come home to America to bring it her art and to get money to keep her beloved school going, and they were asking her the most personal questions. Lenora expected to be acclaimed as an American artist: she was the most acclaimed American artist in Europe, and they were calling her a Greek dancer. She was delighted to see her native land again, fascinated by its fantastic energy, by the way New York had changed and grown, and they were regarding her dancing with the same indifference she had detested ten years ago. She assumed there would be serious discussions of her art; their disinterest struck her as criminal, and her irritation grew. They were preoccupied with her clothes, with her simple sandals and with her loose white Grecian gown which was especially comfortable in the August heat.

She heard one of the reporters whisper to another, "I told you she wore sandals. See them."

Provoked, she stated, "I am only expressing in the dance what everybody who loved it, from Plato to Wagner, said and thought." But still no one applauded. The scornful way they looked when she proclaimed that: did they feel sorry for her? What nerve! Even more provoked, even more determined to show them that Europe had acknowledged her if America hadn't, she announced, "There are many opera houses in Europe that have put my ideas of dance into complete operation."

"Do they dance in that costume?" asked one of the reporters, staring apprehensively at the flimsy Grecian robe she was wearing.

"Of course not. They are still ballet dancers."

"Do you dance in that costume?"

"Naturally," she said with increasing irritation. She was very disappointed by Mama's absence. She had been willing to ask Mama to return, but now it was not so simple.

"And you rely on nothing else?" asked another puzzled reporter.

"On my inspiration."

"But don't you accomplish anything?"

Lenora, not wanting to have murder on her conscience, struggled to control her temper—although it was difficult for they were becoming infuriating—and said, "I accomplish a great deal, especially with children. I wanted to bring them here to dance, but the law prevented that."

A new reporter said, "They are too young, aren't they?"

She retorted, "A child is never too young to dance."

Another reporter said, "It seems impractical to me. As soon as they grow up they'll get married, and then all your efforts will be wasted."

Several of the reporters guffawed at that, and this triggered

Lenora's already touchy temper. She was furious now at Mama's absence, blaming that for the miserable way this interview was going, and further provoked by their stupidity, her own perversity, she declared, "They send people to interview me who know nothing of dancing, nothing of art, nothing of inspiration, and they expect me to tell in five minutes what I have put a lifetime into. Why don't they send me artists? They might understand what I am striving for, what I have been working all these years to accomplish."

"Shall we quote that?"

"Do you think I'm made of wood? It's the truth."

Most of the newspapers the following day referred to her as a freak, since she was neither a ballerina nor an acrobatic dancer, and discussed what she considered irrelevant, that she danced in her bare feet and wore a transparent costume which was shocking. When they did speak of her as a dancer, they stressed what they called "her generous proportions."

This provoked her even more into a determination to do what she pleased. Several days later Lenora strolled down crowded Broadway, thinking she had returned to be crowned by her homeland, many times she had prayed to be crowned here, and Broadway became more crowded with each step she took as people surged toward her to see whether she was really wearing hardly anything. Lenora thought her self most sensible, wearing her flimsy Grecian-style dress and open sandals, which struck her as quite appropriate for the heat wave afflicting New York this August, and everyone seemed scandalized. She created such a commotion she was halted by the police. Even as she insisted this was the natural attire for such hot weather, she was advised it was against the law and that she must wear more.

Outraged, she denounced this in another interview, declaring that America had no appreciation of beauty, that most clothes were worn just to entice men, and the next time she appeared in her flowing but flimsy Grecian-style dress, this time on Fifth Avenue, another mob gathered around her, so large it halted traffic. She was warned that the next time she appeared this way she would be arrested. She replied that the authorities were as coarse and stupid as the Prussian police.

Charles Frohman, who had agreed to manage this artist of Lothar's in America, who was presenting her for twenty weeks—ten at the Criterion Theater on Broadway and ten on the road—was distressed by her behavior. He felt it was fine publicity that she was the first artist devoting an entire evening to dance, unrelieved by song, skit, or recitation, ever to be seen in a dramatic theater in America, but he had no desire to have a censorship battle on his hands. Frohman made light of the agitation over her clothes, calling her garb "merely pink cheesecloth," and that offended her.

By the time she opened at the Criterion Theater she was in a foul mood. It was still August, before the season, the house was half empty, and the heat held New York in its enervating grip and the audience was apathetic. Lenora sought to create her inspiration by thinking of Mama—as she had thought about Niels in Moscow—but Mama's continued absence made her furious, although there was a first-night telegram from Mama wishing her well, and fury had never been one of her effective sources of inspiration. She also felt let down by the heat-wilted audience. If this was what America wanted, it hardly seemed worth while. Even in her own eyes it was an inferior performance, but she felt it was not her fault. The reviews were scathing. They stressed that she was overweight, that her décor was too plain, that she was not a pretty dancer. The critics were disappointed that she was neither sensational nor sensual. Bitter and disgusted, Lenora stated, and the press was delighted to quote her explosive remarks, "America is too crass, too unimaginative to appreciate true art."

Frohman warned her to be more careful, and she retorted, "This is the time for truth. It is crucial. If I don't tell them the truth, who will? You?" Lenora did not wait for his reply, certain what that would be. She was prepared to re-enact Lady Godiva if necessary.

And Frohman thought: how wise is God, to keep out of all this.

He had advertised her as his latest find, but now he feared she would be impossible to sell. It was a pity, he reflected, for there had been great public interest in her until she had opened her mouth. Frohman altered his approach and presented her as commercial theater, and that made matters worse. These critics regarded her as a commodity and went on to say that her dancing was "rusty," that her figure was "faulty," her movements really "physical culture," a remark that infuriated her, that she "swooped" and "capered," that she was "not even pretty," which stunned her, that this was "vaudeville," one of the worst insults, and "Who handed this lemon to Frohman?" which sent pain pouring through her.

She felt the press was united in a conspiracy against her. The ten-week engagement was reduced to three as her audiences dwindled; the receipts were so poor her contract with Charles Frohman ended after a short road tour.

It was impossible to continue when she read a review which stated:

> . . . Miss Malcolm has found a rival, a natural artist in the Tennessee mountains, a milkmaid who has the great advantage of never having worn shoes or stockings, but whose magnificent technique, surpassing even Miss Malcolm's, is the waving of her big toe, the purest revelation of the psyche of the dance.

She decided not to tour to San Francisco, which had been her original intention; the thought of being a failure there was intolerable. Mama's sustained absence had become a gnawing, perpetual sore, and in self-defense she had pretended not to care, not even to Archer, whom she saw occasionally, but she did care—very much.

She spent the next few days in bed, feeling very sorry for herself, although she did manage to issue a statement, on Frohman's urging, in which she said, "I had gone abroad ten years before to wait for the people in my own country to take an interest in me, but I see I had better go back to Europe and wait for ten more years and then come back and try again," but she did not mean it. She resolved never to come back. She booked passage for Europe.

The day she was to sail Walter Damrosch, conductor of the New York Symphony, appeared at her door. She could not wait to get out of the country, and he wanted her to dance with his orchestra at the Metropolitan Opera House.

She said, "They hate me with a virulent hatred."

Damrosch said, "We have a little difficulty, sometimes, recognizing art, but perhaps you have been in the wrong setting. With a symphony orchestra you will attract a different audience."

"For one recital?"

"For one at a time," he said.

"Remember, I will get out of this country as soon as I can if this matinee is not a success." She would give New York one more chance to appreciate her art, but no more. She did not alter her plans to depart; she merely postponed her passage so that she could sail the day after the recital. She was quite surprised when the sale of tickets the day of the recital assured a sold-out house.

Enthusiasm was a wonderful thing to Lenora, and as the Metropolitan Opera House filled to capacity her inspiration revived. She was dancing to the Seventh Symphony of Beethoven; there were one hundred and ten men in the New

York Symphony, and she was all alone on stage and that was absolutely right to her. She felt beautiful again. She felt that since existence was never the same for any two moments, neither was the dance. And, as always, when she danced her best it had the quality of improvisation. Believing that she could trust this audience, she was again the possessed girl with the bare feet hammering on the crust of the world. It was not dancing to many in the audience, they had never seen movements like this before, and when she finished moving to the Beethoven the audience acclaimed her.

More matinees followed to sold-out houses. She became the object of repeated demonstrations of enthusiasm. She forgot about the sneering notices when she read what the *Tribune* said:

Miss Malcolm's style of dancing is now well known. Her grace of rhythm, her poses; her flowing, diaphanous draperies, they were there as ever, and in addition they were carried only by music of a very high order that was in perfect keeping with the dancer's art and classicism.

What had happened under Frohman's management was no longer important. Lenora canceled her passage for Europe and rented a studio in addition to her hotel suite, while Damrosch planned a tour of America's newest artistic sensation. There was no criticism of her garb now in New York; it was regarded as art. No one complained about her bare feet. Artists thronged around her as the symbol of self-expression and used her paraphrase of Whitman as her motto and theirs: "The only artist I compete with is myself."

And when she was informed that her last matinee in the Metropolitan Opera House had taken in over five thousand dollars, a record for a dancer, she was sure that she had triumphed over the Philistines, and she agreed to tour wherever Damrosch suggested.

Lenora became more sculpturesque than voluptuous. She lessened her pagan quality and stressed the spiritual, appearing almost nunlike, dressed with a classical severity, opening each recital with her hands folded in an attitude of prayer, like a Madonna, which she considered more appropriate for America. She was growing heavier, but no one mentioned that now. She was being remembered as the heroine of the Windsor Hotel fire, that was as conspicuous in her reviews as her art. It was stressed that she had saved every pupil in the doomed hotel at the risk of her life.

Boston was a victory, for Boston prided itself on being just as cultural as New York, and it became obligatory to accept "The Malcolm." During the intermission youngsters sold pamphlets up and down the aisles which proclaimed her art as the dance of the future.

Washington was an even greater victory. Lenora was delighted when she read in a newspaper the next day:

> President Roosevelt and many celebrities applauded the dancer and the orchestra. One of the biggest ovations that has been accorded an artist in the National Capital for a long time was given Lenora Malcolm and the New York Symphony this afternoon. The house was filled to its capacity. The President and Mrs. Roosevelt occupied a private box and with them was Nicholas Longworth.

Lenora expected nothing but victories now, having won the President's approval. Milwaukee was, and Minneapolis, and St. Paul.

Philadelphia was another success, and Buffalo and Albany and Cleveland and Grand Rapids and Madison and Baltimore.

Pittsburgh, however, a city of faultless chastity, was shocked at the thought of Lenora Malcolm. A delegation of Sunday-school teachers declared she would endanger the morals of the city and asked that she be suppressed. She replied they might as well suppress Phidias and Plato, and the opposition was overcome and Pittsburgh seemed just as pure after she danced there.

Lenora believed she was performing a great service, bringing art to America. In Columbus, however, she was the one who created the difficulty. Memorial Hall was booked for her recital because it was the largest hall in the city; the day of her recital four thousand people bought seats, four thousand was the capacity. Everyone said they wanted to hear the New York Symphony, but it was obvious that Lenora Malcolm was the real drawing card.

But when Lenora saw the hall she said, "I will not dance in such a hall. I cannot feel anything in such an uninspired setting." The management stormed and threatened, but she was obdurate.

A few minutes before the recital was to start it was transferred to a theater. Fifteen hundred people saw her dance, and twenty-five hundred got their money back. The management thought she was insane, throwing away thousands of dollars. But Lenora was pleased. This had been one of her best recitals. The theater was intimate, quasi-Greek in architecture, and she had been full of inspiration, and afterward the rim of the stage had filled with adorers offering her their homage.

But even now she felt tormented. No one had brought her rapture; Mama was more remote than ever; the tour had had a curious impersonality. Even the painters, poets, and sculptors who had admired her, who had become her friends—some of the foremost in America—had done so like schoolmasters, so learned and grave and too damned polite. Secretly she began to wish for a new lover, a new distraction, a new experience, something personal that related to her as a total person rather than just as a dancer.

The tour, however, had been a financial success, and she was taking back a sizable amount of money, more than enough to re-establish her school in Paris, more than she had ever earned in a single tour.

Lenora stood on the deck of the liner taking her away from America, and the morning mists slowly lifted to show the profile of New York as the liner swung around majestically, pointing its prow down the Hudson. She gazed at the rugged, irregular profile of the city, and suddenly she wanted to embrace it, kiss it, love it. Oh, not just for herself, she cried, but for all Americans. Now that she was leaving it, she felt most American.

Then suddenly, much as she adored America, now that she was leaving it, she adored Paris even more. Paris became her love, drawing her with an overwhelming lure. Mama then would no longer be able to punish her by staying away; Niels could be forgotten, finally. Lenora took a last look at the receding land and thought, now I will find my rightful love, one who will truly shout: Hurrah for Lenora!

She stood like the Statue of Liberty which they were passing and thought, what a wonderful dance that would make the next time she returned to America.

BOOK SEVEN

40

Lenora was in for a surprise when she reached Paris, for Amy, of all people, now seemed to distrust her. They met in Paris to decide the future of the school, and Amy stated, despite Lenora's efforts to keep the school free, that it must become a paid school if they wanted it to survive.

Lenora had earned a large amount of money in America, and already, a few days in Paris, and most of the money was gone. Lenora put the children in a rented château at La Verrières, near Paris, and although Amy liked the vast rooms and the historic architecture she was horrified by the expense.

The school is a failure, that is what Amy is really wailing, thought Lenora. "What kind of a failure do you mean?" said Lenora. "America has acclaimed me, and Paris waits."

"The school is a failure," Amy repeated, "because of the high cost of living and the difficulties of freedom."

Lenora struck resounding airs on the liberty theme. "Think," she said, "of all the lovely children rotting in homes that are no better than dungeons because they cannot afford to learn to dance."

"You cannot educate a whole world."

"We can educate much of it. We must continue with the children. If the school has failed, and I doubt that, it is because we have failed."

Amy thought, children in the eyes of Lenora are an unanswerable argument for beauty, but that is not always true. It is easy to love children at a distance or in the abstract, but when you have to live with them every moment of the day it is impossible. Then children are as individual as fruit, some luscious, some rotten, some ripe, and some spoiled. And some jealous and cruel and self-seeking beyond enduring.

Amy sought to explain this to Lenora, and Lenora stared at her sadly as if there was something wrong with her and said, "Amy, you've been under too much strain lately, worrying about money. When you talk like this, you're not quite yourself."

Amy said, "Even when you were a child you grasped the slightest suggestion of dancing with the comprehension of genius, but the most obvious and prosaic facts of life find you heedless."

"I do not catch the connection."

"You are impractical about money, friends, your own ambitions."

"And, of course, Mama?"

"And Mama! If she were here she would agree with me."

Lenora cried, "But Mama is not here, and it was her own choice!"

Amy said, "Do you really think so!"

Many more words, and many sharper ideas, and it was petty and futile, and they awoke in each other memories of old exasperations: Lenora always believing in justice and equality, as long as it was her justice and equality; Amy inclined to be authoritative, especially about dancing, teaching, and discipline, and seldom winning the arguments about who was right.

The result was that Amy decided to remain in Düsseldorf with a paid school, and Lenora planned to continue her free school in Paris itself.

There was a conference with the children so they could choose with whom they wished to remain. The sisters agreed there were no other issues. The children were alert and animated when the sisters came to present the choice, and Lenora thought, how beautiful they are! Had Mama felt the same way about her own daughters? The past rose up and the years of Mama's service, Mama's enthusiasm, Mama's sincerity; and then Lenora told herself Mama had made her choice and there must be no more regrets. Lenora took one child in her arms, praised another's lovely eyes, was ecstatic about a third child's grace, said Dion needed all of them for inspiration, as she did, and stressed how they, having been with her from the beginning, had become the special ones who bore the authentic *Malcolm flame,* ignoring the faithful care of Amy, who had supervised their upbringing while she had been away on her wanderings. When the majority of the school voted to go with Lenora her step was springier than it had been for months, and she was sure the children had been exceptionally wise. Amy refused to be dismayed, and even managed to congratulate Lenora on her victory, while Lenora said it was not a victory, that Amy was still her favorite teacher, and they were enthusiastic in wishing the other well. Lenora, trying to embrace all the children who were staying, felt as if they had given her a blank check.

It was a check which required constant replenishing. Lenora persuaded Archer to join her in Paris as her personal manager, and Archer quickly discovered that her expenses, as always, exceeded her income. Soon, though he was the calmest member of the family, he was in a state of constant confusion and aggravation, for Lenora could not be taught to keep her spending within reason. When he said, "If you go bankrupt with your earning power, it would be a misfortune," she replied, "Many people are surrounded with misfortune, but we must not succumb."

"Yes," Archer found himself saying, although he did not want to agree.

"This isn't America," Lenora said. "People are not bored in Paris, it is full of *joie de vivre*. They expect an artist to live freely, generously."

Lenora fell in love with Paris once again. The city had hardly changed at all. She told herself that Paris was the greatest artistic city in the world, and she bought herself a fine mansion in Neuilly, one of the finest and most expensive suburbs of Paris. "It is superb," she told Archer, and dragged him over to examine the mansion, after she bought it.

Archer agreed it was superb, but once again he had the feeling of being outwitted. In his mind he felt violated: Lenora was not a millionaire even if she had earned a quarter of a million in the last few years and insisted on living as one. A dancer, even a most successful one, could not expect to be a millionaire, could not squander money like one, it was dangerous, a trap. Yet when he tried to explain this to Lenora, she made him feel pompous and cruel. He went on, however, even as he was aware that the special pleading was in his voice, when she should be pleading with him. He had not had an instant to act or to study acting since he had arrived, as she had promised, and which had been his chief reason for coming. And she was not listening.

She was pointing out the concierge's rooms on the first floor, then dancing up the staircase with the wrought-iron balustrades and exclaiming, "It is just what I have always dreamed of having. We can live full and happy lives here. Look at the workmanship of this wrought iron! Do you realize what genius went into that iron work! The children will love it here. We'll have brilliant parties here. It will be our Temple of Art."

Archer shivered. The upkeep of this mansion would be fabulous.

Lenora, as effervescent as Archer had ever seen her, rushed on, "We have a huge reception hall, a magnificent dining room—we can seat twenty or thirty without difficulty. And the studio, wait until you see that!"

It was the most fantastic studio Archer had ever seen. It was huge, large enough for twice the entire school. A thick, luxurious carpet covered the floor from wall to wall. Couches formed an amphitheater about the stage. They were covered with a deep rose velvet, the only touch in the studio that was not blue. The carpet was blue, the ceiling was a pale blue, heavy blue drapes framed the windows, and the concert grand was adorned with a lovely blue shawl. Archer felt the quick stir of joy which always came when he was moved by beauty. He could not find fault with this, her taste had been sublime.

Lenora read his thoughts. She embraced him and said, "If you hadn't liked it I would have felt awful."

"You see how easy I give in," and thought Lenora had left him no choice.

"We'll manage. But we are wasting time. You must see the rest of the house. And don't get tense, it is all beautiful."

Archer was thankful for one thing: the mansion only had three floors or God knows what further extravagances she would have indulged in. The third floor was devoted to sleeping quarters for the servants, twenty-five children, Dion and his nurse, Lenora, Archer, and guests.

"Isn't it wonderful!" Lenora declared, on her most confident note.

"Extraordinary. I hope you can afford it."

"Of course. And thanks for looking, Archer. You've been quite useful."

Then Lenora engaged one of the most important theaters in Paris, the Théâtre Sarah-Bernhardt, against everybody's advice. She expected to earn enough to provide for her school, but this recital got off on the wrong foot. It was considered sacrilege for an American, and a lone one at that, to think she could fill this tribute to the divine Sarah, when Sarah herself used other performers. Lenora was refused the use of the star's dressing room; she was told that Bernhardt, who owned the theater, reserved that for her own use. Everything was happening as Lothar had predicted. Lothar had broken with her when she had engaged this theater against his advice; he

had warned her it was too risky—the theater was too big and
clumsy for her, and the French would be offended; Bernhardt
was their idol, and they would consider Lenora a rival. And
now, although Lothar was gone like Mama and Amy, his
predictions seemed to be coming true. Lenora said Bernhardt
was her idol too, and no one at the theater believed her. The
more she complained about the sloppy conditions backstage,
the more disagreeable they became. She refused to hire a
claque, which was another sacrilege. Archer knew nothing
about managing a dance recital, and she found herself in
arguments about tickets and advertising, which she hated.
When these demands became stifling she threatened not to go
on. Archer pointed out that if she failed to go on she would
fall deeper in debt, which did not worry her, but when he
added that she would lose her mansion and her school she
ordered the curtain up.

The audience was far smaller than she had expected and
looked lost in the huge theater. When she came down front
she realized she had made another mistake; the seats were
remote from the stage, and there was no sense of intimacy;
the distance might be perfect for an aging Bernhardt but was
quite wrong for her. Some reassurance came when she saw
familiar faces in the audience. Then she thought she saw
Mama, but no, it could not be Mama. Yet as Lenora danced
the image of Mama became real. Lenora grew so convinced it
was Mama that when the woman left in the middle of her
second number it was a catastrophe. Distracted, upset, she
lost her concentration, and when she finished she felt full of
doubt and hesitation. She did not even notice whether there
was much applause.

During the intermission she sipped champagne, which she
had purchased with borrowed money to celebrate her triumph
afterward, and now there was no money to raise the curtain
for a bailiff was at the door. But she believed the curtain had
to go up as long as one person in the audience was watching,
and when it did not rise she appeared before it. Archer had
the presence of mind to dim the lights, the orchestra began
automatically, and the curtain rose as the bailiff admitted he
had lost. Lenora, infuriated but greatly stirred now, was a
little more unclothed than usual and a great deal more passionate.

Exciting, amazing, unpredictable Lenora, thought Archer,
even when the world threatened to smother her, she was able
to recharge herself with such fervor. She did not waver now,
and when the curtain was up she stayed downstage, as close
to the audience as she could get. That was her improvisation,

and the news that Duse was in her audience and several of her old suitors. The recital ended in a triumph doubly precious because it had been snatched from the jaws of disaster.

More recitals were arranged for the Théâtre Sarah-Bernhardt. The bailiff agreed to wait. Even the worshipers of Bernhardt were impressed. But Archer felt that Lenora was not to be trusted. After the recital she gave a huge party, though she could not afford it. When he mentioned this, shocked by the number of guests, pointing out that there were over a hundred in her house right now and that she did not know half of them, she said he was cruel.

He shook his head woefully, "You really do need a very rich man."

Lenora laughed. "You are tired. You can't even think straight. What would I do with such a person?"

"You'd learn."

"I'd be a failure. I couldn't even flatter him."

Then, even as she knew the idea was absurd, one of her guests introduced her to Bayard Royal, an authentic millionaire.

"Be careful," her brother said, turning away.

"Don't be a fool, Archer. I'll see you in the morning, when you can think straight." Her brother was gone then, but not Bayard Royal. He said he had been wanting to meet Lenora Malcolm for such a long time.

41

Lenora had heard of Bayard Royal, that he was a large body of money surrounded by people who wanted some, and that was enough to make her defiant, to show that she did not need him. And she detested obvious compliments which were intended only to flatter, and his had been most obvious. She was prepared to be devastating, but Bayard Royal did not give her a chance. A waltz sounded from her studio, and he took her off without a word. Lenora was startled, she seldom permitted this liberty, and he had not even asked. But he held his hand firmly on her back and made her follow him, and it was difficult to break away from such assurance. He was far taller and better-looking than she had expected. They went on dancing, and gradually it became natural to her. She sensed he was so skillful because he could not condescend to incompetence.

He spoke about her dancing and its relationship to Grecian art with an awareness that surprised and pleased her. Yet he was so self-assured she could not resist the impulse to shock him. A millionaire indeed, did he think she was a piece of work to be regarded as a philanthropy, and she was superstitious but not so superstitious as to assume her need for money could be immediately and conveniently supplied.

She laughed as she asked, "Are you really a millionaire?"

He stopped abruptly, as if he had been struck. "What made you ask?"

"I don't think I've ever met a millionaire before."

He clenched his hands, as if to control a rising temper, and then said softly, "Is that why you are dancing with me?"

"I had no choice. You wouldn't let me go."

"You can go now." His hands were at his sides, and she was free.

They stood face to face, staring at each other. She was determined to be without shame; he was determined not to be outdone. Lenora was all in white, once more, in her simplest and most exquisite gown. Its lines were as clean and austere as those of the Parthenon, but now the glow was not of innocence but of an electric presence. She could feel the excitement springing up wherever she was, which was just the effect she desired.

Then, as Bayard Royal stood there astonished, as the many guests talked, drank, Lenora went dancing through the studio. The pianist, one of the greatest in Europe, was improvising on Chopin, and she was improvising too, as if this were the first time she was dancing this emotion. What she was dancing at this moment could not be bought for money, she thought, and a marvelous quiet prevailed—even the music was quiet in a pervasive way, and she was taking them back to the uplifting of daylight out of darkness.

Bayard Royal was totally unmanned. Lenora had not made one motion toward him, nor had she indicated awareness of his presence in any way, and yet her dancing pierced his heart. It was a vision of a beauty he had not thought possible. There was a certitude in her dancing that made any disbelief in it vulgar and contemptible. Surrendering to the wisdom of her senses, trusting the courage of her faith, Lenora was exacting faith from him who had found no faith in architecture, medicine, science, philanthrophy, although he had pursued them all and had been a scholar too.

She was at his side again and repeating what he had said to her before, "You can go now," and he could not go. He should have been piqued, but he was flustered, and that also was a strange, disturbing feeling. Any competent dancer should be able to suggest love, but she suggested an excitement and fulfillment that was overpowering and yet disquieting. "Bored?" she asked suddenly. "I've heard that you are always bored."

"What else have you heard?"

He assumed that she, like all the others, would talk about his five homes or his two yachts or his many automobiles—he had more automobiles than any man is Paris—but she was saying, "I've heard you think yourself irresistible."

He wanted to strike back then, but that would have exposed his annoyance. So he said, "You are the one who is irresistible."

"Of course." She smiled. "Did you dislike my dancing too?"

"I wanted to." He looked distressed. "But I couldn't."

"I expected you to abuse me."

"No one could abuse your dancing. You are like a wind that changes from moment to moment. When you dance you refresh the body and the spirit."

"Oh, Bayard!" She wanted to embrace him. Now she respected him, he was so poetic in this instant, and so right. Her eyes grew wet with sentiment. She forgot her determination to humble him, to treat his millions with defiance. And though she delighted in having many people about her, like courtiers, and tonight she had invited them in large numbers, preferring a crowd for usually she hated to be alone, she forgot about them also. She said, "You are perceptive. At the theater I pour out my blood for them, and yet many come only to be amused for a few francs, and you can see how ugly that is, but here I can dance a free performance to a free audience. I really wish money wasn't necessary. Beauty does not relate to money in any natural way. No one pays the sea for dancing."

"But you make dancing essential to life."

"Thank you." She held out her hands to him, and when he took them she led him onto the balcony that overlooked her gardens and where they could be alone. Where she could confide in him as she had not confided in anyone for such a long time. She said, "My art is natural because it is not thought out and settled beforehand. While I am dancing it is changing as my feelings change. And when I finish, it is still changing as my audience is changing. A dance lives only through those who are experiencing it. There is no real abstract dancing. You must always start with something, an emotion, a revelation, an inspiring, and that is why academic training in dancing is so often a sham. What we love we must not measure or weigh."

"Yes, to you," he said, intoxicated by her mood, "all should be permitted."

"And forgiven?"

He did not reply, thinking she should have no concern but to be beautiful, and then she could do anything she pleased.

Lenora draped a shawl over her bare shoulders when she was chilled by the night air. She saw herself as a Carmen, for the lovely shawl was a bright red. The pattern was as intricate and dramatic as any he had ever seen. Proud of himself as an art connoisseur, Bayard said it was worthy of Buisson, the most fashionable of Parisian couturiers, and if she wished he would recommend her to this genius. This irritated her—she did not need his recommendation to see Buisson—and suddenly she said she had to visit her children, who were sleeping on the third floor.

"Miss Malcolm . . . just a moment. I would like to go with you. May I?"

Lenora paused and waited for him. He seemed even taller in the dark. "This way," she said. They went up a narrow, dark, winding stairway in the rear of the mansion to avoid the others.

He admired the little girls of the school. He was enchanted with Dion, who was sleeping but who awoke long enough to accept a kiss from his mother. He admired the resemblance, thought it unique, and helped lull the child back to sleep with a pleasant lullaby. He was so capable with Dion that Lenora thought he must be a father.

"I am not a father," he said, reading her thoughts. "Or married."

"You didn't have to tell me."

"I'm glad I did. Then you don't have to ascribe to me any ambiguous motives." He was dazed by the swiftness of his desire.

She could find nothing to say. A curious strangeness seemed to separate them. She led him into the hall and toward the studio where they could hear the sounds of laughter, chatter, glasses clinking loudly, and he halted.

He said suddenly, "I don't want to go back to the studio."

"Why not?" Deep down she knew why not, and he did not answer. She still found him somewhat intimidating, taking himself too seriously, but when he came close she was no longer lonesome or irritable, and he did understand the importance of her art. She also saw that he was annoyed when she took the lead, but when she deferred to his judgment that vanished. This was deplorably familiar, and for a moment she was gloomy.

Then he was saying energetically, "You must tell me about yourself. What do you feel as a woman? As you realize, the public only knows one side of you, but a dancer is a person first to me." He was almost pompous, didactic, yet his interest was genuine. "I have the impression, for instance, that you prefer to offend people. You think it stimulates you."

"People who are easily offended are artificial."

"Is it yes or no?"

"Not so fast."

"Splendid." His eyes were shining, and he took her arm with a grip that nearly squeezed the blood out of it. "I like a resolute woman."

He was like a storm coming up, she thought, how tall and strong he was, how like a Viking. Very tall, about six foot three, she judged, and so vigorous, as if here too he could not condescend to incompetence. He really was a Viking with his blue eyes, his light hair, his fair skin, his Vandyke which added to the strength and prominence of his jaw. He spoke with an assurance she found touching yet absurd. She wondered if he really did know so much. She noticed that his mouth was wide and positive, the mouth of a practical man of power, confident and efficient. Yet now, talking about her children again, saying they deserved the best out of life, he was gentle and generous, two traits Lenora regarded highly.

Nonetheless, Lenora hesitated before the door of her bedroom. Not because it was too quick, it was never too quick to fall in love, but as he stood by her door she studied him more thoughtfully. Impulse was her favorite guide, but tonight she felt she must be more careful. The money did not matter, she told herself, it was his commanding ways and self-assurance that could be difficult, but she could also be a fool and a coward if she lost him now. And perhaps he was not as assured as he pretended, for as she opened her door he seemed as nervous as a schoolboy. Her third-floor bedroom was her studio in miniature. They could hear laughter and music from below as the party went on and on, but when she shut the door it was quiet suddenly.

He was lying on her bed, waiting for her, when all at once she began to dance. One moment she was standing in the center of the room, and the next her gown was at her feet and she was moving as if he were not there. Dancing, she was in a state of withdrawal and then in a state of willingness. She felt she was breaking down the distinctions of body and spirit; she was abandoned to her emotions. She fought to control her excitement as he approached her. She realized this could be a devil of a struggle—he wanted to be masterful, quick, and she could not alter her natural rhythms without creating disharmony.

He spoke of love, and this made her feel she would be the only one for him. Her giving always had been whole, and so her givers always had to be whole, not shared. The dream in her, the reach, the reality and the fantasy had to be realized by such totals. She knew she was not always a good mathematician except in judging results. Suddenly she was shocked that her mind had wandered off while he was kissing her breasts, and she continued to add sums to sums. At last he made her believe she loved him, and now she wanted to ask him if he loved her, yet she did not want to ask but to know, as though asking would be begging and freedom had nothing to do with begging and women were equal to men. She suddenly began to return the fire in him. She kissed his cheeks and found them fragrant as most things in nature were fragrant. She kissed his chest, his stomach, his thighs. She fell to her knees and embraced his legs. There she remained to worship because legs to her had become the gods of the dance. And as she kissed and kissed, making of his legs a tree trunk and all his adjoining parts branches, she spoke her love to the branches and hung it on every branch.

And now he resumed the giving. "I love you," he said, as though he had needed her expression to gain freedom. She was very sensitive to this miracle but would not have dared to expose him to his own egotism.

"I love you," she repeated.

Suddenly two were one.

Afterward he wanted her to sail with him on his yacht in the Mediterranean, and she said, "What about my recitals?"

"I will buy the theater."

"And the children?"

"I have a château where they can stay, and if you don't like that I'll build you a château—for the children and for yourself."

There were the present debts which worried Archer, and when she mentioned them, not as debts, but as a subsidy she gave those she cared for, Bayard laughed and said the amount was trifling. Bayard carried thousand-dollar bills as other men carried dollar bills, and he left a dozen for Archer without hesitation. He said it was a gift, but she insisted it was a loan, and he did not argue although he thought she was being foolish.

Lenora left the money in an envelope beside the sleeping Archer and wrote that she was taking a cruise to restore her health and to inspire new dances and not to worry, she would be back in several weeks. They slipped out of the house while the party went on and on, only by now it was near morning, and she did not know most of the guests there.

The ride south in his luxurious automobile seemed a journey into a time and place beyond measuring. The yacht was ready for them when they arrived, and soon they were in the middle of the Mediterranean.

She lay in his arms for warmth and tried not to think beyond the moment. Yet Lenora had a twinge of guilt, thinking suddenly, I should be living in the poor but free Montmartre with an artist, and he is really a swell in a top hat, and will he suit my dancing?

And when the voyage lengthened into weeks she discovered that he considered her liberal attitudes socialism, a vulgar attitude to him. Yet he was not smug, and he preferred champagne to scotch and soda, and he had a remarkable ability to appreciate. He was a brilliant amateur, but an amateur, too versatile to become professional at anything but spending. He was always on the move, from his country estate in England to his château outside Paris, from metaphysics to impressionism to whatever was new. And for all his importance she soon learned that his life was a perpetual crisis, fighting off aggrievedly aggressive women, paying bills, creating foundations; he also made sure she knew he had had a French mistress and a German mistress and a Russian mistress, but he did not want to hear about any of the men she had known. He declared that the other women had become stupid, wanting only to please his senses, when a real man needed much more. He was positive that Lenora would be different. And Lenora, who had embarked upon this affair as if it were to be the permanent fulfillment of her dreams, wondered why he had to talk so much about the women who had loved him. She was happier when he spoke of his grandiose plans for her, that she would have her Temple of Art—he would attend to that the instant they got back to Paris.

He was determined to take her from her irresponsible Parisian friends and give her the stability she needed. When they returned to Paris after several weeks there was still a party going on at her mansion—it had the look of the same party, although Archer assured her the guests were different. Archer said she had given the word to have open house, and Paris was taking her at her word. But Bayard insisted on getting rid of the guests, and as soon as that was done he came to her and threw himself on her most comfortable couch and said, "Thank God, that is over. Now everyone will believe that you are my love."

42

All for art. All for beauty. And now, all for the millionaire life.

Always the millionaire life. It was impossible now to absorb enough of prodigality, a day without a new extravagance was a day wasted. Bayard gave her a beautiful automobile which she adored and a chauffeur who was always at her disposal. His next gift was an ermine coat which even Lenora thought was outrageously costly, but she loved the glossy black-tail tips against the royal white fur and felt marvelous and dazzling when she wore it. He spared no expense to make her happy. The Lenora of Grunewald and the simple robes and sandals and bare legs found herself wearing costly dresses, silk stockings at many francs a pair, silver-tipped sandals, and all this seemed fitting. Her Viking lifted her in his arms and carried her upstairs when she was tired. Her Viking bestowed his bounty with a princely and open-handed grace. He was enormously in love; he was like a happy boy regarding the universe as a huge playground at their disposal.

Always the millionaire life. When he repeated, "I will give you anything you want," stressing the anything, Lenora said, "Darling, I don't want anything grandiose, not great wealth, not great possessions, I just want a place for my art, where the children and I can be inspired and free," and he reiterated his promise to build her a theater in Paris that would be a temple and school and whatever else she desired. He immersed himself in architecture with an extraordinary nervous energy, but what came off his drawing board was a stately edifice that resembled a villa more than a temple.

Lenora was at his elbow, and when she looked shattered he promised to try again. She exhorted now, praised. Together they mapped out the design of the front of the theater, the most vital portion of the temple, but again a Renaissance villa took shape before their eyes. This time when she said it was not what she wanted he jumped up with a muttered, "Oh, God, what do you want? It's fate!" and wrenched open the door and slammed out of her mansion.

When Bayard returned he said it was obvious that the ideal

place for her temple was Cap Ferrat on the Riviera. It was the afternoon of an early summer day, humid and hot, and her resistance was low and he was very nervous. She said, "Of course, darling, if you think so." They had drawn the curtains against the heat, but even in the darkness it was too hot. She felt oppressed. The mood her Viking brought with him now was a strange mixture of eagerness and scorn.

Always the millionaire life. Months later a huge, Renaissance villa was finished on Cap Ferrat. It was high on a hill where it commanded the entire countryside. It had been built faster than any such villa in the history of the Riviera; he was proud that his damn-the-expense attitude had accomplished this. She admitted the view was magnificent, that the villa was located beautifully, at the perfect juxtaposition of sea and mountains, dominating the countryside. But she was shocked and disappointed. This was more like a mausoleum than a temple.

He explained that the villa was his design. He was especially proud of the iron fence and the roof which had been copied from Versailles just for her. She agreed that the ornate carving of the gigantic iron gate was impressive and decided that he had had this gate built to keep her in, that it was the work of a very jealous man. Bayard had really put his heart into building a new home this time—he had built four in the past ten years, whenever he had begun a new love affair—and he was sure it would stand out because it was unlike anything else. It was part château for their home, part villa for her school. As for her theater, that could come later, he decided, if she went on with her career. He insisted on showing her every bit of brocade, every inch of expensive furniture, the mother-of-pearl door, the gold-inlaid bathroom, the crystal chandeliers, and suddenly it struck her as no use.

Lenora knew she could never get accustomed to such horrors as these pendulous, overweighted chandeliers. With a wicked light in her eyes, angry at the way he had taken for granted she would like his taste without consulting her, she blurted out, "These chandeliers remind me more of a showroom in a New York gas fixture shop than a temple of art."

"They are electric," he retorted proudly. "The most up-to-date on the Riviera, in all of France."

"They are absurd. With one hand you create the pomp of Versailles, with the other you drag us into the twentieth century."

"It will all fit."

"And these mirrors. So many, and such a cunning and cruel arrangement of them. Wherever I look, I see multiplications of myself. Can you fancy a worse hell on earth than that!"

"Lenora, it is for your dancing."

"Not for my dancing, Bayard. I danced Narcissus when I was eighteen, when I was young and naïve. I would be an idiot to live that way now." She stood up, stretching her exquisite white arms above her head in a passionate gesture. "You fell in love with me because I brought you a pagan love."

Yes, he thought, or never would he have permitted such a slur on his taste. Never would he forget their first night, and how she made all their nights a first night. He was drunk once more with the memory of the ecstasy she had aroused, of her astonishing gifts of freshness and improvisation even in love, usually the most repetitive of things. Most women he had once, twice, and it became the same, they bored him, but not Lenora. She was as unique and original in love as she was in everything else; it was as if she could not bear to have the same experience twice. Every experience had to have the excitement of a first; she was so spendthrift she made each time a shattering experience. But now even as the memory held and fascinated him, he felt she was unfair. She possessed him. He could not do without her now.

Lenora agreed that the Riviera had the bluest water in the world, the brightest sun in the world, and this new villa on Cap Ferrat the most brilliant view in the world—and she was bored. He had spent a fortune to satisfy a whim, and she was talking about the Parisian Boulevards and how wonderful to live in a city where streets were named after poets like Dante and Byron, where one could not stroll a hundred yards without coming upon a street named after an artist. She was sure Cap Ferrat would be his home, not hers; he was very angry at her once more, but he consented to return to Paris.

They had their first real quarrel a few days later when he was late at the railroad station and they missed the train to Paris. "It won't make me stay here," she said. "Now what shall we do?"

"So for a change it was my fault. But you are usually the one who is late."

"That's no excuse."

"We'll go to Cannes."

"No," Lenora said sharply. "Cannes bores me too."

"We'll go to Monte Carlo," he said manfully.

"And watch you win or lose money that won't make a bit of difference to you? No. Monte Carlo bores me too."

"But we missed the train, and you said you got carsick when we drove down."

"I know." What he did not know was why she got carsick. If what she suspected was true he might be a very happy man. And it was all the more reason for getting to Paris as soon as possible. She sat down on their luggage and said, "I'm not returning to Cap Ferrat. Not today."

"There is no train to Paris for hours."

"Hire one."

"Are you serious?"

"You say you can give me anything."

For an instant he was furious. He swore, and then the incongruity of the situation struck him and he burst into laughter. "Of course. It's simple. I'll charter a train to Paris."

"I knew you would see reason." The trouble with her Viking was he had so much money he did not know how to spend it.

When they boarded the chartered train all was forgiven. He felt proud; his hero image still glowed, and Lenora regarded him as a true conqueror of time and space, a contemporary Alexander.

Lenora was pregnant as she had suspected, and when she told Bayard it was as if he had built the Eiffel Tower with his bare hands. Overjoyed, he would not let Lenora out of his sight; he waited on her hand and foot although he had given her a dozen servants. He was all agreeableness. He felt as if life existed for his convenience. He still wanted to improve her character, but he decided that could wait until their son was born. He had no doubt it would be a son.

Cathleen was born peacefully, which struck Lenora as an auspicious omen. Four doctors attended her, and this time she did not feel split beyond repairing. It was as if she pressed all of creation within her legs, and then she heard Bayard whispering, "A beautiful girl," and she was submerged under a cloudy reverie. Afterward came the emerging into a happy buoyancy, such a moment she knew she would never forget. And Bayard, once he was over his disappointment that their child was not a son, fell in love with Cathleen's beauty.

Lenora did not deign to name the fathers of her children. It was enough that she loved Dion and Cathleen more than anything else in the world. Her children were love children, and because they were she felt she loved them more. They would be her gift to a brave new world. They were holy.

When she resumed her recitals she gave a free matinee for the art students, and the queue that formed blocked traffic for miles. It had been Bayard's suggestion. He was proud of his generosity which was unlimited now, paying for the theater, the orchestra, the advertising, and her maids. He was proudest of all that everyone was saying, *"C'est la Malcolm."*

Gradually the glimpses of her body through the draperies became more revealing as the draperies became more transparent. But she was the personification of art as she insisted, "My art is a religion, a religion of the beautiful. Ugliness is immoral, it degrades, but beauty uplifts."

Incorrigibly dramatic, her dancing grew more sensual, with a touch of voluptuous abandonment, outraged and outraging. Yet she stimulated in many of her audiences a vision that forced them to see beauty more fully and people more tenderly, to make them feel life was a splendid adventure after all. She was a constant theme for discussion, especially when she danced Beethoven's "Moonlight Sonata," and few recalled how she had deserted Homer and Theocritus for Chopin, and now Chopin was neglected for Beethoven and the sensual Wagner. She expressed the hope that her school would become a fixture in all the artistic cities of the world, such as Paris, and Paris returned her love.

Thus, Lenora was shocked when, dancing the "Bacchanale" from *Tannhäuser,* there were complaints because a safety pin had given way and a large portion of her body had been seen. She was told that the next time she danced in public there would be detectives in attendance, with orders to arrest her, should she dance again merely in a veil and an insecure safety pin. She had been dancing the conception of her children, and when she swore nothing would stop her from dancing as she felt, she was warned that no theater would be available.

Basking in popularity, she did not believe this, but when she went to rent the theater she had danced in last, it was refused her. Other theaters refused her, and then her Viking offered one so much money that cupidity got the better of prudence. By now this recital had become a *cause célèbre,* a symbol of artistic freedom. She invited her friends, and Duse, Pavlova, and Diaghilev, who were also in Paris, and those who accepted invited their friends. As she wrote and informed them, "It is not just my dance, it is for all art."

She might have added what she was also feeling:

All for art. All for beauty. All for the born and the unborn. And, as always now, all for the millionaire life.

43

So there came a day in Paris that was perfect in many ways, and it was then that a kind of exaltation took hold of Lenora which made her feel she could do no wrong. Thousands of Parisians stormed the theater to buy tickets for her next matinee, the one where she was expected to defy the censors and dance nude and which had won the support of artistic Paris. The box office opened early in the morning, but by noon ticket lines still stretched around the theater although all the seats had been sold.

The streets about the theater were flooded with people as she approached. The *Garde Republicaine* had to be called out to create a semblance of order and to force a way for Lenora through the crowd. Her popularity was at a thunderous height, the art students, always enthusiastic, shouted, "Lenora, you are afraid of nothing! Tell them what the artists think!" Beauty was assured, she thought, art was inevitable. For all her triumphs, she had never seen enthusiasm like this.

Clemenceau was in one box, Paul-Boncour in another, Pavlova, Nijinsky, and Diaghilev in a third, Réjane, Duse, and Yvette Guilbert in a fourth. Even Bayard was astonished: he had never seen anything like this, even for Bernhardt.

Then she ordered Bayard out of her dressing room, and the next few minutes Lenora was alone. She drifted into a reverie, to reach a continuous concentration; she sought to concentrate by reaching to the roots of her own centers, by reaching to the roots of understanding. Lenora knew that the closer she came to her roots of feeling and thinking and imagining the greater would be her interpretive powers in her performance. She relaxed on her couch; she permitted a kind of lowering of her being into the depths, lower, lower, lower, until she reached the deepest depth of her feeling. A total relaxation spread over her as she wondered about beginnings: the beginning of her body, the beginning of earth, the beginning of nature, the beginning of relationships between all of these. Gradually her mind and spirit felt itself rise from the depths, felt the earth and nature rising from its depths, from the many beginnings. Still rising, how high, to what pinnacle, to whose pinnacle? Hers was higher than most, but hers was low compared to her need. Her perpetual thirst for the ultimate in beauty, truth, freedom, for the ultimate ultimate was at its strongest now even as she knew that could never be reached or danced to. But Lenora loved this orgasm of concentration. And when she heard her cue she floated out to the stage: inspiration incarnate.

Wild applause greeted her. The stage was dark except for a single beam of light on Lenora. She stood for a moment in total concentration, and then lifted her arms heavenward to embrace them all. And as she danced no one could remain neutral.

Suddenly there was agitation backstage. Detectives stationed in the wings ordered Lenora to halt. Instead, she raised her hands and the lights came up on the detectives. It caught them looking awkward, and the audience laughed, and when several of the detectives started after her the laughter turned to hissing and booing. Stung by this, two of the detectives kept after her until they found themselves dancing in their effort to catch her—"dancing donkeys," the audience yelled. Then Lenora raised her hands once more, and this time the lights came up on the rear of the stage, and there, set in the plastic lines of a Greek frieze, were eight of her children. They were twelve to fifteen in age, at their most virginal. They seemed to be listening to music too ethereal for mortal ears. When the two detectives continued to pursue Lenora she pointed to the children and said, "How can these lovely, innocent children be censorable?" and threats and imprecations were hurled against the detectives, who retreated in disorder.

The audience was intent again, fascinated by the girls in blue and white moving with a fragile beauty toward them, although their upturned faces seemed only to hear the music and to see Lenora. All this time Lenora was dancing also. It seemed unimportant that her body was almost nude; it was vital that as she led the children her body shone like a white candle in a holy place.

The climax of the matinee came when Lenora danced the "Bacchanale" from *Tannhäuser* with all of her accumulated emotion. The children were gone from the stage now, the detectives had retired from the theater, unable to bear the scorn of the audience, and she moved with bolder gestures. Her dancing became a personal manifestation. She danced toward the audience with huge, slow strides. Her arms went up and outward, her legs widened. A wisp of veil fell between her spreading thighs, and there was silence as she stood above the universe with straddling legs.

Just as the audience felt it could not endure this pause any longer, she began to dance again. She was dancing dedication, then fleeing and yielding, denying and surrendering . . .

thinking, often I have said when I dance I am a sexless, un-earthly thing, but not today, today I am dancing the beauty of love, of wanting fiercely and wanting all the time. Wisdom, where else is it to be found? Where else is the place of under-standing? She came as close to the audience as she could then. On the final bars of the music she seemed to give all of herself to the audience.

A blinding storm of emotion arose. The performance had lasted hours, but the audience shouted for more! Bayard was irrepressible, waving from his box, proud and exalted. It was impossible, she had danced longer than was possible or sensi-ble, and she had to keep on dancing. The orchestra had played all their music, and so the piano which was in the wings was dragged on stage. New cheering arose, and a new recital began. Archive Tempora, one of the finest of French pianists, was commandeered to accompany Lenora. The au-dience shared her rapture, unconditionally now. Every time she put out her arms to embrace them, they went into a frenzy. Lenora was expressing what they longed to express, but could not; she was exploring their secret selves. When she fell on her knees in a final encore, confessing she could dance no longer, that she was worn out, only then did the audience accept that the recital was ended and drift out reluctantly.

Thousands wanted to force their way into the gala party her Viking was giving her at Neuilly, but this time Archer stood at the doorway making certain only the invited were admitted. As it was, the number invited threatened to over-whelm them. But Lenora was amused by Archer's concern.

This was still a perfect day, and she was still sure nothing could go wrong.

Her Viking might think her sentimental and foolish, invit-ing so many, but it was far more foolish to measure friend-ship, to worry about the future, especially since the present was so passionately splendid.

"Paris," Lenora told Duse, one of the first guests to arrive, "the very name is an evocation."

Duse did not remind Lenora how Paris had been very cruel to her, could be cruel to Lenora too. Duse was still possessed with an honest melancholy which she thought good for the soul, but there was no changing Lenora.

Lenora said, "We could tour. I will dance the nights you do not act."

Duse said, "Your art is lovely, but together . . . ? They are so different. I do not think they will mix."

"It's the money. You are worried about the money."

"No, Lenora. I'd worry that we'd no longer remain friends."

"That's presumptuous."

"No, that is common sense."

Lenora was in no mood for that. She was so exhilarated, she could hardly contain herself. She was having such a magnificent time being in love with her Viking, her Paris, her friends, she was sure anything she did this evening was right. When Duse did not lose her melancholy or agree with the idea of performing together, Lenora hurried away to greet new guests.

Lenora welcomed Pavlova, Diaghilev, and Nijinsky, embracing Pavlova and insisting that the men must dance with her. She cried, "Nijinsky has wings on his heels . . . he is a modern Mercury!" But when she went to dance with Nijinsky he glanced at Diaghilev, who shook his head No and looked willful. Very quickly, then, her desire to dance with Nijinsky increased. There was something grotesque in Nijinsky's dependence on Diaghilev. Here was one male dancer who was inspired. She took Nijinsky by the arm, and a look of elaborate pain appeared on Diaghilev's face and Nijinsky moved away from her. It annoyed Lenora, for it was not Nijinsky the man she was interested in.

Diaghilev's face had become almost Oriental in its cast, but he still wore the sleek, insolent, pencil-thin Parisian mustache. There was his ever-present cane, his commanding manner, more commanding than ever now that Paris had acclaimed his company. She was irritated because she could not tell whether he was enchanted or bored with her party. As several more male members of his company gathered around him Lenora realized that Diaghilev had an entourage now that no woman could penetrate. She sought to start an animated conversation with Nijinsky but found that difficult. Nijinsky replied hardly at all.

Lenora said to Diaghilev, determined to provoke him as he had provoked her, "I notice in your ballet you are using my long out-and-up-stretched arm."

"Lucky woman," said Diaghilev, "it is more than I noticed."

"You are a critic, not an artist. That's why you didn't notice."

"Today speaks Lenora," said Diaghilev, "and now all will be corrected."

She retorted, "If I were a caricaturist I would draw all critics with big fat ears and no eyes or tongue at all."

"Which means?"

"Which means that some are critics and some are creative."

"Isn't that rather intolerant for such a tolerant artist?"

"I am only tolerant with the truth."

"Whose truth?" He stared at her cynically. "What you call art is often just journalistic dancing that you create out of the mood of the moment."

"You ought to know better. You talk like the nineteenth century."

They stood face to face, as if to eat each other alive, and then Pavlova said, "Sergei thinks the male dancers are the stars in his company."

He said, "I think you are a virtuoso without an equal, Anna, but that is all that matters to you."

Pavlova said, "I have learned from Lenora."

He said, "You have been inspired perhaps, but it is naïve to assume that you have learned from anyone."

Pavlova said, "That is what I like about Sergei, he always has to be sarcastic about the great." She turned directly to Lenora and stressed, "You do have a sense of honor to your art. You are clear about this. And you have brought freedom to us all."

Dear, fragile, exquisite Pavlova, thought Lenora, with the will of iron. She knew Pavlova seldom went out, lived on a frugal diet, remained in bed for twenty-four hours before many performances, believed a true artist must sacrifice herself to her art absolutely, but without the inspiration of a private life what was there to express? And yet Pavlova was even greater now than before.

Lenora was too aroused to subside, however, and, still feeling like a law unto herself, she hurried over to greet her old and new friends, Réjane and Yvette Guilbert. Réjane was second only to Bernhardt in the French theater, Guilbert was the most popular entertainer of the moment, and Lenora knew she would always remember their approval and their coming. Réjane had her own company, and Lenora said, "When my Viking builds my temple, it will be started within the next year, you will play there without any charge." Then to show she was equally in love with Yvette Guilbert's genius, she turned to this tall, slim figure who dominated the cabaret world, and repeated this offer.

A few minutes later Lenora was even happier, greeting her friend and admirer, Anatole France. The writer wore a red skullcap with a long black tassel, reminding her of a charming and witty satyr. He adored paganism and thought that Lenora's dancing had been most amusing and diverting. When he saw that she was truly interested in his ideas—he adored ideas but felt most women incapable of using them—he told her of a demonstration by the Paris socialists which would be honored if she attended. She replied it would be she who would be honored and who would be delighted to attend. But when she suggested to Bayard that he go with her Bayard replied, "Next thing you'll want me to give away my wealth," and she retorted, "In a socialist world you will," and he shouted, "Pouf . . . you talk about going to Greece and living under the olive trees, after you are tired of Paris, but be sure you take plenty of drachmas," which brought on another attack of what he called "Socialist sickness."

Lenora answered, "Imagine a man of your intellect sneering at a genius like Anatole France," and Bayard said, "What do you know about money, you earn a fortune, you spend two fortunes?" But now she was not listening.

Rodin was being announced, and Lenora hurried to welcome him. There was no artist she respected more than Rodin. Greatly pleased but uncertain, Lenora was very quiet, even shy. Rodin made no reference to their previous meeting but spoke of how much he admired her art. He seemed even more of a rock than before, with his enormous white beard, his lumbering gait, his nearsighted eyes. He wanted to talk about her dancing. He said, "You were strong today, ruthless."

"I tried," Lenora said humbly.

"You succeeded," Rodin said vigorously. "You are as mad as I am. You are of that insane race of artists who believe everything they say and who would go to the stake for it. Have you any champagne? I am not an aescetic."

Lenora filled two goblets with champagne—so close to overflowing that Bayard, watching covertly from a corner of the studio, was alarmed. Bayard sought to catch her eye, to have her a minute for himself at least, but she seemed to find Rodin irresistible. Bayard was offended and jealous; he admitted the old man was a fine sculptor, but too extreme and crude for his taste. Lenora's hovering over the sculptor gave him anxiety; her passion was clear in its intention.

Lenora, sensing Bayard's jealousy, told herself he was a tradesman to the backbone although he had never worked a day in his life.

"You have such zest," Rodin whispered confidentially in her ear. "If I were younger . . . ?"

"If you were Methuselah it would not matter."

"But it does," he said, drinking more champagne with her.

"Our French funerals are so woeful, and you would not look distinguished in crepe."

"This champagne makes you melancholy," she said. "We need a better vintage, or perhaps it is not cold enough."

"No," Rodin said, "it makes me truthful. Remember, I am not an aescetic."

They were still laughing with what seemed spiteful complicity to Bayard when more champagne was brought in. Lenora was drinking with automatic deftness, but even more intensely as she and Rodin raised their glasses to repeated toasts to the unaescetic life.

A host of contending emotions took possession of Bayard, and he found an excuse to talk to Lenora alone. Bayard pointed out that she was putting him in a most awkward position. He was not accusing her of being unfaithful, of even thinking of being unfaithful, but look at what people would think?

She exploded, "I don't give a damn what people think!"

Bayard put up his hand for quiet, forced a smile so the guests would think her excitement a happy one. "We don't want people to see us quarreling."

"But it is fine for you to assume I am a liar, an idiot, incapable of a single serious thought. You see nothing great in me because I am a woman. For you I represent, not beauty and art, but obvious sensuality. You are like the critic who judges the dancer by what she wears."

"I was thinking of our children, Dion and Cathleen."

Lenora was touched by his inclusion of her son. She was aware of his abilities as a father, when he was not in a temper. When he wished he could be most attractive. When he sat in their garden caressing Dion with the same affection he gave Cathleen, talking about the brave new world these children would create, she loved him very much and saw him as just the right father for her children. She said, "Darling, you look as if you only half trust me, when I am devoted to you. Just because I insist on living in Paris instead of your magnificent home on the Riviera, you become jealous. But the Riviera, beautiful as it is, is boring after a few weeks, while Paris is a lion's paradise. Remember this in your lion's brain and swear to me that you are not jealous, that you realize how absurd that is."

"Oh, I do."

"Then why are you so uneasy?"

"It is intelligent to assume that now that I have given you position, you will have the good sense to protect it."

She looked out on the famous gathered to do her homage, and he sounded as if he wanted to cut off her legs. Yet he wanted to be her protector, but she did not want a protector. He wanted her to love him for his own sake, but he was always telling her what he was going to do for her. Just as suddenly as she had been attracted to him a moment before, she was repelled.

Bayard said, "I want to marry you."

Lenora said, "Marriage is slavery." Surrounded by friends, feted, what did she need marriage for when she had two beautiful children?

"Marriage will be better for the children," he reminded her.

"Why? If I desire a child why should I ask permission of the law? You are intelligent, you should understand that. Loving you the way I do, that should be enough."

"If you do?" Bayard glanced at Rodin as he spoke.

"Darling, I also have love affairs of the head, which are important to me, and Rodin is a love affair of the head. Do you want to keep me earthbound?"

"Lenora, I want to protect you. And cherish you."

She kissed him then, to put all his doubts to flight.

But a few minutes later she was even more attentive to Rodin, who was saying to her, his tongue loosened by the champagne he continued to drink with her, "They said I was too earthy and explicit, but you are too. You use nature as a source of imagination and inspiration, you understand and interpret nature. You are rhythm, and Pavlova and Nijinsky are rhythm, and rich men—they have their own rhythm, a sexless one."

She burst into laughter and leaned forward, almost embracing Rodin with her breasts. Both gave way to their desire for more champagne. Bayard cautioned her to stop, and she picked up a bottle of champagne with a flourish and drank and cried, "My bottle of blood! My pint of blood!"

Then without warning she became one of her imitators leading a group of little girls. She shouted, "Now dance the moon, girls, dance the sun, dance the sea, don't guess—dance, don't pout—dance, don't pose—dance!" Lenora looked like a fat, awkward schoolgirl waiting for inspiration to strike as if from high; she was breathing contempt on her imitators.

And before anyone could halt her, she was whirling Nijinsky around the room, and the pianist Archive Tempora, as if he had read her mind, was at the piano playing Debussy. Now she could dance Debussy although she did not care for his music. Whatever Nijinsky could dance, she could dance. Now

Nijinsky was articulate. They moved closer. When she had seen Nijinsky leap she had hungered to embrace him, and now they were dancing hand in hand. They circled the studio. They were dancing love, they were traveling from one enchanted place to another, drawing breath and motion from one another, and suddenly she touched him and he dissolved. Nijinsky seemed to fade away, although he bowed in unconscious tribute to her as he did, and the dance was over.

There was tumultuous applause, but Bayard looked as if he had been slapped in the face. Lenora, seeing his anger and feeling it was possessive, looked around for further provocation.

Archer told her there were art students from the *Bal des Quat'z Arts* at her door, creating a joyous commotion, and she ordered him to admit them. Let them drink of the millionaire life, let them revel in this perfect day. Bayard strode across the studio to offer her his arm, but students poured in and she went off dancing with a superbly built art student in a leopard skin. A nude model was carried in, held aloft where she could be the the Venus, rosy and unashamed. The art students rushed through the studio laughing and cheering and dancing; Lenora was their idol, she danced in public the way they did in private.

Lenora was overwrought, voluble and wild—how right, how wonderful, she nodded when the leader in the leopard skin declared he was in love with her, that they were all in love with her. She saw Rodin watching her with obvious admiration. She yearned to dance stark naked for him, and then he would create a statue that would be aptly called: "Saturnalia!" In the mirror she saw Bayard glaring at her fiercely. If he could only renounce his dignity, she thought, but he was growing angrier with each passing moment. To punish him— oh how she would enjoy that—she tried to get Rodin to dance with her. Rodin shook his head No—he was charmed and flattered, he said, but too old.

She took the pianist Archive Tempora then, and although he was clumsy and restrained she could feel his devout expectancy. She leaned against him, her tunic-gown slipping, thinking my Viking is such a criticizer with his top hat and morning dress. She had to lean against Archive, whom she saw now as her Homer—singing sweet songs to her on his lute—to keep herself from falling.

Her Viking caught her, giving her a warning look which she ignored. In a rage he pushed her into an alcove where they were alone, the party going on quite well without her, and shouted, "You are behaving impossibly!"

"Because men have instinct and warmth for me."

"Extraordinarily squalid," he muttered, "and shameless."

"Yes," she answered, "I am human, shamelessly human."

"You're drunk."

"And you're full of moral rubbish."

By now he had a conviction that no one had ever been more wronged. He declared, "You carry on as if you were in a public bed. At least have some sense of privacy."

"That's antediluvian." She had saved him from rot with the power of her love, and he was making fun of it, he was being the snob, and she could forgive almost anything but bad taste and that was what he was showing. When he stated that she did not recognize his faithful, noble qualities and that his wealth conferred upon him a position of public trust, she quoted Whitman: "I do not convince by arguments, I convince by my presence." But if he had not been holding her, she would have fallen down.

She mumbled, "It seems that love is not enough . . . sex has interfered."

He growled, "You did not even know the name of that leopard skin."

She smiled softly, "He danced divinely."

"Lecherously."

"Don't be a bore."

"It's grotesque. You allow these insane students to dance naked in your studio. It is no wonder that . . ." He halted, awkwardly.

"That . . . what?"

"That things happen."

His censorious pose disgusted her, and, more sober now, she said, "In your eyes I'll never be fit for society. But I put on a dance tunic, and my value to you goes up a hundred times. And adds to your desire to see behind the tunic even as you rhapsodize how *spirituelle* I really am, and how divine, while you call that model's nakedness a vice, even as you are thinking what a magnificent pair of thighs, how white, how smooth."

"Lenora!"

"Nietzsche was right when he said, 'Distrust all in whom the impulse to punish is strong.'"

"You did flaunt those students before me in my house."

"I beg your pardon. This is still our house."

Bayard let her go, but now Lenora did not fall down. Because he still desired her desperately and could not admit it now, he hated her for even the nonexistent men she admired. He saw her as insatiably erotic but not toward him, although she had not known any other man since they had met.

Lenora could not admit she was wrong, in any detail, although she knew she had deliberately provoked him to this. To admit that was to admit this was not a perfect day, and it was, it had to be, God, it had to be!

He said, "Tell the guests to go home."

She shook her head No, not trusting herself to words.

"If you don't?"

There was no need to finish.

A moment later he said, "It's our last chance." And he left.

Last chance, what nonsense, but why did such bitterness come when he was gone? Call him back, forgive, before it is too late to forgive. Be generous, do penance if he demands, fight for him, but hurrying to call, his name faded on her lips. Instead, she found herself saying, "Archive will make a faithful lover, look at the talent he displays at the piano, his strong hands, his striking head, the way he plays for me." She was glad no one could hear her, for Bayard had to return, it was inconceivable they could separate for such stupid reasons.

The party went on the next day with Lenora apparently in vigorous health. Now there were many people present whom she did not know, but everybody seemed to love her and were happiest when she was holding forth, or dancing, or offering them champagne. Bayard did not return, but no one asked questions and Archive remained by her side, and when she suggested they transfer the festivities to Nice he was agreeable and so were many of the others. She hired autos to take them to Nice, and when this palled after several days she chartered a yacht to visit Venice.

When the party finally ended, a week after it had begun in Paris, Lenora went to Florence as the guest of Duse. Lenora wanted to rest, for she was planning another tour of America, Russia, and Germany, this time with her school and Cathleen and Dion, desiring them to see the wonders of the world, sure these influences would mold them.

Duse asked, "What about Bayard?"

"He'll come back. If I want him to."

"It could be dangerous. He is a Maecenas. I do not think his Marina will give him up easily."

Lenora smiled. She had heard about this woman, romantically dark, his mistress before and after her and determined not to lose him again, so it was gossiped. But Lenora, reinforced with Duse's regard, proud of her friendship with Rodin which was flowering, the money from her dancing flowing in like champagne, her daughter and son growing up to be beautiful children, was resolved to be unconcerned. With her usual energy she was concentrating on Cathleen and Dion as Mama had concentrated on her. They gave her such rapture with their first words, their first steps; she loved sharing their unfolding wonderment of the world.

Duse was saying, "Please don't go after him if he stays with Marina." Lenora was puzzled. It was unusual for Duse to object to any of her plans. "He is not worth it, and she has a terrible, vindictive temper."

"You're too melancholy. That kind of danger exists only in the imagination. You should see Dion dance. You can't stop him. And Cathleen always wants to follow him, though she's just learning to walk. They are not the least bit afraid of making any motion they feel." Lenora was very happy, talking about her children. Even without Bayard she was positive she had never been happier. She would devote herself to her children. This would be the fullest expression of her personality.

44

For the next year Lenora lived at the top of her emotion, invariably feted and praised, and on the whole she remained happy. Gone were the days when she owned only a ten-franc Venus de Milo in a corner of her studio; now she had a genuine Rodin and had become a close friend of the great man.

Artist, mother, and woman of the world, she had desired all the major pleasures, those of the flesh and those of the spirit, those of the great and those of the humble, and now she had known most of them. A year of such success had given her a deep trust of life and a sense of continuity in her children. She had many more achievements to her credit, and she blessed her own warm, enthusiastic nature for this. She had danced in many cities with her school as a background, although actually these girls did very little dancing, but they had appeal and created a furor with their precocious ability and their naïve and youthful beauty.

Lenora was especially aware of youth now. She took Dion and Cathleen with her wherever she went. They were her defense against disappointment and hurt, and while she was with them she felt she could endure anything.

My children will never be waifs or strays but will have all of my love, she said to herself passionately. She was shocked when anything painful happened to them. They were the romantic illusions of her dream turned into flesh and blood, and so, when Dion stumbled while dancing and fell and cut his leg it spoiled the dream, when Cathleen was hit accidentally by another child's elbow who was imitating Lenora's outflung arms it was a disillusionment. Nothing must happen to them, Lenora thought, whatever happens to me. It was as if she was determined to prohibit even fate from injuring them, even if she had to bear the pain herself.

Their beauty raised great hopes in Lenora. What distinguished them from most children was their radiance. Although all of the children in the school were lovely—Lenora could not have endured them if they had been otherwise—Dion and Cathleen seemed to have a special spontaneity. Lenora attributed this to her having trained them from birth, so they had not come to dancing corrupted as the other children had. They flowed in and out of dancing without any self-consciousness; she had them dancing from the instant they could stand. They did not think of steps; they danced as naturally as most children walk. Lenora gave them everything that would make their spirits sensitive, their minds responsive, their bodies alert. She was scornful of any other kind of bringing up. Dancing was their life, their language, Lenora was absolute about this. She was certain this would make her children secure in their happiness, since their level of happiness had to be inspired and not just happiness.

There were a few hostile elements in this Garden of Eden. No matter how much money Lenora earned, and Archer estimated she had earned several fortunes in the last ten years, there was the inevitable discrepancy between income and expenses. She was tremendously popular, more so than ever. Her recitals, particularly in Paris, were always sold out, and yet she continued to be in debt. Bayard, from the instant he had left her, had withdrawn his support. Yet when Archer pleaded with her to give fewer parties, to lessen her other extravagances, she acted as if he suggested she renounce life itself. She said, "I cannot live poorly. I will die first. Poverty is degrading. Now is the time to reap a little of the beauty and joy we are entitled to."

But as her debts increased she had to give more recitals. She worked harder and harder, often in driving gusts of energy, and often she was very tired. Several times she felt so faint she had to lean against her studio wall to keep from falling. Recognizing finally that she could not rest as long as she stayed at Neuilly, she arranged to go to Versailles for a rest. At the last moment, feeling lonesome without Dion and Cathleen, she took them with her. She had a moment of doubt about this. The children loved Neuilly and preferred to be with the older children, but then she told herself any fears about them were silly. They were in perfect health, and their governess was devoted to them.

The ride to Versailles was peaceful, although Dion and Cathleen missed the other children and did not want to remain at Versailles, especially when Lenora had to leave them the next day to dance.

The Paris recital went as usual: acclaim, many encores, and a full house. Lenora was near exhaustion, disturbed by the children's restlessness at Versailles, and almost satiated with dancing, a feeling she dreaded, when a miracle occurred. Bayard stood in the doorway. A year had passed, and he looked well, but older, a touch of gray on his temple.

He said, "You look tired. Sit down, Lenora, please. Rest."

"It's been a hard recital." She would not have admitted that a year ago.

"You were wonderful. You evoked in me the vision of the birth of the world. It was noble dancing."

She thought her heart would stop beating. She still cared for him, she had always cared for him despite his jealousy and bad temper, she thought, although she had not admitted that, and now he was different. He was calm, as if jealousy had dried up within him, and he could regard her with quiet emotion.

"And, as always," he added, "you were genuine."

"And, as always," she added, "you are perceptive."

"Sitting here, I feel as if I have come back from the dead."

Lenora could not resist asking, "Was Marina that difficult?"

"Marina is Marina," he stated, as if to put an end to that.

"Bayard, you should see the children dance. They've improved so much the last few months."

"I'd be delighted to see them dance."

Beware, her mind said, even as a wave of love flooded her heart. Emotion creates more emotion, and he will eventually try to bully you even as you cannot be a puppet. Bayard made a gesture begging her to continue. What impressed her more than anything else, however, was his new consideration for the children, for Dion too. So she agreed to bring the children to him tomorrow.

This time, she thought, he would not try to reform her, and she would not provoke him. Even so, Lenora awoke that evening at Versailles with the strangest feeling. She heard a child's cry, and then she was sure it was her fatigue and doubts about seeing Bayard again, but no, it was Cathleen crying out, as if in a bad dream. She ran into the next room. Cathleen was sitting up, shaking, but the governess and Dion were sound asleep.

"What woke you up, dear? Was it a noise?"

"I don't know, Mama, a dream, I think. I thought it was you, but then it grew ugly and was going to hurt me. I don't understand, do you, Mama?"

"It's a sign. Be careful, dear, the next few days."

"Do you think it was the devil, Mama?"

"There is no devil, Cathleen. That's an old wives' tale." She took her daughter into her bed. She did not sleep, but Cathleen quickly fell asleep with Mama's arm cradling her. The flush on her face, her trust in her Mama gave her an innocence that filled Lenora with renewed love and hope.

Nonetheless, Lenora took the children to meet Bayard in Paris the next morning with some apprehension. Lenora believed that some things were ordained, she read horoscopes and was certain there was validity in astrology, and perhaps this was a warning, this could be an inauspicious time to see Bayard. He was his most charming, however. He embraced them and was delighted with their gracefulness. Then, as Bayard went to sit down, Dion said, *"Bonjour, monsieur,"* and Cathleen sought to help him to his place. Deeply touched, Bayard kissed them both. He declared he had magnificent plans for the four of them. He was so pleased with the children he wanted them to join him at his home where he could make further plans for them, but Lenora said she had to stop at Neuilly so she could make some adjustments in tomorrow's recital and that the children had to nap, and they wouldn't with him; they would be too excited and he would stuff them with candy and other sweets. Suddenly then he reached over and kissed her as she was stepping into the auto. "Forgive me," he whispered.

"There is nothing to forgive," she said softly.

"I love you," he said, "better than before."

She nodded, too blissful for words.

"You have been wonderful with the children. I am proud of them."

Lenora rode all the way back to Neuilly with a smile that never left her lips. There, she did not want the children apart from her for a single instant, but the governess said, "They ought to go to Versailles. They will not nap here. They will be too distracted."

Lenora knew that was true. They would be occupied with the other children, and she could not be with them anyhow the next few hours. But she sighed, although she told herself it was absurd to be apprehensive.

Cathleen was having such a wonderful time with her hair flying behind her as she danced and played with the other children. While Dion stood thinking, and Lenora was deluged with questions: last week he had wanted to know where the sky came from, and now he wanted to know all about the water and was it the same as the Seine nearby, dark and deep, and what made the water wet? She was captivated by his curiosity; then suddenly, Lenora wondered what possessed Cathleen! Cathleen was watering the lawn with a water can and when Lenora asked why, her daughter said, "Madame Pavlova told me that the girl who handles the watering can most gracefully will be the greatest ballerina," and she went on sprinkling as if she had an audience of thousands.

Lenora stated firmly, "You will not dance ballet."

"It is so pretty, Mama," explained Cathleen, "and Madame Pavlova said——"

"Ballet is wrong, it is against nature," said Lenora, and kissed Cathleen fervently to show her love, and Dion too, for he did not want to be left out. Tomorrow they would see her dance in public for the first time.

The governess promised to look after the children with her life, and Lenora, reassured, told herself it was strictly a matter of principle that the children nap. They blew kisses at her, and she reached out as if to grab the kisses and Cathleen and Dion giggled. They looked so happy, waving good-by, a more cheerful Lenora decided her anxiety must simply be a tension induced by fatigue. It had started to rain, an unpleasant gray drizzle, and the Seine, after a hard winter, had overflowed its banks, but Lenora was not afraid of that. The road to Versailles was much frequented and quite safe. She did wish, however, that the rain would cease. The sky had grown so dark it was becoming increasingly difficult to remain cheerful.

The children were thinking of the Château de Bearn which Bayard had said he would buy for them when the hired auto came to a sudden stop. They had gone just a short distance from their home in Neuilly and onto the Boulevard Bourbon, which flanked the Seine, when the chauffeur pulled up to avoid a collision with another car. He shut off the power so suddenly that he was unable to start the machine again. He got out to crank the car, forgetting that he had left it in gear. The children wanted to join him, but the nurse said it was silly, it was raining and they would get wet. The chauffeur swung the crank around, and the instant the engine started the car sprang forward. He leapt aside, narrowly escaping being knocked over. There was no parapet separating the Seine from the road, and as the chauffeur stood there terrified the auto raced down the gentle grass slope running from the sidewalk to the river's edge. There were brief screams from the children and the governess, almost instantly drowned out by the horrible splash of the auto plunging into the water.

Witnesses gathered immediately. The chauffeur was half praying and half cursing and beating his hands against the road. Then the top of the closed car appeared above the water. Two men, one of them a champion swimmer, dove in. They were unable to open the door and release the prisoners, but as they returned to the shore for strength and air, certain they would succeed the second time—the back door had almost opened and only a short time had passed—a guard held them back. "No," said the guard, "the proper authorities have been notified. Help will be here soon."

Help, however, arrived very late, owing to the fact that it was not applied for at the American Hospital nearby—that was not official—but was brought from the city. Meanwhile, the two swimmers had fought free from the guard and made new efforts to extricate the children and the governess from the car through the windows. But by then it was too late. The auto had sunk totally under the water.

Police and firemen were here now with grappling irons. They worked with frantic speed to get the car out of the river, but it was a long time before the grappling irons were fixed firmly around the auto and it was drawn toward the bank.

Dion was found halfway outside of the door; Cathleen was deep in the protective arms of the governess. The children were still warm but unconscious. As the large crowd watched silently their bodies were taken to a doctor nearby in the hope of saving them. The doctor sought to resuscitate them, trying to blow breath into them, putting his mouth to their mouths to force air into their lungs, wrapping towels about them, holding them tight to his chest to warm them, but none of this helped. It was too late. A few minutes later the children were pronounced dead.

Bayard, informed first and given the task of informing Lenora, approached her saying to himself, I must not break down, I must not lose control, I must be so careful and so cruel. For him this life suddenly seemed like the afterlife; the present had vanished. Lenora was in her study, already missing the children and wishing she had not sent them to Versailles, when Bayard entered. She greeted him affectionately, overjoyed to see him, and he sobbed, "I can't tell you, I can't!" His face was swollen with tears, and he sobbed as if his heart were breaking. "Dion and Cathleen! Oh, Lord!"

Lenora could not hear what he was saying. His voice seemed to echo as if it came from a long way over water. "What is it? You are shivering!"

"They're gone. Forever."

That was a false and foolish idea. Of course she trusted him, like she trusted life, but he was cringing before her and no one should cringe.

"Lenora . . . the Seine . . . that runs behind this house . . . they're in it."

She did not like the look in his eyes. What he was suggesting was insane.

They're gone, he wanted to shout, they're gone, but he could not say it. To say it meant it was true. Yet when he continued to sob, she knew.

She let out a gasp of horror. She could not breathe. A pain started where she had given birth and rose to her heart and struck her like the sharpest of knives. Others were at the door, friends, family, children, but not her children. She screamed, "Bring me my children!"

Bayard was saying, "I don't know how to tell you."

He went to embrace her and she cried, "Please don't touch me!"

It was only a few minutes between Neuilly and the hospital, but for Lenora it was a lifetime. This was the longest journey she had ever taken anywhere, and yet she did not want it to end. She stared ahead, as if into nothing, for there was a mist before her eyes, only able to visualize her children, re-creating their features one by one. She would not take anyone's word until she saw for herself. It was impossible that she would never see them again. That was insane; they had so much yet to do together. But it was growing even harder to breathe as they came closer to the hospital, to the confirming, the never-never again. She sought to hold on to them by recalling their words and smiles and movements, by recalling her last words to them, and what had they answered? She sought to recall her feeling at each child's birth and the great inspiration each brought her, their first cries and their first laughs, when had that been?

Bayard whispered, "It's terrible, Lenora, but it's fate."

"I'm sorry," she mumbled. Her voice was so low that he could not hear it against the noise of the car.

"What?"

"I'm sorry."

"What have you done?"

She had been clumsy and had abused Marina with mimicry, besides taking him away from her, and now Marina had had her revenge. No, she could not say that to anyone, not even to him. It was too far-fetched, too ridiculous, too insane—no one would believe her, yet the children had been so safe. And Marina's whole life was in Bayard; call it self-preservation, and Marina's instinct for preservation was strong.

"How do I live with it?" Lenora cried suddenly. "How do I keep it in my mind without going crazy?"

Even as a father he felt he was intruding, but he had to help. "You were a wonderful mother, dear, remember that."

"Were?" She was horror-stricken at all that conveyed, and suddenly she could not talk.

"They looked beautiful," he said, "simply beautiful."

They still did. They lay there, no fear on their faces. Strange, they were birds in a cage. They could no longer fly. She was not insane; it was life that was insane. This morning she had been sane; this evening she was insane. Genius and madness, too close, too close. And then as Lenora bent and kissed them, as she felt the icy touch of their lips and knew even that was counterfeit, she was filled with an unbearable hopelessness. Mercifully, she fainted then.

During the funeral she thought she would faint again, but Rodin was by her side with a sketch he had done of Cathleen, and Bayard was on the other side whispering she could not give up, it would not be fair to the children.

The three bodies rested on a catafalque in the center of the studio. Nothing was in black, which was her wish. There was no religious ceremony, but the music of Bach and Mozart and Beethoven. The children of her school, dressed in white, filed in to pay their homage. Flowers were everywhere, and mourners, friends she had not seen for years and friends she did not know she had.

Then suddenly she whispered to the orchestra leader to play Liszt's *Funérailles*, and although she had never danced to this she danced before the bodies. A last dance, she thought, her last dance. There was a gasp of astonishment which subsided as her dancing, slow, so slow it was more of a funeral oration than dancing, painted her anguish so movingly that when she finished there was only a hushed and weeping audience.

She stood before their bodies a moment more and uttered a silent prayer:

> *"Rest, rest, rest my babes,*
> *Sleep, sleep, sleep your days,*
> *Rest, rest and save your strength,*
> *The sun will rise at your heads.*
>
> *Rest, rest, rest your eyes,*
> *Mother will turn the moonlight off,*
> *And put a curtain across the skies,*
> *Sleep, sleep, sleep my vines.*
>
> *Sleep, sleep will rest your legs,*
> *Soon you will get up to dance,*
> *Mother will take you by the hands*
> *And we'll dance over lands and death."*

But there was no rest of any kind for Lenora. Exhausted, she hardly had the strength to endure the long drive across Paris to the famous cemetery at Père-Lachaise, where in happier days she had gone sightseeing to visit the graves of Molière, Racine, Balzac, Chopin, and Héloise and Abelard; but she knew she had to go through these rites to the bitter end. Only their cremation was not the end.

There were condolences to be answered. There were hundreds of letters of sympathy. The children in the school had to be sent to Amy in Düsseldorf; every time Lenora saw them she burst into hysterical crying, they were the worst reminders of all. She could not eat or sleep. She announced she was retiring from the stage and devoting the rest of her life to the poor and the sick.

Their death—she was sure it could not have been an accident now—was the only thing she could think of these days. Yet Marina was a clever, beautiful woman who would not kill anybody. There was no way to tell from the fragments of the gear and starter whether it had been tampered with.

One night, about a week after the cremation, when she was alone—it was the first time Lenora had been left alone—she slipped down to the river. She wore a heavy motoring cloak and veil, the veil so she would not be recognized, the cloak so she would sink. Lenora stood on the bank where the auto had gone into the Seine. It would be easy to plunge into the Seine, just as easy as it had been for the auto. Friends said she should cry; they didn't know she could not cry any more. She bowed her head, praying to gods she did and did not believe in. Then she slipped off her sandals. They were superfluous; she would sink just as well without them, and it was a shame to ruin them, so pretty, so useful. She was hardly breathing as she stood over the Seine and imagined her disappearance and final dance in that watery darkness. She could not resist hoping it would be beautifully danced to the music of the sea. Yes, she had danced to sea pieces before by Ethelbert Nevin. She suddenly remembered her passion in these pieces, and her head lifted in its characteristic reach heavenward. Heavenward! Her passion became a glare. The heavens, where she had looked for inspiration so many times, had betrayed her. Irrationally, she cursed the heavens for not halting the disaster, and shouted, "How could you watch them drown!" Yet somehow she could not drown. It would halt the pain around her heart, the aches that would never go away, but it was against everything she had taught herself and believed. Nonetheless, it was a struggle to move slowly away from the river bank. Automatically she picked up her sandals and walked barefooted back toward the house. The sandals hung from her fingers. Her mind seemed to hang just as limply. Not for herself caring, hearing and not hearing the sound of the overflowing river. Not caring that Bayard came rushing toward her, although he threw his arms around her like an anchor and hastily drew her in the direction of the house. He did not conceal his relief, which brought a wry expression to her lips. She said, "I'm all right."

"They're buried now," he said, "and you cannot bring them back, you must go on to other things. To your dancing, your school . . . yes, that's it. I'll build you a school you can dedicate to them."

"They died a bad death. Death was greedy, wanting them."

"Come inside. You'll feel better." She knew she would never feel at home at Neuilly any more, but she went in, just ahead of him. He could not look her in the face, but he asked, "Want a drink?"

She nodded and reached for the whisky. "Pour," she said. "Straight."

Later she was still repeating they died a bad death, and he was repeating that he would build her the most magnificent school and theater in the world. This would be Dion and Cathleen's memorial. Ordinarily his insistence would have made her furious, but she could not argue with him. Arguments were for the strong, and she was exhausted.

It was insane, she thought, but Cathleen and Dion had all the rest they needed now. Rest, children, there is beauty in rest too, she whispered to them. Rest for me. I'll never rest again.

This was the first time Lenora had been able to admit their death to herself. And they had died harder than anyone she had ever known. She turned her face to the wall and wept. And she went on drinking and the pain went on growing and she went on whispering amid her tears, "Rest children. Rest for me. Rest . . ."

45

Rest indeed, but it was impossible for Lenora. The more she rested the more she brooded. So many sleepless nights now, retracing each heartbeat of the last day she had seen Cathleen and Dion, wondering what she had done wrong, how it could have been averted. Even worse were the nights she did sleep, for then she was tortured with nightmarish dreams, more real than reality. Fate, which she had respected hitherto, became a fat stupid witch cheating and mocking her, and life became superfluous, an enormous nothing without them. Had she been too arrogant, as they said?

A few days after their death she had received a fanatical letter, unsigned, which stated in a rough scrawl: "God punished you because your children were illegitimate. God said 'Thou shalt not commit adultery.' "

A great joke that, she thought, but she wondered if she should have admitted publicly that she despised marriage.

Lenora lay in darkness, unable to sleep, exploring the many things that might have caused their death, blaming herself, hating herself, finding less answers rather than more, confusion compounding confusion, not knowing what to do next, to think next. And when she fell asleep finally, it was not sleep as she knew it. She found herself in a vast labyrinth, searching, searching, but there was only water, wherever she looked, and she wept that they were ever born. Then Dion and Cathleen appeared. But it was not good.

Dion was sobbing, "Mama, why do flowers die?"

Cathleen was sobbing, "Mama, I dreamed I lost you."

No, no, she tried to say, but they didn't seem to hear her.

Cathleen was asking, "That's bad, isn't it?"

Dion was saying, "Very bad. Isn't it, Mama?"

They stood like two shiny dolls, but before she could clutch their hands they were gone. She awoke shivering. Unable to fall asleep, afraid to fall asleep now, afraid to face dreams she could no longer endure, she lay thinking, as a human being I am the highest act of the universe, yet I have no real power in the universe. My art is the truest expression of the universe, and this universe has become meaningless, shabby, and indifferent. And this is the worst of all to face.

Lenora felt she had come to the end of the world. She could not even define her pain, or measure it, or confine it—it resided everywhere, in everything. Some people cried when they heard "The Last Rose of Summer," and others were moved only by a Bach chorale, and anything emotional brought her to tears now. She thought people who cared gave such hostages to fortune. If she had had just a last moment with them, but they would not have understood. If she could have held their hands before the last blackness overwhelmed them, and she tried to imagine whether that would have lessened the suffering. This Mama-and-child affair was not that she wanted them to be better than anybody else, but better than herself, to achieve where she had failed, these children who had crushed the commonplace and scorned the obvious, born so perfectly, dead so prematurely. But she had been betrayed, and yet there was no one to punish, not even Marina, for if Marina was guilty it had been provoked. Only herself to punish, self-accused and self-betrayed.

So these spring days curled around her heart like a shroud. In the blue haze of Paris, suddenly, at any time, she was apt to cry, her tears coming at the sight of any child that resembled Cathleen or Dion. At Neuilly their rooms, hushed now—she could not endure anybody else living in them, and yet she could not alter them in any way, as if somehow she must never lose the hope she might see them there—were like a morgue. The gardens where last she had seen them were especially painful to see. A frog sitting there was all skull now, and a dead bird, killed by a preying cat and then discarded, drove her to hysteria. But what was most difficult to bear was the sight of the grass, the simple green growing grass, the grass that was fresh with life, with the luminous rebirth of life, with the compelling vitality of spring, and the imprint of their feet. Crying then, craving death, at the depth of her sorrow, each blade of grass seemed to lay its finger on her heart, and she could not breathe for anguish.

Archer, calm and considerate as always, sought to interest her in a new tour, but she could not dance. After she had danced at the funeral she had sworn never to dance again, inspiration was gone, and faith; and Archer understood and did not accuse her, as Bayard did, of playing ostrich.

Resolute Amy said they must expand their schools, hoping this would revive Lenora, and Lenora agreed that new Malcolm schools would be fine, and the very thought of interviewing new children, no older than her Dion and Cathleen, made her shudder.

But Mama would come to her; Mama would bring comfort.

When Lenora head from Mama the letter stunned her. Mama's mother, her Grandma, had died a short while before the children, and it added to Lenora's sadness, for she had liked her Grandma although in the past few years Grandma had become a remote figure, bleached by time, but that was not what was heartbreaking. Mama wrote:

I read in the newspapers, even before I received Archer's wire, about your tragedy. I was profoundly shocked and even more shocked when I heard the details. It is inconceivable that this could have happened, and yet it did, and I can only add a prayer that the end was quick and painless. Not all ends are. Do we really die once? Or as Shakespeare suggested, a thousand times?

I thank you very much for your touching letter, but I have had to endure also. I saw my Mama die, wasting away for months. I stood near her many hours each day nursing her. It hurt me just as much to see her go in her eighties as a child of seven or younger. She was so full of jokes, though she had to be fed through tubes, incredibly artificial feeding, how much can an infirm body take, but she kept on joking, so we wouldn't be sad, and getting better or so she pretended. I don't think she ever really thought she was going to get better.

Then for a week she lost consciousness, she did not know me or Jessie, but lived her life when she was young, when she crossed the continent and fought the Indians. And so she died with a defiant smile on her face.

That was the hardest thing I have ever lived through.

Look, dear Lenora, there has been no real exchange of feeling between us for years but that does not destroy the happy times we had together. I am sure you are still irresistible, and for your invitation I thank you very much, but right now I hesitate to leave Jessie alone. I call myself fortunate if I get to the theater once a year, I do not mingle with people much any more, and I am no longer your dashing mother. If you want to see me, I'm afraid it will have to be in San Francisco. I know this is small consolation but remember, others have suffered the same as you have.

I do hope that you will return to your dancing. We hear of your success even here in faraway San Francisco, and it will not help your children if you stop now. In any event I have come to the conclusion that we never know what happens to us from one moment to the next. Forgive this poor attempt at philosophy, but what else is there to say, that my memory is full of crumbs of the past, that each of you wanted everything and got it, that life is still a battle here, the same as it is for you, and dear Lenora, let us know when you will come back to our house and we will try to make you welcome.

Lenora thought bitterly, I will never see her again. Mama says it is the same, but no, it is not the same, it is as if the children have been torn off my breast, my breasts torn off. They were young and helpless, and it is worse, much worse.

Now she was possessed with the harsh, voracious thought that if Bayard had not returned to her the children would still be alive. She did not blame him, however, but herself.

Bayard was resolved to cure her melancholy. He gave a condolence party for Lenora, to thank all the people who had been kind to them in this time of sorrow, and to restore her to reason.

He was still a handsome man, taller than anyone else there, with a thick immaculately groomed Vandyke and a fine head of hair, his figure carefully preserved, although it was starting to show some signs of middle age. He regarded everyone with an air of patrician elegance, carrying himself quite erect, feeling fully developed as a person even if Lenora wasn't, with her constant mourning. He was positive he never indulged in self-dramatization as she did; this evening he felt he conveyed a kingly impression of dignity and ease. He was upset that she was so morose and cryptic now, so ugly in her grief. Most of the party were his friends, the rich, the fashionable, and a few artists for her sake. A hundred people were expressing their sympathy, and she stood somber and silent. She was drinking heavily. She did not seem to care how she looked: her hair was disordered, her dress hung unevenly. He felt ridiculed. Nothing about her was elegant, courageous. Everyone was so sincere, so truly sorry for her, and she was saying nothing, not a solitary word. A new group came up to console her and scattered into many pieces on her stoniness.

He cautioned her about her drinking, and she muttered, "Whisky is the best painkiller." He felt this was the final failure, and when he said this drinking would only make her more melancholy she looked at him suspiciously and said, "The best rest is sleep, the best way to get sleep is to relieve pain, and the best way to relieve pain is to take whisky."

The evening became a long-drawn-out torture for Bayard. He found himself hunched over her, to hide her behavior from the others, and she did not care. People were still greeting her, expressing their sympathy, waiting for her answer—and there was nothing. In the darkness of her drinking and the deeper darkness of her spirit people had become the murderer, but if she kept on drinking this would be the sanctuary of her despair. Bayard grew anxious and tired and furious at the spectacle she was making of herself, and finally, filled with an acute depression, he said, when everyone was gone, "You cannot expect me to go on with an association that is not only painful to me but which no longer can be expected to produce any artistic results."

For an instant she was her old self, amused—since when was he an artist? She said, "That's nonsense."

He said in his most elevated manner, "I do not intend to exchange insults with you."

"Don't you realize that if I had to hear another reminder of the children I'd go mad?"

"So you had to drink God knows how much whisky!"

"God doesn't know."

"You're drunk."

"I wish I were. It has to mean something. Their death has to mean something."

"It means they're dead." He sighed, heroically, "And we have to go on."

Glass in hand, she laughed. It was the ugliest sound he had ever heard. Standing in her magnificent studio, the envy of Paris, she wanted to vomit and could not. It was a most agonizing feeling. There was a vile lump in her throat, and she could not get rid of it.

She was saying, actually more to herself than to him, "I don't want to cry, I don't, but if I talk about them I will, I will!"

"Drinking won't bring them back."

Save me, she thought desperately, I am in such a deep, dark, melancholy place; save me, not by moral strictures, not by anger, you don't have to play the offended lover, damn it. Neither of us possess all the truth; I have nothing to cling to if you crumble.

She started toward him in the hope that his embrace would extract some of the bitterness from her heart, but he was recoiling, she was reaching for nothing once more. She saw the look, almost of aversion, that appeared on his handsome face, the look that she had abused him when all she wanted was to be loved, and then she fainted.

When Lenora recovered consciousness, she was in her own bed, Bayard beside her. He was full of remorse. Standing by her side, he was again the beautiful man she loved. He declared he would never leave her. He kissed her gently. He promised they would have another child, many children. She began to cry. This time he did not try to halt her. He patted her hand, agreed it was good for her.

46

Bayard was completely attentive and devoted. With his need to dedicate himself to one enormous enthusiasm to the exclusion of all else, he made her recovery his only concern. It was part solicitude and part vanity, vanity that he could succeed where others had failed, and solicitude for someone he loved . . . when she did not irritate him. He was sure now that nothing but her well-being had ever been his concern. He believed that if anything could restore her to creativity it was the Bellevue château at Meudon that he gave her.

He paid for Bellevue without counting the cost. It was a tremendous château with great, winding imperial stairways. It had been the château of Madame de Pompadour and before that one of the residences of Louis XIV. It was next to the Villa des Brillants, Rodin's home at Meudon. Bayard deliberately chose this location, to show her that he was not jealous of Rodin and to give her the stimulation of an artist she respected, and Meudon was one of the loveliest suburbs of

Paris. It aroused him to the height of passion, like a new love affair, and he set about shaping it to their heart's desire. He was proudest of all about the way in which he introduced it to her.

They drove through the outskirts of Paris, and when they reached the small provincial public square at Meudon got out to walk. Lenora was surprised; Bayard was not one for walking when autos were available, but she did not argue—Bayard was in such a state of anticipation. He led her along an ancient French road and to her delight and amazement his taste fitted hers. Everything was lovely. They strolled by neighboring châteaux, and he pointed out where Rabelais had lived and the son of Napoleon and the Empress Marie Louise. They climbed the hill on which Bellevue was located and she was startled by its size. A castle worthy of a queen, she exclaimed with the first burst of enthusiasm she had shown in months. "You are a queen," he said gallantly, and led her to the lawn which commanded a fine view of Paris. She saw the spires of the city, the winding Seine nearby—her breasts seemed to go flat and hard then, but he did not notice her moment of panic.

Converted by his enthusiasm, Lenora immersed herself in Bellevue. She did not give up Neuilly, to relinquish it was to relinquish the memory of Dion and Cathleen, but she resolved that Bellevue would become their memorial. For the first time they worked with equal excitement on the same project.

The main dancing hall was large enough for a multitude of pupils. Stately columns suggested her beloved Parthenon. A blue velvet carpet softened the stone floor of the main dancing hall. At the far end of the main dancing hall Bayard—who knew her taste well now—placed low divans and covered them with soft cushions.

It was impossible for Lenora to be idle. Bayard was pleased, for he was certain that nothing would make her forget her sorrow but work. She began to feel keenly the absence of the school. She knew it would be difficult to see the children again but that now the step had to be taken. She invited Amy to join her here, and Amy accepted.

A few days later Lenora stood on the lawn and greeted the children who were arriving from Düsseldorf. The girls who had been with her since the founding of the school at Grunewald were almost grown up, and their arrival was not too difficult. But when Lenora saw the younger girls, some of them no older than Cathleen, she was sick with pain and she wanted to flee. She did not move. They were giving her, with bashful solemnity, gifts of flowers. She accepted the gifts with the same solemnity the children presented them, but she had to fight back the tears. The youngest children curtsied before her, and she was thinking, I am deceiving myself, pretending to forget Cathleen and Dion, but it is the only way I can exist. Yet I must be very careful. These children's happiness depends on what I do. Many of them are lovely, but none of them are Cathleen and Dion. Then she knew she must have more children of her own.

Lenora sat rigid on a divan for the first dancing lesson. There were thirty pupils, and she looked frail and sad and wistful as she instructed them, still unable to dance, which upset Bayard, who expected her to be cured now. He had decided earnestly on a program of rehabilitation, and he was determined not to be frustrated. But in the weeks which followed he could not persuade Lenora to dance.

The most she would do was instruct the older girls for the stage. He complained that these girls were too much like her in gesture, in the lilt of their heads, and she said it was because they were not geniuses, but she would discover one yet, or, she thought to herself, create one. By now the idea of having another child had become fixed in her mind, but she had not decided with whom. She resolved she would pick the father with the utmost care.

Bayard's disappointment increased when she still refused to dance. He was disappointed also in their physical relationship. In the past she had been aggressive in a manner which had stirred him more than any woman he had ever known, but now she responded more from a sense of duty than desire. Yet she was more considerate than she had ever been, and she tried to please him. He assured himself she was pouring most of her vitality into recuperating, that he enjoyed her companionship and that was enough, but he began to resent her passivity.

Lenora wanted to respond more passionately, but she could not give herself wholly to him since the death of the children. If she had not gone back to him they would be alive now, she kept thinking, and that reflection plagued her even as he made love. And other irritations developed.

Lenora, who had refused to wear black at the funeral or to show any sign of it afterward, now became absorbed by it, finding black the truest expression of her feeling. This caused an exasperated Bayard to declare, "You can't give up now, you owe it to your career. Everyone knows you've had a tragic time, but that is over now." She was insisting, with all the beauty of Bellevue, on even making love in black. Her bedroom on the third floor of the château had the most funereal aspect. Her drapes, her bedspreads, her negligee were all in black, which went very well with her hair, which she had tinted red. He continued, "I can understand you playing Niobe on stage, but in real life it is absurd." Bayard hummed a few measures of a Chopin waltz, with which he had first courted her, hoping this would cheer her up, and she changed it to a funeral march.

She had made up her mind to mourn, and now she took a morbid pleasure in it. She felt better when she indulged in this self-pity, and when he protested she said, "You resent that someone else is in my thoughts."

"I resent that you are yearning after what is gone for good."

"That's cruel." She grew tearful. "If I remember the dead, they will remain alive in me."

"Lenora, do you always have to quarrel?"

She was on the verge of saying, why don't you return to your mistresses who care about nothing but the jewels you shower on them, but she realized that was wrong—he had showered far more on her—and yet it was as if something in her had to drive him away, had to be as destructive as life had been. And this home was only a make-believe heaven, no matter how much gold he put into it. No wonder he calculated the number and intensity of her embraces. She was seeking a lover who would release her, and that was no longer true of Bayard—the magic was gone, but he was right, they must not quarrel. She kissed him and that evening was almost the Lenora of old.

Gradually, however, she came to seek the father of her child elsewhere, and this led to many stories. Most of these she did not mind, comforted by visits from Duse, Pavlova, and Ellen Terry, but when the stories linked her with Rodin, whom her heart had settled on, she was angry. Rodin, she reflected, would give her child a sense of real existence, his great spirit would not push it into the Seine, he would not destroy the thing he was creating. His art demanded strength too, and her child must have that. Consciousness was selective, and so why shouldn't a father be chosen this way, she argued with herself, and he had such a sensuous awareness of the world, as significant as her own.

She declined Bayard's invitation to go cruising on his new yacht, which he was very proud of, and arranged a private picnic with Rodin. The glade she chose was secluded, and Rodin was happy to picnic with her. They had become firm friends by now, having spent many afternoons together. She had quite decided on her course of action. But when she spoke about her need to have a child Rodin looked surprised and unaware that she preferred him. Rodin said, "Bayard is a good person to speak to when you have a problem."

"He is not an artist, Auguste. And even if he were he'd still lack the creative imagination you have."

"He loves you deeply, Lenora."

"Not enough. Creative imagination is the instrument the child needs to work miracles with, and that Bayard does not have."

"Your genius should find you many such artists."

"Oh yes, Maestro, I wrote Bernard Shaw, mostly as a jest, saying: 'Have you realized what a magnificent child we could create, with your brains and my beauty?' And he replied, 'Yes, Lenora, but supposing the child had my looks and your brains!' "

"He is an aescetic, it cannot be helped, child." Rodin smiled and said, "You should try an artist with more of an inspired body."

"I teased Nijinsky about that, curious to see how he would react, if it would be normal, and Diaghilev almost had a fit. And now they are telling a story about me and Maeterlinck—I am supposed to have gone to Madame Maeterlinck and asked her to loan me her husband so I could have a child who would be a genius, when actually, I wanted her advice whether I should have a child again. Should I, Maestro?"

He shrugged.

Rodin did not understand, she thought, it was her fault, she had been too subtle. "But, Auguste," she declared emotionally, "I want a child and——" She halted so he could pick up his cue.

". . . and love," he finished.

"That is what I have been trying to tell you," she said archly. She leaned toward him as if she were Venus and he was Jupiter, her face flushed, prepared to slip out of her tunic, which was all she was wearing. "Maestro, you have only to say yes."

"I am too old."

"Oh, no!"

"I am old enough to be your grandfather. I am seventy-three."

"You are young in spirit."

"Not young enough."

"But, Maestro, you are the greatest man I know."

"That is most pleasant to hear, but that is not enough for a father."

"Nobody will know about us but you and our child." She

started to disrobe, adding, "You are not going to forsake me, are you?"

Rodin put his hand on hers, to halt her. It was a thick, heavy hand, yellow and wrinkled with age, and she was perturbed by its coarseness although she told herself his warmth would more than compensate. He said with fatherly benignity, "We are too good friends to be lovers."

"We can be friends, afterward," she said hopefully.

"No. Listen to me." He sat down on the picnic bench slowly and awkwardly, and she realized that he felt old, whatever she said. "You may resent me now, but you will be grateful later. I am a veteran sinner, and I know. If you want a father for your child you should have a healthy, uncomplicated young man, one with intelligence and talent, but that is not most important. The real crime, child, is poor health . . . and old age is poor health and I suffer from it. You have a Rubens fleshiness which should be united with the muscular development of a young Hercules. Then, you may not have a charming family, but it should be healthy. You are not an aescetic either, and you should not remain childless."

"I would rather lose my name!"

He was not listening; he was thinking of his age and the uncertainty of his future. He sighed and said, "Everything seems to tire me now. Even my work. I cannot stand any more when I sculpture. I will not be a Methuselah."

"You will live forever, Maestro," she blurted out impulsively.

He shrugged, as if to say that was out of his hands.

She said sadly, "I wanted a child to be a link between us."

"Your work is," he said with a return of some of his former animation. "Your art has influenced my work more than any artist I have known. I think you are the greatest woman artist the world has ever known."

She whispered, "You are trying to console me."

"No, I will always remember with gratitude your proposal. It is a gift to cherish."

She embraced him affectionately and spent the remainder of the picnic talking about the sketches he was making of her.

But she did not lose her determination to find an inspired artist who would make a worthy father. A few weeks later she met a friend of Rodin's who struck her as an ideal choice. Eric was her own age, a muscular, robust Dutch architect, handsome and intriguing, and she was attracted to him at once. Rodin introduced him as a potential Rubens of architecture, and she agreed. She saw Eric's imagination at work in his piercing eyes, in his fierce intensity; every move he made bore the stamp of individuality. His architecture was grandiose, yet dramatic. He had the finest body she had ever seen in an artist. He was fervent in his regard for Rodin and for her. They sat side by side in her salon, and Eric expressed a burning need to be devoted to her. He declared he would be bereft if she denied him, as she would be if she denied herself. She decided this meeting was foreordained, that Eric had the prodigious vitality and talent Rodin had recommended, while he swore that she and her art were magnificent.

Bayard was still away on his new yacht, and she plunged into this affair impetuously. Eric was lavishly romantic, and she gave of herself completely, determined that this child would be the fullest expression of love. But soon Lenora realized that Eric was not truly inspired. He was predictable; he displayed the usual overestimation of the worth of his affections; he was not interested in her social experiments. He saw their love as eternal, although he was not attentive when it came to listening to her opinions. Women were made for love, he declared, not for reflection.

Eric spoke about marriage as if it was the inevitable result of their affair, and Lenora recoiled before his smugness. She had no intention of blighting her art with such a desecration. But she said, since he was her lover and an artist, "It would be a criminal waste, marrying me."

No, she was not mad, she said in response to his indignation. She understood the opportunity he was offering her. But she did not wish to be a betrayer as well as the betrayed. He started to say something about "the practical aspect," and she smiled at his words and said, "Precious heart, you are blind."

He felt like a young bull elephant whose gait was too ponderous for her. His voice grew harsh. He said, "You are a fine one to speak of right and wrong when you reverse all the values."

She always loathed a prig, and then he sulked, something the most ordinary man did habitually, and this she could not bear, an ordinary man. Perhaps he should feel swindled, she thought, but she had wanted to go so deep there would be no memory of previous loves, with an unmeasured plunge so nonconsciousness would come and the imprint would be of a new life.

Eric continued to press in favor of marriage, but she would not talk about it finally, or she would talk her life away. He left early one night, saying he would return, but he did not return. Lenora was not surprised. It was enough that he had loved her dearly, when he had loved her. Feeling the life stirring within her, she was grateful that he had exhibited health and inspiration and had given of his fine body to bring her kingdom closer.

In her pregnancy she did not wish to move. She became passive and very careful, determined that this child must be born peaceful. She did not expect Bayard to forgive her—she did not think she needed forgiveness—but she hoped for understanding. Understanding was something he was an expert at, especially with her, and when she put it on that basis he should not accuse her of infidelity.

She informed him one afternoon after he came in from riding—he was usually in a good humor after riding—and she added, "It was not an affair. I wanted to have a child scientifically. By selection. Selective breeding, the geneticists call it, where genes are controlled through heredity."

Bayard just raised his eyebrows, the picture of an elegant, sophisticated man, although he was exploding with fury. And when she said she had picked the most creative man she knew, his outsized riding crop swung in anger like a scepter. He thought she was impossible, going from bitchery to virtue and back to bitchery with complete aplomb, and utterly lacking in remorse, regarding this child as a scientific experiment when there was nothing scientific about it. Even more infuriating was the way she lay there, in a rapt trance which was even more provoking because it pretended such innocence, expecting compassion, not anger. Such irrationality, wanting understanding from him when she had none herself. What did she understand of his feelings? Suddenly she seemed heartless to him. Yet he wanted to protect his social position, and he could not resist asking who the man was, although he knew that was wrong. "Is it someone I know? So that I can avoid him. That's the only reason I want to know."

"No one you know," she replied. "Not Rodin," she said, seeing the query in his eyes, "or D'Annunzio," with whom she had become friendly.

"Everyone will assume that the child is mine."

"You won't be slandered, but I'd rather not discuss it."

"So this child was just one of those things, like an extra drink." He pretended to be flippant, but his voice had grown harsh.

"I have no obligation to have a child by you."

"That's right. You are the ruler of your divan."

"Thank you." She was casual, ignoring his sarcasm.

He sought to be magnanimous then, for he was proud of

being a worldly man, and the initial shock was over. Moreover, there was a kind of stability in knowing she had had another man; hitherto he had only suspected it, which was worse. But from then on zest was gone from their relationship. Bayard made no effort to take Bellevue from her, but he began to live like a bachelor again, to vist her occasionally, then infrequently, and then rarely. He made no explanations, and she did not ask for any.

Lenora was deeply engrossed in the coming birth, to the exclusion of all else. When she moved, it was gently; when she felt, it was with tranquillity. She realized too, waiting for the child to come, that one of the reasons she had turned to someone else had been as a protection against becoming too dependent on Bayard.

Time flowed imperceptibly until she grew large with child. She tried to feel this was a new beginning, but that summer, as birth came close, Austria attacked Serbia, soon Russia was fighting, and Germany and France and England and most of the world she had danced for and loved.

Bayard wanted her to leave Bellevue, but she refused, although she did not stop him when he took the children for safety to Amy, who was already in America. At this point she did not want to move, to move was to disturb the life within her. Day after day she waited for the child to come, but the fighting, like a witches' brew, came instead. Archer grew frightened. Bellevue was like a huge tomb now. The Germans, advancing on Paris, were at the Marne, on the other side of the city, and there were rumors of flanking movements. Some said the Germans were within an hour's march of Bellevue, but she still could not move, afraid that would injure the child within her. Guns started, German guns and French guns, their thunder rolling across the countryside like an obscene organ, and it became her benediction. She thought herself writhing on the ceiling, and she sought to recall Keats' "Beauty is truth, truth beauty," and she was casting out, faint, dizzy, and then she heard Archer's sympathetic voice, "A girl, a beautiful girl."

She heard a baby's whimper. A surge of exaltation went through her. Dion and Cathleen would have a memorial that mattered, after all. She held up her arms, to caress her child, so tiny and slight, and she saw only Archer standing there. "What's wrong? Why do you look at me like that?"

"You must be brave. You must carry on."

She looked at the open door. Where was her child? Surely they could not deny her now, not after all this anguish. "I just want to look at her."

"It is *Götterdämmerung*," Archer muttered. "The dreadful fighting, all the anxiety. But remember, Lenora, the child did not suffer."

She had a heart too soon made glad. Dion was dead, and Cathleen was dead, and this gift was dead, and whatever excuses were made, life was dead. Her body had failed her; she hated her body.

She lay on her back and wanted to die.

She did not die; they could not let her die; she was Lenora Malcolm; she could not die. But when this child was placed in the ground a great cloud of dust seemed to blow into her eyes.

Death was common these days, as common as flies. The Germans had been stopped at the Marne, she was told, but she did not care. The doctor told her that she would be unable to have any more children because her muscles had become too hard and involved from dancing, and she did not care. She would never dance any more; she was tied to the grave, and people said she was selfish, what was her anguish compared to the world's, to the thousands perishing every day. And so, when she was able to move, she went into Paris and presented her beautiful Bellevue, her temple of art, to France as a hospital for the wounded soldiers who were everywhere.

BOOK EIGHT

47

From this day on, a day bloody and without reason, a day of despair and desperate actions, Lenora felt the world with different feelings. She began to wander, endlessly wander. The world had swallowed her children, and perhaps it would swallow her.

Several months after the death of her last child she boarded a ship for America, unable to find any peace or rest in Europe, and although she was treated with respect and comfort on this luxury liner, she felt naked and alone. The Captain invited her to his table. He was quite flattering. She was a heroine of France with her gift of Bellevue to his nation; he had seen her dance and he desired to talk about her art—did she really feel like an opening flower on stage, and she could not find any answers. There were a few old friends aboard, also leaving war-stricken Europe, who were devoted to her wants and her feeling of loneliness grew. There was a chill in her which came from a deeper cold than the air. Poets had written that her thighs curved like Venus, and they had brought forth only death. What had she done that her children should fall into ash? Amy greeted her at the dock, apparently pert and composed as usual. But Amy went on at a great rate about how everybody was fascinated by the school and that they would have no difficulty winning support, and there was a tenseness in Amy that was unnatural and suddenly Lenora knew why. For a moment she had not known whether to kiss Amy or to shake hands, but now she threw her arms around Amy and cried, "It's so good to see you!"

Lenora looked attractive and thinner, reflected Amy, but haunted by the ghosts of her children. Amy had never seen

Lenora so silent and sad. She sensed that Lenora wanted to let the tears come but was too proud.

Lenora saw no sign of Bayard, although he was in New York. Bellevue had been a kind of dowry, if belated, but the question of support rose at once to plague them. Lenora, automatically, stopped at an expensive hotel. The children from Bellevue added to the mounting bill; there was an immediate need for money.

Amy told Lenora there was immense public sympathy for her, and Lenora replied, "The doctor said death was a scientific fact . . . what can human pity do?" Amy said that a recital by Lenora, announced as the first since the tragic death of her children—the public did not even know about the third child—would fill any theater in America, Lenora would be the artistic voice of a whole generation that was suffering and dying, and Lenora said, "I cannot dance, it would be too painful." Amy replied that nothing else would inspire patrons to support their school, and Lenora looked as if she did not care. Amy noticed a strange distraction in Lenora, as if her mind was elsewhere most of the time. Lenora could hardly do without a drink now. Lenora drank at the hotel, at dinner, afterward.

Amy longed to shout "Don't," but Lenora was too wild to correct; Lenora was, sober or drunk, so high-pitched Amy could not tell the difference.

Tonight, however, Lenora was silent, almost somber. None of Amy's plans made any impression on her until Amy mentioned what an unusual opportunity they had: their children came from such different nationalities, most of them at war with each other, German, French, Austrian, and Russian, and suddenly the audacious idealist in Lenora was aroused. She was animated for the first time since Amy had met her. Her concentration steadied, and she said, "Yes, we must help humanity. We love children, don't we?"

The next day Amy went searching for a location for their school. Amy had the promise of a dozen paid pupils from wealthy New Yorkers who wanted their daughters to be as beautiful as the Malcolm girls, but she did not discuss this with Lenora. By now, she decided, Lenora was not competent to handle financial affairs. Lenora would hold out her hands, charmingly, and the children would run to her enchanted, but she would talk to the parents.

Amy found a place along the Hudson River, some miles above New York, that she thought Lenora would like. They drove up the Hudson, and Lenora grew bored. Then they came to a winding, narrow dirt road above Croton that became rougher as they climbed. The woods were wild, the trees formed an aerial web, Lenora grew more interested. They came around a bend of the road, and there it was: an enormous white Colonial house, two long red coach houses, and an archway that took Lenora's breath away.

"Ruins that they call the barn," said Amy. "It was once a barn, they tell me, until fire burned off the roof. It's called Finney Farm."

Lenora had never seen anything like it. Ruins, barn, call it what they would, it was a perfect outdoor stage for dancing. The four walls were very high, festooned with ivy and flowering vines, and had a striking grandeur. There were two archways, front and rear. The sky was the roof. Through an arch in the woods she saw the Hudson River, seeming to hang in space, a beautiful blue. She stared, fascinated, and felt like dancing for the first time since the children had died.

Amy asked, "Is it right for a school?"

Lenora said, "Perfect."

Amy was relieved. She wanted to embrace Lenora, but she was embarrassed to show any emotion. I will renew her, Amy vowed, she needs me, she is lonely, this will put hope back into her.

Amy raised the money to rent Finney Farm by taking in Social Register children. She did not tell Lenora that part of the school would be a paid school, and Lenora did not ask.

Lenora resolved to prove that her school, composed of many nationalities, could live and work in peace, and thus set an example for the rest of the world. Willa's father was with the Austrian Army; Tamara's brother was with the Czar's forces; Kirsten's father was in the German Army; Brigitte's father was in the French Red Cross. Yet the children were good friends.

Lenora gathered all her pupils about what she called her dancing tree, an enormous three-hundred-year-old ash, whose trunk, a few feet above the ground, branched out into many trunks which resembled legs thrust out, arms thrust out, hips thrust out. The pupils oohed and aahed at the sight of the tree and were impressed by Lenora's example of nature's need to dance.

But after a few days Lenora ran into difficulties. Amy, to attract attention to the school, and since Lenora was still refusing to dance, had Willa and Tamara perform for a specially invited group of parents. Amy was satisfied, the parents were impressed, but Lenora was disgusted and irate.

Willa had imitated her, and the next day Lenora, teaching, suddenly did a parody of Willa that had the girl in tears.

Willa was a lovely plastic girl with a slender neck and graceful arms but without individuality. Then Lenora, reversing her tactics, concentrated on Tamara.

Tamara was one of her favorites; she had adopted Tamara in St. Petersburg, under the noses of the Imperial Ballet. And now Tamara had imitated the ballet à la Pavlova. Lenora led Tamara into her private domain, the cottage behind the open-air barn where the girl had danced.

Lenora waited until Tamara caught her breath, and then she spoke, "Your recital exposed your problem in art, which is your attitude. Your attitude is that you like to dance but not to feel. As Tamara you can't be afraid of anything, not even nightmares. If you feel nightmares then you have to dance nightmares, or you won't be making any contribution to art. And please don't try to make generalities out of what I am saying, it never works. I am only speaking to you as it concerns you. Even if you dance as well as Pavlova, you are not dancing Tamara and you must dance Tamara only, or it won't be art. Sink into yourself, befriend and communicate with your inner self, and by that I mean your sensory self, your intuitive self. I do not mean psychological as most people stupidly use the word. Even psychologists give it the wrong implication. To poets, and a dancer should be a poet, it is the only natural way to experience life. So here's to depth living and to depth dancing, to Tamara, who will not be afraid to feel, to search for the truth."

Tamara cried out, "But what is the truth?"

"It's you. Whatever you feel. How you would express that with your body, with the unique body that is Tamara."

"But I'll never have the experiences you've had."

Tamara looked stricken, and Lenora hugged her and whispered, "Girl, don't you realize you have the most glorious thing of all—youth, that your body is made of elastic? You'll bounce back."

There was no bounce in Lenora, however, for when an exquisite little girl in a white frilly pinafore was brought to Finney Farm the following week as a prospect for admission Lenora thought her heart would break. Marjorie carried a tiny daisy in one chubby hand, a toy rabbit in the other, and her golden hair, cut to fit her lovely head, shone like Cathleen's. There was a tear which glistened like a jewel on her rosy cheek as she saw her Mama leaving. The grass seemed to bend and sigh before the child's short, quick steps, and again Cathleen took shape in Lenora's mind and something broke down inside of her. Suddenly she felt ill, suddenly she wanted to flee.

But there was the parent who had to know at once what Lenora thought about her would-be girl genius. Lenora watched this ten-year-old pirouette in what was supposed to be a copy of herself, and said, "We cannot tell about genius, but talent—she has none."

"She is young," the offended mother protested.

"There is no such thing as young dancers," said Lenora. "There are only young people who never should be dancers."

Finney Farm was dramatic this late autumn season, but shortly afterward Lenora went back to New York. Too many of the origins of life were here, reminding her of the dead husks of her own life. Little cherubic Marjorie was part of the school now. Several of the young children were having birthday parties within the next few weeks. And so although Lenora still cared for the children, and she was grateful to Amy for the intended help, she sought to find her haven in New York.

48

The Lenora Malcolm Studio of the Dance was housed in the heart of the New York business district in a converted loft. The workaday world swirled outside in a daily tumult of noise and confusion, a riotous contrast to the peace and quiet of Finney Farm, yet Lenora felt far more at home here. It was a vast studio, but there were always people in attendance. After the effort at solitude at Finney Farm she wanted people around her constantly.

Lenora became the symbol of free art, and this crowded her studio with artists of all kinds: Robert Henri, George Grey Barnard, Percy Mackaye, David Belasco, Jacob Adler, George Bellows, Edward Arlington Robinson, John Sloan, the musicians Godowsky, Ysaye, Gabrilóvitsch, and Ellen Terry, who was in New York now. There was the usual need for money, for though Bayard was still in New York he had not come to see her and she had sworn not to go to him, and so her friends set out to raise funds to establish a permanent Malcolm school and studio in New York City.

Amy did not quarrel with any of this. The older sister was relieved that Lenora had moved back to the city. Although Amy earnestly wanted to help Lenora she was distressed by Lenora's generosity and outspokenness. Amy was receiving two hundred dollars for each pupil, except for those Lenora had given scholarships to—Lenora would have given everybody a scholarship if she had had her way—and Amy helped her pack before she changed her mind and antagonized more prospective customers. Amy also agreed that Lenora could use the girls from the school at Finney Farm in recital, it would be fine publicity, but Lenora decided to use only the eight older girls.

Lenora, encouraged by the praise of her friends, became violently involved with children and teaching. She decided that if she filled her life with children it would end her melancholy.

Amy thought Lenora was being extreme, one moment she broke down at the sight of a little girl who resembled Cathleen, the next she longed to surround herself with a multitude of children, but Amy said nothing. Thank goodness Lenora had an interest again, a center at least.

There were many suggestions about plans to arouse public interest in Lenora's desire for mass teaching. Friends, influenced by Lenora's eloquence, went so far as to suggest Harvard Stadium or the Yale Bowl, but they were not Grecian enough for Lenora. When all the grandiose plans were on the verge of collapsing, it was agreed that a large New York armory would be useful for a start, would attract public attention, and several influential friends arranged for Lenora to talk to John Mitchel, the mayor of New York, in the hope of interesting him in the needs of the school.

When Lenora heard that the mayor would really come she agreed to talk to him, although she did not think he would actually aid her. The appointment was for the afternoon, and many friends gathered to give her support, which she felt she did not need. Everybody waited anxiously for her to greet Mayor Mitchel—this was quite a coup—but instead of fussing over him, meeting him at the door, she lay on her divan like a mother-earth figure in her simple black gown and waited for him to approach her.

Mayor Mitchel did so awkwardly and solemnly, a lean, long-legged man who looked more like a bookkeeper in her mind than the chief executive of one of the great cities of the world. Lenora sat up suddenly, sensing that he was tense, then reclined again—he should come to her, the artist, she thought. There was a perilous moment of silence, no one else had said a word for Lenora dominated the studio, and then she smiled beneficently upon him. She asked him to sit by her side, but he remained standing, as if to avoid being involved in a compromising situation.

Then she got to her feet, took his hands before he could escape, and said, "What an attractive young man! I expected someone elderly to be mayor, but so young, and good-looking! This is charming!"

"Thank you," he said, "but you are the one, Miss Malcolm, who is charming."

"How nice." She motioned emotionally for him to sit down.

He did, but not on the divan she had arranged for him which commanded the studio, but on a puritanical straight-backed chair. He had expected her to wear white drapes in the Grecian manner, but he realized that she was in black because she was mourning for her two dead children. He noticed that her expression was tragic even when she smiled, there were deep lines about her mouth and dark sad hollows under her green-gray eyes, as if she wept constantly and slept little. He felt sorry for her. He thought she must have been a beautiful woman, before the death of her children. He had been warned to be careful, it was rumored that saturnalia took place here, but now she looked the personification of purity and honesty. And when she smiled at him again, the mayor thought she is still beautiful. A friend carried in caviar, cold lobster, and several buckets of champagne. He was surprised. He had been told that she was impoverished, almost starving. He wondered if Miss Malcolm was always faced with such hardships.

She offered the mayor her glass. He thanked her but said he was not drinking today. She said, "We are drinking in the public interest."

"Of course." He bowed, feeling graceless amid all this grace and beauty, and he took the glass even as he cursed himself for being persuaded.

"You could be an angel, you know," Lenora said suddenly, "giving us an armory to dance in."

"I'm afraid it is more complicated than that."

"Complicated?" Lenora took another sip of champagne and plunged on. "Europe is in chaos, great artists are dying everywhere, art is on the verge of extinction——" She paused to give the mayor her most inspired smile and added, ". . . and you can make New York the heart of the art world. New York must contribute to our school, to our mission for peace. Our children come from all the warring nationalities, but they do not fight. Look, Mayor." She pointed to the eight older girls, poised behind her in a picture of aloof and serene beauty.

He said, "They are beautiful."

She said, "And you can be beautiful too"—he looked startled but she rushed on—"giving us the place to dance, for thousands of children."

"Wait," he said, "I don't want to give you the wrong impression. There are other people who have to be consulted."

"But you are the mayor, aren't you?"

"Yes."

"Then it is settled."

"No, no!" He gulped to recover his breath. "Money has to be allotted, and I'm not sure it can be raised for such a purpose."

She held out her arms with an implacable craving and virtually threw her words at him. "I'm conceding everything. I'm willing to let beautiful children dance in a hideous, warlike armory, and you worry about money. When I was a child I danced by the sea, quite naked, and the sea did not demand money." There was a terrible silence in the studio. "This is an awful city. You send children to school through filthy streets, into horrible schools, when my children are always surrounded with beauty. Isn't that worth more than money?"

"Miss Malcolm . . . ?" The mayor coughed to clear his throat. "I'm only one man and our Department of Sanitation does the best it can."

She stared at him as if he was a schoolboy in a corner, her spendthrift splendor masking an inward desperation, and rushed on, furious that she should be apologizing for what should be wonderful. "Cleanliness is lovely, and you make it sound so dull. Oh, I know that in your eyes I am handicapped because I don't have a husband, because I don't tour the country clucking about my adorable family. I admit I am not a spinster, and I do not cater to a family life, but I am teaching children to be inspired by the arts, not money, I am saving their souls. This is basic, do you deny that?"

His face flushed but he did not answer.

She could feel the rise of excitement in the others, some dismayed at her words but others, especially her girls, proud of her courage. That was what Lenora adored about speaking her mind: it was a quickening of her pulse, it made dull people bearable, it was even a kind of resurrection, and she needed that often now; it tempted the fates, anything could happen and did, and who cared anyhow? She proclaimed, riding the whirlwind, "Give us help and we will give you perfect children, peace-loving children." She gestured eloquently as she moved about, prepared to shed her blood for this cause, and her gown fell a few inches—purposely, it seemed to him—and he was upset by the amount of flesh he saw.

He sought to glance away as he thought he should. But she pressed toward him, and he was embarrassed as he said, "I had hoped to see your pupils dance, but another time perhaps. I have another appointment now, and . . ."

"Oh, New York," she said, ignoring him, "you never listen to me!"

The mayor left a moment later. Lenora, proud that she had displayed her usual integrity, was not surprised or disappointed. What else could you expect from the Philistines! She had retained her freedom. Gaily, as though armed against the worst by her courage, although some of the guests thought it was frivolity, she sought to forget the past few minutes with champagne. Relaxed, she answered all their questions with grace, but afterward there was still the question: who was going to pay for it?

When her newest and best friend, Dorothy Sunbury, invited the renowned and wealthy art patron Otto Kahn to her studio, Lenora promised to be more diplomatic. Lenora could listen to Dorothy, for the latter had no desire to use her friendship with Lenora to improve her own position as so many people did.

Dorothy Sunbury was slight of build, but resolute. She had an unusual strength which was more unusual for being concealed most of the time. She wrote and edited an art magazine, yet imposed none of her career on Lenora. Dorothy's face was almost boyish, although she was going on fifty, and her eyes had a tenderness Lenora had not experienced since the days Lenora and Mama had set out to conquer the world. So when Lenora was with Dorothy she was soft-spoken, gentle instead of belligerent, and inclined to nostalgia.

Otto Kahn was impressed with Lenora Malcolm. Tall candles framed her studio in a gentle light, and everything, thanks to Dorothy, was clean and orderly. Just a few artists were invited, those who would impress Otto Kahn and relax Lenora. Lenora looked lovely. She wore her flowing Grecian robes. She seemed like one whom inspiration had changed into a wise and beautiful Athena.

And when Otto Kahn spoke, thank heavens thought Dorothy, Lenora encouraged him to continue. Lenora listened attentively, as if he knew precisely what her art needed. She agreed with every suggestion he made; she said he had the vision and imagination to comprehend the kind of temple her dancing would flourish in. Soon he was offering her the use of the Century Theater, which he controlled.

Dorothy felt triumphant until Lenora stated that the dance at the funeral of Dion and Cathleen had been her last dance, that she did not intend to dance *Oedipus Rex* herself, which was the program she was planning. Dorothy was shocked and said, "You cannot climb into the grave while you are still alive, just as you cannot force the past to return."

"It is in reverence to their memory that I am not dancing."

"You would honor their memory if you did."

Lenora would not have danced again, however, if not for the continued emptiness of her life. At least when she danced, even in her studio, she was absorbed, some of the pain was less, and she was communicating what was within her, although it was no longer perfect. There was also the continued insistence of her friends, reminding her that life without dancing was meaningless; they said it was a loss that art could not sustain. They convinced her finally, when they pointed out that unless she danced, the recitals at the Century Theater would surely fail.

Lenora decided to feature Archer, who was winning recognition as a character actor, as the narrator of *Oedipus Rex*. She was surprised when she was warned that this was too experimental to be successful. That made her more determined to go ahead with this program. By the time of the opening performance the Malcolm company had swelled to a hundred and ten singers, ninety musicians, forty actors, and Archer. Lenora regarded herself as merely an accompaniment for all these performers, but she was certain the program would be a sensation.

Otto Kahn was stunned when he saw what Lenora had done to his beloved theater. It was the opening performance and he stood at the rear of the Century, and the interior was so altered he did not recognize it. Lenora had taken out the entire orchestra except for a few rows at the back of the theater and converted it into a Grecian amphitheater, so that the performers would be spurred on to new heights, and Otto Kahn thought she was mad. Screens hid the proscenium columns because they were against her prevailing mood. Huge drapes hung at the rear of the stage and set a tone of somber tragedy. Lenora had not consulted anyone; she was determined to transport her audience back to the Greece of Oedipus.

Otto Kahn hurried backstage, resenting that he had not been consulted, resolved to cancel the program, and never got the chance to protest. Lenora met him with outstretched hands, crying out, "Isn't it beautiful!" There was an enormous cluster of lilies in a vase on her dressing-room table, and she seized the flowers and thrust them into his hands as a tribute to his taste and said, "You will love my program!" She was certain of that.

He had to admit *Oedipus* was an extraordinary spectacle, he had never seen so many people on stage at one time; and when Lenora danced he grew absorbed, she opened up a world of experience that was moving and dramatic.

Lenora was a mature Niobe now, legs heavier, body thicker, only her arms were the same. She no longer danced romantic ecstasy; she was death incarnate. She moved less and less in her old manner; she was sculpture now, her face, neck, throat, shoulders, and arms most vital to her expression. Stressing the heroic, her body weeping, she paused suddenly at the end of her final number and instead of looking victorious, she bent as if crucified, going down on her knees in the anguish of death.

There was applause, but she did not receive the unanimous approval she expected. Much of the audience was annoyed that she had disturbed them rather than relaxed them. Others thought her program stuffy, pretentious, dull, and resented that they had been bored. Even those who wrote that "her poses were eloquent," added, "she should have refused the assistance of her brother, who in a voice of doom, insisted on depressing the audience with passages from *Oedipus*, the Bible, and Percy Mackaye."

Lenora was furious, and Amy, to pacify her, suggested that she return to Finney Farm and Lenora declined. She thought some of Amy's pupils badly taught; she was unhappy about Amy's treatment of the children, although she did not say anything. Her sister was catering to the paying children, the Social Register children. Amy pretended she was not interested in politics, that she lived according to the needs of her self, wearing a one-piece ankle-length woolen dress, hanging loose from her shoulders, believing that anything binding at the waist hampered the essential center of gravity, as much the individualist as Lenora, but also aware that money was essential even if Lenora did not. When Lenora came out to Finney Farm the children swarmed about her as if she were a goddess, but several of them were very thin. Lenora thought wealthier children were not necessarily brighter or brighter-eyed. But the problems of the Century preoccupied her, and she did not alter the regime at Finney Farm, but withdrew the children who were her protégés—mainly the foreign-born—and settled them in New York.

This created a new difficulty, for she could not afford to put them in a hotel, having spent far more on her program than she could have possibly taken in at the box office, which did not trouble her, but the indifference of the public did. She remembered Otto Kahn's assurance that they could sleep in the rooms backstage, and so she put her children there, although she was warned this was against the fire laws. Then she thrust herself into preparations for her Easter program with all the energy at her command. She was working like a cyclone, rehearsing, when Bayard came to see her.

Bayard struggled through tremendous masses of drapes backstage, stumbled over high wide flights of steps supposed to represent a Greek temple, which he did not see because they were painted white, and the bedlam backstage was terrifying, but his heart quickened as he saw her rehearsing. Lenora knew just what she was doing, he marveled, despite the chaos backstage. She took a small movement which was insignificant in itself and gave it grandeur with her feeling. She moved with sure, vigorous strides, although she looked as if she had not slept for weeks. Even her rehearsal had the intensity of performance. He stood very still, watching her.

Nonetheless, he was distressed by her dressing room, where he was told to wait for her, for it had a kind of madness. Her clothes were a messy pile on the floor, underthings hung out of her bureau, soiled tunics lay on the couch, there was a bucket of champagne and ice by her dressing table.

She did not look surprised or pleased to see him; he was disappointed.

She carried her casualness to a point of boredom. She had no intention of revealing how excited she was; she felt it would give him too great an advantage. She ignored the disorder and said the recitals were going wonderfully well, although he had heard differently. She said, "I am going to create a permanent school for the benefit of New York."

"How nice," he said. She was so generous, and he loved her for it. He yearned to ask her if she needed help—nothing made him feel better or more fulfilled than when he gave help —but if he implied she was struggling she would hate him. So he said, "I've been thinking of buying some theaters. Would you consider the Century a good investment?"

He thinks himself an expert on real estate, she thought, but he isn't. "It's rather dreary, really. We've had to alter it completely."

"So I notice." Bayard couldn't resist asking, "Does Otto Kahn mind?"

"I didn't ask him. But he has been charming. He trusts my judgment, without trying to be my lord and master."

Bayard had just begun to unbend when she said that. He

banged his cane on the floor although he did not want to show emotion, but damn, she could not avoid being exasperating. He said, "Then you don't need any help."

Darling, she longed to shout, yes, I do, desperately, but if she gave in now he would gain an advantage he would never relinquish. She put her hands on her hips and looked at him in astonishment, as if to say, how could you think such an absurd thing!

Bayard did not wish to quarrel, however, and he was searching for the tactful thing to say when a young man entered her dressing room. Harold was one of the actors supporting Archer, and he had come to obtain her revisions, but now she was very attentive to him. Harold was meaningless to her actually, but he was slim, handsome, and much younger than Bayard, and Harold would make him realize she was still much sought after. She offered both men champagne, suggesting a toast to Oedipus, and Bayard almost choked on his drink.

"Sorry," she said. "Should I open another bottle for you, Bayard?"

"No." Bayard looked like he had been turned to stone.

She ordered champagne for everyone in the company. She said they had been working terribly hard and needed a respite. Only Bayard, for whom she made this gesture, left without another word. There had not been a day or an hour when she had not hoped for some word from him—she had been so lonely without him, but she could not cater to him.

Darkness covered her eyes as he disappeared from sight. How could she tell him money was so low the children had to sleep backstage in painful discomfort, Otto Kahn was withdrawing his support because she had become too controversial, and she did not know whether she could even put on her Easter program? How could she tell him that no matter how she roamed the earth she always wanted to return to him? But he had to humiliate her, have her cry for mercy, forgiveness. He never realized they had different nervous systems. She dismissed Harold now, there was so much rehearsing to complete and so little time to do it.

Time rushed by in an unhappy blur, and the night she opened in Berlioz's *L'Enfance du Christ*, her favorite Easter program, she bought almost every Easter lily in New York to frame this program appropriately. Archer was appalled, they had less than two thousand dollars in the bank—and this was money loaned by friends—and these lilies were fabulously expensive, but she stated flatly that she could not dance without them. The lilies gave the theater a romantic magnificence which was breathtaking, and they took all the cash they possessed. But she could dance emotionally now. Admirers sent her orchids and roses, and these were also placed at the footlights and about the theater. Then she danced death and resurrection, expressing her emotions without stint, believing not in God, yet having to believe that Dion and Cathleen had an existence beyond the grave. When Lenora finished the applause burst forth loudly, spectators picked up the lilies, which had been suffocating them, and strewed the stage at her feet.

Avid for a continuation of the exaltation she had felt on stage, she gave a champagne dinner for her cast and friends backstage. This devoured the receipts for the evening, but she did not care. She was certain there would be other performances, other receipts.

The next morning the fire commissioner told her that she was violating the fire laws, sleeping children backstage at the Century Theater. She tried to reach Otto Kahn, but he was out of town. She tried to talk to the mayor, and he was unavailable. Instead of giving more triumphant recitals, she was evicted from the theater. She was informed that unless she could put up a bond for her foreign-born children they would have to be returned to their native lands. Lenora, feeling trapped, grew ill. The studio on Fourth Avenue was gone now; Amy could not help her; Archer was impoverished because of her. Dorothy Sunbury borrowed money and booked passage on the *Lusitania*, which was sailing for England, for Lenora and her eight older girls, and the day of the departure the tickets were seized for back debts.

Lenora, still shaken by the eviction from the Century, collapsed on her trunks. She was bone weary. Dorothy had gone to such trouble to keep her school alive, arranging passage on a fine ship like the *Lusitania*, and now even this opportunity had been devoured.

So Lenora sat on the dock this May 1915, watching the proud *Lusitania* steam down the Hudson toward Europe, toward freedom, she thought, and was sunk in despair, frightened for one of the few times in her life. The girls crowded around her, German-born and French-born and Russian-born and Austrian-born, and she felt like such a failure. She had always thought of the children as an existence separate from herself, something sacred that had been entrusted to her care, and now they were retreating with no place to go. Darkness was coming, and Lenora could not move, although Dorothy said she could stay with her and the children with Amy, at least temporarily, when a middle-aged woman approached the depressed dancer.

The prim, reserved-looking woman asked, "You are Lenora Malcolm?"

Lenora mumbled, "Yes," as if she had to think twice about it.

"You are short of money for tickets?"

Lenora nodded. She was too exhausted to talk.

Dorothy said, "We've given what we have, but it is not enough."

"What would be enough?"

Dorothy explained, "Passage money, at the least."

The middle-aged woman, who looked like a schoolteacher to Dorothy, plain, inexpensively dressed, handed Lenora four thousand dollars. She said, "I hope that will take care of the passage."

Lenora was crying. She could hardly see this woman's face through her tears, but no one had ever looked more beautiful.

Dorothy said, "The *Dante Alighieri* is sailing today. To Naples."

"Fine," said Lenora. "We'll stay with Eleonora Duse."

The *Dante Alighieri* was sailing in a few hours, and they passed in a whirl of activity, arranging passage, saying good-by.

Then they were on their way to Naples, waving frantic good-bys, throwing kisses, waving American and French and German flags to show that they were true internationalists. Surrounded by the children, Lenora was sure that Europe, as always—whether it would be Italy or Greece or France—would welcome her with open arms. Then she realized she did not even know the name of the middle-aged woman who had saved her.

49

A few days later the *Lusitania* was sunk by a German submarine.

Lenora, hearing of this, felt as cold and limp as a dead woman. It mocked her efforts at neutrality. She had a sick, dismal glimpse of the children drowning, and she would have been responsible. She had sought to stay neutral, but it was very difficult now. And when they arrived in Naples she heard that Italy had just declared war, and the country, instead of being agonized as Lenora expected, was festive. Eleonora Duse was out of reach, performing patriotic duties, and Lenora was afraid this war fever would infect the children. She rushed the school to Switzerland to keep the children neutral, but the instant they were in Switzerland the French girls sang the *"Marseillaise,"* the German girls replied with *"Deutschland Über Alles,"* and the Russian and Austrian girls attacked each other. Zurich, when they got there, was even more depressing. The French girls wanted to hang the Kaiser, the Germans spit on the French, the others continued to scream at each other. Lenora was heartsick. The school had to be disbanded, and all the children were returned to their respective homelands.

Lenora had no desire to go on, but there was a letter from Dorothy telling her that the savior's name was Rachel and that Rachel was not wealthy as Lenora had assumed, but a humble schoolteacher who had given her life savings to the one thing Rachel believed in: the perpetuation of the art of Lenora Malcolm.

But as Lenora said good-by to the children it was as if an apple she had cultivated with great care was crumbling in her hands and none of it was nourishing. She wrote back to Dorothy: "I do not understand the children. They live together in amity for years, and the moment their birthplace, which they have not seen for years, is threatened, they are hostile alley cats."

Paris, when Lenora arrived there, seemed to her depressed spirits like another hallucination. Only the wounded soldiers looked grim. Life seemed much the same as usual, even more hysterically festive if anything during the day, but she was in no mood for pleasantries. Bellevue was thriving as a hospital for French soldiers—although she had suggested originally that it be for the wounded soldiers of all nations—and she returned to her home at Neuilly. There were still many who wanted to study with her, and she accepted a few pupils—paid ones now, for she was living on borrowed money—but somehow the acceptance of paid pupils struck her as a betrayal of her own ideals, and the days were full of confusion and restlessness.

One afternoon, bored with browsing at the bookstalls, she went to a nearby *café* for an *apéritif.* It was a café where she used to meet many old friends, but Rodin was ill and Anatole France was out of Paris, and she sat there in despair as she saw no familiar faces. In the yellow-gray dusk she was chilled.

She had to struggle to keep from screaming. Death had carried off her children, death the all-conqueror, and she saw herself struggling with a shroud that trailed from the shoulders of death, clutching a shroud that would spin her own death. Her drinking increased with the darkening sky. She thought of Ecclesiastes, of dancing to its words, and said them over as if that would answer the question in her: would it have been better not to have been born?

> To everything there is a season,
> And a time to every purpose under the heaven:
> A time to be born, and a time to die;
> A time to plant, and a time to pluck up that which is planted;
> A time to kill, and a time to heal;
> A time to break down, and a time to build up;
> A time to weep, and a time to laugh;
> A time to mourn, and a time to dance . . .

She repeated, "A time to mourn, and a time to dance." Dancing was the rock, the solid rock, the only rock, the conversion and the dedication, and this was the time to return to her rightful home, which was not Paris or New York or any city on earth, but her dancing.

Lenora was contemplating the words of Ecclesiastes when she saw a friendly face. Archive Tempora, the pianist, stood on the pavement outside, listening to the birds, as if they were the intermezzo of twilight. He did not see Lenora. He was in some deep self-communing; he seemed so merged with sound and stem and leaf that he was nature. Here was a strength of spirit she had not realized, such a melodious spirit. He looked almost like a faun with his pointed ears, his alert eyes.

His face was rapt with pleasure when he heard her voice. She held out her hands and he kissed them, a spare, lively little man, his eyes quickly suffused with tears at the joy of seeing her.

He would make the perfect apostle, she thought, he would accompany her wherever she went. There was no bitterness in him.

When they entered her studio there was no need to discuss the next step. He played Chopin for her while she listened with growing emotion. He wanted to play on and on, feeling inspired, but finally she needed other enrichment. She kissed him with a new libertine intimacy. It was a time to love, she thought, and she slipped out of her dress with a single motion.

For an instant neither of them moved.

How desirable she looked, he thought. The time apart had not lessened the excitement of her presence. All his life he had dreamed of a woman like her. How many times he had wondered where she was, whom she was with—he could hardly bear the pain then, and here she stood complete.

"Archive, do you love me?"

"I always have," he said simply, and gulped, as if he had admitted a possible affliction. Then a great shock went through him as she embraced him. There was an abundance of feeling in her that he had never felt before. Even before they reached the huge canopied bed he knew it would be rapture.

No one could possibly have tried more to make her happy than he did the next few weeks. He made no demands on her of any kind but sought to satisfy her every mood. He did not demand that she look up to him, as had so many lovers. He regarded her as an equal in all things, and superior in some. He accepted whatever she did, and this was most important to Lenora.

She sought to have a child by Archive, feeling that he was a genius, after all. She made love at the top of her emotion, thinking the important thing is to desire, to give him all of her feeling, but there was no conceiving. She was wanton and avid, aggressive and receptive, but while the pleasure was great she remained barren.

They strolled through the Paris streets and Lenora was proud to be his *petite amie,* and neither of them had any confusion about sex. He loved her publicly and was not embarrassed by her privately. He helped her with money when she needed it. He became her rehearsal pianist, and she had visions of him touring the world with her. But when she suggested this he frowned.

"Forgive me," she said, "I do not mean to deprive the world of your art."

"I am a fine pianist," he said, "but I will never be a great one. I can play anything efficiently, Bach, Mozart, Liszt, even the Debussy you dislike, but I lack greatness."

"Your hands are as strong as steel."

"Oh yes." He looked at her, as close to envy as he could get. "But your heart has what mine has not. You are a glutton for experience while I am always analyzing. I pull everything to pieces," he said with cheerful derision at himself. "It is sad."

"You've made me happy. You know that."

"I've been happy too. That is why I dislike seeing it end."

"It won't end. We understand each other."

He shook his head in disagreement and said, "You have an appetite for experience I do not think I can keep up with."

"You are in love with me, aren't you?"

He nodded and said, "But that is not enough."

"You have the understanding that matters."

"But not your energy, your impulsiveness." He rushed on, over her protests. "Whoever you care for, you don't ask whether they have the courage or instinct for adventure. You are lavish in your bravery, you assume that your companion, because you have chosen him, must be brave also. You are the giver rather than the taker, the fountain rather than the well. You give of your immediate best, profusely, to whomever you love, without any effort to save yourself, but most people are more cautious."

"You want me to compromise, to practice restraint when my whole philosophy is toward freedom?"

"No. But you are such a strong and colorful personality you tend to make your men colorless."

"It is a defense against being bored."

"I think it is that you cannot take anything for granted. You have that unceasing responsiveness that is part of your genius and one of its burdens. You have to give full measure to every experience, and so, unable to live on plateaus, you have to climb the peaks, but the peaks become harder and harder to climb. Often they are too high, too steep, and too sharp."

"I'm a fool," she said, oscillating between her feeling that he was right and an unwillingness to admit that. "I should stop trying to climb peaks after all the falls I have had, before I really break my neck!"

"You can't stop," he said, striding up and down beside the piano, his face pale but determined. "You are your world. The quality of your behavior is intrinsic, authentic, and entirely your own—your follies, your extravagances, your joys, your loves, your achievements. Every move you make has the signature of your spirit upon it. You are not content to skim the top of your feeling in order to please a box office, you labor always to satisfy an ideal audience, even though that never quite exists, the ideal audience which ultimately is yourself. You respect your genius too much to portray it second-hand, yet this need to give full measure causes you sometimes to overdo the measure. In a way, despite all that has happened to you, you still have an innocence of heart."

"Innocence—after the children!" The blood drained from her face, and she shouted, "Inside, I'm crippled, ugly. I spend my life trying to forget them, but it is impossible. Let me dance naked, does that really matter? I'm heavier now, does that matter? Yes, I can be cruel, I could hurt you, Archive, that's easy, but what's the use? I thought I would live forever in my children, and now I have to struggle to finish each goddamned day!"

Her eyes were swollen with tears but he had to finish, "Nonetheless, Lenora dear, you do have an innocence, you do come to each experience as if it is a first, in spite of whatever has gone before."

"I am a poet," she said slowly.

"And I love you for it, but it makes you try to stretch people to your size, when either they don't want to or lack the ability to stretch."

She went to kiss him, but he pulled away.

He said, "I am too weak. I cannot keep up with you."

"You are not being very flattering."

"I am being most flattering. I say these things because I've come to realize you have a temperament which is like a volcano in constant eruption, and an imagination that is in a perpetual state of susceptibility. With you, thought and action are one, you are a stranger to hesitation."

"And you dislike that?"

"Not at all, but it is difficult to keep up with, quite difficult."

The sun had vanished behind Paris and the streets were quiet and he was sorry for what he had said, thinking he might have been too hasty. It was true, but that was not why he had said it, but to protect himself—he did not want her to emasculate him. He began to play, and she undressed slowly and then danced. She was heavier than she had ever been, but she did not care. She sought to feel their earlier intoxication, but she was disappointed in Archive. He had let her down the last way she expected, by making her better than himself. Her great desire was for a new experience now, one that would enhance her emotion, to live only for the instant, festivities of the flesh swiftly done and swiftly forgotten; and he had to be the psychologist-philosopher, analyzing her freedoms, and that was intolerable.

Archive tried to remain the uncomplaining companion of the previous weeks, but a subtle change took place in their friendship. Restlessness stirred beneath her love. There were sudden moments of silence, distraction, hastily covered by spurts of emotion. And now she wanted a crowd about her, and when she heard that money was needed to furnish Bellevue with new, modern medical equipment she offered her services to France. Although she was in debt and to dance for charity meant she would have to pay for all her own expenses, which would run into thousands of francs, she made this offer gladly. She could no longer feel neutral as more and more wounded French soldiers appeared on the streets of Paris.

Her offer was accepted, and the benefit was arranged. It was the first time Lenora Malcolm was dancing in Paris since the death of her children, and that aroused great curiosity. It was a public occasion: the Minister of War and many other high officials were to be present. And her program caused extravagant interest.

She was dancing the *Rédemption* of Franck for the French, the *"Ave Maria"* of Schubert for her children, the *Symphonie Pathétique* for all the children, and the *"Marseillaise"* for the heroic wounded of France.

The excitement the day of the performance was a surprise even to Lenora. The streets around the theater were a gigantic carnival, thousands clamoring to get in, although all the seats had been sold a week ago. Many outside the theater were waiting just to see, touch "The Malcolm," as if that would bring their loved ones good fortune. She was told that Rodin had gotten out of a sickbed to attend, that all the high officials who had promised to come had kept their word. And when she appeared before the overflowing audience the applause was uproarious. Certain this was a perfect audience, she denied them nothing as she danced, but it was her performance of the *"Marseillaise"* that aroused the audience to a passionate frenzy.

She approached the audience in a tunic the color of blood. Then she cringed as if the enemy was attacking her, retreated a few steps as the enemy continued to advance. Then, although her body moved as if it had been punished beyond enduring, she waved her red silk shawl until it became the flag of France. She caressed the shawl, waved it again and again, and her terror turned to triumph. She rose to her feet, dancing away from the enemy, and pointed to the audience with all of her eloquence and began to march on and on with a victorious emotion that was unstoppable.

It was not dancing but pantomime, Archive whispered to himself, not reason but passion, but he also felt her shuddering flesh, the arching of her body under enemy hands, her victory piercing through proprieties and conventions, nothing counting but victory for *"la belle France."* It is unforgettable, he thought, she is giving France back hope and faith.

The audience stood on their seats and cheered with wild enthusiasm. Soldiers rushed upon the stage and lifted her on their shoulders, war widows kissed her hand, the boxes shouted "Bravo!" It was as if Lenora, singlehanded, had made the tide turn and they believed her.

The recital earned many thousands of francs, which would have paid all her debts, but she said it was her privilege to dance for the France that had given her so much. She gave several more benefit recitals, each time refusing to accept a fee, insisting that all the money should go to the wounded. She felt rewarded by the public adulation; she felt like Joan of Arc when the Minister of War recommended that a statue of this new Joan of France be cast into enduring bronze. He said her unforgettable finale of the *"Marseillaise,"* with her hands clasping the heavens, was as memorable as Washington clasping hands with Lafayette. It seemed that all the moralists who had railed against the scantiness of her attire had been defeated. She was certain that her battle for freedom had won. France was at her feet.

But the statue was never done. Rodin was too ill to do it, as he wished; Bourdelle, Rodin's greatest pupil and a close friend of Lenora's, was quick to conceive a towering monument over a Parisian boulevard, but she did not get the last vote she needed because of her promiscuity. She thought she could always count on the last vote being against her, although Bourdelle went on to use her as a model for his exquisite dancing figures on the Théâtre des Champs-Elysées.

The exultation which had filled her after her contribution to France now became a fierceness, and she became the leader of a group of poets, painters, artists, art appreciators, bohemians, and lovers and mistresses who gathered about her, for she was the figure who stood for freedom above all else, for love above all else, for self above all else, and most importantly, for generosity. Many who would have gone hungry otherwise dined in her home. Many who had no place to stay used her spare rooms. And there were always available beautiful, well-fleshed models for her guests to use in their creations and loves, and noisy parties, where if someone fell down nobody noticed, and if they made love nobody stared, and though music was played often, the favorite instrument was the hunting horn. She danced freely at these parties, demanding nothing but attendance, enthusiasm, and faith. Soldiers, especially those on leave, were especially welcome, and Lenora treated them like a rich woman with a tremendous amount of money—living in a kind of destitute grandeur.

She continued to see Archive, but he found himself competing with younger men—she preferred young men now. She made her studio lovely with candles, incense, heaps of white lilies, although there was never enough money to pay for any of these things.

Finally, when she was threatened with eviction, she arranged to tour South America. Getting her belongings out of the mansion became the chief amusement of her friends. Her five Carrières were the most precious, then her portable gramophone which she carried with her wherever she went, and next her letters and pictures of Niels and Bayard, Dion, Cathleen, and Mama. When she got out with all these possessions, she regarded it as a notable victory.

A few days later she was on her way to South America. It was supposed to be for six months, but the time deteriorated into a nightmarish confusion. A bottle of whisky became her favorite breakfast companion. Archive had said, on parting, that her restlessness had become insatiable and incurable, searching for a substitute for her children that she would never find, but she had replied that he was wrong, that the ocean voyage to South America would cure her of her anguish and restlessness. Yet she could not stop drinking the whisky, furious with Archive for having said what might very well be true. When she paused for reflection, which was seldom these days, she thought her disregard for convention a disregard for an existence which had brutally destroyed everything she had loved. This attitude gave her satisfaction as a kind of revenge; it was also a respite from sorrow. This justification became a way of life. She had an intense urge to smash things, to act without planning, without concern for consequences, to just act, do, drink, flee.

One of the men she slept with on the ship bound for Buenos Aires, an actor whose body she admired, tried to slow up her drinking, and she said, "What's the use . . . broken door here and there, a broken heart here and there, a collection of windmills overthrown, so what, is that what we fight for? Life has learned me, yes, learned me, to survive, that's all, everybody wants to survive, what else . . . !"

South America became many lovers, tepid rain, and boredom. No matter how much she drank she could not forget the day they had come across the lawn to say good-by, to drown, drown deep in sorrow—to do everything as usual, how fantastic! how unsupportable!

And so all these moments, even those reserved for state occasions, such as the taking of a new lover, Lenora never dwelt far from the memory of her lost children. Lying in whatever room he preferred, lying and waiting for no one, lying and waiting to be taken, she was lying in vacancy. It was not only that Dion and Cathleen were the most exquisite children she had ever known, they were the expression of her love, the product of her genius.

Coming back to New York months later, still drinking, not knowing whether it was Thursday, Sunday, or Monday, a phantasmagoria broke over her head. The night before the ship was due in New York she tried to recall what had happened the past few months, but her mind refused to remember. She had no money although she had made thousands in South America. Stranded in New York, that was weird; it had been to avoid such a fate she had sailed for Naples two years ago, although it seemed like a hundred. She tried to distract herself from this awkward fact by drinking, but this revived another bitter memory.

It was the last time she had seen Archive. He had asked, "Forgive me, Lenora, but do you need any money?"

She had laughed. "I always need money."

He had contemplated her thoughtfully and had asked, "How much?"

There had been a brief pause, and then she had said, "It doesn't matter."

"A thousand dollars?"

"I earned that in an hour. I earned a hundred thousand one year."

"I don't understand it. Where did it all go?"

"Where does life go? I've earned a million, or close to it, but it didn't seem that much when I had it. After all, Bayard has many times that."

Bayard? She forced herself back to the present, reviewed her present plight. But Bayard should not have ended there. Then it was impossible to stand on the deck of the ship, the wind came out of the north with such a wintry blast.

50

He came slanting down upon her suddenly, shouting, "Lenora! Lenora!" his arms outstretched as if he knew this welcome on the dock was her wish.

She thought Bayard meant this nest is safe again, but she greeted him more casually, apparently preoccupied with her luggage, saying, "Hello, how are you?"

He smiled expansively to indicate that he felt wonderful, now that he had found her at the dock. Damn it all, he thought, she was still the most exciting woman he knew. Even when she was overweight and did not look beautiful, as now, her genius joined to his taste and elegance formed an impressive combination. He knew there were a hundred Lenoras, but he had to put the one that counted back on her feet. He liked the feeling of being needed, that no matter how many Lenoras she was, he must never lose the Lenora with whom he had fallen in love. If he could shake her out of her hopelessness, return her to the genius-Lenora-self he loved, re-establish her career which he considered the greatest career in the world, the triumph would be gratification enough, he would not ask any other thanks.

"Lenora, Dorothy told me you were coming, and I wanted to welcome you. I've such plans!"

"What do you mean, not warning me? I'm positively green from the voyage."

"Now, dear, don't start one of your speeches."

And she kept smiling despite her effort not to show her pleasure, and she did not know whether she touched him first or not, but suddenly they were embracing and laughing and swaying back and forth with delight.

"You came, Viking, you came!" she cried. "You are the one friend who met me and braved the cold!"

"Dorothy would have come, and others, but I wanted you for myself."

After a lovely dinner, during which she had only two drinks, he spoke of their future. Her cheek against his palm, she looked at him through misty eyes. Nobody compared to her Viking when it came to foresight.

He was saying, "Please dear, dance the *"Marseillaise"* for America. It will arouse the sympathy our beloved France needs."

She did not reply but fell into easy talk, reminiscing about Yvette Guilbert who was singing the *"Marseillaise,"* the genius of Réjane who was acting it, and Bernhardt who had been operated on recently in New York.

"You know, Lenora, there is still no dancer like you. Pavlova is here, and Nijinsky, but none of them move me like you do. But you look tired."

"It was an abominable voyage."

"No, it is something else. Have you been sick?"

"Not any more than usual." She sighed. "But sometimes life is just too unbearable. Our daughter would be seven now."

Something happened to him when the children were mentioned. As she went on about them he looked old and defeated.

"Cathleen was the first to go down," she said. "I met a man in Paris last year who saw the entire incident. They could have been saved, he claimed, if he had been allowed to go in after them."

This was becoming frightening, and he changed the subject. He said, "Suppose you danced the *'Marseillaise'?* What theater would you prefer?"

"The Metropolitan Opera House."

"Some people may resent that."

"Some people resent anything I do." She shrugged indifferently, then grew intense as she said, "This man I met in Paris, who saw the children drown, said the children put up quite a struggle before they died. Why did they fight so hard to live?"

"Lenora, you have too vivid an imagination. You are tired."

He insisted that she vacation at his new home at Palm Beach, and she did not protest. He was proud of his plans to make the Florida resort the Riviera of America, but she was not impressed. He sensed her boredom, but she held in her thoughts, determined to reward his devotion with grace and gratitude. When he rented the Metropolitan Opera House for her, she began to prepare herself for a recital that would please him.

Heavy drinking and lavish eating had pushed her weight to a point that worried even her. She had become positively matronly, she thought, with a shudder, many pounds heavier than her best dancing weight. She went to a bathhouse for massages and became the personal charge of Kid McCoy, the famous prizefighter, now a physical instructor there. These massages, which she had come to depend upon the past few years, were usually an ordeal, but Kid McCoy's constant chatter made them almost bearable. Kid McCoy, once a world champion, many times married, thinking himself a lady-killer extraordinary, amused Lenora with his outspoken comments.

"This Palm Beach," he snarled, "it's a thousand miles from nowhere."

"Does it bother you?" she asked, half agreeing with him.

"Money bothers me," he said, "when I haven't got it. The women around here only talk to you if you got a million dollars."

"You sound bitter," she said.

"I ain't bitter," said Kid McCoy. "I made more than most

of these millionaires with my two hands. But I spent it . . . that's why I'm here."

She nodded. She knew just how he felt.

"And now they put water in my whisky," he said disgustedly, "which I'm supposed to get as a bonus. Or I ask for gin and they give me beer."

Whereupon Lenora used this as an excuse to order champagne for both of them, although the Kid said this would add fat, not take it off, and he was broke, but Lenora said her Viking would take care of it. When the bill came to her Viking, not for one bottle but for a dozen, he was irate. He accused Lenora of having champagne parties with the prize-fighter and implied that she was impressed with the Kid's muscles.

"I certainly am," she said defiantly. "He has some."

Her Viking made a sweeping, dramatic gesture. "He's only a servant."

"You sound concerned."

"I'm disappointed."

"So am I. You're a snob."

"The Kid is a notorious character."

"I am too, they say."

"You are an artist."

"And you are an adult, supposedly. Are you really jealous of the Kid?"

Bayard changed the subject and said, "I'm convinced Palm Beach has the best health in the world."

"It's a place for invalids, and I don't feel like an invalid, not yet."

"Just the same, this could be the American Riviera."

"Or an old folks' haven."

"Nonetheless, people are gossiping about you and Kid McCoy."

"You have your interpretation, I have mine."

But when she lost a few more pounds and returned to New York to dance the *"Marseillaise"* their difficulties seemed to vanish. Bayard, watching her from his box, thought it was impossible to think of this dedicated artist having an affair with the flippant Kid McCoy. She used the Statue of Liberty as her starting motif and draped herself in her red silk shawl. Standing like sculpture, her arm extended against the invader, the audience felt her emotion though she had not yet moved. She was *"la belle France,"* the unshakable. Then she charged imperiously against the enemy, marching on and on until the audience was on its feet, marching with her, singing and yell-

ing. And when she came out for an encore wearing the
French and American flags, looking like a goddess harangu-
ing the audience to battle—America had declared war just a
week before—the audience went wild. This was not dancing;
she did not have to dance. She became a red, white, and blue
Victory of Samothrace. The audience, swept aloft by her ti-
tanic gestures, rose again and cried, "Lenora! Lenora!"

She was as close to America as she had ever been. Recruit-
ing offices were jammed the next day by her converts. It was
said she had made the dance of the *"Marseillaise"* worth a
division. Now no one seemed to mind her outspokenness, her
emotionalism, her overweight, her undress. Even those who
had disliked her dancing, claiming it was impious, were
touched by her patriotism. The press trumpeted: "Lenora has
never been more splendidly, more appropriately the artist;
Miss Malcolm is unquestionably the greatest creative artist
produced by America." If she had halted after this recital or
gone on in the same vein, everything would have been fine
and Lenora and America could have remained in love with
each other.

But she could not halt, having to rush on to new needs. She
felt to just dance patriotism, valuable though it was, was
trivial. She danced for the poor on the East Side of New
York, and when it coincided with the news of the Russian
Revolution, Lenora—thinking this was what she had hoped
for ever since the bloody events of 1905, which she had never
forgotten—insisted on interpreting the "March Slav" as a
tribute to the Russian peasant and worker rising out of slavery. She used the music of "God Save the Czar" as an expression of her delight at the destruction of the Czar's regime. It
was a success on the East Side, where many in her audience
had suffered at the hands of the Czar, but when she repeated
this program at the Metropolitan Opera House, even though
she seemed to clutch the earth with bleeding fingers and she
was sure she had never been better, the reaction was apathetic, and there were a few hisses from the boxes. This was a
shock to Lenora, particularly after the triumph of the *"Marseillaise."* She saw no difference between the *"Marseillaise"*
and the "March Slav"; to her, as she had danced them, they
were both revolutionary hymns to freedom.

At the end of this program she strode downstage and
created a sensation by making a defiant gesture to the boxes
and calling out, "It isn't necessary to sit in the boxes to appreciate art. I care nothing for the boxes, but you act as if you
are the only ones who know anything about art. But you

don't. You put the real lovers of art way up there in the galleries, which are not fit to house human beings." Most of her applause had come from the gallery. "But you people in the boxes, just because you have money, think you are authorities on art. Only you are not, you are blasé and indifferent to beauty and suffering. You express the vulgar snobbery of the rich"—she'd show Bayard, who was seeking to hush her from a front box—"when most of your clothes are unaesthetic and really quite common."

A voice from the gallery shouted, "We appreciate your art!"

"That's right. I danced on the East Side for nothing, and it was so refreshing, the people sat there transfixed, with tears rolling down their cheeks. This is how they cared for my art. The *'Marseillaise'* is beautiful, but so is the 'March Slav.' "

Another voice from the gallery shouted, "How can we help you, Lenora?"

"By building a theater with ten thousand seats where we can give away two thousand seats for nothing every night, where we can sell the remaining eight thousand for five, ten, twenty-five, and fifty cents the top. Where we will have a theater for the people."

Gallery voices yelled, "How perfect!"

"If I say these unkind things about America, it does not mean that I do not love America, it means that I love America more. I once knew a man who was passionately in love with a woman who would have nothing to say to him and who treated him badly, and so every day he wrote her a hard, cruel letter. When she asked him, 'Why do you write such rude things?' he replied, 'Because I love you madly.' That is the way it is with me, it is because I love America deeply. But when I see my native land in the grip of the fox trot, the one-step, the hesitation, I get sick. I see the beautiful art of the dance vulgarized, cheapened, and discouraged."

Bayard finally caught her eyes as she turned back to the boxes, the original source of her wrath, but there was no stopping her.

"I hate the standardization that eats up the lovely American individuality. Only business and politics are important in America. Everything else is regarded as a joke. America will be a fine country after a good revolution."

Applause broke out and more hisses.

She cried out, "Remember, I chide you because I love you!"

Bayard was furious. He stood in her dressing room a few

minutes later and said, "As far as abusing the people in the boxes is concerned, that is a cheap way of attracting attention."

"They were idiots, hissing me."

"God, as a dancer you are certainly becoming a great speaker!"

"I was right. America has no use for the artistic, the beautiful."

"They adored your performances of the *'Marseillaise.'*"

"You mean they adore the patriotism I aroused. The Met ought to hang its head in shame. I never saw such a miserable audience, such amateur appreciation. They just naturally turn away when they see life."

"You are making a mannerism of honesty and integrity."

"I make the most of my art. I always remember the story of Emerson and Margaret Fuller who went to see Elssler dance, and the philosopher said, admiring Elssler, 'This is poetry,' and Margaret Fuller replied, 'Waldo, this is religion.' Bayard, that is the way I dance, but the boxes go to the theater to be relaxed, amused, to ignore whatever is expressed seriously."

He felt as if he stood before a door without a key. She was a snare, a delusion, a hope of paradise that always turned into hell. He thought, this madness will consume us both: she applies her emotions without discrimination or restraint. He gave her a long, hard look, then turned away.

There was no sign of Bayard the next few days, there were no more recitals scheduled at the Metropolitan and she could not afford to rent a theater, with all her success dancing the *"Marseillaise,"* and so she went to Long Beach for a vacation. She was shaken by Bayard's departure, but she assured herself he would return; he always had. She was very lonely at Long Beach, however, although she was with Dorothy Sunbury, until one afternoon she saw Sarah Bernhardt a few yards away.

Bernhardt, who at the age of seventy-three had just had a kidney operation, was convalescing.

Lenora had never met her, and now suddenly she was shy. She said to Dorothy, "I ought to meet her dancing. What am I when I am not dancing? There is nothing I can say to her when I am not dancing."

Dorothy said, "I think she saw you. You cannot avoid her now."

Bernhardt was delighted to meet Lenora Malcolm and insisted on Lenora joining her for lunch. Lenora blushed at the compliment and told Bernhardt that she had adored her since childhood.

Bernhardt said, "We meet so late. And I have never seen you dance. The fates were cruel to keep us apart, yet I can still see it in your face."

"What can you see?" Lenora asked anxiously.

"It's all there, on your face, what you put into your dance. Nothing can erase it. I look at the sea, and I have just seen you dance. If you listen, you'll hear the applause in my heart, my dear Lenora."

Lenora's eyes became moist. She held Bernhardt's hand gently, and an unexpected fulfillment came to feed her need.

The news of this meeting was reported in the press, and when Bayard read about it, although he had resolved not to see Lenora again, he was impressed. He recalled the controversies that had swirled about Bernhardt, and yet now, at seventy-three, she was acknowledged to be the finest actress in the world. He decided it was the nature of the artistic temperament to feel all and to risk all.

This time when Lenora and Bayard met they were both calmer than usual. Some of the stir aroused by her speechmaking had subsided, attributed to the vagaries of genius, although some suspicion remained that she might be a Red, and he rented an enormous studio for her on East 59th Street. He installed a lovely Italian fireplace and a twenty-thousand-dollar marble bathtub that impressed even Lenora. It was inlaid with gold, and she leaned back in it contentedly and thought, it did not really matter what we said—we love each other and that is all that does matter.

He had a new extraordinary plan, but he was keeping this secret from her until it materialized. He gave her a dinner to which he invited their closest friends to hear his announcement. He had resolved to do something epic in stature, that would establish her work for posterity and express his own genius as a patron. He was negotiating for the purchase of Madison Square Garden as a school and art center, to be known as the Lenora Malcolm Temple of Art.

Lenora wore a sensational frock to please him, a lovely white silk with a low neckline and very little back, and a pearl necklace. Jewels bored her, but Bayard had given her the necklace with such pride, she wore it to please him. Her favorite friends were invited: Dorothy Sunbury, Archer, Percy Mackaye, George Grey Barnard, and a few others. She felt it could be a fine evening. The food was lavish, the champagne was the best and unlimited. Conversation flowed in a swift, warm tide; everything one had to say seemed of transcendental importance, until Bayard got the floor.

Lenora thought his speech hideously long. The temple he was talking about, although he had not yet mentioned where, sounded utterly remote, a Babylon rather than an Athens. And he sounded so smug. She grew tense, nervous. She leaned closer to Percy Mackaye, to suggest that she was interested in him, although she wasn't, not as a lover. But Bayard was making himself so prominent, talking about what he was going to do for art, what he was going to do for artists, without revealing the details of his plans until she wanted to shout, Stop it! Only he hated being interrupted and he looked so important, which was ridiculous, the dinner was supposed to be for her, not for him.

Finally however, he said, "And now I come to the *pièce de résistance* of the evening, Lenora's temple." He was angry at her for flirting so obviously and outrageously but he'd be damned if he'd allow her to provoke him, but she was, his face flushing. He announced, "I'm buying Madison Square Garden."

The applause he expected from Lenora did not come. A few people clapped, but she looked stunned.

"Happy?" he asked proudly.

"Do you expect me to dance on a roof garden?" she retorted. She was shocked—why hadn't he consulted her!

He said, "You'll have space for everything."

She said sarcastically, "Prizefighters too."

It was a struggle to hold on to his temper, but he tried. "This is just what you need. I've put down two hundred thousand as a deposit. The property is worth two million. You can hold dance pageants there, and free classes for the children of New York City. You will be able to bring your art to the common people as you have always wanted to."

"Are you serious?"

"I'll tell you all the details later." He was growing embarrassed and annoyed at the way everyone was staring at him.

Lenora's eyes were shining, but not with pleasure. She declared, "I will not dance on a roof garden."

"Please, that is a little hard to believe. Madison Square Garden is the largest auditorium in America. You will have all the space you need. I assumed you would be as excited about this opportunity as I am."

"You are using your hands," she said, "and your voice is strident."

"Lenora, I'll drive you home."

"No. You see yourself in the role of the benefactor, but you don't have any awareness of what my art needs. Dance on a roof garden, like a vaudeville act, with prizefighters. I wouldn't do that when I was sixteen."

He sat for a moment, not saying a word. He had taken many barbs from her, but this, and in public yet! Never had he felt so humiliated! What in the world had come over her? She would never change. But even as he was as angry as he had ever been, he made one last effort. He said, "This is my final offer. Do you want Madison Square Garden, or don't you?"

She turned white, looking as offended as he, then she ripped off her jewels and threw them at his feet and shouted, "I am not a vaudeville performer to dance on a roof garden with peanuts, popcorn, and beer. I, dance on the roof of Madison Square Garden!" She burst into hysterical laughter.

Dark with rage, he pulled the damask cloth from the huge banquet table, dumping thousands of dollars of lavish food, choice wine, crockery, and silver on the floor with a great clatter. Then he rushed out.

Dorothy said, "How could you, Lenora? You've destroyed him."

Lenora said, "Bayard will return. You'll see. As he has before. As he has many times before."

Bayard did not return. Lenora heard through mutual friends that he had felt humiliated in public and that he could not endure. And when she realized that this time he might never return she was stricken with a loneliness and despair worse than any she had felt except at the death of her children. She had to give up her studio on East 59th Street; she had planned to tour the West, to visit San Francisco and Mama, but now there was no money. To avoid being stranded she had to sell the ermine coat he had given her years ago. Then, with some money in her pocket, with all the force of the impulses that were dominating her now, she had to go to San Francisco, she had to see Mama, she had to triumph there, she had to show Bayard, the world, she needed no one and certainly not him. But her heartache did not cease. She stood on the platform, waiting to board the train for the West, and wondered if even Mama would want her bruised, aching, irresponsible—yes, she had to admit it to herself—her damned, irresponsible heart.

51

Lenora stood in Aunt Jessie's old doorway and had the strangest feeling. Aunt Jessie's three-story monument to Victorian splendor had survived the earthquake, and Mama was living here with Jessie, now that Uncle Rufus was dead, and it was as if time had stood still. Over twenty years had passed since Lenora had stepped through this doorway and nothing was changed. There was the same gingerbread scrollwork, the pseudo-Gothic arches, the same dark, dreary rooms, the same dust catchers. But the ornamentations which had shone once upon a time now were grimy, cracked, and had the stench of death, of devotion to a world that no longer existed.

The welcome Lenora had long dreamt of had not happened. There had been no one at the station to greet her, no crowd to acclaim San Francisco's most famous daughter, and here it was as if Mama was asleep or dead. Lenora waited a moment more and then retreated to the entry to ring the bell once more. She heard footsteps a minute later, and suddenly Mama appeared.

Mama looked surprised. Mama said, "I thought you were coming tomorrow."

"I took an earlier train."

"I planned to meet you."

"It doesn't matter." But it did. Lenora had expected an affectionate greeting, but Mama was stiff. Mama had lost weight, her hair was all gray now. Lenora was shocked by the change in Mama.

Mama was shocked by the change in Lenora. Lenora had grown heavy, far heavier than Mama had expected. Mama had assumed it would no longer matter, but she felt a deep sadness for the slim, flashing girl she had loved. Now Lenora was a stout, middle-aged woman, although she still moved like a girl. Lenora would be forty in a few weeks, and this afternoon she looked it. And she had been so beautiful at twenty, even at thirty, when they had last seen each other. But ten years had wrought dreadful alterations, thought Mama. Were the stories of her endless dissipations true? A painful sensation went through Mama, as if all that she had put into her daughter had been a treacherous drug, a fraud. Mama stood in nervous immobility, and then she regained control of herself and led Lenora into the living room.

Lenora stared at the antiquated furniture and the dusty clutter and was appalled. When she saw how Mama had aged she felt even more stricken and remorseful. Mama's body was thin to the point of emaciation. She had lost her tall, majestic quality. And Mama moved so slowly, as if it were such an effort. Lenora longed to reach out and embrace her, but Mama had retreated to her rocker as if that were a refuge.

Lenora saw pictures of herself when she had been seventeen, and she was annoyed by them; Mama should not have reminded her of her lost beauty. She had returned to San Francisco and Mama, yearning to cry out, I have come to the place where my heart is, and the words choked in her throat.

Mama said, "I know we are old-fashioned, living in such an outmoded place, but we have no choice."

"Please, Mama, stop apologizing!" Damn it, she did not want to quarrel, but Mama was stubborn.

"I'm not apologizing." But she was, and that added to her own irritation. "We have very few visitors. San Francisco doesn't know whether to be proud of you, or ashamed."

"Should I stand with my arms at my side and shout hip, hip, hooray?"

"Don't you do that when you dance the *'Marseillaise,'* really?"

"That may be, on the face of it. If you want to be obvious."

"We were pacifists when we went to Europe."

"I still am, but I want this war to end." Lenora raised her arms in one of her grandiloquent gestures. "And the French are civilized."

Mama avoided answering. Suddenly her one desire was to be elsewhere, away from the painful reminders of the past, from the optimism of strong children, of haphazard planning. She thought without gratitude of Lenora's fame, a stranger to her now.

It was not easy to get Mama to talk, thought Lenora. After years of talking Mama had become reticent, as if someone in the family had to be. Lenora said, "Remember how we left San Francisco, laughing and dancing and crying," and Mama turned her head away as if she did not want to listen. "And remember how we were thrown out of that London rooming house, and I climbed in the back window to get our luggage," and Mama did look away. "You were never driven by fear then. The days went quickly then."

"You were in a marvelous hurry," said Mama.

"We were in a marvelous hurry."

"You were dedicated then. You were not spoiled by fame

or money. You accepted the struggle for the principle of being an artist."

"I still do," Lenora said as simply as she knew how. And when Mama looked skeptical she added, "The trouble is, I'm remembered for the extravagant things I do, not the sane."

"But those things you have been quoted as saying!"

"I do not suffer fools, and I merely say so." When Lenora went to put her arm around Mama's shoulder, however, Mama moved away. She felt a dreadful intolerance in Mama. Mama got up anxiously as Jessie entered.

Jessie still possessed her beautiful eyes. Lenora knew the disgust her aunt felt at the thought of unmarried love, and sensed it was only out of consideration for Mama that Jessie was remaining silent. It infuriated Lenora even as she felt intensely the importance of continuing at least a courteous relationship with Mama.

Jessie was proud of her forbearance but shocked also by the change in Lenora. She had expected a maturing, but not this! She wanted to cry, she was so heartsick. Mama had loved Lenora too much: that had been the mistake.

They discussed Lenora's recital. Mama had herself in hand now, although she wondered how Lenora could go through with the program she was planning, it was so long and emotional, it was a program for a young maiden, the one who had started with the bright dream. There was nothing in the world she wouldn't do for this maiden, only this one was dead. The long girlhood was over. At forty Lenora looked intimidated by time. Youth had been one of her greatest skills, and it was gone. Mama was afraid Lenora would flounder, yet she could not ask her to halt.

Lenora came upon the stage with a vision of the far-off time when she had danced on the San Francisco shore and the water had drenched her and she had been dizzy with excitent at six. She recalled the high hills which rose from the bay shore and overlooked the Golden Gate. She thrust upward to catch the flow of this movement. Confident now, and released, she threw across her shoulders the precious red shawl with which she danced the *"Marseillaise"* and "March Slav," but this time she moved slowly and somberly to the music of Schubert's *"Ave Maria,"* dancing as one looking on death.

It had seemed a pose to Mama, dancing at the funeral of Dion and Cathleen, but now she understood. Lenora was dancing not for them, but for herself. This was the long farewell. It was as much pantomime as it was dancing. She

was experiencing death with the anguish of crucifixion. It was
as if she was willing to die so that the children could live.

Mama thought: a beautiful artist, nobly planned, whatever
Lenora was as a woman. The artist and the woman were two
different people. The artist never compromised, the woman
did not care. To gain feeling, Lenora allowed the shadows to
hit her face—indeed, chose it, thought Mama, although it
made her look older, heavier. She was a continuation of her
children. She did not overplay the sadness, but evoked pity
and fear. Death, in the shape of Lenora, made a deep imprint
on Mama's heart.

So as far as Mama was concerned, this recital returned her
daughter to her. It was not one of Lenora's most popular
recitals; many grumbled they would have preferred the stirring *"Marseillaise"* to all these mournful numbers, but Mama
was greatly moved. After the recital Mama welcomed Lenora
as one risen from the dead. Mama kissed her, fussed over her
in a festive ritual of reconciliation. Mama praised the recital
on the note Lenora preferred: her pride in Lenora and the
wisdom of the program Lenora had chosen.

Lenora, stirred also, opened the floodgates of her emotion.
Ordinarily, she would not have bothered to explain, but
Mama was different. "Mama, you can't imagine what the
children's death meant to me."

"I do now . . . but don't talk about it, it'll hurt too
much."

"I want to talk about them. Then I feel closer to them."

"You were wonderful today."

"My dancing is very personal now. I'm a survivor."

"We're all survivors," Mama said dryly.

"That's why I no longer want just to please. People say,
gazing at me, she has the look of a dissolute woman, or they
are sure I am a scandal—does that make for a prosperous
journey? But life is not as rational as this. Let me describe our
nightmares in common, and we will see that what they call
real is often a dream. Then I am not the inventor of a style, I
am the style."

"Dear, you have reached the peaks you set out to climb."

"Perhaps, but they say I prefer the millionaire life," Lenora
said mockingly. "But no one dares to write their own betrayals down. No one admits all their failures, not even to
themselves. At least, we made our dreams come true,
Chicago, New York, London, Paris, Budapest, Munich,
Berlin, Athens . . ." Suddenly all these memories glowed in
the recalling and Lenora was inspired. "Mama, come with me
to Greece!"

Shaken, Mama wanted to shout Yes! But she was too old for impulses, and Jessie needed her and she said, "Right now?" sounding very doubtful.

"Right away."

Mama half started toward Lenora, as though struggling to agree, and then she halted and burst out sobbing. "I can't, dear, I can't." This was the kind of impulse that had worn out her dreams before; she could not risk that again. "You possess nothing material, dear, and you sound as if you possess the wealth of the universe."

"The last time I saw you, Mama, you said that, and I earned several fortunes."

"Where are they now?"

Lenora shrugged. "Everything is ruled by chance. Life is uncertain. We found inspiration in Greece before, we will find it again, or try at least."

Mama shivered. Lenora had not altered but only grown more impulsive and reckless. Yet Mama had to say, "If you ever need me, dear, I promise, I'll come when you call."

Lenora said sharply, "But you can't come with me to Greece?"

"No," Mama whispered, "no. There are some places we must not go back to. The memory will be too painful."

"What's the difference? It'll be a change, less boring than here."

Lenora leaned against the doorway, and everything about her impulse to go to Greece struck Mama as rash. Mama was filled with an even worse fatigue. She uttered a silent prayer: I hope I don't outlive Lenora. For she will only grow more reckless, she will drift only toward the grave. And I, who started her dreaming, cannot acknowledge her myth.

When Lenora's lips touched Mama's, to say good-by a few days later, Mama's lips quivered and a shudder ran through her body. Mama burst out crying again, while Jessie thrust herself hurriedly in front of Mama to halt the tears. The San Francisco recitals had done poorly, and Lenora had been forced to wire Paris for her fare, but that seemed unimportant. Lenora was aggravated by the lack of sympathy she had encountered in her birthplace, but she was much more concerned about Mama.

Mama was repeating, "If you ever need me, dear, call me and I'll come . . . I promise."

Lenora nodded and thought, I should never have come back to this home of my lost laughter, to the time of the happy anticipations and the wonderful dreams. There is nothing to be accomplished here, except anguish.

Then Mama ripped the curtain between them with a sudden embrace, holding Lenora so tightly it seemed as if she would never let her go, crying out, "I ought to give you something. What can I give you?"

"I must go," said Lenora.

"Must you really?" asked Mama.

Lenora nodded, not trusting herself to words, aware now of what Mama feared—that they would never see each other again. Mama was exhausted, she could feel it in Mama's arms: Mama needed rest, and could not rest. It was a terrifying feeling. She said, more for Mama's sake than her own, "I have many dancing years ahead." As she left she waved heroically to Mama. Mama's strained, gaunt face had the distorted, inhuman look of a mask.

52

One cold November morning the war ended, but not Lenora's wanderings. The phrases announcing the peace were pompous and polished, but she felt no peace. She had written Bayard, but he had not answered her. She had written Mama and had received an answer that was almost cheerful, as if Lenora's visit had inspired her. But Lenora was not inspired. Paris was jammed with victorious soldiers, and her nerves throbbed with agitation. When she was offered a good price for Bellevue she accepted it and decided to use the money to sail to Greece and to re-establish her school there.

This was done impulsively, for she had fallen in love again. She was smitten with a new kind of fever; she was infatuated with youth this time. Peter Darou was almost half her age, a brilliant young Greek composer. He had the whitest skin she had ever seen in a man, set off by a noble head of black hair. He was so much younger Lenora did not want to overwhelm him with her experience, yet his love made her magnanimous. When he was with her, she could almost endure anything. Youth was the time you saw the glory of the world, she thought, and his love made her feel younger than she had felt for years.

Peter had no wish to go back to Athens. He yearned to go to New York and build a reputation. He wanted Lenora to come with him and dance to his music, although she never danced to modern music. He did not appreciate her devotion to the classics; he felt that limited her, but if she danced his music he was sure it would benefit both of them. Peter was not certain he loved Lenora, but he admitted she was a remarkable woman in many ways. She was still famous enough to boost his career, and when she danced some of her fire burned undiminished. Although her breasts were softer and larger than he desired, her thighs were still firm, she had a vital rhythm, she evaded nothing in making love, and she had to please. But she refused to go to America, and so finally he agreed to accompany her to Greece.

It was a curious mixture that set out for Athens. In addition to Peter there were the older girls, reunited again, lovely young women now, some children to create a new school, and several artists.

Athens greeted them warmly, there was an official government reception, but Kopanas was a shock. The house she had spent so much money on years before was without a roof, the walls were down, weeds had broken through the floor. Peter tried to look excited, the rest of the party said how charming, and no one wanted to remain at Kopanas.

Tomorrow would be the day they would create the new Parthenon, Lenora declared back in Athens, but tomorrow never seemed to come. She tried to climb the approach to the Parthenon with her old ecstasy, but her breath gave out halfway to the top, and she had to halt. Peter was at the top already with the blond Tamara, and when she saw them silhouetted against the Parthenon she thought her heart would break. There were new lines of weariness about her eyes, but a few minutes later pictures were taken of Lenora in front of the Parthenon with outflung arms, and she announced, "Now I will give you the most beautiful children in the world," but she did not feel beautiful but betrayed.

Peter said to Lenora, "This is like climbing to the sun," and she did not believe him. Tamara was half her age, fair and slim with light hair like a halo, and Peter could not get Tamara out of his eyes.

Lenora ordered Kopanas repaired. Then Lenora gave a recital to celebrate this. But when Tamara imitated her, it was too much. Lenora cried, "Why don't you create your own style! You are wearing a sloppy muslin, chasing sunbeams, and being girlishly interpretive!" In one unbroken motion she ripped the muslin off Tamara, so violently it was in shreds.

Peter swung Lenora away, but it was too late.

Tamara stood half naked, blushing and shaking.

Lenora said, "Your tunic is ruined, and I cannot bear the sight of emotion dripping."

Tamara whispered, "I'm sorry."

Lenora could have smashed Tamara's head against the stone wall, but she said, "Mop your brow, you're sweating. Do you want to catch cold?" She did not even look at Peter.

Tamara said, "I was trying to dance like Lenora Malcolm."

Lenora said, "It takes forty years to become Lenora Malcolm."

In the next few weeks love became a devastated dream and the laughter of the children sounded to Lenora like screeching birds, for Peter was with Tamara always now. He made no effort to conceal his infatuation, and there were nights when Lenora did not see him at all. In her mind he stood like a broken image, for he had fallen in love with bric-a-brac; Tamara was provincial despite her training, talented but uninspired, pretty but immature.

It was arranged for Lenora and her girls to dance in the largest stadium in Greece, and she hoped this would engross her sufficiently to ease the pain of Peter. The crowd was friendly and applauded vigorously—Lenora was dancing for the honor of Greece—but when the government of Venizelos, which had invited her, was overturned, there was the withdrawal of government help, and Lenora felt more isolated than ever.

High principles were all the fashion, however, so Lenora made one more effort to establish her school on Kopanas, but soon it became a lost cause. There was still no water, although the well was very deep now. Food was difficult to store, the only neighbors were goats and their shepherds. There was more talent to the square inch on Kopanas than modern Greece had seen, everyone agreed this new temple of art should be a glorious success, but when Lenora's money ran out no one insisted on remaining.

So Lenora's wanderings resumed. By 1921 her recitals in France, where she was living, irritated her like an old wound. Audiences wanted her soft, pretty performances, and she had come to loathe this kind of dancing. The world, especially Russia, was in turmoil, and she felt about to burst.

One afternoon in Paris, after dancing the *"Marseillaise"* by request, she added the "March Slav" as a tribute to the Russian Revolution. She was certain the bloody days of 1905 were being rectified. But after she danced the "March Slav" there was a riot out front, between those who were for the Soviets and those who hated them, and Lenora hurried before her blue curtains to speak.

"I dance the 'March Slav' because I love Russia, love it as I love France and America and all these countries where freedom is struggling to exist. I see a beautiful future in Russia. Right now she is suffering the anguish of change, but I believe she has a great future for artists and freedom. I say this not for myself—I have an American body, an Irish mind, and a European soul—but for the children of the future. I ask you now, please give me my school. If you don't, I will have to leave my beloved France, I will have to go to Russia. I am not interested in politicians or politics, but for my school I will do anything."

There was no reply to her appeal in France, but several weeks later she received a telegram from the Russian Minister of Public Education, Lunacharsky, asking her to come to Moscow, saying they would give her a fine school, thousands of children, all the facilities she desired, including a private train to meet her, and of course a contract.

Most of Lenora's friends were terrified at the thought of her going to Russia, still torn by revolution and starvation, but Lenora thought they were ridiculous. She was exultant at the thought of bringing the dance to thousands of starving Russian children; she would have enough children to dance the Ninth Symphony. When there was another telegram informing her that she could even take over the former Imperial Ballet, which she had always hated, she wired acceptance and said a contract was unnecessary.

She flew to London where she was to sail for Russia, and announced a farewell concert to commemorate her departure for Moscow.

Mama, hearing of this, feeling this was the worst mistake of all, wired Lenora that she was joining her. Mama hoped this would halt Lenora, for she intended to insist on going with Lenora. Although Mama was past seventy and her health was uncertain she booked immediate passage for London and begged Lenora to wait for her.

Lenora agreed to wait, and prepared eagerly for this farewell recital. Not since the death of her children had she felt such a surge of enthusiasm. Russia had loved her whenever she had danced there; she was sure it would love her now.

A large crowd gathered in the theater to see this recital, many of them curious because of her notoriety, but many were friends. Ellen Terry was in the audience, and Anna Pavlova.

Of all the famous dancers Lenora was the only one Pavlova could honestly admire—they were too far apart in style to be competitive—but this afternoon Pavlova was disturbed. It was the first time she had seen Lenora dance in several years, and though Lenora excited her as usual, she saw flaws. Lenora danced far more slowly than before, and there were moments when she paused because the music became too fast for her. Then Lenora made one of her eloquent gestures and the audience was enthralled, although it was out of keeping with the music. The dancer-Lenora was growing old, Pavlova thought sadly, her drinking and her lack of discipline were destroying her as a dancer, and yet as long as she retained her great pantomime-gifts and essential grace few would notice. And when Lenora concluded with a tribute to those who had died to make the Russian Revolution, using her silk shawl as a red flag, Pavlova—with all her distaste for Communism—was stirred.

Nonetheless, when Pavlova reached Lenora's dressing room after the recital, she begged Lenora not to go to Moscow. "It's dangerous, you will lose your reputation."

"What's dangerous?" asked Lenora, amused rather than provoked. Ordinarily, she would not have even listened, but Pavlova was a genius.

Pavlova said, "When you return here, you'll be called a Communist. The career of every artist is endangered with risks for destroying themselves. This is one of them."

Lenora said, "And the career of every artist depends on having the freedom to express themselves. And space. I need that freedom, that space, without any rules to limit me or small people to pass their judgments."

Pavlova said, "One of the reasons they like your dancing is because you dance what they feel and believe. Should you, however, dance an idea they don't like, you could die on your feet and they won't be moved."

"I'm glad they like my dancing, Anna, but I seldom think about them any more. I don't dance for them, I dance for my children."

"You have a romantic picture of Russia, and it is not true."

"Anna, forgive me, but mine isn't a career, it is a life lived by me to dance. It has no precedents, it is mine to create as it suits me. The first time it will have been lived is when I live it and dance it."

The dressing room grew crowded and loud with the babble of congratulations, the eulogies to Lenora were fulsome, and Pavlova thought warnings were useless—Lenora was a law unto herself, and if she did not break down she would create a new law, and perhaps she would anyway.

But after Pavlova and her other friends were gone Lenora felt sad. She reflected on all the people she had met in Russia, and where were they now? Suddenly she was stricken with nostalgia. Fokine was in America, Diaghilev was in France, Nijinsky was in an asylum, and Pavlova was touring everywhere but her native Russia, and she was an American. Yet also a revolutionary she thought, a revolutionary since the day she had been born.

Lenora waited for Mama to arrive, but finally she could not wait any longer. Passage was booked on a small ship which was sailing immediately; there was no other ship for a month.

Lenora stood on the deck of the ship the next day and searched the dock for Mama, but there was no sign of her. Pavlova was waving good-by and Ellen Terry and many others. Lenora was filled with a great excitement—whatever else anyone said, she thought, this was a pilgrimage, then she felt a sudden loneliness. Mama must have changed her mind, or gotten angry.

Mama arrived the next day, delayed by storms, and heartsick at missing Lenora.

BOOK NINE

53

The journey to Moscow was not as Lenora expected: a journey into an enchanted future. The boat trip to Reval in Estonia took a week and it was barbaric at Reval after years of civil war and the wind sang sad dirges and death was commonplace and the air was cold although it was July. Reval had nothing of hope, and her anticipation became touched with apprehension.

She carried a flask of whisky to keep her cheerful, but that was gone quickly. The boat was small, half the size of an ocean liner, and worried her. Yet the boat was heaven compared to the train to St. Petersburg, now Petrograd. There was no special train awaiting her as promised, but there was an ancient train loaded with lice and other varieties of dirt.

At Petrograd she longed to feel like Aphrodite, rising out of the sea to bring Russia beauty; everyone knew she loved Russia, as she loved all her children. But Petrograd looked like a cyclone had torn the city she knew to shreds—the hours she spent in the city waiting to change trains was disheartening—beautiful homes where she had been entertained in the past were rubble now, so much she had loved was shattered. When she reached Moscow, the journey had taken twice as long as scheduled; she thought one thing had not altered in Russia, the trains were still awful and still late.

It was an oppressive Sunday evening. No one was at the train to greet Lenora. She had imagined a multitude of cheering children dressed in crimson tunics surrounding her at the station, or at least a large delegation from the Ministry of Public Education, but there was not a greeting of any kind, not even a wilted bunch of flowers. All she saw were soldiers, regarding her indifferently. She stood perplexed. Often she had forced herself to feel indestructible, especially in the moments of deepest despair, but this was unbelievable.

There were no carriages or taxis at the station, no attendants or porters of any kind. She stared at Moscow, which looked pitiful and exhausted. There were still a few modern buildings standing, but the streets were full of holes, debris everywhere, and none of the signs of a bustling, alert city.

She was filled with a whirlwind of rebellion. She started walking then, in her red leather Russian boots and her Russian fur hat which she had worn particularly for this occasion. This was even more of an ordeal as she passed more ruined buildings and noticed there were very few stores, many broken windows, and so many signs of war she could have wept. The clothes of the inhabitants, the few who were about, displayed infinite resource—canvas breeches and coats made of rugs and rags for shoes. Her heart sank. She wondered if her hope had been merely an echo of her own need? Moscow looked stripped of all the civilized things she assumed were part of living.

She stood outside of the sixth hotel that had told her there were no rooms and certainly none in the name of Lenora Malcolm, she had telephoned the Ministry of Public Education and there had been no answer this Sunday evening, and with all her courage she felt daunted, when she heard a voice calling, "Lenora! What are you doing here?"

It was Boris Vilkenov, the socialist who she had met in the St. Petersburg of 1905. Boris bowed before her—Boris who had been an early admirer of Gorki. His cheekbones were still broad, but his flesh was drawn and pale. His clothes were of a fashionable, prewar vintage but shabby. When he heard that she had not eaten all day, which did not surprise him, he insisted she dine with him. He had brown bread and caviar he had been hiding for just such an emergency. Boris was amazed to hear that she had come to Moscow to create a free school sponsored by the government. He shook his head, "It's a fine idea, but most of the children are starving. The children survive by stealing, and the best stealers are the best survivors."

Lenora said, aflame with conviction, "That won't stop me. I've been officially chosen to make the children beautiful, healthy, and graceful."

"But there is no money here, nothing can be bought or sold."

"I'll manage. I'm an artist."

"But dancing is an extravagance."

"A religion, Boris."

"In Moscow surviving is the religion. You'll see."

There were no rooms in his hotel either, so he put her up for the night in his room. It was tiny, more appropriate for a closet than for sleeping, but he said they were fortunate, most people in Moscow were sleeping ten to fifteen in a room. The straw mattress was itchy and she slept in all her clothes, but her eyes were shiny. At last she was home in Moscow.

The next day she learned that all the officials at the Ministry of Public Education had been away for the weekend. Lunacharsky was startled to see her, no one expected her, the sophisticated Lunacharsky least of all. He knew nothing about the exchange of telegrams; he had not invited her and he could not find the official who had, but he said her coming was a lovely gesture and they would talk about the school, later, after she was settled.

She was settled in the apartment of Radnova, the leading ballerina of Moscow. How absurd, she thought, she an avowed enemy of the ballet, but they must expect her to displace this vestige of the old order. Instead, Lenora learned that Radnova, who had been acclaimed by Czarist Russia, was an idol of the Soviets and that she had been given this apartment only temporarily while the ballerina was on tour.

Lenora had expected there would be no trace of ballet, yet it was the favorite art of the Communist Party. She had assumed they would give her a simple large studio, a house for herself and her children, but as the days drifted by nothing happened. No one in the government seemed to really care about her. There was still no money, no heat, very little food, and hardly enough space to live. No trading was allowed, so her francs and pounds were useless. Starvation still existed, transportation was erratic when it ran at all, Moscow was even more eroded and exhausted than it had looked at first sight, survival itself was very difficult, many children were barefooted from necessity, not choice. But she felt she would make history; she liked making history. And when she saw the many homeless children roaming the streets she was sure she had to create a beautiful school to occupy these waifs in lovely things. So Lenora waited, although she hated waiting, and often disillusionment and despair overshadowed her dreams of doing great things.

She was growing terribly restless when she was visited by Stanislavsky. He had aged, his hair white, his once fine body marred by a paunch, more the picture of an amiable, middle-aged citizen than the great director, until he spoke. Then his face was mobile and he had all of his old sensibility. They embraced and he asked, "Do you really intend to stay?"

"Of course."

"You're a natural rebel."

"I have my idea of things. Do you know a better way?"

"I am not a politician . . . and I try not to compromise, at least in art."

"You still have your own theater?"

He shrugged. "More or less." He looked withdrawn.

"I fully intend to have a school, though many say that is impossible."

"I wish I had your faith. I can do *The Inspector General* and *The Lower Depths,* but no Chekhov now, he's too bourgeois, the censor says."

"Look, I could speak to Lunacharsky."

"Oh, no!" Then he said, more slowly, "We had the same thing during the Czar's time. When we did Ibsen's *Enemy of the People* and I played Doctor Stockman, they cut out half my speeches. Even so, there was a riot."

She found some vodka which she had been saving for just such an occasion, and he took a sip while she drank on and on. It was obvious she was lonely, he thought, but that was not what shocked him. Her hair had lost its youthful brown sheen and was a dyed red; her body was heavy, opulent, aging. She had lost the look of having stepped out of a Botticelli painting. Where had her beauty gone? She was too young for this. Yet pacing up and down, she looked dedicated, she moved with the free easy grace that was Lenora. It prompted him to come to the point of his visit. "Lenora, we would be honored at the theater if you would teach your art there."

She was touched but she said, "From now on I am devoting myself to the children. I am dancing only for them and to raise money for them."

He said wryly, "There is no money to be raised. And believe me, many of our actors are children, particularly in their ignorance of the other arts, even dancing."

She was tempted. She took his hand, they could still be lovers, but he was withdrawing. He admired her, he was a wonderful man, his invitation was an honor, and he could not give her what she really desired.

"It would be stimulating, Lenora."

"No. I couldn't submit to your discipline."

"Why not?"

Her reply stuck in her throat. Stanislavsky was very kind, as understanding as any friend she had ever known, but how could she say: Death is my constant companion, it is my inspiration, whatever I do with my life I cannot evade it, and only children growing strong and beautiful put it off, and even during dancing I cannot miss a drink, and drinking is not permitted at the Moscow Art Theater, even my good friend Constanin Stanislavsky could not permit it, and I cannot be bound.

"Will you join us, Lenora?"

"Forgive me, I cannot explain . . . but it is impossible."

"You don't owe me any explanation."

"I don't want you to misunderstand. I am very much moved. Look, I have to have another drink."

He said, "I think you will have your school here, as soon as other things are straightened out."

There were conferences with Lunacharsky about the size of the school, the number of pupils she wanted to teach—she spoke in terms of thousands, which stunned him, but he agreed, and no school was forthcoming. Weeks passed, months, and she did not know which way to turn. She saw Stanislavsky occasionally, but he was immersed in his own problems; Boris was busy surviving, which was not inspiring, although he kept her stocked with vodka and whisky. She still did feel she had attached herself to history, which pleased her. There was a letter from Mama, informing her that Mama had missed her just by one day and had gone off to Potsdam to live with Amy.

She wrote to Mama, suggesting that Mama join her in Moscow, and waited for the expected Yes.

Mama answered that she was too ill to journey to Moscow and sounded wretched, but Lenora wondered if Mama was not stressing this to get her to leave Moscow. She could not leave now, for after months of waiting she had her school. The Ministry of Public Education had found a building for her. There were announcements that the Lenora Malcolm Plastic Art School was opening, hundreds of children clamored to be admitted—this was the promise of food and a clean place to sleep—and the State was allowing only fifty.

That was not all. She had just met Nikolai Ivanovich Yarov. She was in love with him. He was so beautiful, such a great poet. She knew she was years older, but that did not matter. Yarov made her feel so vital; she knew he was a genius, that from the strange way they had met he was a kind of good fortune she could not relinquish. And so Lenora, who had been on the verge of departing, wrote Mama that she would come next year, after the school and other things were running properly. Lenora was certain she was right about Nikolai Ivanovich Yarov, he was such a beautiful boy.

54

It was an important party. A hundred people were in attendance, with Lenora the guest of honor, for the party was to celebrate the opening of her school. She took unusual care with her toilette and wore her most attractive gown. She came late, and she surveyed the large salon with eyes that seemed to embrace everyone, and yet did not reveal what she was feeling. She greeted many people, of whom almost all were unknown to her. Most of the compliments were fatuous or shrill with excitement at meeting the great Lenora Malcolm, but she accepted them quietly. The room was a chaos of music, talk, eating and drinking, and a hundred individual desires but none apparently with the possibility of greatness, and she was bored.

Then he entered. Lenora saw him standing in the doorway, surrounded by a group of young men. She looked at him as if obsessed with a vision. She felt invaded, and that she had already surrendered. Someone whispered, "Yarov, the poet." The invader was a boyish Slavic blond, who dazzled her with the violence of his eyes and the beauty of his boyishness. She was seized with a prodigal desire to know this beautiful boy, who seemed to concentrate in himself her idealization of the beauty of Moscow's youth.

What a magnificent meeting, she thought. She felt like Venus now, starting to dance, not for the others, although they were applauding, but for Yarov, the poet.

He muttered something in Russian. She heard a whispered translation, "He thinks you're ugly." But she assumed this was a form of teasing and playfulness, and she was not offended. Suddenly it was half party and half recital. The more she danced, the more he sought to outdance her.

At first she was pleased. He would restore her lost youth, she thought, as she danced before him, tantalizing now. But she was almost knocked over by the savagery of his dancing. He was really struggling to outdo her—how foolish! His oaths sounded superb and dramatic, and he had a fine voice although she did not comprehend what he was saying. She looked straight into his eyes and was upset to see him glaring at her—as if something had to give way. He had blue eyes, and he was shouting, "Dance!"

When Lenora did not dance this time, a friend who had

followed the poet into the party whispered to her in French which she understood, "He says if you ever look at another man again, he will cut out your heart."

How poetic, she thought. He looked like an angel now, until he frowned, and then he was a devil with a cold and sinister beauty. It was more than she could endure. She spoke to him in French, and he did not reply.

A friend of his said, "Nikolai only knows Russian, and the heart."

Nikolai looked angry, since she had not responded to his order to dance, looked as if he despised all these people, as if they were all imbeciles, and he was the only creator of beauty.

Lenora went to dance with him then, but he turned away. She resolved to make herself enchanting. She resumed her dancing. This time her movements were caressing—she laughed as she circled him voluptuously. She heard his friend say, "Beware," and ignored that. She danced even more sensuously and felt she was giving him ecstasy. And now he wanted her furiously. He saw her superbly naked, and his youth rose in him like a storm.

This time she put out her hand to him, smiling, expecting him to kiss it, and he grabbed it and whirled her around, but she danced naturally with him. His body did not have her grace, but it was a young body. Then he took the center of the room from her, darting about vigorously. His imitation of her was obviously unkind. His words were in Russian, something about "ugly, ugly!" and he waved his arms like a mocking banner.

In reply she sought to look like a Madonna when she danced next. She saw him as resembling Dion grown up, the same coloring, the same poetic charm, and she moved with a gentler passion. Gradually, as if in a ritual, in an awakening of love, he came to her and she danced with him in an inviting manner, pressing her body close against his and holding her warm face against his lips. She did it so simply and naturally it became inevitable. After the dance she threw her arms around his neck and kissed him, and that too became natural. He felt relaxed yet intoxicated by her grace and sensuous freedom. She was not beautiful as he expected Lenora Malcolm to be—he had come here searching for her—and he wanted to defy her in his disappointment, yet she looked vital in her ripeness. She made it evident she desired out of life what people were taught to hide.

She sat down, and he sat beside her without another word, quietly, as if she had torn contempt out of his heart. She spoke to him in a soft motherly manner, and though he did not know what the words meant he rested his head on her lap while she caressed him. He was her image of a true Russian youth, her Pushkin, almost too beautiful to be a man and obviously begrudged her by the group of young artists who had come with him.

She said to him in Russian, "Lenora . . . a friend."

Nikolai grinned. She had a bizarre charm, he thought, and the faded beauty of a woman who had aged, yet aged dramatically, with the poignant majesty of a magnificent ruin. He had seen how graceful she was when she danced, despite what he had said. And her eyes, although tired, had power and fascination. What tempted him the most however, were her arms, which were still without flaw, the most beautiful arms he had ever seen. So despite his determination not to succumb to Lenora, to any woman, he found himself succumbing. Such provoking breasts she had, flinging them at him sensuously, yet maternally too. A few minutes later they vanished.

A week later he moved into her apartment. He did not understand her French, she did not understand his Russian, but they understood each other's emotion. She excited him with her love-making; he made her feel free, young.

But when she wanted to listen to Beethoven to express her love, he grew offensive with his comments. He insisted on having his friend Yasha play the balalaika as his national glory. She did not like his friends, most of them would-be poets, surrounding him, diverting him, loving him—the last hardest of all to endure. Yet to protest was to push him away. She found his friends ignorant and warped, but he refused to remain in her apartment unless she allowed them there too.

She resolved to make this love ideal, the truest to nature, and he disliked nature. He had had too much of nature as a peasant boy growing up in dismal poverty. In the sign language they created she sought to get him to tell her anecdotes about his childhood, but he spat when he spoke about his father.

Lenora thought: how her poet must have missed love when he was growing up, which she would bestow on him now. They would be the most wonderful of lovers—she would be mistress and mother and protector and cultivator—but he was drunk most of the time, yet when he kissed her, she was almost frantic with desire. And when he put his arms around her, which was far less than she craved, he shut out pain and bad memories.

Do I love you too much? she longed to ask, when he complained one night about her incessant demands. She wanted to say, just to touch you, caress your tired body, your torn spirit, makes me content.

She said nothing, for he would have exploded with wrath, damning her as a selfish spider. And he was not content. After a month of alternate ecstasy and quarreling she saw that he went rapidly from exaltation to depression. Certain he was going to die young, Nikolai lived in a feverish hurry. He hurried even when he made love. He had burst upon the Russian world of letters at sixteen, a brilliant, uncontrollable boy of unusual intensity and good looks. Acclaimed as a personality, as a precocity, he combined an amazing facility for poetry with a headstrong, passionate craving for excitement. He said he would give experience a new imagery and that *only* a Lenora Malcolm would suffice, yet he resented her greater fame, the way people flocked to her when they were together. But she found the disorder of his mind sacred, thinking of him as a Baudelaire whom she would make well, a visionary who could comprehend evil but see beyond it. His favorite cry—take life and wring its neck—amused her. Thus, while she wanted to feel indispensable, he had to feel worshiped.

Nikolai was jealous when the government announced the official opening of her school and gave her a complete house for it, yet he moved into it with her. The building was monstrous rooms, rococo décor—ugly compared to her previous schools—but she was considered fortunate. Housing was still a major problem in Moscow, and she did have space.

Accordingly Lenora announced auditions for her school, and several thousand children arrived for admission, for food and clothing and a place to sleep. Finding a way to turn away those who could not be admitted was a defeating experience for Lenora, knowing that those who failed would remain half starved. She was told she could accept only fifty—there would not be food for any more—although she had space for several hundred. The government also said she had to take in only orphans, to which she objected. She did not resent that they were orphans, but she resented that as a reason for admission. She was not establishing an orphanage, she told Lunacharsky, but a school for talent and beauty. The government was adamant, however, so all those admitted were orphans, mainly on the basis of malnutrition. Worse, just as she had the school organized she was informed that due to a major change in government policy the State could no longer support the school. Private trading was returning; if she wanted to keep the school going, she would have to earn the money.

Lenora wired Paris for money she had put aside for Mama,

feeling that Mama would understand and that Amy would take care of her. This money did not last long, however, and finally she had to dance to support the school, although she had come to Russia to give her art without charge.

Lenora did dance once without charge, on the anniversary of the Russian Revolution. Even then, however, there was controversy. The censor did not want her to dance the "March Slav." He said it contained the Czarist hymn, "God Protect the Czar," which shocked her. She insisted on waking up Lunacharsky, although it was midnight, but if they could intrude on her dress rehearsal she could intrude on his rest. She danced her version of the "March Slav" for him, improvising in his parlor, and he said, "My dear, you have made it sufficiently revolutionary."

The audience was tense, hearing about the argument over the "March Slav," which added to the excitement. Lenora used the music to depict the destruction of the Czar, reworking the hymn into a sardonic commentary on the Czar's mercy, certain no one would misunderstand her. The Bolshoi Theater became her platform. Her flair for improvisation was never more phenomenal, for she sensed from her first movement that this audience was with her. She repeated nothing she had done before, but made her performance a call to action. When she raised her arms to lead them in the singing of the "*Internationale*," although it was not dancing, the audience was stirred. Encore followed encore, and this performance was a triumph.

But the economic situation continued to grow worse. By Christmas the children were living on one meal a day, and that was mostly black bread. Much time was spent in frantic bed-bug hunts. Nikolai was never around at such times, or was sleeping. They rehearsed in an enormous studio which had been a Napoleonic ballroom, and it snowed a great deal that winter and the children were always cold. So Lenora gave a Christmas party, hoping to give them a little joy. The party became a pathetic Christmas tree and sad holly, and she felt lonely for Mama, although the children clustered about the tree even with the room five degrees below zero and looked happier than she had ever seen them. She kissed each one of them. She could not cry, for they would, but she felt overwhelmed with the enormity of the task ahead of her.

Boris, who had found the tree, was saying, "Give it up, Lenora, you'll have to support the school totally yourself, and you can't. No one can."

He was a warm, pleasant man, devoted to her, with a true paternal feeling for the children, but he lacked her poet's passion. Yet there was truth in what he was saying. Lenora had given up a famous European career, perhaps for good, to come here, and now the government had not kept its word. Yet if she returned to her career in Europe, the children would be homeless again. She told Boris, "I have to keep the school going, this is beauty and health, and the children need it."

She gave a series of paid recitals in Moscow and Petrograd, using the Petrograd performances as a honeymoon with her poet. They stopped at the finest hotel, as Lenora always did, and he acted as if she were wealthy. Lenora told him to order whatever he desired, and Nikolai exhibited a taste for luxury that even surpassed hers. Although she earned enough money to help the school, he spent all of it. She came to feel that the only way she could keep the school open was to tour abroad, preferably in rich America.

As spring approached this idea gathered substance. She decided to stop off in Potsdam and see Mama; she would show her poet the wonders of the world and get him away from his companions, particularly Yasha, who never seemed to leave Nikolai's side.

Yasha was an ordeal. Yasha was the balalaika-poet-philosopher who appointed himself Nikolai's constant companion. Lenora seldom hated anyone, but she could have dissolved him instantly if it had been within her power. He was short, stocky, with the horny, muscular hands of the coal miner although he had never done a hard day's work in his life. She had never seen any of Yasha's poetry, but Nikolai was devoted to him. Yasha adopted a most important air when he was with Nikolai, playing the role of his herald. Yasha was even more lavish than Lenora in his praise of Nikolai, and Nikolai reveled in his hero worship. Yasha was Ukrainian, like her poet, and when he stroked his thick mustache his arrogance and vanity matched Nikolai's.

Lenora would lie on her divan waiting for her poet to appear as he had promised, and many evenings he broke these appointments to be with Yasha. He did this with an unholy glee. This was particularly painful. Those evenings were dreadful. She hated being alone. Her memories overwhelmed her, she was too restless to read, to listen to music alone—that only made her more melancholy. Seeking to be loyal to Nikolai, she found herself with too much free time. In her increasing loneliness she was drawn to Mama once more. She began to dream frequently of Mama.

There came an evening when she could not sleep, distraught with a dream of Mama bound to a bed. Nikolai was out drinking with Yasha, and she was baffled. It was impossible to tell whether this was an ordinary friendship with Yasha, but it was not beautiful or to her advantage, that was evident. Then Mama came back to her as she tossed in her dream and, not content with disturbing her, pulled her toward a black gulf. Lenora awoke stricken with terror. The next day she was told that Mama had died in Amy's house in Potsdam the night before.

All day the wind beat at Lenora's window, but it was Mama she heard, Mama singing old songs, Mama entertaining them with Blake and Homer. Mama such a spiritual energy, so determined that none of her children be stillborn souls, there had been no other Mama like Mama, trotting at her heels all over the world, and yet if she had been the favorite, Mama had tried not to show it. Mama always saying, when asked, "I love all my children, they are the best luck I have, we must always be neighbors in happiness."

Homesickness assailed her, and America became home. She thought of Dion and Cathleen and the child never named and how Mama would have loved them all because they were Malcolms, whatever the circumstances of their birth. She hoped then that Mama had died quickly, and prayed that when she went it would be swift and painless.

She arranged to tour America and planned to take Nikolai with her. Action, that was it. Move, move, move, they'd see everything, do everything, there would be no time to cry, to think, to feel, to realize she would never see Mama again, and never was such a long time.

To take Nikolai out of Russia, she had to marry him. She considered this stupid, but in spite of her dislike of the institution, she married Nikolai. She would heal her poet's spirit, which had grown turbulent lately, on the rainbow of the world's art.

Her visa said she was thirty-eight, although she was forty-four; his said he was twenty-eight. He stood aloof during the civil marriage ceremony. Nikolai was even more disdainful of marriage than she was, but if it would get him to Berlin, Paris, and New York, he would endure it.

55

Thus begins the Grand Tour. This is not the Grand Tour of the rich, thinks Lenora, this is the exploration of the artist. This is to be the art galleries of Berlin and the music of Bayreuth and the sculpture of Florence and the antiquity of Rome and the hazy blue beauty of Paris. This is to be opening the eyes of the child, making the visions of the poet real, walking the world from sun to sun.

Her poet did not want to walk up and down the streets of Florence, to plod through the art galleries of Berlin, to explore the beauties of Rome. Each time he felt in an alien land, and he insisted on stopping at the fashionable Adlon hotel in Berlin, at the fashionable watering place of Weisbaden, and then to Leipzig, to Weimar, to Salzburg, always by the most fashionable auto Lenora could hire, always at the most fashionable hotel he could find.

Nikolai was arrogant about European art. He declared it was decadent, had no vitality. He regarded only two things with deference: money and what he could buy with it. He shopped insatiably in fashionable Ostend and Brussels and Venice. He made a Grand Tour of the most expensive shops in Europe.

Lenora thought this was charming. Thank goodness he was having such a good time, and that made her happy. But she was not amused by Yasha. Yasha appeared in Berlin, and that was the end of her honeymoon in Berlin. Wherever Yasha wanted to go, her poet went. Only when Lenora was being interviewed and photographed was Nikolai attentive. Then he stood close to her, made sure the camera angle favored him, resented when the focus was on her and not on him, and stood on tiptoe to show that he was taller than she.

Lenora decided these were the faults of a schoolboy and to enlarge the honeymoon moved on to other cities. They lost Yasha when they went to Florence and Venice, but Nikolai was restless there and he was happy when she suggested Paris.

She reacquired possession of her house in Neuilly, but he said it was too run-down to live in and insisted on staying at the luxurious Hotel Crillon, where he ordered the best champagne, the best food, and sent telegrams to all his friends and relatives in Moscow. He sent them like one might write poems. Lenora thought this rather singular, but when her friends said this would put her in the poorhouse, she replied, "It is his poetic spirit." He did learn a few French words—money, caviar, champagne, the necessities of life—but when Lenora tried to teach him French he grew sullen.

"My God!" he said, puffing out his chest with awesome dignity. "I am understood by Yasha!" It was in Russian, but she understood his heroic gestures and was distressed by his wild, almost hysterical laugh.

He spent the next few days accumulating a multitude of silk shirts, silk socks, silk ties, silk pajamas, and silk robes and handkerchiefs. Money only had one purpose for Lenora, to be spent, and she was delighted that he was enjoying himself, although she was unaware of the extent of his purchases. She did notice that wherever they went they acquired more luggage. By the time they moved into the Hotel Crillon they needed so many porters for their trunks they looked like a royal entourage.

It was summer, so he bought summer suits. He developed a love for champagne that far exceeded hers. She was drinking less when with him, for when he got drunk his moods got dark. But when they settled finally at the Hotel Crillon she thought now their honeymoon would really start. She still loved people and parties and food and drink and causes and talk, but Nikolai acted as if he was trapped. He broke up several parties with his drinking. She took him to the Louvre, and they had a terrible argument.

Jeering, he pointed at Carrière and said, "Rotten, soft!" She showed him her favorite Rodin pieces and he sneered, "Trash." Yawning from lack of sleep, having been drunk all last night, he took off his shoes in the Louvre and muttered, "I do not like this art, it's the corpse of the past." Their quarrel ended when she arranged for publication of his poems in German and French. He was almost amiable to her. He titled the German translation: *Confessions of a Roughneck*; the French translation: *The Confessions of an Uncouth*. He was proud of his ruthlessness. He was not going to succumb to the decadent standards of the West, of these non-Asiatics.

Then, one afternoon, he vanished. She was miserable. He did not return for dinner, and suddenly she knew: Yasha had come to Paris.

She refused to show anger, although she did say when he got in very late that night, "I was worried."

He acted as if he did not understand her, though she was sure he did.

The next few weeks it was as if she was excommunicated. She wondered when Nikolai slept, he was at the hotel so seldom now. The whole structure of their life was coming to nothing. This had become such a hit-or-miss arrangement. Lenora had been slack about appointments with most people but not with those she loved. She halted her thoughts with a gesture of despair, her eyes filled with tears.

One evening, however, unable to suffer his absences in silence, she begged him to stay, saying, "I have a special surprise for you, Nikolai."

He understood her, although she said it in French, and he paused. After considerable arguing, by way of sign language, for she did not want any intruders around—not even an interpreter—he agreed to remain.

When he emerged from his toilette, she reclined on a chaise longue in a stunning white gown. There was iced champagne on a small table.

He motioned: what surprise? She pulled his head down to hers, kissed him, and said, "Our anniversary, dear. We have been married three months."

He was irate when he understood her. He grew truculent. He pulled away from her abruptly. She felt hopeless, he was so angry. Then two tables laden with food were wheeled in: cold chicken and lobsters, caviar and roast beef. He stopped retreating and reached avidly for the food.

She could not resist asking, "Anything else you want?"

"Too many men have loved you."

Surprised by this attack, and troubled, she stared at him and realized that his beautiful face was in some ways more effeminate than masculine. But the glow in his eyes, his youthful delicacy, his wavy hair, his fair skin . . . how could any woman resist him? She said, in French, "Your eyes are so blue, Nikolai . . . has anyone told you how handsome you are tonight?"

As she suspected, he understood this—he had been told this before—but he said, "Give me some champagne," without answering her question.

She obeyed, thinking it was odd: Nikolai never seemed able to talk naturally to her or any other woman, although he had been married before, had had mistresses before—which he had explained to her in detail, being quite articulate then in a rough but basic sign language.

"More champagne," he said, deigning to use French.

He drank this champagne ferociously. His world seemed to brighten, although he did not smile. She thought his drinking phenomenal. She quit her own drinking to watch.

Nikolai saw no need to be sociable. He had come to the West to take whatever he desired. He was determined to be an

Asiatic, to prove he was better than any of these decadent Westerners. Anything else rasped his raw nerves. Fools, thinking poetry was genteel. Poetry was brutal, arrogant, and Lenora would be smart when she realized that. Her dancing sought to inspire pity and compassion, but he was not that stupid, his poetry inspired fear and terror. Then, and only then, his footing felt steadfast.

She wound her arms around him and he bit her hand. She drew back her hand to slap him, then paused. It was his youth, she thought, his intensity. She said in French, "What's the matter, Nikolai?"

He shrugged, said in Russian, "Your Russian is awful."

She said, "Learn French."

He said, still in Russian although he understood her French, "It is a decadent language, soft, weak." He returned to his drinking, grim-lipped and sardonic, when a husky male voice sounded outside the door. Nikolai said, "It's Yasha." His eyes gleamed, and for a moment she hated him.

"You have an engagement with him?" she asked, her voice growing hard.

He shrugged, muttering in Russian that she did not need a translation.

"When will you be back?"

"I need money," he said in French.

Yasha stood in the doorway, waiting and grinning.

"Suppose I have no money," she said, still in French.

"Lenora!" he shouted, "Do not make jokes!"

"Suppose I say—'No money, never more.' "

She waited for a towering rage, but he was merely scornful now, saying, "I charge. I charge everything. What do I care?"

She had to do the handsome thing. She stuffed his hands full of francs, insisting, "You know you can have anything I have."

He said nothing, sticking the money into his pockets with a gesture of disdain, but Yasha said in precise French, "I must say I hate dancing."

Then they were gone, arm in arm, swaggering down the hallway.

Lenora felt like an abandoned ruin. They were not even friends, she thought, she was merely dragging Nikolai about the world.

Yet the heart of Nikolai was unpredictable. She huddled on the chaise longue, thoroughly drunk, miserable, wanting to obliterate all thoughts of him, and a week later, when they were given passports to enter America and an extensive concert tour was arranged for her, starting in Carnegie Hall in

New York, he embraced her and said, "Good! Good! You will get thousands of dollars a concert!" It was the only English he knew.

She sought to look detached, but when he kissed her with sudden devotion she felt split asunder, one half clamoring to clutch him, the other half resolved not to show she cared. Yet she had to ask, "What about Yasha?"

He said in Russian, "I see him later, maybe."

"We sail on a good ship," she said in her usual French.

"I know," he said in understandable French.

She booked the finest suite, and he was impressed. He became so peaceful now, she encouraged him once more to buy whatever he craved. When friends pointed out that she had to borrow for passage and there was no assurance that the tour would be profitable—there were mutterings in America about Lenora Malcolm being a Bolshevik—she said, "Nikolai needs a little luxury, he was so deprived as a boy." But they required many porters to move them, he purchased so much new luggage. Nikolai thought the way porters swarmed around them a most magnificent compliment.

Then they were off for America. As Lenora led him into their lavish suite, the finest on the ship, he was as cheerful as she had ever seen him.

She was certain that when they reached America and she showed him the grandeur and beauty of her native land, he would be his true self, he would love America's vitality, and their honeymoon would really start.

56

Lenora's eyes searched the pier: there was Dorothy Sunbury, and Archer, proud of his triumph on Broadway as a character actor, and Percy Mackaye and George Grey Barnard and many other old friends. Full of joy and anticipation, feeling sentimental, she prepared to greet them as she and Nikolai looked the picture of married bliss, when she was interrupted by an officer of the ship. The officer was embarrassed. He mumbled, "I beg your pardon, Miss Malcolm, but you and your husband are wanted in the captain's cabin."

"What about all the people waiting for me?"

He said, "It is important."

She found herself being led to the captain's cabin although

she did not wish to go. The captain looked tired and even more embarrassed than his officer. He talked about what an honor it was to have her as a passenger with such an excess of emotion she knew at once something was wrong. He spoke about her fame until she seemed to have no other identity.

Banal, she thought, this making himself important by cultivating her. "But why the delay?" she demanded, growing impatient.

Finally he stopped vacillating and said, "The immigration authorities."

Through the half-open door she saw an authoritative-looking man. He was the immigration inspector, the captain informed her. The immigration inspector told her, "We find it necessary to detain you and your husband on Ellis Island for a special board of inquiry which will be held tomorrow morning."

Bewildered and angry, she said, "You mean we cannot land?"

"Not until your passports are approved. You are no longer an American citizen. You lost your American citizenship when you married a Russian."

"Ridiculous! I was born in America, I dance America, I am American!"

"It is the law, Mrs. Yarov," said the immigration inspector.

The captain deplored the delay, and the officer who had hailed her whispered, "They say it is because of the Russian opinions you have."

"Nonsense," she said, "I am an artist, not a politician." Damn it, she thought, I come with such high hopes, and already America and I are snarling at each other. And Nikolai looked upset, although he nodded approval of her remarks, which he did not comprehend since they were in English, but he liked her vehemence. "I am an American, and proud of it, but I will return to Europe before I allow myself to be imprisoned on Ellis Island."

The captain suggested, "We would be happy to accommodate Miss Malcolm for the evening if it is acceptable to the authorities."

It was, after some discussion.

She said to the captain, "You will take this great risk with me?"

The captain said, "I saw you dance the 'Marseillaise' in Paris during the war. It was magnificent."

The reporters were clamoring to see her, and she agreed to be interviewed. They found her sitting disconsolately in the gilded salon of the ship. But when she saw the reporters approaching she grew more cheerful. Now she reclined on a couch in her customary pose, next to Nikolai, and looked chiefly concerned with him. She told him in French not to worry and then said to the reporters, "I must confess I am the most surprised person here. Why am I being detained?"

A reporter said, "There is a notion here that you are a Communist."

"We are artists, not politicians." She brought forth a statement she had prepared for a triumphant welcome, which she considered remarkably tactful. She read: "Here we are on American territory. Gratitude, that is our first thought. We are the representatives of the young Russia. We are not mixing in political questions. Our concern is with art. We have come to America with only one idea, to work for the rapprochement of two great countries. No politics, no propaganda. May it be that art will be the medium for a new friendship. May the American woman with her keen intelligence help in this task. On our journey here we have crossed all of Europe. In Berlin, Vienna, Paris, everywhere, we found nothing but death and disenchantment. America is our last, our greatest hope."

Another reporter asked, "But you do favor revolutions, don't you?"

"I am astonished to hear that America has no sympathy with revolutions. Our country was started by a revolution in which my great-great-grandfather General William Malcolm played an important part."

"Then you do approve of the Soviet system?"

"I approve of children dancing. There are at least twenty thousand girls all over America who are dancing now the free dances I brought into fashion twenty years ago. Why, I have never even seen Lenin or Trotsky in all the time I have been in Russia. A Bolshevik, indeed! How can they be so stupid?"

"What about the Soviet opinions you have been expressing?"

"I came here to raise money for children starving in Russia."

"Haven't you been called the Queen of the Reds?"

"The President of France said I was worth an army to France, and now, because I love children, whatever their nationality, I am regarded as a lost soul." Seeing Nikolai stirring restlessly, she said, "You should be more interested in Nikolai. He is the greatest Russian poet since Pushkin. Poor boy, he was so happy when he saw the New York skyline. Heaven knows this child is innocent. He wants to bring beauty to America, that is all."

Several reporters applauded, sympathetically.

Nikolai grinned and was delighted to pose with his arm around her.

She asked the reporters, "What will you say in your papers?"

A friendly reporter said, "That you were a good sport."

Most of the newspapers were indignant about what they called, "the unwarranted detention of America's greatest dancer." Public sympathy was on her side. Editorials criticized the immigration authorities. She resolved to keep the press on her side.

The next morning when she was questioned by the immigration authorities at Ellis Island she sought to be gracious and courteous, but it was difficult. Nikolai looked afraid, hurt, and bewildered, and that added to her tension. Finally, unable to endure this any longer, she asked point-blank, "Why am I being questioned?"

"You have expressed revolutionary beliefs, or so it has been reported."

She laughed. "As I've said before, I'm a dancer, not a politician."

"Are you a revolutionary dancer?"

"How should I know! I don't dance out of a textbook! I dance what I feel!" She did not care how much they dragged her political opinions around, but when they disparaged her art it was difficult to keep from exploding.

"But you do call yourself a revolutionary dancer, yes?"

"I am a free dancer."

"What kind of a dancer is that?"

"You might as well have asked Rodin what kind of a sculptor he was."

"Why have you returned to America?"

"Because I want it to know Russia better, because it is my homeland and I love it, even if it does not always reciprocate." She turned to her poet and added, "This is Nikolai Yarov. He is a genius, and he will do much for the poets of America."

"Are you and Mr. Yarov legally married?"

"But of course. Russia is not that different."

"What do you intend to dance at Carnegie Hall?"

"Tchaikovsky and Wagner. I want to heal the scars of war."

"Mrs. Yarov, are you a Bolshevik?"

"Nonsense. That's utter, complete nonsense!"

The Board of Inquiry permitted Lenora and her party to enter the United States without any further restrictions. Lenora said she was treated courteously, still seeking to be tactful for the sake of Nikolai, but she was irate.

There were more editorials denouncing her detention; there was the usual story reminding the public she was the heroine of the Windsor Hotel fire and had saved many children at the risk of her own life; she was told that her recitals, which up to the moment she had been detained had done no business, were selling out now; yet her anger grew. She felt a withering scorn for the Philistines who had opposed her entry. She swore to show America she could not be muffled.

They landed at the Battery where they were greeted by an applauding crowd. Lenora had promised the immigration authorities she would say nothing political, but she managed to scold those who had detained her and stated she was a defender of freedom everywhere.

At the Waldorf-Astoria, where she was staying, she gave another speech. It was a new version of her ideas of freedom. Surrounded by the approval of her friends who had gathered to welcome her, she became a woman of formidable opinions. Several reporters were present, regarding her as good copy, and when she saw them she stressed the genius of her poet. He stood the epitome of male fashion in pearl-gray spats and a light blue suit, to match his eyes, and Lenora stated, "He will be a classic soon. You will see."

Dorothy, much as she loved Lenora, noticed that Lenora's hair was a brightly dyed red now and far less attractive than its original reddish brown, although she knew this was to keep it from turning white. She was unhappy about the amount of rouge Lenora was using. Yet when Dorothy got a few minutes alone with Lenora, Lenora was her old natural, simple, sweet self. But the instant there were more than three or four people in the hotel suite, Lenora had to make a speech.

A reporter baited her, saying, "I understand you intend to dance wrapped in the red flag," and Lenora retorted angrily, "I will wear what is appropriate. Nothing—if that is appropriate. Clothes are not as important as the person in them, or out of them."

"What about public opinion? Suppose it is offended by what you wear?"

"I choose my own clothes, and if any reporter tells me how to speak I say No, and No, and No, and don't tell me I am ruining American morals."

"Even if you dance, say—eh, without any clothes?"

"Even if I dance naked. Can't you say the word!" She was contemptuous.

Dorothy agreed with what Lenora was saying but felt it would have been wiser to have said nothing, for this could be blown up until it became something sensational. This forth-rightness was a luxury Lenora could no longer afford, thought Dorothy, but when she suggested this to Lenora—quietly, Lenora looked betrayed and so Dorothy changed the subject.

Nikolai approved of Lenora's forthrightness. After he learned a few words they'd hear from him. Meanwhile, pleased with their hotel suite at the Waldorf-Astoria, he was the aggressor in their love-making for the first time since Russia. He even kissed her of his own volition. Tenderly, in a sudden spurt of emotion, when she promised to obtain an American publication of his poetry. There was just one major problem: keeping him supplied with liquor. Due to prohibition, champagne was especially difficult to obtain.

From morning to midnight their valet and maid labored to find a druggist, speak-easy, or bootlegger who could supply them with uncut whisky and good champagne. In the middle of the most intense rehearsals Lenora would suddenly be interrupted for a hurried whispered conference—they would have to pay fifty dollars for genuine champagne, but gin and rye were cheaper—and the hotel bellhop, who knew most of the local outlets, had to be called in to approve. Then the valet or maid or both would dash out for the champagne before Nikolai went into a frantic rage—Lenora saying the price was not important, she would earn another fortune on this tour—and she needed champagne, too, for her rehearsing and recitals.

It was frightening, she thought, the bad liquor you could be stuck with if you were not careful. Her spine tingled when she had genuine champagne, her eyes shone, she could reach a bright inspired feeling then without any enormous soul search-ing. And her poet lost his anguish when he had vintage cham-pagne, it was whisky that made him unhappy, disagreeable, that drove him to throw things, to give her a black eye just before her opening concert but eye shadow hid that and made her seem even more tragic, which suited the mood of the concert. But the morning of the first recital she did suggest, "Nikolai, don't drink too much today. You know what always happens."

Carnegie Hall was jammed for her opening performance. The crowd stood up to show its approval. She bowed and slowly began to dance. The program was Wagner, and she had turned the stage into immense proportions by hanging towering curtains and placing the symphony orchestra on the floor of Carnegie Hall.

The contrast of the hundred musicians setting off the single artist on the vast stage was dramatic and flattering and focused all the attention on Lenora. But Dorothy had a sudden pang of sadness. Lenora was no longer beautiful. Her art had become more pantomime than dancing; she was not moving with her old grace—there had been too much lavish living, weight, and age. She showed exhaustion quickly now, thought Dorothy, as if, whatever she pretended, she was bone weary. Yet she still had her beautiful movements, and when she arched her back and stretched her arms skyward, holding this movement three minutes, there was an astonishing instant of exaltation and the emotional suspense was almost unbearable. She stood as one who had looked on death; she danced death; she was death. And she was still brave. Age showed in her body, but there was still a great sense of honor to her art, she was concerned only with expressing honestly what she felt.

There were many bravos, although there was a sizable minority who thought she had grown fat, sloppy, and rather dreary.

At her last New York recital in this sold-out series she asked Nikolai to take a bow with her. "As my inspiration," she told the audience. He had been very difficult lately, drinking heavily, snarling at her, bitter that everywhere they went it was *Lenora the celebrated, Lenora the genius,* and no one spoke of his poetry, many did not even know he was a poet, Russia's newest and greatest genius by his own admission. But as he stood beside her on the stage of Carnegie Hall, on tiptoe so he would look the taller, and the applause rang out for him too, he even managed a warm smile and felt rejuvenated. Lenora had to push him off stage before he would stop taking bows. She was proud of him, however; he had looked so handsome beside her.

Her next engagement was Boston. It was a Tchaikovsky program, and when she danced the "March Slav" as a tribute to the Russian Revolution, Nikolai—having shared a bottle of genuine champagne with her and feeling just as inspired—stepped out of the wings holding her famous red shawl and shouted, "Comrades! Comrades!" There was a dead silence, then a few boos, but he had learned a few more American words by now. He waved the precious red shawl, half imitating Lenora, half trying to outdo her, and yelled, "Hurray for Communism!"

The impact of what he had done struck the audience with full force then, and the house shook with boos and hisses and applause. The audience became two armed camps. There were jeers, then cheers when she began the Tchaikovsky, and when the jeering seemed to be winning her poet burst out of the wings again. For an appalling instant an outbreak of mass hysteria seemed certain. He was in the uniform of a Cossack officer. The orchestra paused. Lenora stood in the center of the stage as if transfixed. He brandished an old-fashioned Russian cavalry revolver and shouted at the audience, "You stink, pigs! Shut up!"

Instead, when the audience realized the revolver was empty it began to laugh. It was as much from hysterical relief as anything else, but Lenora was furious. She sprang forward, grabbed the red shawl from her poet, and in the scuffle—he did not want to surrender it with everybody focused on him— her red tunic was torn at the shoulder. The booing rose in volume, there was loud whispering about the breast that was showing, and suddenly, hearing this, Lenora, with a wild gesture of defiance, tore her tunic down to reveal both her breasts fully and, waving the shawl like a red flag, proclaimed, "Of course I'm a Red, my blood is Red, the sun is Red, do you think I would stoop so low as to do a strip tease!"

Supporters in the audience, standing up to applaud, hollered, "Hurray for Lenora!" They were mainly students from Harvard, and for a moment they dominated the audience, but as she saw a number of people fleeing from the auditorium she turned to address them.

She negligently draped the red shawl over her shoulders, part of her breasts still showing, and began a tirade. She shouted, "Bostonians are afraid of the truth. They want to satisfy baseness without admitting it. A suggestively clothed body delights them, but they are shocked by the beauty of a body the greatest artists in the world have admired. There is a Puritanical instinct for concealed lust in Boston. To expose one's body is art, concealment is the vulgarity. When I dance my object is to inspire reverence, not suggest anything vulgar. All my life I have sought the emancipation of women from the hidebound conventions of New England Puritanism."

Her poet had subsided in the wings, and everyone was listening to her, or staring at her, and the thought of dancing naked gave her a curious excitement. But then, although she was not one to make light of her emotions, she realized it would end all her dancing in America. The manager was leaning out of the wings, imploring her to get off, and so, to show him that no one could halt her free speech, she hurried down to the footlights and with her breasts exposed, defiantly, she shouted, "I am speaking the truth. Nobody is going to shut me up!" Her back arched, her body tilted toward the audience, and the curtain came down with a bang.

The next day Mayor Curley issued an order prohibiting her from ever appearing again in Boston. Pittsfield canceled her scheduled concert; there were rumors of cancellations elsewhere. Everything she said poured gasoline on the fires of disapproval. Editorials recalled her criticisms of marriage; she was called "The Red Peril," which struck her as absurd. Other cities canceled her concerts, although Philadelphia was willing to take the risk, Indianapolis stationed policemen on stage to make sure there was no repetition of the Boston incident, Milwaukee booed her off the stage, Brooklyn was a catastrophe although the house was crowded, for once again her breasts showed. By now she did not care, but everybody else seemed to, and so when she planned to dance Christmas Eve at the church of St. Mark's-in-the-Bouwerie at the invitation of its minister, and to speak on "the moralizing effects of dancing on the human soul," it was forbidden by Bishop Manning of the diocese of New York. When it came time for her last concert in America that January 1923, she had assured herself of one thing: she would never be allowed to dance in America again.

Lenora felt like Joan of Arc, however—that she had lost all but the truth. It was Nikolai who made her very ill. After Boston she had expected him to adore her for defending him. Instead, he resented that she had taken the spotlight away from him just as he had stepped into it. The tour became a series of drunken orgies, smashed hotel rooms, battling and reconciling, and the increased realization that he was miserable in America. They returned to the Waldorf-Astoria when they got back to New York, and one night her poet got very drunk, he went running down the hallways sans clothes, sans all but a lusty yell, and Lenora got him back to their suite before anybody except the hotel employees saw him. But the next day they had to move.

She attributed this outburst to an excess of boyish spirits. When she sought to lessen his drinking, however, he said he carried an ancient poison in his pocket which would bring instant death. He was always talking about death now. He enjoyed telling her of the strange and supernatural ways he would leave the earth. He said, in a mixture of French, English, and Russian she could understand, "I will die in such a way as to make the whole world wonder and tremble. I shall never rot in a common grave." And when she tried to reason him out of such moods he insisted, "No, I will have a short life."

That evening the only liquor they could obtain was gin, and he got drunk immediately. He screamed, demanded champagne, and then he threw himself at her feet, clinging to her legs, begging her to love him.

This caused Lenora to resolve more than ever to bring him peace and love.

A few days later, however, just before they were to sail, the explosion that occurred terrified even Lenora. A party was given in honor of Nikolai by the Russian-Jewish poets of New York. He was supposed to be the guest of honor, but when Lenora arrived with him, he felt eviscerated. Inevitably, everyone converged on her—she was their symbol of freedom, of beauty, and suddenly he could not endure watching it. She began to dance, and he knocked her down. She rose wearily, looking her age in this dreadful moment, too stricken to go on. She could not stop shivering. But when someone sought to console her, saying, "Nikolai had some bad liquor," she refused to blame him.

They asked her to dance again, but she refused. She took Nikolai by the arm, hoping to dance with him, and he pushed her away. A friend of Lenora's admonished him and he spat. A minute later, in a terrible rage, he was trying to pull off all his clothes, intending to dance naked, shouting, "Lenora does . . . I do!" She sought to cover him with her red shawl. It took a dozen men to subdue him, to keep him from disrobing totally. Then, just as he seemed quiet, he went through the window of the ground-floor apartment and into the snow outside, and as Lenora followed him, afraid that he had hurt himself, he turned and shouted, "I'll beat you if you follow me!"

It was morning when he arrived at their hotel on lower Fifth Ave. He was soaked to the skin, he had lost his shoes somewhere, but he was clinging to Lenora's red shawl. Lenora was waiting for him, more coldly sober than she had been for a long time. He slapped her face, and she did not move. He raised his hand again, and her eyes seemed to shine at him with an unholy brilliance and tenderness, and he was flooded with a great wave of giddiness.

"Lenora . . . Lenora . . . I'm mad . . . mad . . . "

She put her arms around him, and he seemed to disintegrate in her embrace, mumbling that he had a terrible headache, and now they sat on the floor and she rocked him back and forth like a baby, whispering, "You will be all right, darling, all right."

"What is wrong with me, Lenora?" he asked in understandable French.

"Nothing wrong. You are a genius. You feel too intensely, that's all."

He smiled like a little boy then, and said, "I wish . . ."

"What, darling?"

He did not answer. He was looking off in space, and then he fell asleep in her arms and she did not move for many hours. Some of the sun had exploded into this boy, she thought and must be understood.

At the dock, however, when the majority of people came to see her off, not him, he frowned, looked disdainful, and began to drink again.

"Nikolai, darling, please . . . easy," she said, her face as pale as death.

But by the time it came to say good-by he was sneering at everything American, and he had to be escorted to the cabin by members of the crew before he became impossibly abusive. He collapsed on the bunk, cursing, and she locked him in and went to say her last farewells.

Dorothy thew her arms around Lenora, begging Lenora to take care, and Lenora began to cry. Lenora, who had been poised and proud saying to the reporters that she was glad to return to a Europe that appreciated her, that prohibition and bootleg liquor had poisoned her poet, wept bitterly.

Dorothy said, "Lenora, Lenora, he's a sick boy."

"It's only a temporary condition."

"Let's be sensible. He'll only get worse. You must have some instinct for self-preservation," implored Dorothy.

"Do I have to?"

"You are an artist."

"I care as an artist. But as a person? I pretend when I am with Nikolai I have my children back, I am as loving as Mama, but it is a fraud, I'll never see any of them again. I've given my heart to him, but . . . ?"

"He can't give his to you."

"He tries, Dorothy, really he does—sometimes. But he's had too much chaos around him, inside of him. Maybe that is why we are so well matched."

"Take care, Lenora."

"I'll try."

Nikolai lay sleeping heavily, his breath reeking of whisky, and Lenora, who could no longer endure feeling alone, felt dreadfully alone. I, she thought, who have been the most illustrious representative of America dancing, am walking blindly down a road which leads only to the grave. The coming years do not belong to me. I have had my day. A few more moments of triumph perhaps, and I will be of the past. For who really cares about another's freedom?

So her wandering resumed. This time without plan or design.

57

The trip back to Paris was an ordeal. Nikolai was never sober aboard the ship, although Lenora had taken it because it was American and was supposed to observe the prohibition laws, and she had to watch him constantly. She ended the voyage so exhausted every nerve in her body seemed about to shatter.

But she did not have to stand more than a moment in the lovely lobby of the Hotel Crillon to know this was the place to stay again. She could not move into her fine mansion at Neuilly because she had rented it for the six months she had expected to be in America, and now she was back in four, but the Crillon had the comfort she craved.

They moved into the hotel like a royal entourage. They still had their maid and valet, and her poet had several followers whom he had picked up on the boat train. He was sober now, proudly and busily supervising the handling of their luggage as a general commanding an army. He loved the silk drapes, silk cushions, silk bedspread, which Lenora had chosen to please him. He approved of the polished Louis XIV living-room furniture, the Empire chandeliers. The gigantic mirrors, however, brought him to a sudden halt. Lenora was startled by his agonizing vehemence—he was staring in the mirror as if he was staring at a stranger. He shouted at his image with loathing, "You're not beautiful, not beautiful!"

She wondered: had he gone mad? Mad or not, he was continuing to glare at himself with such a passionate dislike it was terrifying. "What's wrong?"

"I am the greatest poet since Pushkin, and it brings me no joy, no joy!"

"Darling," she said in French he could comprehend, "I love you."

"Do you mean I don't love you, Lenora?" he cried in

French. "I'm not your son, I don't have to be your son." He
began to sob. Her lingering vitality was partly responsible for
this resentment. Her hair was white when she didn't dye it,
she was stout and middle-aged again, now that she was not
dancing, but sexually she had a youngness which was surpris-
ing, which often surpassed his strength. It sent him off on
spasms of anger, for that made him feel ineffectual yet increased his desire for her.

Dismayed, she thought, now I've done it. My need to be
maternal, to keep Dion alive has made me blunder. She said,
"It is just that I love you so much it has to express itself in
many ways."

He said, "You are not beautiful."

"I don't care," she replied in French.

"I don't either."

"Then why do you say it, Nikolai?"

"Who knows what to say any more?"

"What do you have to know, darling? It is what you feel,
feel, feel."

He flung his arm around her, half threatening, half
courting. They drained their champagne, and she pressed
close to him. She vibrated with desire. Did he have any idea
just how much she wanted him?

In her eagerness she was very close to him, and the light
fell on her and he paused. She looked so old, he thought, I
must be very drunk indeed. Still, once they were in bed—as
now, not recollecting how they had got there, she had led him
almost imperceptibly in the dark—she was lovely and young,
tender yet searching, and there was a rushing force.

"Happy?" she asked softly.

"Do I have to be? That question, do you know how many
times you ask it?"

"I love you. Do you believe me?"

Her body moved toward him, and his body, pressing down
upon her, down upon the human plane, seemed outside an
important part of him. Then he forced her back into his
imprint and into the occasion. He was breathing hard, the
whole room was thrown into a gray shifting confusion of
desire and distaste. He felt avid, yet mutilated.

"Do you love me, Nikolai? I love you."

He paused.

She said, "If you believe that I love you as a man, not a
son, it will be better for both of us."

He stood up suddenly, a surge of futility and anger rising in
him, and shame that his desires had another life he could not
reveal to her.

She watched him moving about and wondered what out-rage she had committed. He was irritable, disturbed. She said, "Lovers should be kind to each other."

"Yes." He took the rest of the champagne and drained it with his usual vigorous gulp. It seemed profane to her, to drink champagne this way, but she did not say a word. He was going to take her again, this time violently, without urging, but instead he fell asleep against her, like one who was dead, away from her wish for love and affection.

To alter the atmosphere of their love, Lenora gave a small party to celebrate their return to Paris, and she sought to make herself look beautiful for him. Her weight, however, annoyed her, although she had no intention of doing anything about it. And she felt stupid when she allowed vodka to be served. Vodka inflamed him, and he was insatiable for it. She tried to make him cheerful as friends appeared, but a fog drifted across the salon—part alcohol, part irritation. She kissed him, before all the guests, and he pushed her away. Yasha had entered. Goddamn Yasha! She said to Nikolai, "I thought he went back to Russia."

"He heard I was returning."

What kind of a bluenosed Puritan was she becoming? I'm not afraid of Yasha, she thought, of any man. I will not compete with Yasha for Nikolai, she resolved, but she was full of pain when Nikolai regarded Yasha with an affectionate attention he had not given her for days. She greeted Archive Tempora with outflung arms, her emotion greater and more demonstrative because of the presence of Yasha. But Archive looked small and insufficient beside Nikolai, although he still moved with grace and aplomb, tanned and well preserved and cheerful. His lucid eyes regarded her with interest.

He said, "You look well, Lenora, and still the elemental force."

"Let there be nature, Archive, always nature." And she laughed.

"You can be too natural, you know."

"America thought I was too voluptuous. I guess I excited the old ladies when I wanted to arouse the young men."

"You feel that on every occasion you must dance a master-piece, you believe that to compromise is to corrupt your art, that to keep quiet is slavery. But tact isn't slavery, tact is a skill as dancing is a skill." Lenora stood motionless, absorbing this without a word. "You never could settle for the merely attainable however, and the unattainable——"

Lenora interrupted, "leads to inevitable defeat. But your

tact is a lie and has nothing to do with inspiration. If I should fall out of the sky you can lift up my reputation and put it back where it belongs."

"It may be too late then."

"So I make an occasional overstatement; it's my defiance and they incite it. But most of the time I'm simply being truthful."

"Truthful, except with Yaròv. There you must be a master of tact."

"He's suffered enough. I want to banish poverty and worry from his life so he can create in peace. That doesn't have to be unattainable."

They were interrupted by people flocking around her—even Nikolai's friends wanted to meet Lenora Malcolm. Nikolai, alone except for Yasha, glowered like a storm cloud. He became quickly drunk. He recited his poetry and commanded everybody to listen to him. She felt the bitterness of his emotion although she did not understand the Russian metaphors and symbols of his poetry. When she suggested that he drink less, slower, he shouted, "You think I am a jackass!" Before she could deny that accusation a new grievance came at her in a torrent of Russian, French, and gestures. He informed her he was making this scene because Yasha had told him this was not the finest suite in the Crillon, and then his rage turned against the hotel. He took deliberate aim at the gigantic mirror which had brought him to tears earlier, uttered a vile name in Russian, and shattered it with a savage kick. The china went next, and when the guests tried to halt him, he kicked and fought with the strength of ten men.

Only the arrival of the French police halted Nikolai. Then he was like a little whimpering boy when they led him off to jail, showing a respect and fear for the police he had not shown to anyone else.

Her poet had accomplished his objective: their suite was a shambles. He had shattered the mirrors, the Louis XIV chairs, chipped the chandelier, wrecked the bed, ripped the bedding, and dented the walls with the smashed china.

And made history: never in the history of the Crillon had so much damage been done by one man.

Lenora was ordered to leave the Crillon at once; she was told Nikolai would be released from jail only if she paid for the damage and guaranteed that he would leave the country at once. The damage ran into thousands of francs. Lenora had to sell one of her precious Carrières to raise the money. That was very painful, but she resolved not to cry over spilt champagne and vodka. The Carrière also brought enough money to pay for Nikolai's trip to Berlin, where there was a large Russian colony.

Nikolai was sober when he kissed her good-by, and quiet. Two policemen stood beside him, and she wished she could command such respect, just once.

She tried to endure his absence by getting her business affairs straightened out. Only she still could not enter her house at Neuilly, and she had to move into a small, drab hotel, and for weeks there was no word from her poet. She became drunk, full of tears for all of humanity and herself. So very drunk, and salvation was in drinking and reading Heine, and the mystic German sorrow had a wonderfully lyrical sound and the bills dissolved and her blue drapes embraced her, only the blue had become garish. Why she did not collapse from all this drinking, she could not understand, but she did not halt until she heard from him about a month after he had left.

Then, all at once, he overwhelmed her with telegrams begging her to join him in Berlin, to bring champagne and vodka, and he would pay her fare but he didn't have any money and he loved her very much, eternally, and he would never leave her again, never, never, never!

This slowed up her drinking, but she did not decide to join him until he wired: "I dream about you and want you very much. You will find my arms open to receive your body and soul. Do not refuse me. Your darling."

Archive was shocked when she prepared to join Nikolai. He was willing to lend her a thousand francs for fare and incidentals, it was all he could spare, but he had to say, "How can you go back to him?"

"We are lovers. It is natural for lovers to quarrel."

"But you are not happy with him. No one could be after what I saw at the hotel. He is mad or childish or both."

"Not always. It was the bad liquor he got in America, that damned prohibition liquor, that drove him wild. But he'll be fine now."

Archive's thousand francs were a trifle compared to what she needed. She sold two Carrières this time, which left her with just two paintings and this shook her—they had given her so many transfigured hours and represented a part of her life that she had loved—but their sale enabled her to hire an auto, a chauffeur, and to have a few thousand francs over.

Nikolai was waiting for her in front of the Hotel Adlon in Berlin. She lifted her head imperiously, and he forgot all about the imperfections which annoyed him. No one could capture the tone of a Lenora, but a Lenora. They were in each other's arms in an instant.

It would have been simpler to have stayed at a small, inexpensive hotel, but Lenora insisted on the Adlon. The Adlon was just as plush as the Crillon, one of the few German hotels which held on to its prewar elegance, and she had to celebrate their reconciliation with earth-shaking enthusiasm. She insisted on a grand party for her poet, ignoring the disaster of the last one. Lenora was such a fervent lover. She loved parties, friends, liquor, art, everything that helped her forget.

Lenora was loving this party, until she saw the way Nikolai was looking at Yasha. Nikolai's eyes said Yes in response to Yasha's enticing glance. She almost jumped out of her skin then; she had the urge to smash things. There was a better solution, however, she thought: divert Yasha. She had managed even more difficult men than him.

A minute later she invited Yasha to tango with her. Yasha did not like her, but she was Lenora Malcolm—it was an honor, and he was curious whether she could really still dance. Yasha was vain; he was sure he could match whatever step she tried. And she moved so gracefully despite her size that he grew fascinated. He found himself dancing with her unaware of when they had started. Her dancing was so sensuous that his flesh tingled. There was an opulent, voluptuous satisfaction in her that was suggesting to him a new form of physical love. Yasha was fancying himself a Nijinsky when Nikolai interrupted them. She did not want to drink now, but Nikolai insisted—to toast her art. He had never been more attentive. He spent the next few minutes getting her drunk. He was doing it deliberately, to assert his supremacy; he knew a few drinks made her gay, inspiring, but many drinks made her melancholy and impaired her dancing.

Now Lenora was overwrought, giddy, and wild. How right, how powerful, how wonderful to be in love with him! They would start afresh, like a first time. She felt as if they were alone, although the hotel salon held almost a hundred people at this moment.

But suddenly Nikolai was doing a Russian dance with Yasha. He was making fun of her, challenging her, and she swore to meet his challenge.

So it started. She threw a dish, went on. Her aim was not as accurate as his at first—she had not had as much practice—but gradually, after the beginning dishes, she began to hit the lights, the mirror. He yelled, "Darling, what are you doing?" He was merely surprised, not angry.

She shouted, "This is wonderful! If I had known it was so

much fun I'd have done it with you!" She took aim at him until he yelled for mercy, until the whole hotel was awake. People gathered outside their doors wondering who was getting killed—the crash of the plates sounded like gunshot. Victim, stoic, mother, she was rebelling against the roles he had forced her into, close to hysteria now, unthinking now, laughing like a banshee, crying out, "He's a darling . . . and I'm mad about him! What am I to do!" But she wanted to kill Yasha.

All at once dish throwing struck her poet as sordid, such a mess she was making. He told the hotel authorities that Mrs. Yarov was ill—the party had scattered out of range, especially Yasha—and only when they were all gone did she cease. Nikolai said, "Lenora, how could you?"

"Be quiet."

"Are you trying to get rid of me?"

"Don't be nauseating!"

"All this roaring and ranting!" He was so disgusted he forgot he was speaking understandable French. "Are you mad?"

"Propaganda, Russian propaganda, being mad. Why don't you protect me?"

He had never heard her speak so sharply to him before. She was very attractive in her outrage. The hotel manager was at the door, asking if Miss Malcolm was sick, and she retorted, "Certainly not!"

The next morning they were asked to leave the Adlon. Lenora did not mind—Nikolai had come to her with a fierceness that was adorable. He had held her thighs until all of her had yielded.

Her big hysterical scene, however, did not have a lasting effect. They returned to Paris to sell things from her house so she could bring money back to the school in Moscow, and once more there was the inevitable party and the inevitable explosion. Through influential friends she had obtained special permission for Nikolai to enter France, but she was unable to say no to a social engagement, to a party—and so, when he brought a few friends back to her house at Neuilly, although she had no intention of succumbing it became a party. Her house was empty now, and she was hoping to rent it and she did not want anything damaged.

Nikolai said the house was like a wailing wall without company, and by the middle of the evening the house was jammed. Lenora felt benevolent after three glasses of champagne and thought this party might be like her old ones, a success—they always said Lenora Malcolm gave the best, most exotic parties in Paris—when she saw Nikolai with his arm around a pretty young brunette. He was drinking heavily, and Lenora wanted to say, steady, my love, steady, I'll do the drinking here, but he would be furious at any such remarks. Yasha was playing his balalaika loudly, as if he too resented this diversion of Nikolai, and when Yasha finished, Nikolai applauded.

Soon after, however, Nikolai disappeared into a back room with the brunette. There was a sudden thump, a thunderous creak of springs as if two bodies had fallen abruptly upon the couch in the rear. Suddenly everything—the crowd in the house, the flicker of the lights on the walls, the pulse of her blood—seemed strange and remote. She had endured much infidelity, but in the next room! It was as if they were lying beside her. She could see even Yasha looking revolted, goddamn Yasha!

Lenora snatched a bottle of whisky and drank savagely. She had married her poet because she needed him, but what did he need? Yet he had kissed her earlier with as much love as he had ever shown, but she could not assess her misery, her heart ached with thinking of it.

Nikolai did not return for an hour, and by then Lenora had retired, the party going on without her. He was breathing heavily when he came into the bedroom. Why did she mind so much? It had been a moment of nonsense. But when she did not answer his "Are you sleeping?" he slapped her. Her whole body was trembling, but she said to herself: his whole world is in turmoil, I must be generous, a look, a word can make him my enemy. He said, "You must listen," and she turned on her face, her back to him, which drove him mad. He pulled the telephone out by the roots and sent it hurtling against the wall. The crash brought her around. She sat up with a start.

"Money! Money! That's all you think about!" he yelled.

"Darling."

He pulled out the revolver he had brandished at Symphony Hall, pointed it at her, pulled the trigger, and to her surprise it went off. The shot landed in the ceiling above her. Then he was stricken with remorse, and she was kissing his hand, saying he didn't mean it, he couldn't have meant it, and he mumbled that he was a miserable dog but if she would only stop insisting life was beautiful!

"Darling, are you sick?"

"Sixty hammers are pounding in my skull."

"Rest a moment." She cradled him in her arms, while she sat trembling.

"What's wrong with me?" he said, speaking for once with

the utmost sincerity. "I'm cursed." His face was contorted
with torment and guilt, and she was too weary to argue.

They reached Moscow barely able to travel. Nikolai was
drunk, he had been drunk continuously from Paris to Moscow. There was still a school, but before she could resume her
classes he made her sick to the death.

The day after she arrived she began to unpack their luggage. They had arrived with a dozen trunks, and Nikolai had
locked them, but she had nothing to wear and so, after considerable difficulty, she forced open the trunks. They were a
shock. Suddenly she stood still. She did not want to go on,
only she had no choice. The trunks were filled with the most
costly clothing, and worse, most of her clothing intended for
his sister and mother. Several were packed with face and hand
creams, all kind of colognes and hair tonics, bath salts, hair
brushes, and nail polish, all of the very best quality. Then, as
she tried to put one of the drawers of a trunk back in place, it
was very heavy, it slipped out of her hands and crashed on
the floor. Money spilled out from behind the hair brushes,
dollars and francs in such an abundance she was shocked.
There were thousands of dollars in front of her, and she could
not touch any of it. Her hands felt withered at their roots. He
entered a few minutes later, and when he saw her sitting on
the floor amid his loot, weeping over what she had discovered,
over pictures of Dion and Cathleen, he lost control of himself.

"I'll kill you!" he cried in a drunken rage. He rushed at her,
to hit her, then saw pictures of her children. He paused,
laughed in a nightmarish way, and pulled the pictures out of
her hands, tore them into a thousand pieces, and thrust them
into the fire. And when she tried to reach them, feeling desolate, alone, all alone in a wide wide desert, her soul in agony,
putting her hands in the fire to save her precious pictures, he
let her fingers burn a moment, and then he pulled her back,
saying, "They're dead. Good and dead."

She felt witless. She tried to stand erect. Then she fainted,
and when she awoke she thought she was dead. There was the
slow crackling of the dying fire. But she was not dead, for she
could hear his voice, saying, "Do you hate me, Lenora?"

He stood above her, waiting, and she had no answer.

"You do! You do! I tore your pictures, I took your
money."

"Our money."

In the dark she heard him sobbing.

She whispered, "Dion and Cathleen did you no harm."

"I loved you, Lenora. I have, but it is no good. I am no good."

"Please."

"No, I tell you, no, no, no!"

"Where are you going, Nikolai?"

She saw him pick up the money that was scattered on the floor, she heard him say something about sending for the clothes, and then he was gone. A new wave of anguish swept over her. She lay on the floor and felt herself sliding down into the past: she saw Mama's vision, a bright little girl with clean pink legs, clean pink cheeks, and a white pinafore. She saw Cathleen and Dion and their soft, red lips, the torture of the years since their death. And she had died too, this was the last death but one, and as she reached for them, she saw their pictures curling to a sad brittle ash. Her hands lovingly picked up the ash, and it melted into indecent dust. She felt as if her flesh had burned away to cinder. She lay there and did not want to get up.

58

A month later Lenora went on tour, hoping to earn millions of rubles for her school. She was very depressed, her heart felt numb, but she had the school to sustain and she could not quit.

Private trading was in full force now, and she owed the State for rent, gas, electric, water, heat, food, teachers' salaries, and costumes, but the State promised to allow her a few more weeks to pay these debts before they closed the school. She was giving of herself freely, and there was nothing in this State that was free. But she was given permission to tour the Caucasus, the Volga region, and the Central Asia Republics.

She was warned that her itinerary included places no American had ever visited, that many of the towns were savage, primitive, a hell, but that made her more interested in the tour. She liked the risk, and nothing was worse than the hell she had been in since her poet had torn the pictures and vanished. Love had become such a lie, dissolving her heart and mind; love that had been sacred was now a ghastly caricature.

She had an accompanist and a manager, the accompanist a

young capable pianist, but for once she made no effort to
beguile either of them. The next few weeks there were many
defeats. The Caucasus were striking, the Georgian people
were attractive and dramatic, she wore high Russian boots, a
large felt black hat, a high-necked embroidered Russian
blouse to show the natives she was one of them, but they
regarded her as a doubtful blessing. Most of the audiences
came free, since she was a comrade and was dancing for
comrades. Much of the time she shared common meals of
herring, onions, black bread, cucumbers, and weak tea to
wash it down. Many were apathetic; there had been a devastating famine just several years ago, and the effects were still
felt. Officials ignored her or had no appetite for her dancing,
and no one wanted to crown her with flowers.

Baku to Tiflis to Batum, it was as if she went from one
bawdy house to another, yet she went on and on, into the
Volga region—to Samara, far to the east of Moscow, to
Orenburg and into Central Asia, where no American woman
had been, to Tashkent, Ekaterinburg—where the Czar and his
family had been executed—to Uralsk, Kazan, Vyatka, Perm,
Bokhara, and Samarkand, the legendary cities of Tamerlane's
empire. But there was one victory.

At Samara she was rehearsing the "March Slav" when two
secret police ordered her to remove it from her program because it contained the hymn to the Czar. The leader's head
was as shiny as a gigantic billard ball. The second one was a
corpulent little man, one of the few fat men she had seen in
hungry Russia, and his head was shaven too. They looked
quite willing to use the revolvers at their sides. She stared at
their shaven skulls and thought, how ugly, and she did not
deign to answer them. She would be damned if she would
dance what they ordered her to dance: she would dance what
she wanted to dance, as she wanted to dance it.

But when she saw the room she had to dress in for her
concert, she was shaken. The walls were smeared with the
stains of squashed bedbugs. There was one naked, fly-stained
electric light bulb. There was no running water, just a washba-
sin, and when she asked for a shower or a bath they laughed
at her. She fell into a state of dreadful depression, felt forsaken even by her dancing. She came upon a mirror, and she
stood for a moment wondering what had happened to the
slim young dancer whose height had stressed her slimness,
whose face had had an almost classic purity, whose soft
brown hair had shimmered in the sunlight, whose every
movement had had a wistful, touching quality. Who had deceived whom? Spring would begin again, but nothing would

make her a nymph again. She drank glass after glass of vodka which she had been saving for a special crisis. She held her head higher than usual when she approached the stage, which was a converted lecture platform, and smiled mockingly as the two secret police accosted her.

The leader of the Cheka repeated that she could not dance the "March Slav," and she cut him short, declaring, "I'll be damned if I can't. Don't instruct me!"

"Who are you?" shouted the leader, furious. Nobody defied him.

"Lenora Malcolm."

He gave her an implacable look. He said in Russian, "Who the hell is Lenora Malcolm!"

His pig-small blue eyes glared at her, and she shouted at the translator, "I'm more of a revolutionary than you Bolsheviks. When you were peasants cringing before the Czar, I was smashing tradition, I was creating new dances. Dog!"

The little fat Cheka took his hat off and wiped his perspiring forehead. He muttered, "Only idiots make such statements!"

But Lenora, delighted with a Russian word she knew and still irate at their stupidity, kept shouting in Russian, "Dog! Dog!"

The leader threatened her with prison, and she turned to her audience, waiting impatiently—they had heard about the argument over the "March Slav"—and she enticed the secret police on stage and pointed to them and said to the audience, "They want to throw me in jail!"

She saw the amazement on the faces of the Cheka that she would dare to make a public issue of it, she saw their hands reach for the revolvers at their sides. She braced herself, to keep from fleeing, let them kill her, by God that would be the final irony. Then she raised her head, feeling like Danton under the guillotine, motioned for her accompanist to start, and plunged into the "March Slav." The secret police did not move for a minute, and then the audience yelled at them to get off, they were spoiling the entertainment, and they retreated. The applause was thunderous, but afterward people avoided her, and her manager drew her aside and said she had been foolish—they could all be shot, quickly, before Moscow would hear a word, and they had better move on, while they had the opportunity.

The tour resumed on a more normal tempo: it continued to be one defeat after another. There was never the right scenery, never the right lights, never the right stage, never the right audience, never the right understanding, never the right transportation, never the right curtains, and never enough money. The heat was terrible, the accommodations grew worse and worse the farther away they went from Moscow.

She plunged deeper into the interior, and several weeks later arrived at Bokhara, far in the heart of Central Asia. Bokhara had been one of the most famed Moslem towns of antiquity, but now it was a grievous disappointment. It had been Russian for just a little more than fifty years, it was more Oriental than Western, it was where the dust of dead Emirs and Empires blew in the street, where the kingdom of heaven was Islam and the people Asiatics. They had no comprehension of her dancing. She stood upon a stage but felt in a quicksand. The whole framework of this world was simply to survive.

Then on the way from Bokhara to Samarkand, the most famed of all these Oriental cities, she hired a dilapidated auto, unable to put up with the fourth-class railroad carriages. She curled up in the back of the ancient auto. The driver was black-haired, with a swarthy skin, and a beard like a shrub, which was dyed red. He wore a turban, he was handsome in a primitive vigorous way, but when she tried to talk to him in her curious mixture of Russian, French, German, and Italian, he shook his head. He said, *"Nyet, nyet, nyet,"* which was the only Russian word he knew.

As they climbed the hills that surrounded Samarkand, puffing along a road that took the strongest character to keep from getting out and walking, Lenora wondered if she had been wise to avoid the train, disagreeable though it was, when the car suddenly came apart. One moment she and her two companions were sitting in the rear seat while the driver struggled with the dust, the next the driver was fifty feet ahead of them. It broke in the middle, and the rear half turned over and over. By all the rules they should have been killed. Instead, they found themselves standing beside the driver, who was very sad, who kept saying, *"Nyet, nyet, nyet."*

So this was it, she thought, the final stupid rejection. Not even a hideous car and a horrible road could kill her.

A rattling Tartar cart picked them up, but a few miles outside of Samarkand a wheel came off. Finally, she found herself entering Samarkand on the back of a camel, holding on for dear life. She forgot her discomfort when she saw the beautiful mosque, the minarets, the gilded domes, the imposing ruins. There was the lovely chapel in which Tamerlane was buried. A gigantic saber stood over the tomb and the marble imprint of a book.

She was deeply moved until she entered the dark hotel

assigned her and noticed by the smell that there were other people in her room. She wanted to run out screaming. Instead, she asked for another room and was informed that all rooms had to be shared. She sought refuge in the park, and that night slept on a bench. She was weeks away from Moscow, even by train. She felt back in the time of Tamerlane, in the fourteenth century.

She tried to talk to the natives, but most of them did not even know Russian. She met one little boy who attached himself to her, and she was touched until he vanished after she gave him money for food.

There was one official, a native of Samarkand, who, knowing a few words of French, understood her request for vodka and obtained some. Dinner that night, to which he added some caviar and fresh fruit, took on the air of a party. His skin was the color of tobacco juice, and he had a red beard.

He toasted, "Miss Malcolm!" but he knew nothing about the arrangements for her recital, and she found herself dancing in the public square. Behind her, while she danced, merchants haggled over turban cloth, a snake charmer had a crowd around him, old men squatted and smoked their ancient pipes, a beggar asked for alms, a little boy was selling coins with the head of Alexander on them, for Alexander had conquered Samarkand too. Her tunic was soiled and creased from the constant traveling and the endless dust. No one applauded, but afterward she was offered more vodka as a reward.

The remainder of the tour became one vast chaotic jumble of impressions, of no soap except kitchen soap, of fighting invisible evils—vermin and Soviet inertia, and blistering heat —of peasants regarding her expressionless as stone, of places where even onions and black bread were luxuries, of no dye for her hair—let alone shampoo. Her hair turned white without henna shampoo, and by the time the tour was half over it was all white and frightening. She could not endure this sudden onrush of age. And the traveling was most impossible of all. Wherever she went, by train, boat, auto, wagon cart, camel, on foot, it was overcrowded. The railroad waiting rooms were jammed and stinking with people sleeping on the stone floors surrounded by their baskets, bundles, goats, and children. She learned to sleep standing, sitting up, lying on boards. Many evenings she was intense with desire to sit with friendly children, but the children were too hungry to be affectionate. Yet she continued to dance Chopin, Schubert, Gluck, and the "March Slav" and the *Internationale*," and wore her beloved red shawl which floated behind her in the wind. She found herself dancing finally to earn enough money to get back to Moscow.

There was no interest in her when she returned to the school. With the recent death of Lenin there was a desperate struggle going on between Stalin and Trotsky, and none of the important officials could be bothered with a dancer's problems. Nobody in the Ministry of Public Education could aid her. The year she had gone to America a hundred thousand children had died from starvation; they could not worry about fifty.

Then came the final blow of all. The government turned off her gas, water, electricity, and padlocked the door of her school because she owed them rent.

She stood before the ancient mansion which had housed the Lenora Malcolm Plastic Art School and thought, I was wrong. I thought Nikolai was the last death but one, only it isn't, there are many deaths still, as long as I live.

When she was offered an engagement in Berlin she accepted it at once. She did not question the terms, the manager. She had to dance, not out of desire but out of desperation. She had to flee. Lost, she thought. No, that was too easy, too simple. If that was all, she could manage.

Stanislavsky came to say good-by. He asked, "You'll come back?"

"What for?"

"For my sake, for our sake . . . Russia . . . Moscow . . ."

"For good or bad?" she asked.

"We need you."

"Do you?"

"Yes, please. You will return?"

"No," said Lenora.

BOOK TEN

59

The distinguished, graying gentleman, a sophisticate by inclination and a successful painter by necessity, sat in the Berlin café gossiping leisurely about the decadence of modern art with a banker friend when a stout, middle-aged woman entered and found a place at a nearby table. She was alone, but the painter looked embarrassed and stole a furtive glance at the woman. Suddenly, although the beer in this café was the best in Berlin, he slipped out of the café with his friend. Safely outside, he explained, "I didn't want to be seen by her. I knew her quite well before the war, and the moment she saw me she'd want to borrow money."

Lenora did not see the departing painter, an acquaintance from happier days. She was sunk in melancholy. She had come into the café to find relief from her despair.

Lenora, remembering the past, had expected a joyous reception, and Berlin had become a continuation of despair. She sat there, seeking to cleanse her thoughts with the cold beer, recalling each moment with a frightening clarity, and the recalling of it made it worse. A month ago—had it been just a month ago, it semed years ago now!—she had danced a program out of the past, purposely nonpolitical, Grecian, picturing an Olympian people in joy and sorrow. She had also danced with heroism and erotic abandon, in what she assumed was the mood of Berlin 1924, and the audiences had jeered her. In her heart she had shouted back, but outside she had stood with clasped hands and shining eyes as in the past, and the jeering had increased. In her encores she had sought to be delicate and beautiful, the divine and sainted Lenora who had transfigured Germany twenty years ago, and the audience had shouted, "She's fat—a Bolshevik—*kaput!*"

This was a different generation, she thought, fondling her beer, they were bitter, disillusioned, but she knew it was more than that. Her impresario had vanished with all the receipts, and she had very little money. She owned a valuable property in Paris, worth hundreds of thousands of francs, and it was tied up by debts and litigation. She had sought to arrange more concerts, but impresarios who had clamored for her in the past refused to see her. Lothar was dead. The artists who had worshiped her were gone or out-of-date. And she was being blacklisted as a Bolshevik, Germany claiming she was a Red, and yet she had danced Wagner during the war when no one else would and the Soviets had said she was too bourgeois.

She could not get into the Hotel Adlon because of the havoc she and her poet had done. This was now a historic occasion in Berlin; people still spoke with awe of the damage they had done, as if unable to believe that two people could have caused so much wreckage, especially when one was a woman.

She had moved into the palatial Hotel Esplande where she had stayed many times, intending to remain just a week, and now she could not afford to move, she could not pay the bill that would be submitted. Yet Amy was visiting her, Amy who had re-established a very successful school in one of the Kaiser's old palaces at Potsdam, and Lenora, although she was sick at heart, was determined to put on a great show for her sister.

So Lenora invited Amy to the expensive tea gardens of the Esplande for lunch, although she could not afford this either, and the moment they met she was talking about how thin Amy had gotten, because she was defensive about being fat. But Amy had not altered much actually, she thought, but she had—she could tell by the sudden blink of Amy's eyes.

Amy asked, after they kissed each other on the cheek, "What happened to the Revolution?"

"They buried it in Red Square, with Lenin."

"How does it feel to be an ex-proletarian?"

"How does an eagle feel when someone calls him a sparrow?" Amy did not reply, but stood like marble, cool and firm. Lenora thought, Amy's pupils are wealthy, Amy always has been clever at attracting rich patrons and holding on to them, Amy must have saved thousands and I'll be damned if I'll ask her for a sou. "In any case, Berlin is dismal these days."

Amy said, "Germany is still an art-loving country."

"Ah, most of the children are interested only in Swedish gymnastics."

"I have some beautiful children," Amy said, a little testy.

"Of course," said Lenora, realizing she was antagonizing her sister and not wanting to. "You've always been a brilliant teacher, one of the best."

"Possibly," said Amy, looking more relaxed. "How have you been?"

"Fine."

"Your dancing is still quite exciting, your style still unique."

Lenora's face lit up. Amy was as forthright as she was, although more diplomatic in public.

"But the situation is quite different today," continued Amy. "How are things with you, Lenora?"

"I said everything is fine, things are *gemütlich*, plenty of *Guten Tag* and *Guten Appetit!*" She hadn't eaten sausages for weeks, but now she ordered them, reminded of the happy, wonderful days of prewar Munich and Bayreuth. She saw Amy frown when the waiter brought the sausages, disapproving of such a heavy meal so early in the day, but she ordered more wine for Amy and beer for herself—Amy was not in the mood for beer at midday.

Amy said, "I gather that basically you haven't changed."

"Why should I change?"

Amy shrugged.

"Do you want me to dance hymns to celibacy, the monastic life? That's hardly my style."

"How true that is."

"Deep down, you agree with me."

Amy did not answer.

Then Lenora, wanting to recapture the joys of their childhood, spoke about Mama and how much she missed her and those wonderful growing-up days.

Amy did not want to talk about Mama. Amy did not regard their growing up as magical. Amy said, "I'm in no mood for *Weltschmerz*. That's the prerogative of old age, and I don't feel old."

"But suppose you thought you were going to die tomorrow?"

"You are still too emotional, but it still helps your dancing."

"A couple of million people have seen my dancing."

"Yes," said Amy. "You must have given over a thousand recitals. It's unbelievable. How you go on and on."

And Lenora, feeling with a sudden start of fear that this was the last chance to reach Amy, blurted out, "But now I can't get another recital, they say I'm a Communist. Other women can dance naked here, wave their breasts, and they watch them voraciously, but try to give them art and . . ."

"Are your speeches art?"

"They're the truth, as I see it."

"Well, I suppose you've enjoyed your extravagances."

Lenora wavered, afraid to face another rejection.

Amy thought, Lenora is still obsessed with the beauty of the flesh despite her age, still believes in its lasting freshness and inspiration, still desires to press it violently close. Amy asked, "Are you really serious about being unable to give any more recitals?"

"I can't find the impresario. He vanished with everything I earned."

"I wish I could help you."

"I didn't ask for help!"

"But we are enlarging the school, and I haven't any money available. Why don't you go on to Paris? You were always a great favorite there."

Flushing darkly, Lenora's impulse was to jump to her feet and stride out. Instead, determined not to quarrel with Amy whatever the provocation, she said, "I intend to go to Paris, once I find the impresario."

"You may be throwing good money after bad."

"Oh, Amy!" If she really asked for a loan, if she really told her sister how desperate she was, Amy wouldn't refuse her.

"Yes?"

Lenora hesitated—Amy looked so curt, disapproving.

"What is it, Lenora?"

"Maybe I could visit you at Potsdam."

"Maybe?"

Lenora ordered champagne now; she'd be damned if she'd cringe before anyone and certainly not Amy. They chatted a little while longer, about nothing at all, and then Amy was gone as formally as she had come.

That evening when Lenora was going to bed she found a note from the hotel management, politely but firmly requesting payment of her bill. She had nowhere near the amount owed, it was increasing at an astronomical rate, and the next morning she wrote letters to friends asking for a loan.

When there were no answers, yet none of the letters came back, she wrote more letters, their tone becoming desperate. There was still no trace of the impresario, no possibility of any concerts, she was living on beer and gin now, unable to practice, to dance, growing fatter and fatter. Her blanket was like her shroud now, she did not want to emerge out of it.

Finally she was forced to leave the hotel. She went from hotel to hotel, each cheaper and more run-down, until she had only enough money for fare to Amy's school in Potsdam. She telephoned Potsdam, and when she got Amy she asked, "Could I stay a few days? I don't feel well."

"What's wrong?" Amy sounded remote.

She wanted to say an overdose of humiliation, but she said, "I'm short of money."

"Why don't you move to a cheaper hotel?"

"I have."

"The Esplande was too expensive, but you liked being reckless."

"Amy! Why are you trying to punish me?" Anything would be better than the way she was living now.

"I am not trying to punish you. But I have to be in Dresden to see some people about moving the school there."

"I could go along, and handle this school."

"Oh no!" Amy was shocked, certain that a person with her sister's Bolshevik reputation would alienate the wealthy people she was courting. Moreover, she considered any money given to Lenora a waste, as good as thrown away. "I'll send you some money and see you when I return, in several weeks. What is your address now?"

Lenora could not answer I have none, I have been sitting in the park all day. She shouted over the telephone, "I'd love to see your school . . . I'm sure it is beautiful!"

"Realistically, Lenora, I've no room. I'll send you money. What did you say your address was?"

But Lenora had hung up and was hailing a taxi to take her to Potsdam. The school was beautiful, surrounded with a magnificent iron fence and a wrought-iron gate. The taxi driver waited, for she did not have enough for fare. The gate was locked, and she banged on it.

Abruptly, one of Amy's assistants stood in front of Lenora. Lenora knew Sarah—Sarah had wanted to be one of her girls but had been too old, too homely. Sarah said, "Amy is gone."

"I'm in no hurry. I can wait."

"Amy won't be back for a month."

"A month?"

"Sorry, and she left instructions not to admit you."

Lenora stood there and thought, I should run, I have rushed here like a lamb come to slaughter. But one death or another, it is impossible to say which to choose.

"But there is an envelope for you, which Amy left." Sarah

thrust it through the iron bars of the gate, and Lenora ignored it. The envelope fell into the mud. Lenora intended to let it lay there, but the taxi driver picked it up, took out his fare both ways, glad it was in francs—marks were no good—and handed it back to Lenora. She was unaware the envelope was in her hand until she was back in Berlin.

This was Amy's generosity? Lenora had just enough for fare to Paris—Amy had been clever, but Lenora's throat was parched and she stopped for a bracer and by the time she finished, hours later, the fare to Paris was gone and she had just enough to rent the cheapest room in the cheapest hotel she could find. Then she lay down on the rickety bed and was very, very sick.

Lenora was there a week later, with nothing to drink and nothing to eat. She tried to subsist on tea and bread, but it was the absence of liquor that almost choked her. She did not move out of the room; she resolved to lock the door if they tried to evict her, to turn on the gas if they broke down the door. She kept the shades to the sill, shutting out all the daylight. She almost liked the worn-out, dizzy feeling that doused her; it drove everything else away. Time had no velocity, she might never have moved out of this room if she had not heard a piano nearby. It was in the next room actually, and the Chopin was rather charming, she thought, if too sentimental. It made her cry, and she did not want to cry.

"No cry . . . no more," she whispered to herself. "No more." More maudlin than reasonable, and wishing he would play something that was an antidote for her melancholy, she wandered down the hallway and banged on the door.

Suddenly she was sober. What a sight he was, this pianist, his face fair, well formed, his hair as blond as her poet's. Actually he was not the image of her poet as she thought, his face oval rather than square, his body far slighter, his accent British, his amazement obvious.

All at once he blurted out, "I know you. You're—— Oh, really, I have seen your face before."

"Could you pour me a drink?"

"I've only got beer."

She made a face, but she took the beer. Then she got dizzy; she had not eaten for several days.

He sensed that and said, "I'm on short rations myself, but I have some cheese." He gave her a slice, and she ate it in one ravenous gulp. "Say, you are famished." He found more cheese and bread, although this meant less for himself tonight, and then he introduced himself as Derek Hughes, an English pianist studying in Berlin. And as she smiled wistfully he knew who she was. He said, "Are you Lenora Malcolm? I heard you were in Berlin," and she said, "It doesn't matter," but when she moved over to the piano to examine the instrument, her face illuminated at the sight of her favorite musical instrument, he saw the remnant of the artist.

"Oh, it's the truth," she said, seeing the shock on his face, "I'm Lenora Malcolm . . . and so forth."

"Ill?" he asked.

"And stranded." Her face lit up with a lovely smile when she saw that he had Scriabine. "Would you play Scriabine?" she asked, as if that were the greatest favor in the world. "I haven't heard his music for such a long time." As he played and as she listened he forgot her puffy features, her shapeless body, feeling only the vitality of her attention. She seemed to have completely forgotten the shabby hotel, and only the beauty of the music mattered, and his feeling.

But the moment he finished she asked, "Do you have any whisky?"

"I said I only have beer."

"I forgot. I forget many things these days."

"But not Scriabine."

"Not Scriabine." She smiled; he was a kindred spirit as she had thought.

For quite a while then she existed on what food Derek could spare her. Finally, however, unable to help her any longer, he decided to get outside help. One day he came into her room very excited. He had a newspaperman who had a proposition for her, although he called it "an offer," not wanting to offend her. Derek said the newspaperman knew her, but he would not tell her who it was, wanting it to be a surprise. It was. Brian Pomeroy stood in her doorway, his hair gray, his face lined, but still impeccably dressed, still the diplomat, so unlike most of the newspapermen she had known.

This was fantastic, Brian thought, and he was shocked, but he did not show that, looking imperturbable. Her rouged cheeks, her red hair struck him as a translation of Rubens into a far coarser idiom. There was a Flemish exuberance of flesh, she had grown so heavy. He was certain she had lost touch with reality, but even as he stared at her blatant red hair, her overrouged features, she smiled and said in her soft American voice, "It's been a long time, Brian."

"Too long, Lenora." He bent and kissed her hand, which was still lovely.

She motioned for him to sit down and he did. "What's on your mind, Brian? An obituary?"

"You're jesting. You have many years ahead of you."

"Of course. Inevitably." She smiled wryly. "I am just as popular as I was twenty years ago, when I met you."

"Just as famous. In fact, that is one of the reasons I am here. A book from you, or your letters . . ."

"Love letters?"

"That would be worth a considerable amount of money, published."

"Pour me a drink. Do you have any whisky?"

"I can get some."

"Do. Then we can discuss the letters."

Derek looked embarrassed, but Lenora looked indifferent.

The following day Brian returned with a bottle of whisky, and saw her in Derek's dingy room. She thanked him for his contribution but said she had changed her mind. To publish her love letters would be to betray their love, she declared, and she would prefer to starve before doing that.

Brian regarded her with exasperated affection. Was this integrity or a need to be perverse? He said, "Is this a joke?" How could she love what had died? "Lenora, I've wired my newspaper, they seem interested, they suggested an advance, say fifty pounds or thereabouts."

"No. I loved my lovers for themselves and not for what I could get out of them." Her lovers represented all her freedoms, and to take money for her freedoms was impossible, whatever she had promised in a moment of weakness.

Derek had sacrificed many decent meals for her sake, and suddenly he longed to shake her. So many of her love affairs were public property, she had made them so herself—who would she hurt?

Brian was still a very polite man, inclined now to be fatherly and kind, and he knew he was a constant reminder of a past that had turned to ashes, but she was being ridiculous. He asked, "Is it a matter of money? I might be able to arrange a larger advance."

"Since I've never cared for money in itself," she said, "it follows that the money is of no consequence to me." She took another large, quick gulp of whisky. Her robe was disorderly, her red shawl shabby.

Brian thought, the kindest way to describe her appearance was to call it embarrassing. The celestial dancer had become a colossal mess. Then she rose from the dingy couch. He thought, this is the end, she waddles rather than walks.

Lenora said, "Play, Derek. Chopin, without sentiment." She raised her arms with a majesty that transformed the ugly room. She went as if to embrace the heavens, then recoiled, then danced across the room as if fleeing from evil. There was no rhythm in her dancing, no attempt to follow the exact beat of the music, but she moved with the grandeur of a goddess. Doom went with her: she was Cassandra. After Derek finished she stood motionless. Tears rolled down her cheeks. She stood like a human sacrifice. She had loved life with a passionate faith, and now there was no love left. She had danced as a naked blade, and now she had been thrown aside.

Held by her hypnotic intensity, Brian and Derek watched fascinated. Then when she went to sit down they approached her as one, each took an arm, and escorted her to the dingy couch as if she were a queen. No one mentioned the letters. Brian said, without thinking, "How can the world forget?"

Lenora said softly, "Perhaps they are wise after all. I have death in me, especially when I dance, and they don't want to be reminded of death. Once I was going to dance to Duse's acting, a duet of a kind. Today Duse is dead. I loved Duse. I cannot dance without dancing her death."

"But you say it so poignantly," Derek declared.

"Many poets have said it better," Lenora replied. "Donne, Wilde . . . Oh, I see you smile, they strike you as an absurd pairing, but in this they are not."

"And you are a poet," Derek said emotionally. "The most poetic dancer I have ever seen."

"And now I have to struggle to just stay alive," she said.

"You must dance again," Derek said, "on the stage, for many people."

"Without money? Oh, I know, Brian, you could get me some, but it would destroy whatever inspiration I have left to dance."

Derek asked impulsively, "Don't you have any material resources? You made so much money. Surely, many people are indebted to you."

Lenora said sadly, "Don't you know that people are never so watchful as when they owe you money? But I never lent money, I gave it, thousands and thousands. I gave it away as if it were going to be obsolete the next day."

Brian said thoughtfully, "There must be somebody who could help you."

"My friend Dorothy Sunbury, but she has her own needs, and perhaps my brother Archer, but he's far away."

Brian said, "Look, could I wire Archer? I could help you for a little while, but I'm returning to London soon."

"Thanks, Brian, but I'll manage somehow. Perhaps find myself another millionaire, or re-establish my school. Yes, I know what you are thinking. Poor Lenora, she is back in her dreams, full of self-pity, she doesn't make any sense at all."

"You make very good sense, in some ways," said Brian. But not in all, he thought. That evening he cabled Archer and told him about Lenora's situation. A week later Archer sent her enough to take her to Paris, to pay all her expenses for a month, if she would be careful, and promised to continue this each month as long as he was working.

60

The following year was a desperate pilgrimage to nowhere.

"I must dance again," Lenora told herself, once she reached her beloved Paris and stood outside her lovely house at Neuilly, which she could not enter, and added, "Then I will reclaim my house, reestablish my school," but she did not dance that year or the next.

She lived as if in a dream. She had the wish, but not the energy. She had the image, but not the reality. Then, although her friends had many plans to reclaim her property, none of them materialized. The money Archer sent her, at great sacrifice, for he was having trouble with his eyesight and losing important roles, was just enough to subsist on.

Instead of Paris becoming her salvation, it drove her to the breaking point. She moved into a tiny, shabby hotel on the Left Bank and lived there as if she knew no one in Paris. Friends lost touch with her, or did not know where she was, and she made no effort to see them.

The concierge was friendly and knew that this stout, middle-aged woman must have suffered, for she was always looking at pictures of two pretty children and crying, but the only thing that seemed to make her smile was an occasional absinthe.

Often Lenora saw no one for days. When she did go out it was at dusk. Frequently she stayed in bed for days. Then the world seemed as far away as the vanished hours of the past. The only person she wrote was Archer, to thank him for his aid. His replies were all that kept her in touch with the world. Her desire to flee from everyone was accentuated when Archer wrote her that Nikolai had set fire to himself in Red Square in an effort to kill himself. This sapped the rest of her strength. It struck her as the final rejection. She was as one immobilized. She was lost, and she withered without love, without dancing. Her first vision of Paris had been so wonderful, and, recalling that, she fell ill. She was trying to live without emotion, and it was all she had left.

Poor Lenora, it became her battle cry, she was seduced by this self-pity, it was her one luxury. She could not even afford a decent brand of whisky, she could not even impress herself. Yet she had the need to justify herself, but not the energy. In some ways this was the worst loss of all. Always before, whatever had happened, she had had energy, but now, no matter what the circumstances, she had none. She felt used up, that life had become a foolishness.

Then Dorothy Sunbury found her. Dorothy had heard from Archer about Lenora's depressed, isolated state; Dorothy had come to save Lenora.

Lenora sat in a rocking chair, looking twice her age, rocking back and forth, back and forth, not hearing the knock on the door, the door opening, not hearing anything but the shrill laughter of children in the small courtyard below, reminding her of Dion and Cathleen. Dorothy felt a cold wave of terror down her back, but she forced a smile, took a deep breath to regain her courage, and, assuming her most cheerful manner, approached Lenora from the rear, embraced her, and cried, "Surprise!"

"Mama!" Lenora cried, then shuddered, realizing what she had said, and faced Dorothy. It was as if she had been away on a long journey and still could not believe Dorothy was really there and was holding her tight.

Lenora began to cry.

"You mustn't," said Dorothy. "You've cried enough."

"You do love me?"

"I'm here."

"Thousands have loved me, but now . . . ?" Lenora shook her head woefully.

"You've got to dance again."

"That's a sentimentality. I can't dance any more."

"Why not?"

"If you are going to browbeat me . . ."

"As it happens, I am. Do you want me to leave?"

"Yes!" Lenora rose from her rocking chair. They stood facing each other, and then they fell into each other's arms.

Dorothy was right, Lenora admitted afterward, she ought to dance. She was shaken when Dorothy showed her an article which said: "What has happened to Lenora Malcolm? Is she ill? Has she given up her art? Her disappearance is causing many of her most fervent supporters to think she is finished with dancing forever." Lenora agreed to practice, to plan a new concert tour. The loneliness was gone with Dorothy by her side, and she felt better than she had for some time.

In a month Dorothy raised enough money to take them to Nice and to rent a studio in Lenora's name on the Promenade des Anglais with the marvelous blue sea in front of it and the magnificent hills behind it and the superb sunshine overhead.

It could have been a reinvigoration, but when she heard that Nikolai had killed himself it became impossible to practice. Lenora did not cry, but the news made her very tired, and the details made it worse. He had gone to the suite in the hotel in Petrograd where they had spent their first honeymoon, had cut his wrist, written his last poem with blood from this bleeding wrist, and then hung himself on an enormous hook in the bedroom.

The poem said:

> *To a Friend*
> *Good-by, my friend, good-by!*
> *This fated parting*
> *Holds for us a meeting in the future.*
>
> *Good-by, my friend, without hand or word.*
> *Be not sad nor lower your brow.*
> *In this life to die is not new*
> *And to live, surely, is not any newer.*

She cried to Dorothy, thinking of her poet's death, "They've buried me . . . they've buried me." And when Dorothy said, "Please, dear, I don't want you to say that ever again," Lenora replied, "Let me joke, let me joke."

Now, however, she could not muster the energy or will to dance.

Lenora was notified that as his legal widow she inherited his estate, which was worth three hundred thousand francs in copyrights and royalites. And although she was partly responsible for his large royalties, she refused this legacy and said Nikolai's mother and sister needed and deserved it more. This left Dorothy with a hopeless feeling, but she continued the struggle to regain Lenora's property. Finally, Dorothy and some friends regained the property and put it in Lenora's name. But Lenora was not allowed to possess it. The committee who had regained it were afraid she would dissipate it as she dissipated everything else, and so it was planned as a memorial.

The moment Lenora got any money she spent it. Given a hundred dollars for an article she wrote, she spent two hundred on a party to celebrate the sale. Given the company of a friend in a café, she insisted on making friends of all the young men about. Given a bottle of whisky for her ills, real and fancied, she drank it immediately.

She shuttled back and forth between a flat in Paris and the studio in Nice, going nowhere, arriving nowhere, spending time without living it. She sun-bathed at Juan-les-Pins and picked up young men whenever she could, but none of them were permanent.

The beginning of 1927, after several years of this, Dorothy said, "I cannot continue this mad pace to nowhere." She stared at Lenora and the latter's shabby brown fur coat, split down the back, her old felt hat pulled down over her blatant red hair, her pale features overrouged, at Lenora changing her mind whether to stay in Nice, whether to go back to Paris. Dorothy added, "You must be more practical, or I'll have to go back to America." Or, she did not add but thought, I'll be as deep in debt as you are.

Lenora replied, "What is a fact, that Tuesday follows Monday, that death follows life. You are all so practical, everybody is so practical but poor Lenora, so obviously mad."

"But you will never be able to dance again if you keep this up."

"Deterioration is part of the flower, a flower has to fade, wilt, and die. We have to accept that."

"If only you would stay on a diet."

"Talk away."

"I know, you're not listening."

"Poor Dorothy, Lenora runs away from everything now, and you have to try to keep up with her," said Lenora, detached suddenly, as if she were speaking of a stranger.

"For most people, survival is still the primary instinct, but for you . . . ?"

"Do you want to be discharged as my companion?"

"I don't feel very flattered when you talk this way."

"Dorothy, you sound like Amy, calling me a 'helpless genius,' and then washing her hands of me."

"That's a terrible thing to say."

"Sometimes you sound like Mama, disapproving of me yet afraid to say so."

"That's not true. Your mother was not afraid of anything except what might happen to you."

Very softly then, Lenora said, "We had a perfectly beautiful childhood. Do you think I'll see her and the children when it is all over?"

Dorothy paused. How could she predict what would come after? She would have liked being a sibyl of the arts too, and to dance as if it were the revelation. But she had been too short and awkward, barely five foot one, inclined to be gaunt, the same age as Lenora but always looking older. She was a fine swimmer and an excellent hiker, but she looked scrawny beside Lenora. She knew that often she had the manner of an able head nurse, although they had met as equals, unlike many of Lenora's friends. She had succeeded as an art editor, and now she was retired. Dorothy was a combination of the worldly and the aesthetic, and now she felt baffled.

Lenora was saying, "I can only create when I am inspired. And nothing inspires me now. The spirit does not move me."

Then, all at once, the spirit did move Lenora. Lindbergh took off for Paris, and Lenora became part of the crowd waiting for him at Le Bourget, and when many shouted, "He will fail!" she stood up on the fender of an auto and announced, "He will make it! He is an American!" Everyone knew Lenora, they shrugged—anything was expected of "The Malcolm." When Lindbergh arrived at Le Bourget, Lenora was proud of being an American; she could almost believe in heroism again.

A few days later she placed herself in front of the American Embassy in Paris and led a crowd defending Sacco and Vanzetti. She raised her arms in protest, calling forth a fantastic emotional response from those around her, and, catching this flow, she was further aroused. She understood their response—she had used this many times in her dancing—and her arms took on their old thrust and arch. Lenora, never doubtful in such moments, then dangled her arms and pleaded in her American accented French, "With our hearts, our voices we must uphold justice." The crowd swept toward the American Embassy, and the police had to disperse them, but Lenora felt triumphant. America had heard the voice of the people; Sacco and Vanzetti could still be snatched from the jaws of disaster. The next day she told Dorothy, "Self-pity is useless as inspiration. I will dance again, for Lindbergh and Sacco and Vanzetti," and she saw no contradiction in this.

61

The first rehearsal was the moment Lenora knew she should have listened to Dorothy, who had warned her to keep her body firm yet limber. For the harsh truth was that one hour of rehearsing and every muscle ached. The front of her legs ached, the back of her legs ached, her shoulders ached and her arms. There were shooting pains across her waist. She felt clumsy, and motion seemed alien to her sluggish, heavy body.

She anticipated some muscle fatigue and strain, but not this. Once, impaled against the floor in one of her stretching movements, she felt inept, which she hated; she was furious suddenly at her body, such a frail accomplice. She sought to concentrate on her emotions, on her sense of triumph that Lindbergh had evoked, and she grew tense and her shoulders throbbed when she lifted her arms. She felt like the instrument of her own humiliation. She was forty-nine, and she felt every minute of it.

But she could not halt. Dorothy was at her constantly now, prodding, encouraging, inspiring, and reminding her of a slighter, younger version of Mama. The theater in Paris had been rented for July, just a short time away now, and too many friends were coming for her to cancel. This is my come-back, she repeated to herself, and she struggled on.

After several weeks her rehearsing improved, though during this time she moved in a haze of pain, with the constant, nagging fear that her legs were gone. It was as if her body had acquired a disdainful immobility, denying her all it had given her in the past. She was still far too heavy, she knew, but she still had poetry and imagination in her but very little agility or energy.

Then Dorothy persuaded her to visit a masseur. For several weeks Lenora went to him frequently and sought to subsist on one thick slice of roast beef a day, orange juice, and hot tea, but she insisted on some whisky before each rehearsal. She came to hate the rehearsals. She was losing weight, but she was still far heavier than she should be for the program she planned. The massages were an ordeal and made her miserable. Finally, a week before the recital, she refused to endure any more massages, although she was still many pounds over her best dancing weight.

Dorothy, who was dismayed by Lenora's weight, said, when

she also began to drink more—the pain in her back was killing her— "You'll spoil your dancing."

"I'm on the verge of dying and you reproach me."

"I don't want you to make a fool of yourself on stage."

"I? Lenora Malcolm? I'm surprised at you, Dorothy. For God's sake, pour me another drink."

Dorothy did, but added, "Dear, this is not a normal concert. This is your first long program in several years. You'll need all your strength."

"How dreadfully depressing! I care only for my dancing now, and you want to condemn me to dullness and starvation."

As had happened before, Dorothy had a baffled sense of trying to penetrate a mind already made up. But she sought fervently to persuade Lenora, saying, "I could give you a dozen rational reasons, but one should be enough. Your whole future depends on this concert. I want you to be a success——"

Lenora interrupted Dorothy sharply. "Of course, you want. You're too sensible to make a fool of yourself. You want me to be without a frown or wrinkle."

"I want you to dance beautifully, as you always have."

"Dorothy, have I ever been faithless to my art?" Dorothy did not reply. "You know as well as I do that creation is not a kind of chastity or living in a desert. Creation does not occur like the sun, rising every morning, bright and refreshed, always plentiful, always sufficient. It has its good days, and its bad days, days when nothing goes right and days when it flourishes like a miracle. That is why I have never danced unless I was up to it, unless I could give of my best. And if I feel sad I dance sadness, if I feel gay I dance gaiety. I never dance what I do not feel. Creation is not a faint and fretful mistress, but a triumph, yes, even a triumph over death and dissolution."

Dorothy, who was finding it very difficult to be as stern as she felt she should be, said encouragingly, "Creation triumphs over all."

"Not always. But when it does, we are all possessed, the artist and the audience."

"And when it does not?"

"We should never be forgiven." Lenora paused a moment, then added, "Creation must be the expression of the best in us, even when it expresses servitude or death, even if we have to stand naked, even if we have to step over our own corpses."

Dorothy was silent. The way Lenora looked was heartbreaking. Lenora was at the point of tears. Dorothy thought for a moment Lenora was going to break down.

Then Lenora said, "Do we have any more whisky?"

Dorothy nodded and poured her some.

Lenora gulped it down. She said, "Friendship." She laughed, "Sometimes I think whisky is the best friend I have."

Dorothy thought that Lenora would get hysterical, but she began to dance. For the first time since she had begun rehearsing, her overweight did not seem a handicap. She was using her size to express the tragedy of Schubert's *"Ave Maria"* with a ponderous grandeur.

The matinee was given with the Pasdeloup Orchestra, conducted by Albert Wolff, and the program was impressive. So impressive indeed, thought Dorothy, it was impossible considering Lenora's present state, even as she prayed that this recital would be a kind of deliverance. Despite the announced program being different in several details, Lenora planned to dance her famous *"Rédemption,"* the *"Ave Maria,"* and for the second half of her program the *Tannhäuser* overture, and finally, the *"Liebestod"* of Isolde.

It was too much for today's Lenora, thought Dorothy, it was like building the Alps by hand. Moreover, the deficiencies of her body were so obvious, whatever the resources of her spirit. Dorothy stood in the wings, afraid that Lenora would collapse at any moment, wondering whether she should have encouraged her to this point, yet admiring the inner incentives that drove her to such demoniac effort.

Lenora waited in the wings for the music to start, and she was stricken with a dread she had never felt before. There was a tense feeling in the back of her neck, her shoulders ached despite the champagne she had absorbed a minute ago. For once she had no confidence in her body. She thought, in a moment of dreadful lucidity, I am betraying my art, myself, my body is no longer able to bear the burden, there is no inner equanimity. Quite unexpectedly then, Lenora moved before the front curtains. The music waited, assuming she would make one of her customary speeches. And there, as if hanging in space, Lenora stared at the hundreds of faces, held out her arms to embrace them all, and bowed her head in supplication. She was fighting for breath, her lungs desperate for air, her legs wobbly, but the applause was loud and strong.

Standing there, Lenora remembered this was the anniversary of Dion's birth, a painful, exhausting time, and she had not conformed to the proper social pattern and they had said she was not a good mother, that she was cold-blooded, indifferent. Indifferent! The winds of summer swept over her, and she relived the day that had made her the creator of so much sorrow. And yet her tremendous vitality, which in happier days had flooded the stage, was gone. The world had turned dark, dark forever, dark with a design stronger than her own. It was her tears now which flooded the stage, which dominated the *"Ave Maria,"* which created the cradle her arms formed, the empty cradle. She paused and wound her red shawl about her head like a shroud. She turned to her audience as if they stood beside her and said, without speaking, whatever dies lives in me.

She has become a consummate actor, Dorothy thought, her performance far more acting than dancing now, unhurried, establishing a mood with a single gesture, with unlimited confidence, far different from her rehearsals. And even as Dorothy wondered whether Lenora could maintain this mood for the rest of the program, she felt a sadness she could not put into words and found herself filled with tears.

When Lenora came out for the second half of her program, which began with the overture to *Tannhäuser*, her face was transfigured. There was an incandescent animation about her, as if to herald the resurrection of Lenora. No longer did she feel extinction creeping over her; once again she felt shaped to a mighty purpose. But as she moved suddenly a pain shot across her back. Her body was a fraudulence, she thought angrily. Tired, weak, unhappy in this instant, she felt changed and yet not changed, lost and yet not lost. She saw her famous blue draperies, shabby now, hanging as if they had the palsy, but they were the fundamental structure of her life. So she was a ruin, she told herself, but she would be a magnificent ruin. She would dance the *"Liebestod"* even if all the bricks fell.

This final number became a hymn to love, an evocation of a love that endured beyond dissolution. As the strains of the music grew intense she became love's martyr. She was dancing her life, dancing it away she thought, with each infirmity, and that was fitting; she had lived by love and so she would die by it. For now she feared nothing. On the final strains of the music the lights dimmed and all that could be seen was her red shawl like a flame melting.

Dorothy felt she had witnessed an execution. The applause was as loud as Dorothy had ever heard, and Lenora looked exhausted, on the verge of collapse. Then Lenora held out her still beautiful arms as if to embrace everyone, bent her head slightly in acknowledgment, and that was all.

Dorothy rushed backstage and found Lenora stretched out

on a couch. Her flesh sagged, and her robes were scattered on the floor. Dorothy had a sense of a body forsaken, though the place was jammed with friends telling Lenora that she had been magnificent, her career would resume in all its glory now, and Lenora, so unlike herself, said hardly a word.

Lenora had decided that if she could ever dance again, she could make a comeback, and now she had danced and it had almost killed her. She was torn between the knowledge that one more recital would kill her and the knowledge that no more recitals would kill her. But what was the use of talking about it. Dorothy was saying, "You were right, Lenora, your program was perfect," and she was silent for a moment and then said, "I'm very pleased."

Friends wanted to celebrate, but Lenora, to their surprise, begged off. She would never dance in public again, but whom could she tell? Her friends looked so happy, she could not disappoint them. Dorothy suspected, yet Dorothy would say she was exaggerating.

For God's sake, if they would only stop talking about the future!

Dorothy, sensing her mood, got rid of everybody and, feeling that Lenora needed the illusion of *going on* more than ever now, said, "I was unjust. You were completely up to the program."

"Please, stop apologizing. Pour me a drink."

"What about your next recital?"

"What about it? Is there any champagne left?"

"A little." She sighed. "I don't like your drinking so much."

"Did you like my dancing?"

"You made me so emotional I forgot where I was."

"Remember that, remember it when I am no longer here."

"Lenora, dear, don't be morbid. You'll dance again. Of course."

"Of course."

"How do you feel?"

"Wonderful. But a little tired."

"You danced a long time."

Lenora said nothing for the moment. A shudder deep in her shook her being. There was an involuntary estrangement between her flesh and her spirit that was too terrible to face. The feeling, horrifying, that nothing she could do would have any significance any more, was unthinkable. She began crying, to her own dismay, with a desolate abandon and thought, why can't I die? Why can't I be free of all this pain?

Dorothy embraced her and sought to soothe her, asking, "What's wrong?"

"I'm so tired. Let's go back to Nice, right away."

"Aren't you going to arrange any more concerts?"

"We'll arrange them at Nice."

Dorothy did not argue. For once, she was at a loss for words.

62

Lenora felt now that each day was a day nearer death. It became her hope. It was all that mattered. She had no direction except to avoid pain and lonesomeness, and she was rich in both. She returned to Nice with Dorothy, without a penny, for the concert had failed to earn any money, and Dorothy's modest income was quite insufficient to support both of them. She owed several months' rent at her studio, but she entered with such assurance the owner did not dare suggest she pay up or vacate.

She had no money of her own at all now, for Archer, going blind, had been forced to halt his monthly payments. The loss of the money did not trouble her much; even when he had sent her money she had spent it at once and had been impoverished the rest of the month. She was worried about his impending blindness, as worried as she could be about anyone, but she did not have the energy to do anything about it.

She regarded the world as if she were a stranger in it and looked at it with a curious detachment, as if Lenora Malcolm, for better or worse, was a historic relic, and it did not matter what she did any more.

All she owned now was her ancient gramophone of prewar vintage, some cracked records of Wagner, Chopin, and Schubert, her worn blue drapes, her long red shawl, her shabby old brown fur coat split down the back, and an enormous red leather handbag which contained a miscellany of mementos, letters, an album of pictures, several of her holding Dion and Cathleen that had escaped Nikolai's wrath, a few of Niels, Bayard, Nikolai, and Mama, and some maxims of hers on the dance that Mama had kept for many years.

She agreed to rehearse if Dorothy remained with her, although neither of them believed in it. The day Lenora was supposed to resume rehearsing Dorothy found her standing with her head thrown back, her arms by her sides, looking strangely stiff and sad. For a moment Dorothy had the feeling that Lenora was an alien here. This was saddest of all. It struck Dorothy that Lenora's black pessimism had gotten worse. Dorothy went to open the windows which opened on the sea, and Lenora halted her, saying, "The sun will spoil my mood."

"What number are you going to rehearse?"

"I don't know."

Lenora did not rehearse that day, or the next. The trouble was she did not rest either, or control her drinking. Lenora's restlessness was incessant now. The next few days she cultivated any attractive young man she could find; she drank whenever there was someone about to pay for the drinks; she avoided the studio every chance she got. She had to be on the go now. It was as if it was a ritual. Nothing else seemed to make any sense to her.

Often Dorothy could not keep up with her uncontrolled actions, and it was very trying. Dorothy developed new misgivings. She felt drenched with emotion. Tired to death after a week of this, and despondent because Lenora had done no rehearsing since they had returned to Nice, Dorothy suggested they go to a party being given for a group of Hollywood people. Dorothy had suddenly got inspired with the idea of Lenora making a film of her dancing, and while that idea struck Lenora as silly, the idea of the party did appeal to her.

But the party went badly from the start. The producer Dorothy approached, a short, burly, round-faced man, recognized as one of the most astute businessmen in Hollywood, thought Dorothy's idea idiotic.

"Why she's an anarchist bitch," the producer said.

Their backs were to Lenora, and they did not see her approaching them, but the producer had the kind of voice that carried, and as she heard this remark she edged closer. Ordinarily she did not give a damn what people said, but this was so obviously ridiculous, and what right did he have to assume such nonsense!

Then suddenly Lenora realized that everyone about the producer was agreeing with him, except Dorothy. Dorothy's usually calm free was flushed, and she was trying to halt the producer, who was denouncing Lenora Malcolm as "old, fat, impossible, not even the youngsters would be interested in her, most of them have never heard of her, she's a has-been, finished, completely finished! Yep," repeated the producer, pleased with the approval his words were receiving, "she's an anarchist bitch. She was no more fitted to be a mother than my collie bitch."

Lenora did not hear Dorothy's irate protest. She stood awkwardly, arms hanging, staring apparently at nothing. She felt like a discarded grotesque. Then suddenly, with a numbing shock, she understood: she was too different, too unique for all of them. No, she thought fiercely, I cannot give in. Yet it frightened her to feel such hatred, especially of life.

Lenora flung herself out of the room, past caring that her feelings were naked. She walked into the Mediterranean, she had come from the sea, she would go into the sea, she would join her children. But the water was chilly, her clothes clung to her, in the same instant revulsion in her body slowed her. A reckless excitement took possession of her, however, she'd be free soon, free, free. The sea was almost completely dark now and very cold. She went on and on, up to her hips, then paused. She took a deep breath, hoping she would not look too awful afterward, when they found her drowned.

Moments later, when she was pulled out, she was in a state of shock, clutching the rescuer's coat as if it were the earth itself. It was a long time before she realized she was back on land.

She wanted to laugh: was dying that difficult? But when she was brought into the house where the party had been, to rest and recover, a horrible feeling seized her. It is all so useless, so futile and absurd. The meaningless chaos she had sunk into, and this cold sea, the hills mounting above the beach, the indifferent stars. She could not stop shivering. She remembered the crab crawling across the beach and that the sea was so dark, she found that more frightening than anything else. Lying on a bed, having water pumped out of her, she steadied herself and said, although she felt nightmarish, "It was a joke. I wanted to get my inspiration back."

Dorothy stood looking at her anxiously, wanting to kiss her, to comfort her, but afraid it would bring a flood of tears.

"How do I look?" Lenora smiled feebly.

"I've seen you look more dashing. Are you ready to go home?"

"No, no, I can manage myself."

"Lenora, dear, the dishonor is not yours." Dorothy wanted to shout that Lenora was also gentle, loyal, sensitive, especially with children, but they were surrounded with little men and women and it would be no use. "I'll wait until you're ready."

From then on Dorothy tried to avoid criticism of any kind, but it did not help. Lenora felt alone despite Dorothy, and she could not endure that. Many nights she found herself trying to communicate with Mama, grinding out memories as she could not sleep, but they were mostly nightmarish.

She was grateful for the attention of any young man now. She borrowed money from whoever would give it, and the moment she had it in her hand it was gone. She did this with the instinct to seize each instant as if it were the last. The drinking, the spending, the young men were the only reality because she was the unreality, everything else was crumbling like her body. Any attempt to engage her in a responsibility was futile. Now Lenora had two dominating obsessions: the death of her children and the death of her beautiful art.

Dorothy was even more patient and understanding, but the extravagances did not cease. Lenora got a sizable advance on an article she was writing on the dance, and she squandered it in one quick meal of champagne, caviar, and roast beef. And after that dinner they returned to her studio where she drank gin avidly and searched haphazardly amid the confusion on her desk for the article, for she wanted to finish it so she could get more money for another feast, and then, unable to find it, she shouted, "The hell with it!" and ordered Dorothy to go out and buy more gin and was annoyed that Dorothy had no more money.

Several days later Dorothy found a heap of papers thrown into a corner, dirty and tear-stained. They were the article Lenora had been searching for, but when Dorothy suggested that Lenora rewrite it, the papers were in no condition to submit to anyone, Lenora refused. The next moment she was ordering champagne, although her debts were enormous. There was a nasty argument at the door about the bill, but when Lenora put on her grandest manner, as if she were about to inherit a million dollars, the champagne came. Then Lenora insisted on inviting several young men she had just met.

Dorothy felt so utterly hopeless it showed on her face, and a moment later Lenora was embracing her, saying, "Darling, I love you as I've loved nobody but Mama, but what does it matter? It is better not to know what's going to happen tomorrow." Slightly drunk, but with sudden vivacity, she said, "Suppose Charles Frohman had not died on the Lusitania, suppose Charles Frohman was announcing, as he once did, 'It is with great pleasure I present Lenora Malcolm,' should I stand on my head, or say, 'Ladies, dance the moon, dance the sky, dance the sea.'" Dorothy watched with horrified enjoyment while Lenora did a savage imitation of herself. Then, just as suddenly, Lenora said dryly, "That's what I'll leave behind me."

But the financial situation was serious. The owner of the studio was threatening to evict Lenora now, and Lenora's craving for extravagance was increasing at a terrifying rate. And so Dorothy, hearing that Bayard was at nearby Cap Ferrat, decided to ask him for help. Bayard had always given Dorothy affection and hospitality, for he respected her as one of Lenora's levelheaded friends. Yet she approached him with trepidation.

Bayard greeted Dorothy warmly, kissing her on the cheek. He wore striking Côte d'Azur trousers, a brightly striped Riviera shirt, but his hair was gray and his tall figure was a little stooped. He knew all about Lenora. He said, "Such a pity."

Dorothy said, "Yet she deserves to survive."

"That's the least of it," said Bayard, "but can I halt the landslide she's on?"

"I don't know. But if we don't she'll collapse completely."

He knew that was true and that he had no choice. He agreed to visit Lenora and do what he could.

Lenora did not expect Bayard to come, but when he did, delighted though she was to see him, she was seized with a scandalous desire to laugh. Bayard looked so solemn, so dedicated, and then he smiled reassuringly, and she came to him in a beautiful movement as if he were one of God's messengers. She took him by the hands and led him to the one uncluttered part of her room.

She asked, "Shall we sit here? I think it is comfortable."

"Please."

"You haven't changed. Not much."

"Thanks. Neither have you, Lenora."

She shook her head in wonder. "I can't believe you're here. It's wonderful. Strange, one can be so happy one minute, and the next." Her eyes filled with tears. I'm going to cry, she thought, and I mustn't.

Bayard delivered a gallant speech about what her art meant to the world, and she almost believed him. He insisted that she have dinner with him. As they drove through the lovely country, there was so much beauty Lenora was almost hopeful. The dinner was excellent, and by the time they reached the final course he was her Viking again; he declared he would subsidize her so she could have an accompanist, a studio rent-free, and whatever other expenses she needed to resume her concerts. She would have preferred aid for her school, but she decided to mention that later, subtly. She could not tell him that she was never going to dance in public again, that was impossible.

When he took her back to her studio he said, "I've thought of you many times, but you've traveled so much it was difficult to keep up with you."

But all that mattered now was did he care for her still, not his money not his promise of help, and she cried out, "Do you love me?"

He smiled gently and said, "I always have. I always will."

"Forgive me," she said, "for asking."

"There's nothing to forgive. I would have been hurt if you didn't want to know."

"Outside of you and Nikolai and Neils, there's never been anybody who really mattered. I've shared more of my life with you than with anyone else. You always believed in my art."

"I still do."

"I wish I did. I think if I had any children now that showed any signs of genius I'd shoot them."

He longed to say something that would allay her bitterness but found nothing and was silent. Her bitterness had a devastating impact upon him. It was as if she was pulling apart a beautiful temple that he had built.

"Oh, you can pass judgment on me—everybody else does," she shot out, uncomfortable in his silence.

He said gently, "I didn't come for that."

"So I've caught my Viking being Christ. I must kiss you for that." He sat there while she did, on the forehead. Then suddenly she sat beside him, pressed his hands to her heart, and repeated, "You do love me?"

"I told you—I always have."

"Yes, you loved other women, and I have loved other men, and yet we do love each other and it will be forever. You understand that."

"I understand many things I didn't understand years ago." It had been more than feeling like a Medici, an illustrious patron endowing a great artist, although that had given him vast satisfaction. There had been the hushed expectancy before her recitals, and never quite knowing what was coming next. It was the feeling she was dancing directly to him. It was her transformation of the world into a dancing cosmos and how it transformed him. But being so close, he reflected, had had its hazards. Her dancing had been so stimulating and overwhelming they had not paid enough attention to anything else. "We were too proud," he said, "and it pushed us apart."

"I continued to dance."

Yes, he thought, now that these days were gone, he would give anything to regain them.

"You're not listening!"

"I was thinking, Lenora, how nice it would be to see you dance again."

"Is that an order?" God, how could she tell him of her final humiliation, that she would never dance again!

"No, no, just a wish." He stood up. "I must go now, really."

"When will I see you again?"

"Tomorrow. I'll telephone. And I'll bring you a check."

"Please, that isn't necessary."

"If anybody else said that I wouldn't believe them. But nobody was ever more forthright than you."

She kissed him with all her honesty, on his lips. This was the first gratifying moment she had had in weeks. Then he was gone.

There was a whole evening ahead of her, but for once it did not seem a torture to endure. She was able to bear herself for a change, to sit at her desk and start to rewrite the article on the dance she had left dangling a week ago.

But when Bayard did not come the next day, telephoning that he had been detained and would come the day after, her bitterness returned and she did not believe him, certain he had no intention of seeing her any more. She wondered if it had been her intense faith in love that had betrayed her. Perhaps love was a swindle too. She had loved life too much, she thought, and it had been unable to return such love.

Overcome with restlessness, feeling a weight on her heart that she had to be rid of, she rushed off to the most exotic café she could find in Nice. Dorothy hurried after her, afraid Lenora would do something especially reckless. Seldom had she seen Lenora so frustrated, so determined to break out of bonds, imagined and otherwise. Lenora drank feverishly, announcing she needed a ride urgently, anywhere, the faster the better. An attractive young Spaniard, dressed in racing togs, heard her and asked if he could join her. "Of course!" She motioned for more whisky, although Dorothy was trying to restrain her.

The young Spaniard, who looked in his twenties, dark, slim, and quick of speech, explained that he had a racing car which he would be delighted to demonstrate for Madame, and if she liked it perhaps she might want to buy it. Lenora became far more excited than Dorothy thought sensible, but Lenora was willing to buy it, rent it, ride in it, whatever was necessary, he was so attractive.

The young Spanish driver agreed to pick up Lenora at her studio the following evening. Dorothy reminded her that Bayard might come then also, but Lenora was not to be dissuaded. She was in a state of hysterical excitement at the thought of racing through the mountains with this attractive young man; it was too painful to sit still.

The next morning, just as Lenora was feeling particularly wretched, certain that neither man would appear, the young Spaniard dropped by to confirm their appointment—very anxious to sell this grand lady his car.

They were sitting on her little balcony, and Lenora was saying she required a chauffeur-handyman to manage her affairs when Bayard strode in. There was an ominous hush.

Then Bayard said, "Is this the devotion you were telling me about?"

Lenora said, "I was just discussing a car I might need for business."

Bayard sighed, "I guess you are incurable."

Lenora said, "How silly." She confirmed the appointment with the owner of the racing car for the early evening for a test spin of the racing car. Then the young man, looking awestruck before the imposing Bayard, who was his most commanding and aristocratic self now, bowed out.

Bayard said, "You shouldn't see that boy. He's no better than a mechanic. Small wonder people gossip about you."

Lenora, who was amused by his anger, who thought his jealousy a healthy sign, indicating he continued to care about her, did not like the assumption, however, that this was a rival. She said, "There is no reason why I shouldn't test the car."

"A racing car? What do you need that for?"

"I like to drive fast, the faster the better."

"You don't even know whether he is a competent driver."

"He was an aviator in the war, he said. He's an expert."

"And you believe him?"

She longed to shriek, I don't believe anyone, not even you, it is all farcical, each day is only a day nearer death and death assumes many faces, and I have died many times already. But Bayard meant well, perhaps, and so she managed to control herself and say, "I appreciate your interest, Bayard, but it is a little late to make me over."

"A strong person must keep fighting."

"Remember, you said you love me and always will. Remember."

"But to see you betray yourself?"

"What else have you come for?"

He glanced at his watch. "I must go. But I'll have a check for you in a day or so."

"Do you resent me, Bayard?"

He stared at her and thought, she has lost her life-enhancing energy, she is cursed with self-pity now, and she is no longer beautiful, not even attractive, except in rare moments, her flame is flickering, she is pathetic and vulnerable, and the look in her eyes sank deep into him. Her love had made him a giant. He wanted to weep for her. Let their arguments go on, she had nourished him as no one else had. Yes, life was two-faced. Suddenly he bent low, took her hand and kissed it as if she were a queen, and whispered, "I would no more think of resenting you than resenting the wind for blowing."

Lenora sat motionless for a long time after Bayard was gone. Although daylight was still in the sky, the atmosphere was that of evening. She wanted to hold herself upright, but it was such an effort. She looked up at her drapes which had been her blue clouds. She smiled bitterly, with a desperate pride. His coming was providential, or was it? He would come back; he had said he would, and he always kept his word. But what would he find?

The concierge was at her door, informing Miss Malcolm that a young man was waiting for her outside. The concierge had a little boy with him, his son, golden-haired and fairskinned, so resembling Dion that Lenora's heart almost stopped. They were gone a minute later, but Dorothy, who had entered on their departure, found Lenora crying again, wildly and uncontrollably.

"I can't bear it," Lenora sobbed. "My children want me to die, my children want me to die . . . because they want me."

"Nonsense," said Dorothy, although she was shaken by the resemblance.

"Don't you see I can't go on!"

"It's wicked to talk this way." Even the calm Dorothy was horrified.

"I've tried . . . oh, I've really tried. But I can't go on this way any longer. What can I do? Dorothy, what am I going to do?"

"Did Bayard turn you down?"

"No. He made me feel as if I still have *joie de vivre,* and I haven't."

"I don't think you ought to go out tonight. You're so moody, it'll only make you feel worse."

"The boy is waiting, and I can't disappoint him."

Dorothy asked her to wear a coat instead of the old red

shawl, it would be too cold with just a shawl, but Lenora, defiant once more, not giving a damn, thinking, what's the difference anyway, and if she drove fast enough and rashly enough all would be blotted out, said the shawl would be perfect.

Lenora wound the shawl around her throat, the shawl that had always meant the beginning of creation to her, and even more so now, since the death of her children and the appearance of the new patterns she called the end of creation. All the new patterns like the death of Nikolai, all the new deaths while climbing the mountain toward the pinnacle of love. She looked in the mirror and pulled down the short end of the red silk, with which she had danced the *"Marseillaise"* and the "March Slav" and "America the Beautiful." The mirror was a challenge and a threat and the whole world of the past, the present and future, the unending, timeless future with herself a red silk shawl floating uncertainly. She saw the future as merely a state of floating alone, separate, isolated. Lenora sighed so loudly she surprised herself. She gave the room a contemptuous look and walked out too boldly, too engendered with the fires of memories.

The dark young driver smiled at her like a cavalier, and she liked his free and easy manner. She did not notice that this was not even the auto that had caught her attention. It did not matter. Or that she did not know his name. She stepped out on the beautiful Promenade des Anglais. It was a good-to-be-alive September evening, Bayard had said I love you and always will. She made herself secure in the seat beside the driver.

Then Lenora turned to Dorothy and several friends who stood on the Promenade des Anglais and shouted emotionally, "Good-by, my friends, I'm off to glory!"

It was twilight, almost dark but not quite. The auto gathered momentum, and Lenora, with her characteristic gesture of defiance, whirled her red shawl around her neck and over her shoulder. The shawl dragged a few feet like a snake alongside the rear of the auto. Her face was silhouetted in the dusk, sharp and shining and striking in the rush of air, in the joy of motion, her beloved motion, the shawl tight around her neck, the shawl clinging to her as her children had clung, as Mama. Then the shawl twisted suddenly, tightened ferociously. She felt a fearful jolt against her neck, a blinding light, so blinding it blotted everything else out, and then, nothing.

The shawl had caught on the rear wheel and broken her neck.

Lenora was dead.

"Good-by, my friends, I'm off to glory."

Dorothy moaned, oh resurrection! and fought to push life back into the limp body that had held so much life, but Lenora's face had been smashed out of shape and recognition, and death, which Lenora had desired so frequently since that dreadful afternoon her children had drowned, had been instantaneous.

Now the legends could begin. Now the world could praise her again. They could put her back into the sky. Now they could call her America's greatest dancer. And her motions were not lost. They were in the trees, in the flowers, in the wind, in her beloved sea.

She had created beauty and who could say she was wrong.